THE PUPPET MAKER'S DAUGHTER

Shoes on the Danube Memorial
Photo by Dennis Jarvis from Halifax, Canada, CC BY-SA 2.0
https://creativecommons.org/licenses/by-sa/2.0, via Wikimedia Commons

- KARLA M. JAY -

This is a work of fiction. Although some of the characters, events, and organizations are real as described in the Author's Notes in the back, the rest of the story is based on the author's imagination or used fictionally.

Printed in the United States of America
Book Circle Press

Cover designed by Emma F. Mayo

Photo by Lynda Smart-Brown

Paperback ISBN: 979-8-9853222-0-0

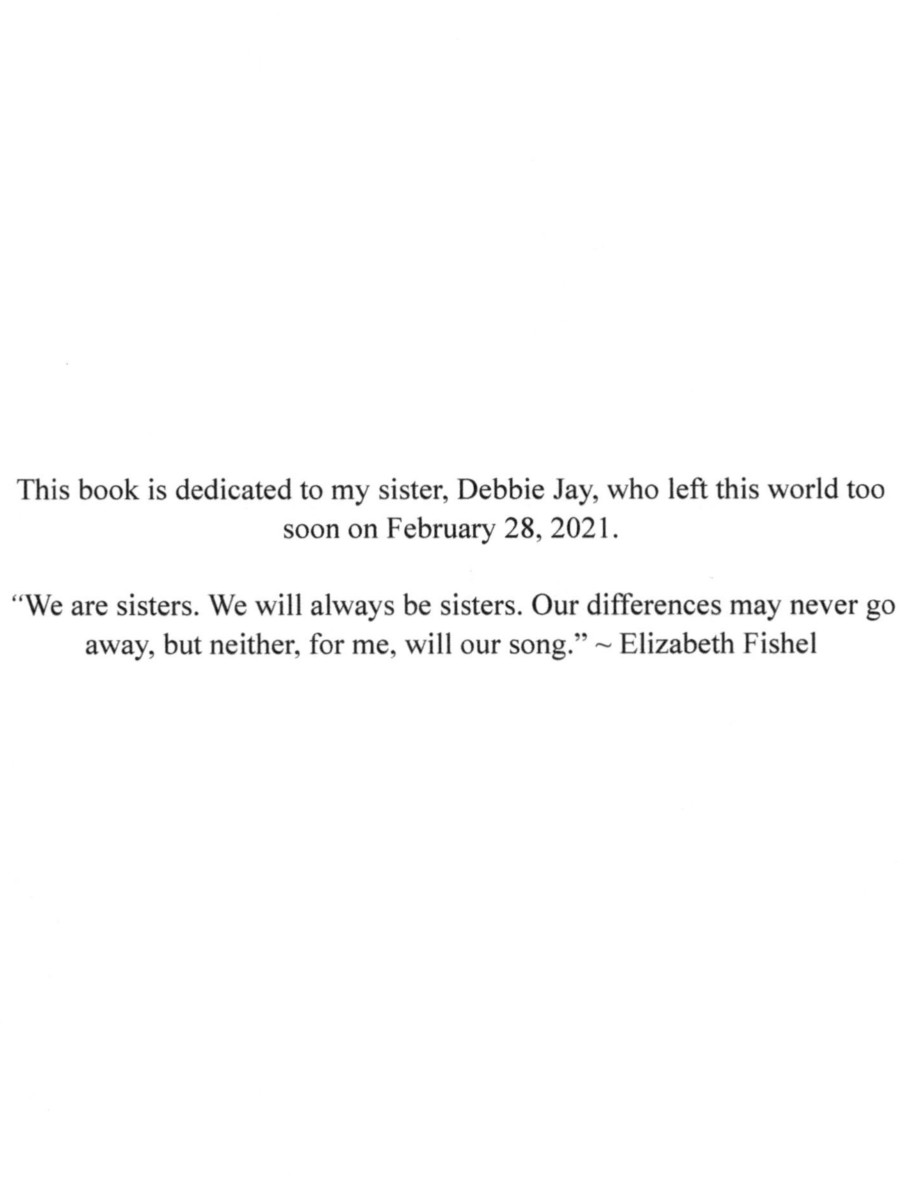

This book is dedicated to my sister, Debbie Jay, who left this world too soon on February 28, 2021.

"We are sisters. We will always be sisters. Our differences may never go away, but neither, for me, will our song." ~ Elizabeth Fishel

"When we are no longer able to change a situation,
we are challenged to change ourselves."
~ Viktor Frankl

"Monsters exist, but they are too few in number
to be truly dangerous. More dangerous are the
common men, the functionaries ready to believe
and to act without asking questions."
~ Primo Levi

Other books by Karla M. Jay

When We Were Brave
It Happened in Silence

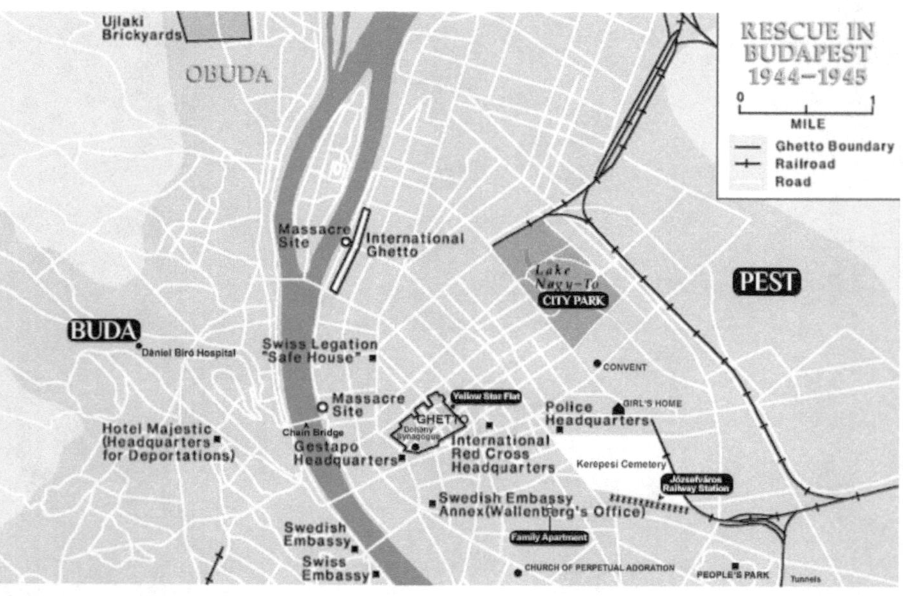

Ujlaki Brickyards
OBUDA
RESCUE IN BUDAPEST 1944-1945
0 1
MILE
Ghetto Boundary
Railroad
Road
Massacre Site
International Ghetto
Lake Nagy-To
CITY PARK
PEST
BUDA
Dániel Biró Hospital
Swiss Legation "Safe House"
CONVENT
Massacre Site
Yellow Star Flat
Police Headquarters
GIRL'S HOME
Hotel Majestic (Headquarters for Deportations)
Chain Bridge
Dohány Synagogue
GHETTO
Gestapo Headquarters
International Red Cross Headquarters
Kerepesi Cemetery
Józsefváros Railway Station
Swedish Embassy Annex (Wallenberg's Office)
Swedish Embassy
Family Apartment
Swiss Embassy
CHURCH OF PERPETUAL ADORATION
PEOPLE'S PARK
Tunnels

-1-

Budapest, Hungary

March 19, 1944

MARIKA TAUSIG

"The Germans have arrived," my father says.

I'm enjoying an unusually warm spring day with my family on an outdoor restaurant terrace in Széchenyi Square when my father, Endre Tausig, speaks. His words remain adrift in my mind, like clouds struggling to arrange themselves, a pleated pattern across the blue expanses, not yet noticed. I close my eyes and tilt my face toward the warm sun, the moment draped in the clinking of silverware against fine china and bubbly conversation floating above the restaurant's outdoor dining area. The fresh air is infused with the smells of chicken paprikash, fisherman's soup, and warm bread. This Sunday morning the restaurant is packed, like all the other cafés, beer gardens, and coffee houses in the city. Everyone in Budapest is ready to shrug off winter's dark layers for the transformative embrace of spring.

"The Germans have arrived," my father repeats, this time with more urgency.

Awash in faint scents of paint and turpentine, the telltale aromas of one who creates puppets as a hobby, he is a soft-spoken man. But the way he lays out these four words, cold and evenly placed like headstones in a cemetery, grabs my attention. That and the increasingly closer sound of drumbeats.

"They're always here, Father." I set down my flute of sparkling wine. Hungary remains a safe island in the middle of the world war thanks to our

Regent, Miklós Horthy. By now, the third year into the war, Hungarians are used to seeing German military. They've been crossing through our country on their way to other fights they started. Recent rumors of British and American victories give us hope the three-year war between everyone else will end soon.

István, my older brother by four years, scoffs. "They're doing what they always do." He and his wife, Erzsébet, and their baby son have come into the city for this special luncheon.

"Showing off," he continues. "Trying to discredit the rumors that they're losing, pretending they're soon-to-be victors." He and my father stand and walk to the terrace railing, studying the Danube and the bridges leading from the west.

István refuses to say much about his time in the 2nd Hungarian Army that Russia crushed last year. His and his wife's conversion to Catholicism two years ago probably saved him from a worse fate. At least he came home whole. Two months ago, my fiancé, Gellert, and five others escaped the forced labor battalion, solely made up of Jews. They made their way back to Budapest after the Germans turned and ran, leaving them all to fend for themselves against the Russians. Gellert is trained as a medic, one year shy of becoming a doctor, yet the Hungarian Army put the Jews at the front, creating a shield of *unimportant* flesh, with limited weapons and food as they tried to hold the Don River and take Stalingrad. Nothing but a complete failure. Forty thousand Hungarian soldiers dead with thousands missing. The Jewish laborers like Gellert fared even worse. They were given suicide duty, burying the dead on the front lines with no protection while bullets from both sides traced across the bloody scene. They wielded only wooden sticks to clear minefields ahead of the rest of the troops or risk a bullet in the back for disloyalty.

Gellert returned with the help of the resistance group and is confined to the Dániel Bíró Hospital until he recuperates from a serious head wound and a troubling darkness that seems to rule his sleep.

"Is that a band I hear?" Across the table, Erzsébet stops feeding two-year-old József, who is the reason for this name-day celebration. We have a long tradition of celebrating the day of the year that matches a family member's first name and decided today should be no different. Father paid for the added pleasure of a champagne brunch founded by another József, Mr. József Törley, a local winemaker.

"It sounds like one," my mother, Leichi, says. As always she's elegantly dressed, today wearing a silky grey-and-pink-plaid dress bought in Paris when she and Father traveled there in '38 to sell one of his specialty puppets in the Latin Quarter. She twists her wedding ring, a nervous habit. "Maybe it's a celebration we didn't know about."

The ensemble is closer now. Drums and horns. We take the two daily Jewish newspapers that are still secretly published, so I doubt we wouldn't be aware of a scheduled parade through the city. My mother is always the positive one and tries to share the light from a match not yet lit.

I didn't inherit that kind of trust. The slightest breath can snuff a flame. I'm like my father in this regard—deal with whatever comes head-on, even if it means there's nothing good about the situation.

"This isn't any celebration," Father says, turning his head toward our table. "At least not for us."

I join my father and brother at the brass railing overlooking the streets. Budapest, the capital of The Kingdom of Hungary, was created in 1873 by the merger of three cities—Buda, Óbuda, and Pest. The town spreads along the banks of the river Danube and is divided into twenty-three districts, sixteen of which are located on the Pest side, six in Buda, and one on Csepel Island on the Danube. We live in Pest.

My gaze travels just north of the Chain Bridge along the Danube, stopping at The Parliament, known as one of the most beautiful government buildings in the world, inspired by the British Palace of Westminster. It's described as resembling a long ornate cathedral, although a few blocks away sits the city's largest church, St. Stephen's Basilica, another architectural beauty.

But the Chain Bridge connecting our Pest side of the Danube to Buda and Castle Hill on the other is where the action is today. Of course, the Germans would cross into Pest on this bridge, the grandest of them all. Built in 1849, it became the first permanent span linking Buda and Pest and is a popular nighttime destination as couples and families stroll across its 375-meter-long suspension under hundreds of lights.

"Oh dear," I say. "You're right. This is something else."

The troops—hundreds, perhaps thousands of them—walk six abreast behind a strutting band. The musicians play German military marches as the grey-green slither of officers and soldiers flows across the bridge and pours through the main streets, like sewer water overtaking our beautiful city. The hair on my arms rises. Why are they here now? The Germans have Parliament's permission to take all our resources, and they've been doing that for years out in the bauxite mines and oil fields.

"Looks like they've sent their SS officers too," István says. "This has to be bad news."

Father often warns him about being too open with his disdain for the Germans. The enemy has friends in Parliament and throughout the Hungarian government, all eager to arrest and remove malcontents, and especially outspoken Jews or *Fake Catholics*, as some call any one of the seventeen thousand who converted in the last three years.

Four months ago, István came home from the war an exhausted, thinner version of himself after surviving two years embedded with the army. The winter of '43 was particularly brutal. I asked, but he never saw Gellert when they both were out there. The front was massive, tens of thousands of workers spread thin. Erzsébet—pregnant when he was swept up in the war—has almost healed him since his return.

Almost.

They live near Győr and run my mother's ancestral sheep farm, famous for its thick Stark wool. My grandparents left it to my brother when he married four years earlier. My grandmother and grandfather Stark have since passed away, merely months apart. Pneumonia and a broken heart were the verdicts, with my mema leaving us first. My grandparents went by Mema and Bepa, based on what István first called them when he was learning to talk. The names stuck.

With István off fighting, Erzsébet struggled to run the estate alone with its fifty sheep, a dozen prize horses, and chickens while she suffered severe morning sickness. She hired some local men to help, and my parents and I took turns working there while my brother was away.

I still drive out. Last week, the hourlong trip was almost a religious journey, a soul-cleansing experience, washed by the scent of cold soil and green sprouts coaxed upward, ripening under the warm spring rays. A rebirth, especially this time of year. The bare trees have finished their winter self-reflection and are now brave enough again to push forth buds. If they can put trust in another year, that's the only sign I need that nature knows best. Never quit living even after a bleak, cold stretch.

First, I worried for months that Gellert would never return after a letter saying he'd escaped the Labor Force and was making his way back. Then, I received the call that he was injured and hospitalized. A short-lived celebration.

His head injury is severe, but he's improving, not as delirious now. But I still alternate between waves of happiness and despair. Unlike the trees this time of year, I'm afraid to push forth hopeful blooms, in case they find no sun and die.

We've been together three years and planned to marry next year. That would've marked the end of his residency, and I'd have my nursing degree. Now we wait for this war to end, and we'll make new plans, maybe marry right away, skip the big wedding, and move to America. Gellert's dream place would be where he could eat a hot dog loaded with sour cabbage while watching an American baseball game. I blame the cinema for showing American movies like *Alibi Ike* when Gellert was younger, planting these images in his head. But I'll go wherever he goes, and my parents know a move across the ocean is a possibility. My mother encourages my impulsive ideas, and I think she would agree to a quick wedding, recognizing that tiny bit of herself in me.

Until Gellert is well enough to walk, or we figure out why he won't try, all I can do on my visits is wrap him in a warm hug and whisper, "*Szeretlek*"—I love you. I keep those elopement thoughts to myself and stay focused on each centimeter of improvement he makes in his long kilometer of recovery.

It's the hardest part of being unable to communicate in depth with him right now. He knows who I am. He knows we care for each other, but something he witnessed made his mind snap, and he's in and out of reality.

While memories and future plans circle inside my head, they have no exit since he can't discuss them yet.

Before he was taken into the Labor Force, Gellert was the kind of guy who listened to understand, not to ready his next reply. And I know that man I love is still in there. He's just temporarily stuck behind scrambled thoughts caused by his head injury.

"Times are about to get interesting," my father says. "The war has arrived."

A long motorcade of black vehicles crosses the Chain Bridge, Nazi flags flapping on the fenders of each vehicle. The Waffen-SS—Hitler's elite force—immaculately dressed in grey and black, stand stiff, immobile in the open cars while locals wave and cheer.

I snort. None of the crowd celebrating the Germans really want them here, but the Nazis are less feared than the Russians. Unless you're a Jew. Then you can't trust anyone but family and friends. Although we Hungarian Jews have remained safe from what's going on in the rest of Europe, so have people who've arrived in Budapest fleeing persecution. But tales circulate of massive roundups to help the German war effort, stories of crowded work camps, and long hours in warehouses.

Women and children too. Who needs mothers and babies in war production plants?

My heart aches imagining these poor families. They wake up each day and open their eyes to a world where they're enslaved for another exhausting day. At least, that's what we hear on Father's secret radio. The BBC verifies information coming out of a dozen cities where the Germans imprisoned the Jewish population into areas called ghettos. They say it's to protect them from the bombing, but the British report the ghettos have little food, no medical help, and disease runs rampant. Hundreds, perhaps thousands have died.

I turn to my father. "Have you heard any of this from your friends?"

He'd worked as a professor in the engineering department at the Budapest Technical University until all Jewish persons were let go two years ago. He still consults clandestinely with his colleagues on urban infrastructure projects, such as water supply, sewage systems, and gas works.

He likes to say that while Budapest may be nicknamed the Queen of the Danube, under her throne, rats rule the connected cellars and tunnels beneath the city's splendor.

"Ferenc said Regent Horthy was called to meet with Hitler." My father's forehead knits together. "A discussion about taking over the remaining bauxite mines."

Ferenc Zambos is my father's best friend from childhood. They attended lower school then university together. He is the city's transportation supervisor, a deacon in his Lutheran church, and president of one of the local chess clubs. Most sunny days find him in our apartment's courtyard with my father hunched over a Knubbel chessboard, shot glasses and a bottle of Unicum on a side table. Ferenc shares the latest news with Father as the two fight a micro battle with wooden carved figures.

"One of the drivers for Regent Horthy told Ferenc about the upcoming meeting in Vienna," my father says. "Horthy didn't want to meet with Hitler in Austria, but it's for two days only. He'll return Monday."

Tomorrow.

I turn to my brother. "You might be right. This is bad. The Germans are here but Horthy isn't."

"Knowing them, he may not come back." István leans closer to Father and me. He takes after my mother with his dark features and brown eyes. His hair lifts ever so slightly in the warm breeze. "I've seen what happens when a person opposes the Germans."

One Jewish newspaper wrote of my brother's army detail while he was in the thick of the fight. They were tasked with burying several dozen men taken from a small village near the Carpathian Mountains, all shot when they resisted the order to turn over their Jewish citizens. The Germans first stuffed pages from the Torah in their mouths, then further gagged them with cloth restraints and shot them.

I swallow hard. The shine on the day has dulled. Has the Regent made a secret deal with Hitler? Did he let the Germans swoop in while he was out of the country so he wouldn't be blamed?

"Horthy will be back." My father stands taller and gently touches my back. "We carry on as always."

His touch is reassuring.

"Right now," he continues, "we have this special occasion to celebrate. We're not going to think about tomorrow just yet." Father gives me a quick hug. He puts more affection into a simple embrace than a thousand kind words.

He's right, of course. Although Horthy is anti-Semitic, he's not turned over any Jews as Adolf Eichmann, one of Hitler's top men, demanded. Horthy's concession to Hitler and his henchman's demands was the Jewish labor unit and the dozens of regulations limiting our businesses and cultural involvement. These regulations also satisfied most Parliament members that we Jews are kept in our place. There's no pleasing the far-right government party, but they aren't in the majority and remain trivial, really no more than background static. My family has discussed this before. We only need to hang on for a few more months until the Red Army arrives.

We return to the table set with fresh daffodils, and I sink into my leather seat. A young pianist plays muted Chopin on a Victorian baby grand, the notes mixing with laughter and talk, a goulash for my soul.

I pray nothing awful touches my family's lives and that Gellert heals soon.

A long bar framed by mirrors runs along the far wall. Bartenders buzz around behind the counter, ambidextrous artists, pouring and garnishing many multicolored drinks at the same time.

The patrons don't seem to have heard the commotion from the streets below, but my mother's eyes search our faces, and she's gone pale. Father calls her his Hedy Lamarr, with her large doe eyes and wavy dark hair. She blushes at the reference, but how could she not be pleased with the comparison to the Austrian-born actress?

"What's happening, Endre?" My mother reaches for my father's hand. "Shouldn't we leave?" They are best friends after twenty-four years of marriage that has had its rough patches. They've shown that love is about dedication to each other's happiness over and above oneself.

"No. We'll stay and finish our celebration." He forces a smile, one I've seen many times since the Jewish laws were enacted. "The Dobos cake and poppy seed strudel will be ready soon. Would anyone like coffee?" He raises his hand to signal the waiter. "And I have a riddle for all of you."

My father is the master of these. For as long as I can remember, he's shared a riddle every few days.

"What disappears the moment you say its name?" He looks to each of us as we ponder our answers. I can't remember one riddle he has ever retold in all these years.

When it's clear we have no guesses, he says, "Silence," and smiles.

I nod and a small laugh escapes me. "Good one, Father." But the light moment soon passes. Inside, my stomach quivers. Another flute or two of champagne may calm my nerves, but coffee is more practical. The rapid drumbeats from the street match my thumping heart, and the cheering sets my teeth on edge. Horthy has promised the Jewish people he will oppose our deportation to labor camps if we obey the new racial laws. We're all defined as *Jews* due to race, not religion. Intermarriage between Jews and Christians is now forbidden, although thousands fit in to that mixed-marriage category.

I've stuffed away the anger from when my friends and I were forced out of university when the quotas for Jewish students were cut. I'll finish nursing school later. These new laws pushed my father out of his job, my mother out of her riding club, and Gellert out of medical school.

We've been doing what's demanded of us. We pray Horthy keeps his side of the bargain. With Germans swarming the city, we need more answers. Everyone in the family has gossip connections either in Pest or over on the Buda side where Castle Hill rises. The day is young, but each of us will reach out to friends and colleagues to test the rumors floating on the wind.

Hopefully, the Germans are here only for a respite from the fighting, to eat our food and drink the beer, and then blow back to wherever they came from.

But if their real purpose is more nefarious, all our people, about seven hundred thousand in the country, will be no more than a spindly fence trying to hold back a raging storm.

And if we're not one step ahead of their plans, we'll be swept up in a dark whirlwind, scattered helplessly about while they play out their evil war games.

-2-

BUDAPEST, HUNGARY

March 19, 1944

The walk back to our apartment building on Szerdahelyi Street is a quiet one. On the way, my parents and I say goodbye to my brother and his family many blocks back at the Andrássy Street car park. Father makes them promise to ring as soon as they make it to Győr.

Baby József pouts when I hand him over to Erzsébet, calling out "Mika"—his way of saying Marika. "Go with Mika," he wails, his arms stretched back to me as his father and mother carry him toward their Ford Taunus, one of the first touring cars made in the Ford plant in Hungary. Henry Ford made his anti-Semitic attitudes well-known by his writings in *The International Jew,* but István's father-in-law insisted it was the best car to protect his daughter and grandson, so István bought it.

If the Germans now are spreading throughout Hungary, it may be unsafe for me to travel to Győr by train, my preferred mode. I'll miss the baby, but in the meantime, I have hundreds of children at the orphanages where I volunteer, offering me their too-tight hugs, slobbery kisses, and that cheek-to-cheek press of dewy skin.

Father unlocks the front gate to our five-story building. He bought it in 1935 and had the eight apartments modernized with central hot water. Floor 0 houses a laundry, canning shelves, the mechanicals, and the air-raid shelter. The courtyard off Floor 1 extends behind the building and is larger than most on the block, spacious enough for individual gardening plots. Everyone plants their choice of flowers, herbs, and vegetables so that in the summer, from my window seat above it all, the area looks like a colorful puzzle. The pieces are separated by narrow walkways, yet somehow form a complete picture, a many-hued Monet painting from above.

On Floor 1, the janitor's three-room apartment is on the right, behind his concierge desk. János Schlesinger is the keeper of the keys for all the apartments except ours and maintains the building's repairs. For this, he receives a discount on his lease.

János, his wife, Ilona, and their daughter, Raakel, my good friend from when we were classmates in primary and secondary schools, live there. Raakel works at the famous Café Gerbeaud that draws people from the highest social strata, including back in the day when Sissy, the wife of Emperor Franz Joseph and Queen of Hungary, stopped in whenever visiting Budapest.

Not that long ago, we met there for coffee on Raakel's day off, gossiping about the girls we went to school with and the choices they'd made. We perused magazines for the newest fashion styles, and of course we imagined our futures—marriage, children, our careers. Under the crystal chandeliers and sitting at gilded tables against silk wallpaper, every crazy idea was possible.

That was before Jews were told which establishments they were forbidden to enter. The Gerbeaud Café is not for the *undesirables*. Raakel brings day-old pastries to us when she can. Sugar is in short supply in the city, and Jews are issued ration cards, one-fifth what Christians are allotted so her treats are a welcome gift.

"Sweets for the sweetest," she always says when she hands them to my mother. Raakel spent hundreds of nights at our apartment for sleepovers all through our teen years. She calls my mother, *második anya*, or second mother, and at one time, we thought she might become part of the family when Raakel and István dated.

The building's residents are a mix of professional Jews and Christians, with not much turnover since we moved in when I was ten. German is the *lingua franca*, though many residents speak a little English, Russian, and of course Hungarian.

A hallway divides the building in half and runs straight back to the courtyard. Across the hallway from the Schlesingers, a small bicycle repair shop faces the street, with the owner's three rooms behind. Herr Belko Dely and his son, Benedek, live there. They're standoffish and keep to themselves. We've never learned where Piroska, the wife and mother, goes, but she is rarely at home. The father and son don't speak of her unless we ask and then they are quite tight-lipped about what she does or where she stays. The bicycle workspace smells of axle grease and spiced sausages. The aromas often float along the hallways, reminding me of helping Bepa fix mowers and tractors on the estate, not an unpleasant smell at all. Bikes are a necessity now that the war has rationed petrol, and Herr Dely labors in the shop all hours of the day and night.

Benedek is a few years older than I am and has made it clear that he's interested in taking me out, but I feign that I'm too busy to date. Besides, he knows I'm engaged to Gellert. Benedek pilots tugboats on the Danube and once agreed to carry furniture to my brother's estate at his stop in Győr. I was relieved he didn't expect *compensation* beyond what Father paid him.

The other six apartments are stacked atop these two sides, the larger apartments with five rooms on the right like ours, the four-room flats on the left.

Ilona is sweeping the front sidewalk and looks up when my father calls out to her.

"Good morning, Frau Schlesinger. Have you or János had the radio on?"

Ilona is tall for a woman, with auburn hair that peeks out from the green scarf tied around her head. She has a ready smile and is always busy, usually cooking or embroidering.

"Hello there. János might be listening to his in the courtyard." She leans on the broom handle. "He's planting lettuce and onions"—she tilts her head—"why do you ask?"

"A large group of German soldiers entered the city," my mother says, her voice strained. "No one on the street seems worried, but we're just wondering what it means."

"I'll get János, and we can listen to the news together," Ilona says. "I've just taken apricot kolaches out of the oven."

"You're so kind, but we're stuffed," my father says, patting his trim midsection. "We just celebrated name day with István and his family."

"Oh, how is little József doing?"

"Getting bigger every day it seems." My mother wrings her hands and offers a fixed smile. "We need to be upstairs for István's call to let us know he returned home safely. I'll pop down later and help you finish up the aprons for the Aid Society."

"I'd like that." Ilona squeezes my mother's hand as we pass.

"Is Raakel in?" I ask. The Café Gerbeaud is Swiss-owned and often a place for rumors to safely circulate through the heady aromas of coffee and yeasty bread.

"She's off at two." Her eyes crinkle at the sides as she smiles. "I'll tell her to ring you when she's back."

"Thank you." I return her smile. She's like a second mother to me too.

Inside the building, my mother's heels echo on the centrally located stairs as she is already climbing to the fourth floor. I follow, stealthily, trying to walk on the balls of my feet. Not sure why, but I imagine the building is holding its breath so I must be quiet as well.

I'm the last inside, and I close the door behind me. The kitchen is to the left, open to the blue and gold upholstered sitting room on the right. A game table is near the floor-to-ceiling windows overlooking the garden area. The soft light brushes a buttery hue on our wall of bookcases and the two navy-colored chairs that face the fire grate a short distance away. Even on a gloomy winter day, this room is warmed in the glow of two floor lamps as mother or I sit wrapped in a Stark wool blanket, the brand made on mother's family farm. I glance at the domino tiles that remain in place on the table where Father and I finished our last game, now a sprawling black pattern, resembling a skeleton of some yet undiscovered creature.

My father is a quiet man, but it would be naïve to judge him as superficial. He's a deep thinker and keeps us all organized. Tall with light brown hair peppered with fine silver threads, I get my lighter coloring from him. His kind and calming spirit usually relaxes those around him, but right now as he paces the apartment, his silence is different, almost too loud to ignore.

Mother drops into her favorite chair near the bookshelf. She picks up her needlework, but her gaze isn't on the embroidery. Her stare is fixed, as though the apartment walls have disappeared, and she wills the future beyond to reveal itself.

We're all worried about what awaits us. We should have insisted that my brother and his family stay here. What were we thinking? The country-side must be crawling with Nazis if they've reached our city. What would stop them from swooping up all the men they can find to work alongside the army? I'm not sure István could survive returning to the fight.

I perch on a kitchen chair, staring down on the street below where a shard of sunlight separates the buildings, turning the grey cobblestones to gold. My mouth is dry, my nerves raw as scraped flesh. The loud insistence of the mantel clock makes it worse. Do we need the reminder that time, and whatever is unfolding under its scrutiny, is beyond our control?

"He'll call," I say to my father, but his sidelong glances at the telephone on the kitchen wall are now more frequent. "The roads leaving the city will be slow-going."

A commotion erupts in the distance, and its sound draws closer. I turn to the window to see hundreds of people round the corner and enter our street. It's a cheery parade of young women giggling merrily, moving off to the side as military convoys move through. The steel-helmeted German soldiers still remain standing in the vehicles next to their rifles. At this distance, they remind me of moving blocks of green metal spikes, warning that whichever way we turn, we may find ourselves impaled.

The sight is unsettling. I'm unsettled.

Holding on to optimism in the face of uncertainty is like cupping a cracked egg. You don't dare move too much, so you sit, holding on to what you can, confident you will keep it together.

We're almost frozen as we barely dare move, awaiting the call.

An hour and a half later, the jangling phone startles us all. Mother gasps, and I place my hand on my chest, an attempt to reassure my pounding heart everything is all right.

My father has never left the kitchen table, so he's there to answer the call. "You've made it," he says, his shoulders sagging. "Good, good."

I stand and move to his side, and my mother flanks him on the other. He holds the phone away from his ear so we can hear.

"We had to take backroads. The main highways are full of Germans. They're still heading your way." Even through the phone, István's tinny voice sounds frightened. "A friend who lives on Buda Hill says the palace is already surrounded. There are machine guns set up everywhere, a couple of cannons outside the gates."

"Will you be safe out there?" Father asks.

"Yes. Seems so. The farm looks unchanged." He's talking between quick breaths. "The foreman says we should be able to continue with the shearing. Get the wool to market as planned."

When we were children, István and I loved March and shearing season because it meant baby lambs were right around the corner. We carried them in feed-sack slings we made, their warm bodies held against our chests. We bottle-fed the weakest, and our grandparents chastised us for trying to dress some in our old baby clothes. Bepa sheared pregnant sheep about a month before their lambs were due to encourage ewes to take shelter, so their lambs wouldn't freeze to death if born outside.

István follows that tradition.

"Please come here if it starts to look bad," my mother says into the phone's mouthpiece. "The hired hands know how to keep the place running."

"I've seen no Germans in town." As he keeps talking, István's voice becomes muffled. He must be speaking to his wife before he addresses us again. "Oh. Erzsébet's father called to say he saw Regent Horthy's procession of cars go by, so he's probably back in Budapest."

Erzsébet's father, an inspector in the national milk cooperative under the Ministry of Agriculture, has connections in Parliament.

"Maybe Horthy will broadcast something soon." My father clears his throat. "Son. We want to hear from you every day. And, who knows, maybe we'll be coming to stay with you if it gets too…let's say, too crowded here."

"Be glad to have you all. Besides, I can't leave. We're about to harvest possibly seven thousand kilograms of wool this year. We'll need that money." He draws in a big breath. "I'll call each day, but you do the same if for some reason I don't."

After we hang up, Father crosses to a side table and turns the radio to the BBC. "We should hear something about the Germans' plans with so many arriving here."

We take seats in chairs, newly upholstered in gold-tone velvet, and stare at the device like it's about to deliver a missive from God.

Turns out the news is anything but informative or inspiring. After an advertisement for KIWI black boot polish, there comes a reminder that we would hear Oscar Wilde's play, *An Ideal Husband,* tonight. We wait for the General Forces Programme, but it only updates the blackout times throughout the British Isles today. Then the London Studio Players take to the airwaves with their orchestra.

"Nothing," I say, trying to keep the irritation out of my voice. I draw in a long breath. "Maybe this is a good sign. Surely an invasion would warrant an immediate announcement."

"Keep listening." Father puts on his hat. "I'm going to talk to János." He glances at his watch. "And if the world hasn't tipped sideways, Ferenc will be here in a short while for our chess match. He's sure to have information he's picked up from the bus and trolley drivers."

I leave my mother to listen to the news as I wander through the apartment and open the door into what was István's room before he married. It's now Father's workshop, and the scents of paint, wood, and glue invade my nose. Puppet parts, in all sizes, are in boxes or spread out on tables. Filling the shelves are strings and paddles used to make the marionettes move, and scraps of bright cloth for the richly decorated folklore costumes.

My father shared how he wanted to be an artist growing up. His father, a harsh man I never met because he shot himself after WWI, chastised him for wanting to make a living by "drawing on paper what can be seen for free by any idiot."

While studying engineering at university, my father took graphic arts classes in his free time and fell under the spell of crafting lifelike people out of wood. Before the war, he sold many intricately painted string marionettes to world-famous theatres throughout Europe. The Arc-en-Ciel Theatre in Paris often bought from him, up until the Germans invaded. Now the National Puppet Theatre in Budapest, from time to time, asks for his creative help, but more often than not, he makes them for the family.

His newest project is for baby József. A prince will be dressed in the national colors—red, white, and green—holding a sword in one hand and book in the other.

One wall of his workshop holds several awards, and on another wall hang numerous festive marionettes, including the first puppet he ever attempted. He calls him *Moshe*, or Moses. Father carried him from place to place in his twenties after he carved the foot-tall, disjointed figure. But with the puppet's scars and scrapes, it looks as if it must have wandered the Earth for two thousand years instead of forty.

My father is a city engineer by trade, but his heart is in creating figures so lifelike that when his marionettes are attached to the hand controller and hung from nine strings above, an audience could almost believe the performers are living beings.

Since the war started, our lives have been controlled as if we are the marionettes with mad puppeteers holding our strings. Here in Hungary, we're quietly singing and dancing, and still celebrate special occasions, as long as we follow city regulations. But now more than ever, when night drops her curtain of darkness over the city, it seems my family prefers sorting through our memories rather than pondering the future. A laugh here, a head shake there, as familiar stories are retold. There's even room to accept the embellishment we add because the exaggerated details remind us of what was real. That *we* are real. Memories hold us in place and will surely outlast our daily fears. What else could we cherish more than these as we all move toward uncertainty?

This is what I miss most—creating new memories with Gellert. I replay our long talks, mostly about medical research but also about places in the world we'd like to visit. I miss dancing with him. He won many folk dancing awards when he was younger. We spent hours every Friday night at the city hall where famous Hungarian musicians took to the stage. Hundreds filled the floor, everyone moving in rhythm to our most cherished folk songs. I long to do that again. Gellert, folding me in his arms after every dance, his familiar spicy scent filling my head, our clothes damp, our chests heaving.

Right now, I'd settle for a short walk with him down the hospital corridor. Physically there is nothing wrong with his legs. The doctors are as baffled as I am about why he can't walk. As a nurse in training for three years, I've seen miracles happen, and I'm not giving up. There could be another one around the corner.

Maybe I am a bit like my mother after all.

If outside rumors are true—and it's hard to believe they can be—the Germans have already cut the strings and cleared the performance stages in other European countries of marionettes they determined unworthy. Will the same tragedy play out here before the war ends?

I shake the thoughts away, needing to press my skirt for work tomorrow. I leave Father's workroom and head for my bedroom closet.

Because no matter what is to come, my father has taught me if you're meant to take the stage, you should always look the part.

-3-

BUDAPEST, HUNGARY

March 22, 1944

It appears the Germans have taken the matter into their own hands and begun to play games with Regent Horthy. For days, the radio reports nothing from him, and the silence in the streets is worse than if there were shouting and gunfire. A foreboding gloom descends, and the weather changes to match the mood. It's hard to stay positive when a cold wind is blowing across the country. Through the treetops it may sound musical, but we Jews hear nothing more than a high-pitched howl, and shivers race up our spines as the wind courses through the streets, sending bits of paper and cigarette butts with it.

Earlier today, a friend of Father's called with more information. The entire city is overrun by Germans. They've settled into our nicest hotels and now dine at the best restaurants and coffee houses. The palace is surrounded by their troops, and the Regent's hands are tied. He either needs to appoint a new right-wing government more pleasing to the Germans or face the bombardment and destruction of our city.

Not one bomb has fallen on us during the first three years of the war. If we turn a deaf ear to the radio broadcasts, we wouldn't realize a war rages around us.

We're seated at our kitchen table, finishing our breakfast of tomato and pepper ragout with scrambled eggs.

"They've arrested Caelen." My father scrubs a napkin across his mouth. "And hundreds of others."

Caelen is Father's distant cousin, a top manager at the Hungária

Elastic Fabrics and Bandage Factory. Like so many Jews, he converted to Christianity decades ago. And it isn't as if our family is all that devout in the first place. We rarely attend synagogue and only celebrate Rosh Hashanah and Yom Kippur. When I was younger, I asked Mother about it, and she said it was Father's choice.

Mother's Jewish family was always highly accepted in the mixed religious Győr community. But Father came from a life of persecution by other Jews when his father was thought to support the Bolshevik cause in the early 1900s. When he was a teenager, Father was spit on and beaten for his father's political beliefs. The harassment ended with my grandfather's suicide, and my father couldn't forget how he was treated.

"Their souls are full of scars," my mother once said. "Oppression will do that to a person even though deep down, your father believes."

"Why take Caelen?" My father is on his feet now, pacing the apartment.

My mother pushes her food around on her plate as if trying to rearrange the breakfast, along with what's happening outside.

"Sister Sára Salkaházi talked about this just last night." I volunteer at the Sisters of the Social Service orphanages, and Sister Sára oversees them all. She allows people of all religions to work there, not only women from their order. We learned she sees holiness in anyone offering service to another person in need. I trace the coffee cup rim with my finger, my nails bit ragged, an unwomanly sight my mother likes to point out. "She said they took away Social Democrats and any prominent Jew who is an artist, musician, or businessman."

"But took them where?" My mother's face pales, and she shoots a quick look toward Father who's staring out the front window. He's both an artist and a businessman. I can almost read the question in her eyes. *Will they come for him?*

"To the Nyugati railway station," Father says, pulling the lace curtain fully aside to peer out. "I'll make some calls again. I know the supervisor there."

Was another Labor Force being created? Thousands of men are still missing or haven't made it back like Gellert. There's no question that if this is the case, the men in Budapest will need to hide.

"I'm off to the hospital then to work." I stand and kiss both my parents on the cheek. "We're expecting a new shipment today at the orphanage."

Shipment means refugees. And now more than ever, the Sisters of Social Service will need to be extra careful with the *cargo* the village wagons and trucks unload at the Working Girls' Homes and Orphanages spread throughout the city. I've been volunteering there for two years, using what I've learned so far in nursing school to help.

I leave the apartment with my parents' wishes for my safety following me out the door.

If they knew I have been helping the Resistance for the past few months by meeting families on the run and bringing them to the orphanage, they'd be much more worried.

The Germans have made it clear—they won't tolerate anyone helping a Jew and threaten arrest if discovered. But I fell into helping the underground by accident and I stayed because I need to do something other than worry. And what safer place than the cover of working with nuns protected by the Pope.

I ride the tram across the Margit Bridge, making sure to sit in the roped off area at the back. Then I take the cogwheel railway tram up Castle Hill. Not more than a ten-minute walk farther sits the Dániel Bíró Hospital and attached sanatorium. The main building is three stories tall, the first level in red stone and the upper two floors in yellow brick. Continuing along the block, a yellow stone wall surrounds the inner grounds. The sanatorium. The side where Gellert was first admitted into with his ravings and combative issues. He's now in the main hospital in a private room.

Inside, antiseptic scents surround me, and I relax. This is where I thrive, in a hospital with someone needing my help. I square my shoulders and plant a smile on my lips before stepping into Gellert's room.

He sits in a wheelchair with his back to me. A bandage circles his head directly above his ears. It will be removed soon. When he arrived two weeks ago, it still seeped blood, but his head gash is nearly healed now. The sight of him always makes me tear up. Some nurse I am. *Show no emotion. Be a vision of calmness at all times.*

I move to his side and drop to my knees, so our heads are at the same level. "Hey there, handsome."

He slowly turns, his eyes searching around in space before stopping on my face. "Marika?" He speaks slowly, his speech drugged, most likely the pain medication.

"Yes, Gellert." I grab his hands. "How are you today?"

"I've been right here waiting." His smile is weak, unfocused like his eyes. "Right here…" His voice trails off into incoherent words.

"I enjoyed seeing you yesterday. Do you remember our visit?" I run the back of my hand down his cheek. This is the caring face I remember. And with guilty relief I'm again happy he's whole, not outwardly damaged except for the head wound. "We talked about how we could go for a walk since spring is here."

The knuckles on his hands appear extra white under his skin, and he grips the chair arms as if he could tumble out if he releases his hold. He looks as if he wants to say something but stops himself and turns his head away. "I tried to help them."

He's back on the subject of whatever happened while he was in the Labor Force.

I know you did." I press my face against his chest and listen to the beat of his heart, the thumps coming faster and harder as his memories must be resurfacing. "The doctor instinct in you won over your own safety."

"I waited too long," he says. And just like that, he's sobbing.

His sadness makes me cry in tandem. Before the war, I'd rarely seen him fall apart, even under the goriest of situations. A trolley wreck two years ago sent me vomiting in the gutter, but he remained coolheaded and in charge among severed legs and arms.

"We've heard the terrible stories. The Germans put your Labor Divisions out front without ammunition or supplies."

"Russians. Women. Children." His face crumples. He cries harder and begins to wail like a severely wounded animal. It's hard to hear, cutting through me.

He's regressed since yesterday when he was more clear, more planted in the here and now. This change scares me. What if this is his future, riding this emotional rollercoaster, reaching a high, and then plunging back down into the depths of despair?

"Gellert. Try not to think of what you saw." He's broken, barely holding himself together. He must have seen the horrors the Germans inflicted on innocent Russian civilians. "As soon as the doctors say you can leave, you're coming home with me." Gently I wrap him in a hug, but his arms remain limp in his lap. "And we only need to hang on a short time more. The Allies are pushing in from the West, the Russians from the East. The Germans are losing."

He bangs his hands on the arms of the wheelchair. "We have to go!"

What is he talking about? There's no safe place for us to go with the fighting all around. His delirium must have him still on the run from the front. The story of how he escaped and arrived here will come out one day, but now is not the time.

"Sweetheart." I take his hand in mine. "I'll be back every day to visit. I need you to focus on getting better. On what we'll do when the war is over."

He slumps in his chair again and weakly squeezes my hand. "Marika," he whispers and glances at me with what I think is an apology. "Too late."

"No, Gellert. It is *not* too late." Tears build again and blur my vision. "You are stronger than that. *We* are stronger than that."

He drops his head to his chest and closes his eyes. I must speak to the doctor about the pain medication he's on. Many of them can cause delusions and increased emotions. This forlorn, anxious side of him had been gone this week. He's obviously been traumatized, I accept that, but a head injury can amplify all he witnessed. I admit that when I received the news he was back and in the hospital, I pictured a happy reunion, with renewed love and affection, him taking care of me, offering me hope.

My selfishness saddens me.

I also wasn't prepared for this version. Did I really think Gellert would act the same way as when I last saw him? Free of all shock and horrors?

This isn't about me and what I need. It's about facing reality and getting him healed. Buried under the layers of hurt and pain is the man I love. And if not exactly the same man I said goodbye to, then a man I nevertheless still want to build my life around. I was young when I met him, a mere sixteen, but we've been committed to each other since. I won't give up.

A tapping on the doorframe directs my thoughts back to the here and now.

A nurse stands there, her curly dark hair so thickly piled on top of her head that her nurse's white scarf tied at the top is barely visible. "It's time for his therapy."

"How's he doing?" I ask, keeping my tone upbeat. "He told me yesterday he was ready to go for a walk with me."

"He's not quite there yet." The nurse's smile is sympathetic. "He needs to convince himself there's nothing preventing him from walking."

Once again, I'm reminded his inability to stand or walk baffles us all since every test indicates nothing has impaired his legs.

"You can do it, sweetheart. As soon as you're walking, you're coming home with me, okay?" I have told him this before. I kiss his forehead. "I'll be back tomorrow." And like yesterday, I spot a glimmer of life in his eyes.

"I'll wait right here." He's groggy and his words slur, but his attempt at humor relieves me.

I chuckle and kiss him again.

I still believe he will recover and make a great doctor one day. And a good husband. I smile when I think about the effort he always put into his gifts. He'd spend hours fastidiously wrapping them, tying the most unique items onto the top—an antique button, a pine cone, a rolled-up theatre program from a play we attended. He's unselfish to a fault, and that's what I think hurt him during his escape back to Budapest. He must have stopped to help someone and something went wrong.

I leave the hospital, heading back to Pest.

For the first time in days, the dour grey clouds are gone. The sun rises, embracing the sky, as if it missed its long-lost friend, the blue of day. The sun rakes its warm fingers across the buildings' rooftops and onto the uplifted faces of school children making their way to class, the bright morning reminding me I have another day to appreciate.

Sure, not everything is going as I wish it would, but I know while speaking with the refugees flooding into the city, my situation could be so much worse.

$-4-$

BUDAPEST, HUNGARY

March 22, 1944

Once across the Danube, it's only a fifteen-block walk to the Girls' Home on Kerepesi. The Catholic Church supports Sister Sára, the head nurse over the many homes. And she's so much more than a nurse. The woman wears everyone out with her tireless energy. At age forty-four, she's been a teacher, bookbinder, milliner, and journalist. One day, I'll be happy to simply practice as a nurse.

The Catholic nuns running the large program changed their original focus from helping Catholic girls in need by providing food, offering shelter, and teaching them a skill, to helping anyone fleeing persecution who arrives in Hungary scared and scarred.

One day as I was driving our family car back from Győr, two young women rushed from the bushes and waved me down. They were from Yugoslavia and had been on the run for weeks—now gaunt and dirty—trying to stay ahead of the Nazis who rounded up their family and shot them all at the edge of town.

I hid them in the car and delivered them to Sister Sára, and just like that, I was working with the Zionists Youth in the Resistance.

As the group shepherded more refugees into Budapest, we believed Hungary was one of the last safe places for Jews and gypsies in Europe.

Or it was. Now that the Germans are here, uncertainty hangs like a grey curtain around our city.

I push through the front door of the three-story brick building and instantly bump into Sister Margit Slachta. She is the first woman elected to the Hungarian Parliament, where most of her speeches focus on the poor conditions of women and children. She's carrying a crying toddler with a blotchy red face and hair fuzzed out like a dandelion gone to seed.

"Sister Marika." Sister Slachta smiles my way, her shoulders holding a self-confident pose. "You're just in time. This little one is running a temperature."

Everyone here is called Sister- or Brother-something. If asked, we're all Catholics. I have an identification card that says as much.

"Let me take her," I say. The girl is sweaty and limp as I carry her up the wide stone stairs to the infirmary on the second floor. The third floor is the dormitory for fifty-five residents, now divided into adult and child sections because the home is no longer just for girls.

I greet another nurse volunteer as I lay the girl on a bed and cover her with a sheet. I brush damp hair off her face and note her listless eyes. With flushed cheeks and pale skin around her lips, I pull up her shirt knowing I'll find a rash. She has scarlet fever.

"Go Mama?" the tiny child cries and searches my face for an answer. "Want Mama."

I haven't seen this child before, so I don't know her history. Within a few steps, I retrieve an aspirin, crush it, and feed her the medicine in a spoonful of apricot jam. After I know she has swallowed the mixture, she drinks the water I offer.

She cries again for her mother. I shoot a quick glance to Anna, the other worker, and she shakes her head, her downturned mouth saying it all. The child won't see her mother again.

"I'm here with you," I say, my throat painfully tight. I've followed Sister Sára and Margit's examples and learned not to cry in front of the children or refugees. They need soothing reassurance, but some days I believe my larynx will burst apart from all the pain stifled there. Maybe that's why I cry so easily at the hospital with Gellert. It's a safe place to release my pain.

I rub the child's back after she turns on her side and begins to suck her thumb. Soon she is asleep. Surveying the room, I'm glad to see only six beds filled, down from fourteen a week ago. Once they're healthy, the new arrivals move to any one of the dozen Girls' Homes or orphanages in the system. The primary condition we treat is starvation since we're often the first stop. Some people arrive having eaten bark or food scraps left for pigs as they made their way here from the countryside.

I stand and turn to Anna. "Do you need any help?" She's not much older than my nineteen years, with dove-grey eyes and long lashes set on a pockmarked face, most likely from chickenpox. Her family is from the town of Vác, along the Danube north of here.

"I'm fine," Anna whispers. She rubs her hands down her tan skirt, a habit even when she's not nervous, but today she has a steady rhythm going.

I walk to her side and touch her arm. "Are you okay?" Asking about a person's former life is frowned upon. Sister Margit will scold an inquisitive newcomer. *"A person should not cast his thoughts to the past, for God has placed our eyes on our face for a good reason."* However, asking about current feelings is encouraged.

"The Germans," she says. "I try not to be, but I'm afraid."

News about the invasion ripples through the street like bad cigar smoke. The unknown stink of what's next. There's always that cold finger tracing fear down our spines if we let it. And in a new safety move, the nuns no longer dress in their grey habits but don simple streetwear. They're able to move without recourse through the city and report what they've learned to the Catholic leaders.

Shockingly, not all bishops are willing to listen or help the Jews, but there are a few.

I give Anna's arm a squeeze. "Well, then you have also heard that the Russians are winning the East, right?"

She nods, her mouth set in a firm line.

"They've reached Romania. The Americans and British are also winning back countries. It's a matter of hanging on, and to keep helping out here until the Germans are defeated." Half the time I believe my own words, and today is one of those days. I offer a smile I've practiced in the mirror. It says, *I'm not worried and you should trust me.* "I'll check back with you later."

"Thank you." She wipes her hands again, but the tension has left her face. "Will you come see Sister Sára's play tonight?"

The busy nun managed to write a play on the life of St. Margaret of Hungary, and the opening show is tonight in the more spacious orphanage nearby.

I'd almost forgotten about it with all the apprehension of the last few days. "Of course, I'll be there. What a nice treat for our children. And the visitors."

Which reminds me, I need to check on the new refugees. If anyone asks, and so far no one has, the "visitors" are here to check on the health of a child they had to give up because they could no longer feed him or her. Abandoning children has become common practice throughout Budapest, so it doesn't raise any questions. We workers know that's not why these people are here. Running for your life is a whole different story.

The intake room is located in the basement, where refugees are brought into the building through the root-cellar doors keeping them away from prying eyes on the main street. Only last week, I rode up front in a truck while nine people hid under piles of produce in the wagon we towed, the farmers receiving extra money for the additional cargo.

A boy of about seven is on the linoleum floor, playing with a carved wooden horse. He doesn't look up when I enter the room. Behind him is an older girl. Her print dress is so ragged on her emaciated form, it's hard to guess her age. She could be twelve or sixteen. They both have dark ash-blond hair, and the girl's wary eyes are light brown. The smudges of dirt on their skin and bits of twigs and dead leaves in their hair tell a recent survival story involving hiding in the forest.

The Girls' Home matches the nuns with arriving foreign refugees. Sister Aleksandra is Polish, so she's kneeling in front of the pair, speaking softly in their language. The boy doesn't appear to be listening, but the girl is as she stares at nothing, her face void of emotion although her ear is turned toward Sister Aleksandra.

I've seen this expression before, and it's terrible. The girl's feelings, either shoved away or forced deep into a dark recess of her mind, may one day tear her to pieces. It's like struggling to keep a deadly poison inside. The body will try to expel it in every way it can, but if prevented, it will kill the person from the inside out. My father believes this is why my grandfather shot himself. He'd seen too much horror in the Great War but refused to talk about it.

I cross to the wooden chest in the corner and choose a few items. Local families are generous in donating their used games and toys to the Sisters' Society. Although we're grateful, we need to sort through them to remove the soldier figures, boxcars, and lifelike guns.

On the floor next to the boy, I set up a cow, two pigs, and a small water bucket to go along with his horse. Slowly, I walk the cow toward him and say hello in Polish. "Cześć." I only know a half dozen words and phrases as my family's preferred languages are German, English, and Hungarian in that order.

He stops his horse and studies my cow.

"Welcome to our home," I say. I bend lower and try to see his face as he continues to stare at the floor.

His hands are grimy, and the nails are torn. His sister's match. They must've dug through the cold ground for roots.

"Where have they come from?" I ask Sister Aleksandra in German.

"They lived with their father at an uncle's house in Eger."

"That's way in the northeast. And?"

This is the question that always unearths the saddest part of the tale. The segment of *What happened next?* reveals the reason they're here.

"Their father heard the Germans were about to take Hungary. The uncle who's not Jewish was afraid to house them any longer…although it doesn't sound like he offered them more than a shed and meager food these last few years."

"Years?" A scowl knots my forehead. Who keeps relatives in dismal conditions for that long, especially when children are involved?

"Yes, it seems so. This is Zofia and her brother, Jakub. Zofia won't say how they came to be at the uncle's house from their town of Jedwabne in Northern Poland."

At the mention of the town's name, the girl's eyes grow to the size of plums and dart back and forth from my face to Sister Aleksandra's.

The Sister gently reaches toward the girl, but Zofia curls into herself, avoiding the touch. "You are safe," Sister Aleksandra whispers.

Zofia's reaction says she witnessed unimaginable atrocities.

"They set out on foot five days ago," the Sister says. "Near Hatvan, the father fell into the river and drowned. The children were found crying, and the local priest drove them here."

"Poor dears," I say. The smile on my face is the practiced one, but inside I'm heartbroken for them. Asking about other relatives will have to wait. The children need a bath and a medical examination before we can assign them beds.

Sister Aleksandra explains to them they will get food, a warm bath, and clean clothes, and that I'll see them again later.

The boy looks at me for the first time. His lower face and neck are covered with twists of burn scars that appear to have healed on their own. His lower lip pulls downward on the left side, and his bottom teeth show the frozen skin on his chin unyielding.

As I stand, I rub my hand along his cheek. A shiver races across his skin, like the twitch of a horse's flank at the touch of a fly, or from a person expecting to be hurt.

I now fight the tears as I climb the stairs to the main office.

The play we'll see later today is about St. Margaret, a Dominican nun who wore scratchy hair shirts and put tacks in her shoes to try to experience the pain of others. She is attributed with dozens of miracles before her death at age twenty-eight, and if I understand it correctly, she prayed and fasted herself into an early grave.

I would gladly don such an uncomfortable shirt right now if I could conjure a miracle to take away the pain Jakub and Zofia have suffered.

The soles of my leather shoes make scuffing sounds on the steps. I'd like to think I could walk on tacks as well, but I know my limits. And I know I'll never be pious enough to have an island named after me in the middle of the Danube like St. Margaret.

The Torah teaches, "If you are not a better person tomorrow than you are today, what need have you for a tomorrow?"

Since I have every plan to see tomorrow and the days after, all I can do is try to be a better person.

I go in search of the other refugees. It will take most of the day to assess and get them ready for their new home assignments. For me, the children are always the special cases, holding a sense of promise, of a hopeful future, and that gives me comfort when they teem around me. I'd argue there is no sound more heavenly than an infectious giggle.

When I get a break, I must call my parents and tell them I'll be out late. They've always worried about me, a single woman on the streets at night. With the enemy now in our city, they'll be more apprehensive. It's only nine blocks home, and I know all the secret alleys, so I'm not concerned.

I bring my fist to my mouth, stifling a yawn. It's after 10 p.m., and I'm back at the Girls' Home performing a final check on all the patients before I leave. The little girl with scarlet fever is doing better. Her temperature is down, and she's eaten several bites of stew. A few more days and she'll be playing in the nursery with others her age.

Sister Sára's play was a success. Eighty attendees made up of children, nuns, and a few adults crowded into the theatre for the one-hour production, an uplifting glimpse at a life well-lived in the service to others. The hearty applause at the end was inspiring. I've missed live acting since we were banned from all cinemas and theatre houses.

I sigh. And I miss the Opera House. Ours is purported to be one of the finest in the world, a theory I'd like to test out one day. The foyer has marble columns while wrought iron lamps illuminate the wide stone staircase and main entrance. The vast, sweeping staircase was an important element of the evening's events as it allowed ladies to show off their new gowns. I would like to have been around when the Opera House first opened in the nineteenth century.

The day will come when we'll step foot in that beautiful building again.

I call my goodnights and leave the Girls' Home. The brisk night revives my sleepy senses. The streets are mostly quiet, except for the clink of bottles dropped into a container and the far-off wail of a siren. The trees along Fiumei Street sway overhead as I follow the road alongside the sprawling Kerepesi Cemetery. As the largest Jewish cemetery in Budapest, it's known for the towering mausoleums that line the inner avenues.

My father often comes here to think. He says he finds peace among Hungary's most prominent citizens.

I startle when I hear scraping behind me and whirl around, my hand to my chest. A German soldier is my first worry. My identification papers show I work under the protection of the Catholic Church, but would that mean anything to a drunken attacker?

My eyes search the shadows behind me. A stray dog scrambles across the intersection and disappears down the street, along with my bravery. Maybe walking home so late wasn't such a good idea.

"What are you doing out?" A man's voice.

My heart leaps into my throat. I press against the cold stone of a building and strain to see who's approaching under the dim lights.

A deep laugh comes from him. "Marika. It's me." He steps closer, and I sag in relief.

"Benedek!" I release a long-held breath. "You frightened me."

"I was at a meeting." My downstairs neighbor, the tugboat operator, takes my arm and steadies me.

"For work?" I fall into step beside him as we head to the apartment building. "Awfully late, isn't it?"

"It wasn't for work." He clears his throat. His familiar scent of bike oil and sausage waft from him. "I joined a group of men. Street safety and all that."

"That's good." I want to say that's what the police are for but hold my tongue. I'm just so relieved he wasn't a German.

"You need to be careful, Marika. Times are about to change."

"They've already changed for some of us. We've got rules and more rules coming at us all the time."

"Well"—he stuffs his hands in his coat pockets—"about to change *more*. If you need someone on your side, you can always come to me."

My side? "We're all trying to stay calm and not take sides." I stop near our front gate and face him. "What have you heard?"

"This Adolf Eichmann. He's here now." He motions for me to pull out my key to open the locked gate. "He appointed Döme Sztójay as our new prime minister."

I fumble with the key and turn the lock. The gate's hinges squeak. "I don't know who he is."

"A professional soldier. Loves the Germans, hates the...well, he's against the non-Christians."

I shake my head. This growing hatred over the last few years is preached from pulpits and published in Christian newspapers—Jews are the cursed who turned from the true faith. And now, some are considered dishonest, scheming to seek earthly happiness by converting to Christianity. Top government leadership never repeated these radical right views...until now.

And *"earthly happiness"*? Isn't that what all humans seek for themselves and their families?

"What help can you offer?" We reach the front door to our building. Our apartment window upstairs has a light on, but the others are dark, including his. "Protection by your new group?"

"Maybe." He runs a hand at the back of his neck and looks skyward. "But better yet, you could convert to Catholicism while that's still allowed. And then marry a Christian."

Again, I shake my head. I didn't see any reason for this, although thousands converted like my brother and his wife. From what I hear, the Germans loathe our race, not our religion. "I'll keep that in mind."

"Good"—he smiles—"and I'll gladly volunteer when you're ready."

A shiver runs through me. His offer comes across as more like a demand than a proposition. I swallow hard and form a flat line with my lips. I can't force them into a smile.

"Thank you for walking me home." Before he can say anything else, I thump up the stairs, leaving him in front of his door.

We're friends with all our neighbors and Christian acquaintances, even as we're limited now in some joint activities. Monthly, many of us enjoyed potluck dinner in the garden before attending theatre together, but half of us are now no longer allowed.

Benedek's suggestion—that I convert—worries me that his opinion of Jews has changed. And if it has, what does that mean for all of us living in the same building?

~5~

BUDAPEST, HUNGARY

April 1, 1944

On this late Saturday evening, we've just come upstairs from a celebratory dinner at the Schlesingers' apartment. It's János's fiftieth birthday, and Raakel and I pulled off a gathering for her father. The building's residents brought dishes to share and arrived at exactly seven o'clock. János was taken completely by surprise and quickly swiped at his moist eyes. He then reached for and popped open two bottles of local wine my father handed him. During his toast, he thanked everyone for coming.

Father's riddle for the gathering was, "This belongs to you, but everyone else uses it."

After a moment, Raakel won with the answer, "Your name."

The only missing guests were Benedek Dely and his father, although the light was on in the bicycle repair shop and shining beneath their apartment door. It's been a week since he walked me home, and we haven't spoken again. I slipped the invitation to the party under their door days ago, glad not to have to talk to him. His offer of marriage still sends a shiver through me. How arrogant. He knows I'm engaged to Gellert.

And speaking of my guy, Gellert took several steps today with the use of a wheeled walker. At this rate of recovery, he should be discharged soon. He's had no trance-like episodes this whole week, and the doctors believe that phase is behind him. Although he has an apartment, living alone won't be an option. My parents heartily agree he'll move in with us.

A warm breeze pushes through our open living room windows, gently lifting the ivory lace curtains, the ghostly rhythm infused with scents of lilac and lily-of-the-valley.

My father heads into his workshop where he has spent many hours in the past month. He's working hard to get baby József's puppet finished.

We're trying to stay busy, to act as if our lives haven't changed. Yet a greasy flutter fills my chest daily, a constant warning that our safety can shift on a whim. We call to the farm each morning, and István assures us all is well.

I change out of my dress into my nightclothes. Short bursts of jazz mixed with a hissing sound come from Father's workroom as he tunes the radio, trying to find news. Since yesterday, telephone and telegraph communication with other countries is now blocked. We're sealed off from the world, and if not for the BBC on our illicit radio, we'd hear nothing.

Last night, we quietly celebrated a report that Allies are bombing more German cities. But we also prayed for the injured or dead citizens trapped below while the war is fought from above.

"Leichi, Marika," my father calls. "Come quick!"

Mother and I enter his workroom at the same time. He points at the radio as if it were a bomb ready to explode.

We lean closer and listen to Radio Budapest, the national station.

"...This government decision means that all Jews of either sex above the age of six are required to bear on the left side of the breast of their outer garment, a yellow six-pointed star no less than ten centimeters square. This will help the government of the Kingdom of Hungary identify the Jews upon whose loyalty we cannot rely. This action is not taken out of hatred or revenge, but rather only in a self-defense move that benefits all the citizens of our fine country."

Mother has her fist to her mouth. Father shakes his head as the broadcast adds that Jewish persons caught out in public without it will be arrested.

During this unsettling news, I'm gnawing on my thumbnail and realize I've nibbled to the point of making it bleed. I keep my focus on the radio but cut my eyes back and forth to my parents' faces. Have we been naïve, assuming we're safe from what transpired in other countries? Now that we're to be labeled, branded like animals on a farm, how much time will we have before fences are built here?

"A Central Jewish Council is now established as a go-between in Budapest," the announcer says. He's emotionless, as if announcing a stalled weather pattern with no foreseeable change in the near future. "The Germans have reassured the Jewish leaders that if their people comply, they will come to no harm."

"Huh." Father slowly rocks back and forth, toward the radio and away, his hands clenched behind his back. "I must hear what the rabbis at Dohány say. First thing in the morning I'll visit, but it seems as if we need to comply for now."

The Dohány temple is the main synagogue for all Jews in Hungary, the touchstone where we gather, religious or not. With its red-and-yellow striped façade, lavish décor, and two tall spires topped by gilded onion domes, sometimes we go there simply to enjoy its beauty. The fact it was designed by a Christian architect in the last century, we remain optimistic about the tolerance the gentile world has for our religion.

"I don't think we have any yellow fabric," my mother says. Tiny lines have formed around her eyes in the last four weeks. "And we need to put more food into storage."

I'm saddened by how quickly my mother is ready to comply with this demand that we wear a star. She's more defiant than that. But this is her way—stay positive against the ugly face of aversion.

"I'll stop by the fabric shop after I meet Raakel tomorrow," I say, "and buy enough for this building and whoever else needs it."

A strange noise comes from the street below. Two plops, like someone dropped and smashed Greek melons. Then someone screams, a hysterical high-pitched wail that tapers to a strangled ending with a call for help.

We rush into the kitchen, and Father pushes the window wider. Now shouts for an ambulance rise from below. I lean out with my parents at my side. Under the eerie wash of a streetlight, a few people are gathered around two people splayed like broken puppets on the street.

"Oh no," I say, realizing the answer and I shiver as I glance to the roofline. Then the disturbing plops echo in my ears. These people have jumped from the roof terrace next door that connects to ours. We've been to that apartment building's shared upper terrace many times to enjoy summer parties for the residents of both buildings. "I think it's the Grubers." The hair on my arms stands on end at the thought this older couple, who secretly arrived here four years ago from Austria, has come to this end.

"Frau Gruber?" Tears build in my mother's eyes and slide down her face. She snakes her shaky hand into mine. "We talked only a day ago. She seemed fine. She had me try her new recipe for cherry crepes."

"Nothing short of a tragedy," my father says. "Herr Gruber never got over their son still missing after the fight on the Don. He hated the Germans for putting our sons out in front and leaving them there." He sighs and it's one for the ages. "This news of the new regulations. It must have been too much."

I didn't know their son Karl well. He was years older than I was when they arrived in Budapest, and within a short period of time, he was swept up in the Jewish Labor Force like Gellert. Karl has yet to return. The Grubers never lock their door, even though it is on the first floor, and everyone passes it on the way to their apartments. When warned that one-third of the population in Budapest was hungry and looking for opportunities to steal and sell valuables, the Grubers always said, "Karl could return when we aren't here," or "We know he will make it home one day, God willing. He should not be locked out."

But they gave up, climbed to the terrace, and left the world together.

I know the emptiness of missing someone. I waited months for Gellert to walk through our door. Some days, profound doubt threatened that hope, but I found that having no hope at all left me hollowed out, desolate. That's the agony they've suffered.

My father pulls us away from the window and holds our hands. "We will pray."

We bow our heads as he begins. "God, full of mercy, who dwells in the heights, provide a sure rest for our neighbors and friends…"

I know the prayer by heart, and although one part of my mind follows along, the other part tries to picture my family walking around our beautiful city with a star sewn on our coats. We're singled out as different, unwanted in the name of self-defense. Such a senseless demand.

Why deem us as unnecessary in a city where our culture is highly praised because of its artists, musicians, scientists, and financiers? All Jewish people. All made to feel ashamed now.

I think of our friends the Schlesingers and our other Christian neighbors. They've never viewed us as different from them. Our religions and cultures have intermingled in Budapest and throughout Hungary for centuries. Sure, there have always been the extremists who want Hungary to remain one race, but their group is so small. Besides, they dislike everyone.

"We're going to get through this," I say. "Sister Sára said only two hundred Germans remain in the city now. Their big show of conquering The Kingdom of Hungary is over. A million people live here. Surely, there are tens of thousands who will see the unfairness of these regulations and step up to protect us if the situation gets worse."

"We'll wear the star with pride." This is the mother I know—the daughter of a wealthy landowner, who once tamed a horse no one dared ride. The woman who married my father even as her parents rebuffed that decision, saying my father was not affluent enough. If I know her, she'll sew a quarter-million stars, one for every Jewish person in Budapest, and tell them to smile while she pins it on their coats.

"We will," I say.

"Let's make sure ours are extra-large." Mother has a mischievous glimmer in her eye as she spreads her hands fifteen centimeters apart. "Hate to have them go unnoticed."

My father traces in the air a huge Star of David that would cover his entire suit coat if made real. "Make mine this big."

We all chuckle but our eyes say we aren't as sure of ourselves as our words seem to boast. We'll wear the proper marking, but we'll stay away from the Germans and wait out the war.

It surely will end any day now.

The next morning, walking back to our apartment carrying a bolt of yellow cloth, I'm surprisingly optimistic. The chestnut trees along the street are starting to leaf out in their bright green buds, springing to life. Every day is one step closer to our lives returning to normal.

Suddenly, a tremendous roaring builds in the sky. Then, explosions rock me at the exact moment deafening blasts drown out every sound. The thump of bombs striking somewhere nearby comes up through the sidewalk, through my shoes, into my chest. In an instant, air-raid sirens wail, and people scream and run to clear the streets.

My heart pounds as the bombing continues and planes fill the sky, giant insects buzzing across the city. I run toward home, the continual burst of explosions muting the sounds of my erratic breathing and my shoes slapping the pavement. Between the deafening noises, I catch pieces of conversation from people I pass, "The railway yard…airplane factory…Hamburg."

Would the Americans and British create a fire tornado like in Hamburg last year? Nearly sixty thousand burned to death. The destruction from the air described by the BBC war correspondent was that nothing was left but whole neighborhoods resembling blackened honeycombs.

My hands shake so hard I fumble with the key to our gate, but once through I rush inside.

"Marika!" János is at the end of the hallway, pacing. "I've made everyone go to the cellar. Your parents are worried sick, so hurry down."

The circular stairway takes me another twenty feet below into a long, arched room, with high windows and dull-colored, stacked-stone walls. Years ago, Father ran electricity down the center of the ceiling to prevent an accidental oil fire from the old lanterns, but now the lights are extinguished. Sporadically placed candles sputter, flickering off jars of canned goods stored on the floor-to-ceiling shelving. My eyes adjust, and I spot Father in the group of our building's residents.

"Father!" I move into his embrace.

"Good Lord." His voice cracks. "We didn't know where to look for you."

Mother is at my side, trembling, like a captive bird held in a stranger's hands. "We must check on István and the family."

"As soon as the bombing stops," Father says and pulls her into our embrace.

Would the Americans waste their bombs on sprawling estates across the countryside? I doubt it. But major cities will be targets, and Győr is large.

I'm thankful Gellert isn't still out in the countryside trying to make it home. In his twenty-four years, he's suffered enough tragedy. His parents, grandparents, and his uncle—his only extended family—were killed a few years ago in the Bucharest earthquake that took hundreds of lives. He'd just started medical school when his parents traveled to Romania to bring Gellert's grandparents and uncle to Budapest. Rumors that Romania was about to side with Germany forced their spur-of-the-moment trip to bring the family to Hungary. When the earthquake struck, the family lived in the Carlton Bloc, the tallest building in Bucharest. In the few days it took to unearth the bodies, Romania indeed signed on with the Axis powers.

His parents had the right idea but the wrong timing.

We'd just started dating. Gellert, so overcome with grief, nearly left medical school. The emotional weeks after their deaths solidified our relationship. His parents had worked hard and saved every pengő they could spare for their only son to become a doctor—quitting was not an option.

My eyes adjust to the dimness. Benedek and his father must have made it to the basement first because they're at the farthest wall from the entrance door. They're talking to Herr Griess, a manager at Gedeon Richter pharmaceutical plant, and his wife, Greta. Their two children go to the Gymnasium, the same university preparation high school István and I attended. Right now I imagine they would be safe in the building's cellars where Raakel and I tried our first cigarette at the urging of some older girls. We both turned green around the gills and swore off trying to impress the upper classmates.

More thumps rock the ground. In a split second, my hands are sweaty as I realize who's missing.

"Raakel's still out there," I say to my parents, choking on emotion. "She left for the café early. It's why I went shopping alone."

"János is waiting for her," my father says.

"The Germans love Café Gerbeaud. What if it's the Americans' main bombing target?" I could go find her. Thanks to my father's years advising the transportation department, I know all the tunnels under the city. We'd be safe coming home that way. "I can get to her through the underground passages." I squeeze my mother's hands as if to say I'll be fine as I turn to leave.

"You'll do no such thing!" Father grabs my arm. "Those tunnels may have been hit and could be filled with water."

Footsteps descending the stairs stop the whispered murmur of conversation in the room. We all turn in uncertainty.

Raakel and János hurry in, and Ilona runs to her daughter and husband.

I let out a held breath. What would I do if something happened to her? She's the sister I never had and the friend everyone deserves.

They walk farther into the cellar, and my mother pulls her into a hug. "We thank God. May we all cheat death a thousand more times."

"Thank you, but I was fine," Raakel says. Her face is blotchy from exertion. "They closed the café. Most of the bombing was at the armament works, but someone said a block of apartments was also hit." She swallows hard. "People are hurt, possibly dead."

The ousting of all Jewish doctors and nurses has left a shortage of trained medical professionals in Budapest. Part of me wants to offer help, but would the local hospitals allow me inside their wards? But they may decide to change their minds and accept Jews during a state of emergency.

"You're safe now." János appears shrunken. Only moments ago, the fear expelled from his rigid appearance seems to have left less of him behind.

Raakel shakes her head. "We may be safe, but you"—she turns to my family—"need to stay inside for a while. Gossips have already started saying that Jews are signaling Americans and British planes from the rooftops."

"Preposterous," my mother says. "Who would believe this?"

"Lies. Always a trifling spark that ignites so much more," Father says, his face set hard. "If this gets fueled by repetition, it'll grow into an inferno. We'll remain home as much as possible."

"We can shop for you," Ilona says. "That's no problem."

I don't mention it, but I'm needed in the underground and at the Girls' Home and orphanages. Maybe now more than ever with the bombings. I'll figure out a way to get there.

The all-clear siren bleats from above. The residents appear to collectively sigh before shaking hands with each other and heading upstairs to their apartments. As the building's owner, our family will wait for everyone to leave before us. Father shakes the men's hands, and Mother smiles. Young or old, Gentile or Jew, we're fortunate to have a diverse building that lives in harmony, sharing each other's trials and successes all these years. Many apartment buildings in Budapest are connected, block after block, however, the same cohesiveness is not always transmuted through their walls. Perhaps if our elderly neighbors had not isolated themselves after their son went missing, they'd still be alive. Or was it their bad luck that others in the building couldn't ease their despair before they decided to jump to their deaths?

Belko Dely and Benedek are last to leave.

Herr Dely does not meet my father's eyes as he shakes his hand, but mutters we should have a good day. Benedek stays behind his father's back, avoiding the polite goodbye. Before ascending the steps, he sends a probing look my way.

Why is he not at work today, moving barges up and down the Danube? He usually has only Sundays off. Could he have been warned to stay home and away from the river? The Dely father and son have always been secretive about where Piroska Dely, Benedek's mother stays when she's not with them. Herr Dely and Benedek moved in two years ago. The story was their previous apartment near Central Park had no space for Herr Dely to open his bicycle repair shop. On rare occasions, Frau Dely stays in the apartment but even less frequently speaks to any of us while she's in the building. She comes off as morose, and I'm sure I've never seen her smile.

A new air of distrust comes from the Delys. But what have they to fear from us?

"Let's get busy cleaning out my workspace," Father says. "We've got to make room for István's family if they need to move in."

"No, Father," I say. He needs his creative outlet. "They can have my room."

"Where will you sleep?" My mother's smooth forehead knots in the center. "Endre can move his workspace into our room."

That's a nice offer, but his workspace now fills a whole room, and even the smallest table wouldn't fit in there.

"I can spend some nights at the Girls' Homes. They need more overnight help." I offer my most reassuring smile. "And you know how often I fall asleep on the couch."

"It'll only be for a short while," Mother says. "The bombing means this terrible war is almost over."

Hungarians have a saying, *He who trusts is happy; but the doubter is wiser.* I'll let my mother enjoy her happiness. For me, with the Germans' determined push toward supremacy, my doubting mind says we haven't seen the end of the war just yet.

—6—

BUDAPEST, HUNGARY

April 10, 1944

I t's been a week of sporadic bombing, and we scurry from place to place and back like rats on trash day. We've blacked out the windows, dimmed our hand torches if we even dare venture out at night, and spend at least part of every day in the cellars. Sirens and radio alerts blare all the time.

And we wear our yellow stars. There's no pride being labeled inferior, a scourge upon the city, but getting caught without the emblem on the left side of our coats means immediate arrest and a fine. A second arrest means imprisonment.

And the news worsens.

Hungary is asked to bear the burden of financing the German occupation. Had Regent Horthy seen that coming when he welcomed the devil as his bed partner? Now, the Hungarian government needs to pay two hundred million pengö monthly for the German troops. To avoid a complete collapse of the economy, their answer is to steal wealth from the Jews.

Suicide is rampant. Hundreds have ended it all, especially those who arrived in Budapest thinking it a safe, last resort.

János was forced, as was every building janitor, to list each Jewish family in the building, with the excuse the sugar and soap ration coupons would be replaced by newer ones. He hung his head in shame and apologized over and over the day he came to tell Father this and that he needed a record of our bank accounts and assets.

Not to be left penniless, Father devised a plan to withdraw some of his money from the bank before János handed in the paperwork and our assets were frozen or taken. He wrote out a large check to János, calling it a bonus for his years as building manager. The janitor cashed it and brought Father the money, now hidden in the apartment. Father didn't tell us where he put the cash, and the rest of us are fine with that. He said it's to protect us should anyone try to force us to speak out.

István moved their bank accounts, now under Erzsébet's father's name, in case someone cares that István was born a Jew. He insists they are safe in Győr, although some Jewish men have been forced to build fences and sheds outside the city. Father Andrew at their church promises protection for all converts in his parish. Zoltan, a Jewish worker on the farm, is a hardworking man with a wife and six children. He also helps clean the local synagogue. István said he asked if he could hide their valuables on our family's property.

"They only had two silver bowls, a small bag with a few rings, and a gold watch passed down three generations." István's voice lowered as he told us the story over the phone. "We told them where we will bury the box and assured them we'd be returning it as soon as it's safe. But their faces. I think they're not so sure they will be back."

"We can put them in houses if they can get to Budapest," I offer. "The International Red Cross stepped up and is providing shelter to anyone arriving who's in danger."

The Red Cross has been here since October of 1943, mainly involved in blood drives for wounded citizens or supplying food. Now their focus has shifted. Their counterparts in other countries have warned them of what happened to the Jews who were rounded up, so they are readying safe places here to hide if it comes to that.

"I'll walk over later today and tell Zoltan," István says.

But there are good times in this chaos too. Tucked safely in the apartment, Mother, Ilona, Raakel, and I spend many hours, talking and laughing while we dry meats and sausages and bottle fruits and vegetables for possible lean days ahead. We've had to hand over our food coupons, but Ilona still shops for us.

I've learned so much about my mother I didn't know before. She bested her older brother in running races, stuck sheep's wool to her chin, pretending to be an old man, and drove the family crazy at meals as she acted out the part. She learned to ride a horse at four and won six riding competitions before age ten. Once, when angry at her parents, she ran away, riding her horse Lily thirty kilometers north of Győr, hoping to reach the North Pole she'd read about.

"I couldn't sit a horse for a week after the whipping your Bepa Stark gave me," she says with a wistful look in her eye.

Today we've just finished canning more bitter cucumbers and beets. It's only Mother and Ilona left inside to clean as Raakel and I leave. Father is in the courtyard, playing chess with Ferenc and catching up on the latest updates of what Ferenc hears along the transportation routes.

Father and Ferenc's voices carry in from the doors opening onto the courtyard as Raakel and I sit on the cool cement stairs of the first floor. She takes a bite of the apple kiffle she's brought from the bakery and passes the sweet to me. The cream cheese dough tastes amazing. This is a treat we've had no means to make for over a year.

"I saw a smart skirt in the hotel shop the other day," she says, touching a tiny rip in mine. "I can pick it up for you."

I swallow the pastry bite and hand the rest back to her. "You're so thoughtful. I wear this one to the orphanages because the children climb all over me." For years, she's borrowed my clothes and knows I have more in the closet than I can ever wear. "I do miss shopping with you, though."

"Me too. Hey. Guess who came sneaking around the other night?" As she talks, her blonde curls bounce around her face. The blue of her eyes makes people stop to stare for a moment, the color an arresting pale azure.

"Let me guess." I nudge her with my shoulder, nearly knocking the pastry out of her hand. "Béla Lugosi." Raakel has had a mad crush on him ever since we watched *Dracula*. A few years back, we went to the cinema every week, especially if an American movie was playing. Sure, he's a Hungarian living in Hollywood, but of all the choices of men to make her swoon, I never understood this one. Give me Clark Gable any day.

"Yes, and he bit me on the neck, and soon I can only be out at night." She laughs. "He's just as strong and domineering as I'd hoped."

"You *would* like that." My reply carries no malice. We've had this discussion many times before. I prefer a man to treat me as an equal, while she would like hers to be in charge.

"It was that creepy Mrs. Dely. I was coming back from the laundry room when she rang the gate to get in. It was dark when she came up the walkway, but I swear she was dressed in men's slacks."

"God's zoo grows bigger every day." I chuff. "Did you talk to her?"

"She barely said good evening before entering their apartment. No more than thirty minutes later I heard the gate clang shut out front."

"Benedek offered to marry me and make me a Christian." I reach down and rub a scuff mark off the side of my black shoe. "As if. And he knows about Gellert."

Raakel's smile drops away, and she takes my hand. "How is he doing?"

"A bit better"—I shake my head—"but he still can't come home. Yesterday he seemed more like himself, calm, making a few jokes. It's been a good week though, and the doctors believe the crisis is passed."

"That's good to hear. He's such a sweetie." She snudges my shoulder. "You wait. He'll be discharged soon."

"What would I do without you?" Raakel and I have grown up together, swimming at the local spas, riding bikes, laughing. I turn to her and force a smile. "Tell me what's new with you. You look happier today."

She bobs her head, and her smile is dreamy. "I've met a waiter…Sándor Saamik. He works at a posh restaurant in the Gresham Palace Hotel, a block from my work."

I grab her hand and lean closer. "What? You must tell me everything."

"There's not much right now." Color rises in her cheeks. "We sit on the benches outside the hotel and watch the boats on the river or the comings and goings across the Chain Bridge."

"Has he kissed you?"

"Just last night, when he walked me home." She wiggles her eyebrows. "It was amazing." Then she places her hands over her heart.

"Well. I need more than that. What's he look like? Is he dark like your Lugosi dream man or what?"

"Believe it or not, no. He's blond. Blue-eyed." She shrugs. "He's only been here a short while from Paris."

"Paris, how fancy." Then I think about the travel restrictions across those war-torn countries to arrive here. "Gosh. He could have gone to Spain or Portugal a whole lot easier. Why here?"

"I assume it's because Budapest has hardly been touched by the war." She shrugs again. "I've been too busy swooning over him to ask those questions just yet."

"Strange that he's not been enlisted," I say. "Clearly he's Christian or he wouldn't have traveled so safely."

"He is." Her facial expression is now serious, and she wraps her arms around me. "You know we'll protect you and your family, right?"

"I do know that." I lean into her embrace. "And one of these times, I want to meet your Sándor."

"Count on it." She kisses my cheek and stands up. "I have to get ready for work."

Ilona is leaving as I return to the apartment. We kiss goodbye. I find Mother in the kitchen, doing nothing, a rare image.

"Mother, may I take the toy farm set to the orphanage?" Our childhood toys are in a box in my parents' closet, waiting for József when he's older. "There's a boy there I think may enjoy it."

"Anything you need to take, sure." Mother unties her floral apron. "Do you want Ferenc to escort you to work?"

Now that we Jews stand out so clearly with our yellow stars, we've been taunted, spit on, and some beaten for supposedly bringing the wrath of the war to Budapest. Such illogical rubbish.

"I'll be fine. It's not that much farther than the Girls' Home."

I find the farm set and take the barn and tractor. Jakub hasn't let go of that toy horse since he arrived, even insisting it bathe with him.

As I'm about to close the storage container lid, I spot the square wooden box Father made for István and me. It has three holes on the top and sides. We'd drop a wooden ball into one of the top holes and wait for it to circle around inside before it rolled out the side hole and raced across the floor. The ball's appearance used to surprise us every time.

And there's the Jack-in-the-Box we let József play with the last time he stayed over. He started crying when the yellow-haired clown popped out.

"Mika, no more!" he yelled as I sat with him to rewind the tiny handle. We packed it away. Seems we've all been startled enough, even the baby.

I drop the farm toys into my bag and shrug on a light green coat. I've illegally attached the yellow star to my coat with snaps. When working on behalf of the Sisters' Society, I remove it.

Not permanently attaching it is a piddly defiance I find quite satisfying.

A bunchy blanket of white and grey clouds adorns the sky, with sporadic rips that let the sun peek through for a split second.

The streets appear extra busy today. Like the clouds, we in Budapest are a mixed bag who slide together but remain independent, each carrying our worries, our fears, along with the hope we'll be safe in the end.

Today, I'm heading to a large convent the closest to City Park, northwest of our apartment. Inside the many buildings surrounded by high brick walls are two hundred fifty beds, housing lost or orphaned children. The gardens with trees and flowers are peaceful, even with all the children filling the grounds. Jakub and Zofia, the Polish children who lost their father, live here now.

Inside the front gates, a nun sits on a bench, holding a boy with his stuffed toy dog. At her feet are a dozen other children, some with dolls. A game of dreidel is well underway, with the stones for the game pieces collected in the pot. Months past Hanukkah, there's no sin in playing this game of chance, especially if it's a happy activity for so many children.

Have I met this nun before? I smile and wave. She returns the greeting. Sister Sára's cheerfulness is infused in all her charity homes and every worker's demeanor. She's never sad, it seems. Her motto, "Every new day is a gift to be used to serve the poor," is evident in each home she oversees.

None of the Girls' Homes or orphanages sustained damage during the bombings. However, many new arrivals lost parents who lived near the railroad yards when their houses were hit. Another Sister and I rescued several devastated families yesterday whose misfortune set them under the bombs. The uninjured came with me while the others were rushed to the makeshift hospital in a Jewish school on 44 Wesselényi Street. The Waffen-SS soldiers captured the buildings of the famous and important Jewish hospital on Szabolcs Street when they swarmed the town and now treat their soldiers there.

I head to the dormitory where Jakub and Zofia have their beds. The hallways carry mixed scents of cleansers, and freshly baked bread, stuffed cabbage, and near the infant wing, dirty diapers. Volunteers come to hold the babies, but there are never enough cradling arms.

I'm excited to give Jakub the new items for his horse. He still hasn't spoken but has begun to play with the other children as long as Zofia is at his side.

The children aren't in the bedroom, but I find them in the sizeable playroom with forty other orphans. The tall windows let the sunlight in and brighten the area. It's divided with tables for arts and embroidery, a cement floor for bouncing balls and riding scooters, and a carpeted area for playing with toys from a wall of shelves.

Zofia is dressed in donated clothes, but the buttoned-up sweater and proper skirt age her well beyond her twelve years. She's putting a jigsaw puzzle together with Jakub, a colorful picture of a man playing an accordion in front of a row of seated women in fancy hats.

I drop down next to them. "Hello," I say in Polish. "Pretty picture."

Zofia's expression is vacant but she meets my gaze. I took it as a breakthrough when she let me braid her long hair yesterday. Tiny hairs have now escaped the plaiting. The daily report says Zofia is a restless sleeper and often has nightmares or stays awake all night, napping during daylight hours.

Jakub snaps the last puzzle piece into place and smiles at me. His horse is gripped firmly in his left hand.

"Very good," I say. I pull my bag closer to reach inside for the green tractor. The boy's eyes grow wider when I set it on the carpet and drive it in a winding path toward him, popping my lips to create *putt putt* noises.

He makes his horse rear on its hind legs and then walks it over to sniff the tractor. Out of the corner of my eye, I see a tiny lift at the edges of Zofia's usually tight lips. I need to think of something she'd like to have. The Sisters say she hasn't shown any interest in books, sewing, or cooking, although she most certainly has done those activities before. Fending off nightmares, sticking close to her brother, and lack of interest in simple activities—she's reliving some terrible event. Hopefully, she'll feel safe enough to talk about it with one of us. An accepting listener will help her make sense of the roaring words and images stuck inside her head.

Sister Sára tells every refugee, "We are here…use us." I pray she does.

One more surprise for Jakub. I lift out the barn. It's big enough for the horse to fit inside, so I slowly drop it over the wooden figure, and he releases it. The barn door opening is in the front. I bend over and wave to the horse. "New home," I say in my limited Polish.

Jakub then bends over and peeks inside at his horse.

In a snakelike strike, Zofia grabs the barn and hurls it across the room. Her eyes are wide, and her chest is hitching, forcing a strangled cry from between her pursed lips.

I reach for her, and she slaps my hands away. She pops to her feet, visibly trembling, and grabs Jakub, lifts him by the arm, and runs through the door and down the hallway.

Oh, my goodness. How have I upset her so badly? Is she jealous because I'm giving gifts to her brother? Perhaps some unscrupulous person did this before and lured them into a cruel situation.

I have to make this right. My job is to soothe their fears, not upset them needlessly.

On my way out of the playroom, the Polish nun, Sister Aleksandra, hurries to my side.

"You need to speak to Sister Sára." Her expression is grim. "She's learned about the children's past"— she touches my arm—"You couldn't have known."

Known what? That playing with a farm, something I've done each day with Jakub, would upset Zofia so terribly?

Shame sits heavy on my shoulders. I should have talked to Sister Sára first. As head nun, she asks us to check in with her each day to make sure we're fine since most of us are Jewish. It's also how we catch up on information about the children currently here and learn about new guests.

In my haste to find Jakub, I broke the rule to try to make him like me.

Sister Sára's office is along a tiled hallway connected to the small chapel. Before I reach her door with a confession of the sin of self-importance on my lips, I suddenly stop. Men's voices, speaking in German, come from inside her office.

The nuns work with the Zionists and many resistance groups, but they always meet her secretly in the alley or convent cellars, away from watchful eyes.

"We trust you will follow orders," a man says. "You are doing fine work here with the Christian children. A bright woman like you understands the reason we hope to trust you."

"I understand we are to trust each other." Sister Sára's voice lacks its customary merriment.

A soft chuckle comes from one man, but it's not a kind sound.

My neck now throbs. Is the Sister in danger? Should I walk in to disrupt the meeting?

"Yes," the other man says. "We have our orders, and you have yours."

There's a long pause before she speaks. "And what are your orders? We hear so many rumors. It's nice to learn the truth from you, Herr Eichmann."

The feared Adolph Eichmann is here? We heard he ruled from Castle Hill, and unless driven to a restaurant, he never ventures out among the populace he considers beneath him. What has happened that he's come to the convent in person?

"I am in Budapest as the director of transportation should we need to move the Jewish residents to a place of their own."

"Like forced labor camps?" Sister Sára's tone doesn't waver.

"In war, there is always so much to build and repair. Jewish men make amends for their historical sins by helping us win this fight." He clears his throat. "The new Jewish Council is the organization that imparts the orders for everything else. I am in contact with the eldest Jew there who reports to me."

"Then why is he not the one telling me to immediately stop showing the Saint Margaret play?"

"I wanted to meet the famous nun who has done so much in her short life."

"I have been blessed."

"We worry, as well. Someone with your writing skills might think to put up a…um, a resistance to change." His voice carries an edge.

"My calling is to help the children and the poor."

"As it should remain." I hear chairs scrape the wood floor.

I do *not* want to meet this evil man. I hurry back the way I came and exit the main door in desperate need of fresh air to calm down. Someone has tipped off the Nazis to the Sister's network of hiding Jews. He didn't come here to stop a religious play that doesn't affect him. He came to deliver a warning.

I need to talk to Sister Sára about Jakub and Zofia, but first I must compose myself. I turn in the direction of City Park. A quick jaunt among the beds of tulips or under the flowering quince will lift my spirits.

Rounding the corner of the building, I stop dead in my tracks. Ahead ten meters sits a line of highly polished black cars. German soldiers guard them, guns at the ready. As two men exit the convent's side door, I notice a back door sitting open on the center car.

I slowly backtrack. This must be Eichmann, although both men are of slight build, not imposing as I imagined.

A few more steps backward and I'll be out of sight.

One of the men calls to me. "Fräulein!" Then they all turn my way. "Come here," he says in German.

The hair on my neck rises. I've had no time to take off my coat, but I've stuck the yellow star in my pocket, not where it should be.

"Come." The man's tone is less friendly, gruff. His hand gesture is impatient, waggling it as if commanding me to match its speed.

I have no choice. Trying for casual, I will my shaking legs to move toward the men.

My greeting is in German, wishing them a good morning.

"Do you work here?" the other slight man says, and I recognize his voice. Adolf Eichmann.

"Yes, sir. I'm a Catholic nurse." This is the lie we've been given permission to use.

"Perfect. I'm looking for girls of good virtue to work for me." His face is narrow with a sharp nose. Dressed in his grey leather coat, he resembles a bird of prey, waiting for the right moment to pounce on a mouse with its menacing claws. The most conspicuous thing about him is his reddish hair. Not at all the formidable Aryan German I pictured.

I realize he doesn't suspect my heritage, considering I have my father's light brown hair and light grey eyes.

"Thank you, but my place is here with the children." I bow my head, hoping to exude humility.

"I need a hundred typists to work for the Jewish Council. We have thousands of names to put on lists." His eyes have darkened. "You will receive extra food ration cards, work in a clean office, and if you prove yourself, could work personally for me." His smile is thin, wolflike. "Who knows when I may need a nurse?"

I swallow. Once he learns who I am, I'll be in one of the prisons they've built below the town hall. I'm the one who will need a nurse. Or a mortician.

"You're a foolish girl," the other man by his side says. "Do you know who this man is?"

I shake my head, feigning ignorance, and enjoy the scowl on Eichmann's face. He believes he's so important everyone should know him.

"This man, single-handedly, has fulfilled Hitler's dream," the aide says, his eyebrows raised. "Anyone would be honored to work for him. He does not ask just any young woman to be …um, close to him."

My stomach churns as I realize what this proposition means. Refugees tell of the Gestapo and SS officers, all married, taking women to soothe their sexual desires, a prize for the conquerors. The rumor here is that a plane arrives regularly from France with young women and wine aboard, specifically for this horrible man.

How am I to get away? If I tell him I'm Jewish to repel him, I put myself in grave danger for lying about being Catholic. My mind turns over a list of diseases. Which one should I say I have?

Eichmann points to the open car door and sweeps his gloved hand toward the interior. "Then it's settled."

Oh no. My silence is interpreted as acquiescence.

"You will accompany me now. We'll let the good Sister know she needs to find a new nurse."

I take a step back, but the aide rushes me, grabs my arm, and tugs me to the car. The dark interior might as well be the drooling maw of a bear, ready to devour me. My heart is thumping so hard. Surely, he can feel it through his black leather gloves. I think of Gellert and imagine him leaving the hospital only to find me missing.

"What are you doing with my fiancée?" A young Hungarian soldier, dressed in an officer's uniform, appears in front of the car. He strides toward us and gently pulls me away from the man. "Darling." He wraps one arm around my waist.

I've *never* seen this soldier before. Could he know István or Gellert? But right now, I don't care either way. He's rescuing me.

"I came looking when you weren't at the restaurant." The soldier plants a kiss on my cheek and smiles at the men. "She is lovely but so very forgetful with appointments. I hope she has not kept you from your important business."

Eichmann's face is dark, his eyes small ebony beads. "What is your name and unit?"

The young man steps forward and offers the Heil Hitler salute. "Sergeant Peter Wertz, Second Army, sir. I've fought with your General Fretter-Pico. A good statistician."

I may be in more trouble than I thought. This man fought alongside the Germans. He may want from me what Eichmann planned.

Eichmann waves the soldier away, a dismissive gesture. "Your fiancée should be more careful."

"I will keep her close," the soldier says and takes my hand as he pulls me back the way I came. "We'll have to have a talk, darling," he says loud enough for the Germans to hear.

Once we turn the corner, I pry my hand away and step back. "Who are you?"

He's about eight centimeters taller than I am, with blond hair and blue eyes.

"You're welcome." A smile plays on his lips, and his eyes are full of kindness. "Obviously, I'm the man who is in the right place at the right time to come to the aid of a Catholic girl."

"Yes. Thank you"—I lift my chin but speak quietly—"that was very kind, but you need to know, I'm not Catholic." I want to ward off any idea we could attend church together.

"Congratulations." He leans closer. "You need to know, I'm not a soldier."

"Then who are you?" I study him. Why has he helped me? "Is your name really Peter Wertz?"

He adjusts his military hat. "It's my name for now. And since you're masquerading as a Catholic, that tells me something. If you or your family need a safe place, look me up. We're working out of the Swiss Embassy on Szabadság Square, or in the office of the Weiss Company at Twenty-nine Vadász Street."

He walks me to the convent back door, his hand on my lower back. "What do you do here?"

"I'm a nurse, or rather a nurse's aide since I haven't completely finished the program."

"We can always use a good nurse."

"Who is 'we'?" I ask before opening the door. I have a feeling he's with the Resistance although I've never met him during my participation. And I have reason to worry. Some underground groups are safe to be involved with and some are life-threatening.

"Let's just say, a group that cares." He looks to the right and then left. "Please know, the Germans are lying to the Jewish Council. Like in all the other countries, they plan to eliminate every last Jew in Hungary." He shrugs. "Just in case you know any Jewish people."

Eliminate? Sourness hits the back of my throat. Surely, he can't mean kill. He must be exaggerating to impress me.

"You've been very nice. I'll let my fiancé know you helped me."

He inhales slowly and for a moment, appears sad. Dimples in his cheeks disappear when he isn't smiling.

But it's not my mention of a fiancé that sobered him.

He shakes his head. "I know of the murders firsthand but have no time to explain. The truth is that the situation here is about to get a whole lot worse. Hungary is to be Eichmann's crowning achievement, and he has thrown himself into it with gusto." His eyes meet mine and I shudder. Their intensity nearly knocks me back a step.

I almost ask how can you trust the truth, but the question is vast, unspeakable, and my throat refuses to release it. Maybe I don't want to know.

"Thank you again for saving me." I touch the door handle. "And for the warning."

"Come see me if you want to learn more…bring your fiancé."

I'm not sure why but I quickly tell him about Gellert, his escape from the Labor Force, his injury. "He's a lucky one that made it back."

"He *is* the lucky guy." He smiles. "But more than that, having a nurse to hold him close. That's all the medicine he'll need."

I'm touched by his kindness. This day, that not so long ago reeked of desperation, has turned hopeful. "I'll do that, Peter Wertz."

"And who have I had the too-short pleasure of being engaged to?" His face brightens and warmth returns to his eyes. And the dimples are back. "Just a first name, please."

I laugh. He's flirting. There are so few feel-good moments these days not to appreciate one for what it is—harmless.

"Marika."

"Pretty." He takes a step away. "Remember, every day until the Germans leave is dangerous. But, as my faith—and most likely yours—teaches, every day is also a miracle."

I watch him take confident steps as he walks away. Self-assured. Willing to defy the elite German leaders without a waver in his voice. But what has made him join the Resistance? He doesn't look any older than I am. And his accent is from Austria or Germany, not Hungary.

Our sages tell us that each good deed creates an angel who serves us as a guide and protector.

I forgot to ask Peter how he came to be at the convent the precise moment I needed him.

It doesn't really matter.

On the day I reach heaven, I'll thank him or her for sending Peter at the right time.

I tremble to think what Eichmann had in mind.

-7-

BUDAPEST, HUNGARY

April 15, 1944

Father, Mother, and I sit in the living room listening to *Hungarian Rhapsody* in three parts by composer Franz Liszt, playing on the phonograph. The rain hasn't stopped all day. Its silver drops splash a lullaby on the roof and windowpanes.

These days, I prefer the phonograph to the radio, one emitting a beautiful melody, the other disastrous news.

One thousand seventy-three people died in explosions when apartments near the industrial plants were hit by Allied bombings. The Jewish Council, at the demand of Eichmann, ordered fifteen hundred Jewish apartments in nicer neighborhoods vacated to relocate Christians left homeless. We've been lucky so far that our building isn't on that list.

The apartments are handed over furnished and ready for immediate use by non-Jewish families, so sufficient furniture and cooking implements need to remain. Rumor of the start of a ghetto is circulating as Jews are forced to move into District VI and VII. These districts are in the Jewish quarter next to our District VIII.

Yesterday, the newspaper, *Pesti Hírlap*, ran with a disturbing headline.

The Heart of the City Cleansed of Dirtying Jews

The article explained that for too long, the privileged but childless Jew lived in six-to-eight-room flats or villas while hardworking Christians raised a family of six in two rooms. It concluded with the proclamation that decades of unfair housing distribution will finally be made fairer.

They didn't print a word about how every family—Jewish or Christian—worked hard in their occupations and could purchase better apartments over the years. It's evident that after a decade of anti-Semitic propaganda, the local population isn't entirely against the attack on Jews and their property. This dissatisfaction has grown steadily over the years.

My father looks older than his forty-four years. New age lines have appeared around his eyes, and he has a slump to his shoulders as if carrying a loaded sack of worries on his back. And the care he takes to force brightness into every statement isn't lost on Mother or me. He's gone, often for hours, saying he's meeting with former transportation colleagues trying to stay ahead of the German's plans.

Then there's my mother. Although her hair is always elegant and she looks so put together, the dark circles under her eyes attest to the soft footfalls I hear in the apartment late at night. I've joined her many times for a cup of tea. We talk about books, past get-togethers, and dishes we'd like to cook once rationing is over. The Germans confiscated our coupon for paprika, knowing it's the main ingredient we use in so many dishes. We also have no sugar or meat, although we're fortunate enough to travel to the family farm and get what we need from there. At least we *were* able to, but don't dare now with the new Jewish regulation. We're forbidden to travel five kilometers outside our residential area. And within our neighborhoods, we can't go to the bathhouses or parks.

These late-night talks with Mother remind me what really matters. The special moments seeded in these dark days will bloom later in stories we retell our children and grandchildren. I've always drawn strength from Mother's feistiness and peace from her positive attitude. The Germans may be whittling away at our freedoms and want to bring us down with their hatred, but the times with my mother, in the velvet grey of night, are moments they will never steal.

"I have a riddle," my father says. He stands and closes the lid on the ornate phonograph, a gift to my mother from her parents when my brother was born. She received a gold-plated soup spoon for my birth.

Father makes sure we set our embroidery aside before he begins.

"The maiden has seven dresses, and the one who takes them all off ends up crying. Who is this maiden?"

He makes me smile. He delivers riddles with a stern tone, as if he's sharing wisdom I can spread throughout the world.

Minutes tick by.

"I have no guess," Mother says. I'm never certain she hasn't heard these riddles before, but she won't spoil the anticipation of an answer.

My mind runs wild with this one. Why would someone cry when seeing a naked maiden? Unless…

"A young man has dressed up like a maiden?" I ask. "Like in a farcical play?"

My father's face freezes as he ponders my answer then laughs. "You get points for creativity, but no."

I say the words he longs to hear. "I give up."

He spreads his hands out in front, offering the gift of an answer. "The maiden is an onion."

I roll my eyes as my mother speaks. "That's a good one, Endre."

The phone rings, and he crosses the room to the kitchen in eight quick strides. István checks in each day, but this call comes earlier than usual.

We will take turns talking to him, Erzsébet, and József, so I'm surprised to hear Father say Erzsébet's name.

"When did they say this?" He sinks to the kitchen chair below the phone. His face has greyed, and he runs his free hand through his hair. His voice is threaded with love and concern, as always when he talks to a family member.

"Oh, dear," Mother whispers, her hand to her throat. "Something has gone wrong."

In the space between our leather armchairs, I reach for her hand. Strength moves through our entwined fingers.

Moments seem to drag, and Father nods and then shakes his head at my sister-in-law's story.

"We'll figure out how to come get you." He stands and stretches to his full height. "Pack only what you would for a weekend. Tell the foreman one of us is ill but you'll be back in a few days."

He barely hangs up before we pepper him with questions.

"The Germans are combing through the large estates, taking food, and asking if any Jews live in the big houses. They took the car. István says other men have been rounded up to help clear the bombed-out residential areas near the airport. I guess the Allies hit the maternity hospital too."

"That's awful." I'm suddenly nauseated. "Those poor mothers and babies. We'll take them in at the Girls' Homes if they have no place." István said he would go into hiding before he'd suffer slave labor again. He could more easily hide here in the city versus in the generally flat, treeless, and anti-Semitic Hungarian countryside.

"Endre, can you find someone to drive out to get them?" Mother is on her feet. "And how *dare* they steal from my family's estate."

"I'll get a car from Ferenc. But we need a driver who can leave the area. If I'm stopped while at the wheel, I'll be arrested."

Peter, with his secret connections, pops into my head. "That young man who helped me at the convent. I failed to mention it, but he's with a group that seems pretty industrious when it comes to giving assistance. Let me ask him."

"Do you mean the underground? They'll shoot anyone working for them, Marika." My father shakes his head, his lips now a grim line. "While meeting with the rabbis, they warned me about the arrests and killings, even if a person is simply rumored to know someone in the Resistance."

This level of concern is why I've never mentioned to him what I do when rescuing refugees. It seems safe enough to me. It's not like I'm passing weapons around.

"Peter says they drive out to labor camps and the countryside all the time to rescue people. They must know what they're doing. Besides, he looks German."

My father considers this. "How will he know where to go? He can't very well be asking around without raising suspicion."

The words leave my mouth before I know I'm forming them. "I'll go with him."

I told my parents only a teeny-tiny portion of the Eichmann story and how I got away with Peter's help. They would never let me out of the apartment again if they knew how close I came to being shoved into that car.

"I look Aryan enough for Eichmann to want to hire me." I don't add what else he wanted to do. "And I have my Catholic identification card."

"No, darling"—my mother's chin quivers—"it's just too dangerous."

"Not for Hungarian citizens," I say. "They're going about their lives, unaffected by all these stupid rules." I glance at the clock. If I can find Peter at one of the buildings he mentioned, and if he has an available car, we could be in Győr by early afternoon and back an hour later. "Let me try to find him, Father. Then you won't have to get Ferenc involved, and one fewer person will know where István is." I reach for my purse and pull out the yellow star and drop it on the end table. "I'll be back with the rest of our family this afternoon."

I leave my parents in the doorway, holding each other in a tight embrace.

On my walk to the Weiss Company office, I keep to the back alleys and practice what I will say to request Peter's help to bring my brother and his family home.

In the distance, an ambulance siren wails. I flinch at random noises that arise behind me. They're innocent enough. An iron gate squealing open as a mother and little boy exit their house and the rattling wheel of a newspaper cart pushed by an elderly man. I try to act like I'm not breaking the law, but everything makes me jumpy. The walk is about three kilometers to the northwest, near the Parliament building, but with danger all around, the distance strikes me as expansive.

Once I turn onto Vadász Street, I release a held breath. With its long rows of windows, the three-story Weiss building is wedged between two taller brick buildings. When I told Father where I was going, he said Artúr Weiss and his sons ran a wholesale plate glass business there. They abandoned the building two years earlier when he could no longer own the large company he and his family created.

Two policemen guard the front door. Had I heard Peter wrong? Why would local policemen guard an empty building?

I stop and try to figure out what to do.

If I go home now, I fail my family and put István's family in danger.

The policemen don't look menacing. One is casually smoking against the wall while the other has his face tilted upward, his cap pushed back, taking in the warm sun.

Asking a question shouldn't raise any suspicions.

I straighten my shoulders and approach the men.

"Good afternoon," I say in Hungarian since they wear the local uniform. "I have a question."

"Yes, miss?" The taller one drops his cigarette onto the street and twists the toe of his black boot over it.

"My family wonders if the glass company still sells to the public." I point to the building with its varicolored windows.

"The company is closed for business," the other policeman says. His voice is rough, like it's dragged across stones to reach his lips. "Carl Lutz, the Swiss vice-consul for Hungary, occupies it now."

Again, I doubt I heard Peter correctly. Would the Swiss Government be involved in underground activities? Highly unlikely, I think. I need to get inside and ask if anyone knows Peter. I concoct the quickest lie I can.

"How lovely. My grandmother is from Switzerland." I shake my head and sigh. "I miss her. Her cooking. It's been too long since I've had her delicious apple strudel."

They study me, probably wondering why I'm going on about my grandmother's food.

"Are you Jewish?" the smoker asks. There is no malice in his voice, but I'm in violation of the law without my yellow star.

"I have Jewish friends." I tilt my head. "Why do you ask?"

"The Swiss Council has protective letters for eight thousand Hungarian Jews to emigrate," the short man with the gravelly voice says quietly. "Tell your friends if they feel they are in danger to come here and apply."

This is great news. "Emigrate to where?"

"Palestine," the man answers. "But hurry, Eichmann is clear about the number he's allowing to leave."

Eight thousand. A drop in a lake compared to the two hundred thousand in Budapest.

I smile. "May I go inside and ask for the paperwork for my friends?" Once inside, I still need to find a way to either get a driver to Győr or meet Peter.

"Just speak to the receptionist." They each pull a door wide, and just like that, I'm in the building the people of Budapest nicknamed the Glass House. The building is bright with an open ceiling. Colorful glass panels fill the wall along the stairway leading to a second level.

"May I help you?" A young man sits behind a counter in a small room off to the left. He's thin with hollow cheeks, chestnut-brown eyes, and long fingers. He'd make a great pianist.

"Someone told me to meet him here. A Peter Wertz. Do you know him?"

He freezes in place, and a pencil he reached for remains inches from his hand on the white counter. His eyes bore into mine. I hold his gaze. Have I just signaled the enemy? Should I have gone to another door, to a secret entrance like the convents have?

He leans closer. "And how did you meet this man?" he whispers, his eyebrows lifted.

"He was dressed as a Hungarian officer and saved me from a dangerous situation last week." My father always says to tell the truth, or someone will tell it for you. I'm putting my trust in his words, although this might cost me everything.

"I see." He nods slowly. "I'll be right back."

He hurries away, and I hear his footsteps descending stairs. The cellars of the building would be the storage rooms for the glass products when the business operated. There must be another entrance down there.

Moments later, I hear voices approaching. Two men speak and then appear around the corner.

I can't contain my relief when I spot Peter. "I'm glad I have the right place."

He's dressed in a casual suit, his tie askew, looking every bit a businessman just home from work. "It's good to see you again, Marta."

A second before I remind him what my name is, he imperceptibly shakes his head. He's using a false name, and I realize he's protecting me by giving me one too. I'm glad I didn't give my name to the door guards. That could have come back to hurt my family and me. I'm such an amateur at this deception business.

"Yes, Peter. It's nice to see you again." I pause and glance at the receptionist. "I need to follow up on something you said." Suddenly, I'm worried. What if he was boasting to get me to like him, and he can't really help my family?

He motions for me to follow him farther into the building. The hallways are busy with people carrying papers and briefcases. Typing sounds and conversations come from somewhere inside a row of open doors.

We stop in a small room with plush chairs covered in yellow velvet, but remain standing. My impression is he has no time to sit. A long table holds a spill of maps, a telephone, and stacks of papers and envelopes.

"Let me guess?" His eyes are mischievous. "You need a place for your fiancé?"

"I may need that soon, but my family…and as you guessed, we're Jewish and have a more pressing matter." I decide to trust him and explain the situation with my brother and his family in Győr. "I was hoping you'd have a way to get them back here. Today."

"The stories from the countryside have worsened." He crosses his arms. "Your brother is smart to get out now."

Relief washes over me. "You're saying we can go rescue them?"

"Wait. You want to go too?" His brow lowers over his eyes. "What if we're stopped? I have dozens of identities. But what can we say about you?"

I pause, searching for a purpose. "The maternity hospital was bombed. We'll say I've come on behalf of the Sisters' Society to offer housing." I dig in my bag and hand him my church identification.

He studies the card and turns it over before handing it back. "This will have to do for now. When we get back, I'll order a new Hungarian citizenship card that says you're Aryan."

"You can do that?" His message makes me perk up. A tingle of hope moves through me. Maybe there is hope my family will survive to the end of the war.

He leans close. A clean scent comes from his clothes. "Oh, I can do that and so much more."

A laugh escapes me, and I nod. I won't pretend he's not charming because he is. He's good-looking, but it's his air of confidence that's winning me over. And it makes sense he's devised secret schemes to protect himself. But his willingness to help my family, to protect others he doesn't know, is his most attractive trait.

"I'm ready," I say. "My father always says, 'God gives us the wheat, but He doesn't bake the bread. Let's roll up our sleeves and get at it.'"

He laughs. It's a throaty sound. Warm. "My father used to say almost the same. God gives us barley, but He doesn't brew the beer."

"Let me guess? You're from Germany." His family must have fled before the Germans declared war. "Is your family also here?"

"Close. I'm from Austria." His eyes take on a faraway gaze. Lines of pain appear on his face. "And no. They're not here."

Digging into his past creates a space between us where none existed a moment ago. "I'm sorry to have asked." I know better than this. Never ask about someone's past unless they volunteer to speak about it.

His face shifts from darkness to a neutral smile. "One day I'll tell you about my family. Right now, *Marta*…let's go rescue yours."

$-8-$

GYŐR, HUNGARY

April 15, 1944

It's most likely a miracle, but we aren't stopped by guards as Peter drives across the Széchenyi Chain Bridge and heads up into the hills, traveling northwest. I think of my Gellert as we pass the hill bearing his name. I send a grateful prayer skyward he didn't meet a similar fate as the saint the hill is named after. Pagans stuffed St. Gellért into a spiked barrel and pushed it down the mountainside.

I slip a sideways glance at Peter. He's comfortable behind the wheel of this big car, borrowed from a storehouse fleet of donated vehicles. An underground cellar in a building near the Glass House is spacious enough to park several cars and store barrels of black-market petrol.

We drive through District XI and leave the crowded city behind, heading into the forested area. It now feels safe to ask a question.

"You said you could get Aryan papers for me. Is that part of the Swiss government deal?"

"It's a different process." His eyes shine bright blue in the sun coming through the windshield. "Are you sure you want to know the details?" He taps his forefinger on the side of his head. "The less you store up in that pretty little head, the safer you are."

"Well, I'll need to tell my family *something* if we're all to get documents."

"That's true." He pauses, as if weighing a decision. "Okay. We send a young person into the population registry office looking for a made-up Aryan name. My girlfriend Ariel is very good at orchestrating this."

I smile. Of course, he has a girlfriend. No wonder he gave me the impression he's a happy man.

"They're allowed to look through the lists and they write down other names of Aryan citizens," he continues. "Then, a few days later, another person goes back with a stolen name, asking for *their* documents with the story they've lost theirs."

"That's clever."

"It's easy now with all the turmoil. The local government is barely holding itself together. There's a Zionist youth group serving as a liaison between all our resistance movements." He crosses his arms. "If you want to help, the Swedish or Swiss forged-documentation operation at Perczel Mór Street could use another hand, even for a few hours a day. You also may like working with the children and mothers hiding there."

Another place I haven't heard of. "How many are there?" I'm ready to do more than help bring refugees to the orphanages.

"I'd guess they have over a hundred children but sadly only a dozen mothers."

"I've been working for Hashomer Hatzair but would love to do more. I'd also like to meet your girlfriend."

He raises his eyebrows. Is he surprised I'm involved or that I want to meet his girlfriend?

"I'm with Maccabi Hatzair," he says. "And you'll get along great with Ariel." He smiles. "You're both strong-willed."

"Hey. That's not a bad thing."

He briefly lifts his hands from the wheel as if to ward off an attack, but he's grinning. "I didn't say it was."

I flash a smile and return to what he said about the mothers and children in hiding. "Is everyone coming in from the countryside?" I can't contain the instant distress painting my voice. There must be a few thousand orphans in the city now, and those are in the few places I know of.

"That's who we're trying to get through." He rolls the window lower, and cool spring scents fill the car. "Out here, every Jew is being driven out of their homes. We work to free them from the new ghettos built outside the towns. It's baffling though. We offer these forged documents that look so real they're never questioned, yet so often the people actually say no and refuse their chance at freedom."

"What? Why won't they take the documents?" I see the broken families and hear the cries of the children every day. If only the parents were offered an escape into the city.

He sighs. "They don't believe us when we tell them what happens after they're deported. It's not a new town like the Germans promise. Or a labor camp where the family will work side by side in the fields. The reality is too unbelievable."

I nod. "We've heard about those places. Work camps where everyone is driven too hard, with poor housing and only a few doctors on staff."

He grips the wheel with both hands, and he stares ahead for a long moment. "Two prisoners recently escaped a camp named Auschwitz-Birkenau. In Poland. They reported that there are workgroups for farms and coal mines, but this camp's main purpose is to kill most of the Jews who arrive."

"Wait. They're actually killing them? On purpose? That can't be true. We hear on the BBC the workers are dying from disease and exhaustion." My pulse thumps in my neck. I try to picture people disembarking from a train and then killed. Surely some must be able to run away when the shooting starts.

His jaws clench and unclench. "The report just reached Rudolph Kasztner, the head of the Hungarian Jewish Underground. He called us into a meeting yesterday and read parts of the testimony." Peter studies me. Is he wondering how much he wants to share? "We're doubling our efforts in the countryside. The report said the camp commanders gas ninety percent of the arrivals, then cremate them. The escapees claim there are six-foot-high mounds of eyeglasses and shoes next to the crematoriums."

That would mean thousands were killed there.

"Gas?" My father rarely talks about my grandfather's time in The Great War, and refuses to own a gun, especially after his father took his life that way. But this horrible way to die by mustard gas came up if he ever spoke of those days. I picture my family walking into this unimaginable scene. Baby József in his mother's arms. Burning gas filling our nose and air passages. "Like the mustard kind used in the first war?"

We pass a small town where along the field two oxen pull a wagon full of stones. There's enough rock to build a small structure. Or perhaps they're rebuilding a damaged home. Life in the countryside hasn't changed much for the farmers—it's a hard existence, often without modern conveniences like running water or electricity.

"This gas is more deadly." His words sound thick, as if they're too big to speak. "The prisoners believe they are going to have a shower before changing into work clothes. Mainly the elderly, the women, and children. The door is locked, then they're killed, and dragged out the other side and taken to the furnaces."

This is *pure* evil. These men, I suppose who look and act like Eichmann, know exactly what will happen to the thousands they've deported, yet they do it in every country, every town. And Peter's family? Had they met their end there? I'm not going to ask.

"It *is* too hard to believe," I say. I fight to control my trembling lips. "This is a war between countries. We understood the Germans needed workers, but not this…outright killing."

"It's being called Germany's best-kept secret." He snorts. "Or the worst act against humanity." He looks my way for a moment. "Eichmann brags he will use this coming summer to send the Hungarian Jews—in his words, 'spiced with paprika'—to the Auschwitz mill."

"America. Britain. They need to know about this so they can get to those camps."

He's quiet and softly chuffs. "I'm not counting on them, especially not the United States."

Gellert and I have always looked up to the United States. Peter says the country's name as if he's ridding himself of a foul taste. "Have you been there?"

"Almost…"—he slowly shakes his head—"Let's just say I've viewed her sunny shores up close. But never set foot there." His expression is a mask of self-control. "Again, a story for another day." He draws in a long breath then slowly exhales. "Concerning your family. You're getting them to safety just in time. This camp in Poland...the two escapees report that they're building new death showers and crematoriums, preparing to receive and gas the remaining Jews in Europe."

I brace for it, although it's clear what he's about to say.

"The Hungarians."

We travel in silence for half an hour. The roads remain undamaged, but we pass several pastures with huge craters, a pox on the fields that are still bare and cold but sprout a haze of green. Willows in the creeks are turning yellow. A man balances on a ladder against his whitewashed stone house, rethatching the roof, the lighter colored straw the newest addition. The yard is a disaster of mud, but a boy and girl chase each other, their high-pitched voices afloat on the breeze.

"Were you raised on your family farm?" Peter asks.

"I've always lived in the city, but we spent many weekends out here. When István and I were younger, we stayed with my grandparents for weeks at a time believing we were helping with chores, but looking back, I'm not so sure we weren't just in the way."

Peter chuckles. "Sounds like a good childhood."

"It was, even though my grandparents were painfully formal. Who eats fruit, including apples, with a knife and fork? They did. Bepa could take ten minutes to eat a fried egg, slowly cutting, setting down the knife, raising the fork. At least it seemed that way when we were younger. Meals took forever, and all we wanted to do was get back outside to swim in the pond or play with the lambs."

His face is thoughtful as he keeps his eyes focused on the road, probably imagining my story.

I twist in my seat to face him. "How about you? Do you remember your grandparents?" Asking about one generation back has to be a safe subject.

A grin grows as he nods. "Both were enormously generous. And my grandmother cooked heroically, like someone feeding an army. Even when she was well into her seventies, she worked a six-day week at their shoe store in Salzburg, and still found time to visit the poor and take food to our neighbors." He stops and gets a faraway look in his eye, and then swallows hard before forcing a smile. "I probably wouldn't be here without them."

His story is slowly emerging, but his cracked voice comes from a different lifetime. I won't ask any more questions.

"Mema made the best pancakes filled with cream cheese, lemon rind, and raisins." I shrug. "I've tried to follow her recipe, but something is missing."

"Sounds like she has passed away?" He slows the car to ease around a boy walking two cows alongside the road. The bells around their necks clang out a steady side-to-side rhythm.

"She and my Bepa both passed around the same time four years ago."

"That's what's missing then." His gaze softens, as if sympathizing with my loss. "It's not the food, but it's always about the people we hold dear."

I turn away, afraid I'm about to cry. It's hard not to miss my grandparents. They are everywhere in my memories, except not here today, and that hurts.

We're nearing the farm, passing through a small village with a smattering of houses. Most locals work their meager parcels of land or are craftsmen, butchers, or pub owners. Women dress in traditional long, drab-colored dresses, with scarves tied around their heads, carrying heavy pails from the town well. Poverty is on everyone's plate, yet hope is sowed every spring that the crops will grow and the animals will reproduce. Community is everything, and gossip holds it together.

Our estate spans one thousand *hold* which Gellert used to say was a measurement equal to over fourteen hundred acres in the United States. The land is broken up into the logging operation near the forest, the grain and produce fields, and the sheep farm. The prized horses we grew up with are still here, although mother's horse, Lily, has long since died. I'm nervous about what we'll find when we arrive. Hopefully, István and the family are packed and ready to go in case the Germans are nearby or coming back.

"There's the turn." I direct Peter to the entrance off the road. The circular drive leads past a two-car garage, now empty after the car was stolen. Attached is a good-sized tool shed. Next, we head to the main house.

"A beautiful setting," Peter says, taking in the view. "So well cared for."

The main house is built of ochre-painted stone and has typical arched doorways and windows on the ground level and square windows on the upper floors. The door and window frames are painted dark green, stark against light-yellow walls.

"My brother employs dozens of workers to keep the place running."

"Hmm." Peter studies the land.

I spot the storks on the barn's sunny side of the thatched rooftop. "Look…" I touch his arm and then point. "They come here every year, the same pair, Jeno and Rezi, to lay and hatch their eggs."

He leans across the center of the car to see out my window and lets out a low whistle. "That nest is big enough for a person to hide in."

I nod. "Probably two meters across. Jeno returns from their southern migration a few days before Rezi and fixes the winter damage and makes the nest bigger."

"Smart guy." He gives the two birds one more glance then moves back to the driver's side. His clean, soapy scent lingers. "You know, I didn't realize storks could fly, and I sure didn't know they migrate."

"Who would believe it? We always think of them standing in water, fishing. They're smart to build their nests up high for protection." I pause, recalling how we'd bet on how many babies would be hatched each June. "I love their soft clattering and chirping in the morning."

Peter waits for me to finish before speaking. "Does it seem too quiet to you?" He turns his head from one side of the estate to the other. "Where are the workers?"

My breath stops. He's right. Usually, men are busy filling feed bins, moving hay, or repairing a fence. The quiet is eerie—no voices, no hammering—just my ears straining to hear anything in this muted world.

"Erzsébet said they would hide if the Germans came back." I swallow hard. "I pray we find them inside, safely concealed."

Peter is out of the car and at my door, opening it before I have a chance to do the same. "If there are Germans inside," he whispers, "our story is we've stopped to buy eggs."

"I'll let you do the talking."

The air is thicker, like the heaviness that precedes a thunderstorm as we climb the steps to the wide porch. Two clay pots sprouting winter kale sit on either side of the door. The only sound is our shoes on the wooden planks.

The scents of manure, grasses, and livestock register in my brain where stored smells from childhood remind me of happy days. Now a struggle begins, pitting the past against the present, contentment against fear.

Peter glances at me as he reaches for the ornate lever on the iron doorplate.

I nod. Perhaps István sent the workers home and locked the doors until we arrived.

But the lever moves, and the door opens inward.

"Hello," Peter calls in German as we enter the sweeping foyer. The staircase runs up the wall to the right, and an archway at the base leads to the sitting room. The study is beyond the archway to the left. Straight ahead are the kitchen, dining room, and a specially built cold-storage chamber. Before the house had electricity, the small room with half-meter thick walls remained ice-cold throughout the summer months.

There's no answer to Peter's greeting. The house is deathly quiet. I point to the kitchen and lead the way.

The passageway wall is covered with ornately framed photographs of our family and the early days on the estate. I pause for a moment next to the one of my grandparents, seated shoulder to shoulder, probably in their fifties when it was taken. They are a handsome couple, but the photograph does them no justice. In life they were known for their expressive hand gestures, public shows of emotion, and too-loud laughter. But here they posed big-eyebrowed, the fierce heirs of Dracula and Attila the Hun, with tiny, knowing smiles.

Below on a narrow table, postcards yellowing with age lay next to a crystal bell we were never allowed to touch. And Mema's detailed embroidered cloths are everywhere.

Movement outside catches my eye, and in an instant, I stifle a gasp as I point to the scene beyond the kitchen windows.

"They're stealing our animals!" However, it's not the Germans but our neighbors, the Qurjesz family. My family has helped them through the years when one of their seven children was sickly or when their crops suffered poorly for a season. But here they are, leading our two prized horses from the barn. Several of their children carry chickens, and one boy tugs along Corn Cob, our main breeding pig, with a dingy rope.

Reality hits. We've come too late. The floor seems to move, and I reach for Peter to steady myself.

"My brother and his family must be gone." Spots swim before my eyes. Peter's stories of gas chambers and of mass cremation spin through my mind. How did it happen this fast?

After making sure I'll stay upright, Peter leaves my side and exits the back door. He yells for the neighbors to stop and return our livestock. I arrive at his side just as the father Odon Qurjesz, speaks.

"We've been asked to watch over the animals." He's lying. His close-set eyes never meet ours.

"Where are István, Erzsébet, and the baby?" I reach for the lead rope on King, a jet-black Nonius, my horse when I was younger. He nickers as if to say thank you.

Odon pulls the rope out of my hand leaving a burn across my palm. He takes a few steps away. "The Germans are looking for your kind right now." His hands are grimy, his neck unwashed.

My face reddens. Not because of any shame based on his words, but because I'm angry. "Our kind? You mean generous to your family over the years, helpful, concerned?"

"We have no choice." He shrugs. "Who will take care of them with your family gone?"

"You always have a choice." Peter shakes his head. "I don't know you or your family, but your decision reflects who you really are."

"Helpful," Odon says, and spits something brown to the side.

"Greedy," Peter counters. "Your family could come here to feed these animals, and in turn help yourself to the eggs and milk. Give the animals back right now." He reaches for the rope and Odon pushes him back several steps.

Peter lunges and gets in a hard punch to the man's gut before I step in to stop him.

"We can't," I whisper as I pull him away. "They only need to call the local police and we're gone too."

Peter stares at the offensive man but backs away with me. "You will pay one day."

"We've suffered for years." The man turns and leads the horses away.

Odon's wife exits the drying sheds carrying a dozen stringers of dried chili peppers. She wears a printed blue kerchief, and her arms are bright pink to the elbow. She's a washerwoman for several estates in the area.

"Do you know where they've been taken?" I struggle to sound accepting of this situation while I'm fuming inside. Who plunders another's home and possessions within a matter of a few hours? Have the Germans given permission for this behavior?

"Your brother and the Jewish workers were taken away in a big truck." The woman scratches at a red area on her arm. "I never saw the wife and baby leave."

If they haven't left the property, then I know where Erzsébet and József are. Before I return to the house, I can't let this common thievery go without a final pronouncement. I call out to Odon. "Mr. Qurjesz, I hope you'll change your mind about taking what belongs to my family. You'll have to answer for stealing when István returns."

He stops walking. "I doubt it. The town council made an announcement." He smiles. His missing upper teeth give him a ghoulish cast. "The Germans are creating fairer land ownership. Leveling out who has what. It's been unfair for too long."

"Come on," I say, touching Peter's back. "We can't reason with corruption."

Tears brim in my eyes as King glances back over his shoulder, bearing a wild expression, his ears forward and fixed. Does he sense the fear in the air? I vow to come back here when it's safe and collect every last animal taken.

Once inside the house, I cross to the cold-storage room with Peter at my side. The entrance is through a small pantry, with shelving on three sides. However, a shelf to the left pushes inward to reveal a door, nearly invisible unless one notices the faint scrape marks on the floor.

And there inside, cowering on the floor, is my sister-in-law holding József to her chest. Her crestfallen face is blotchy from crying, and she's visibly shaking, I suppose both from the room's frigid temperature and outright fear.

"They've taken him!" she cries in anguish.

"We heard." I bend down and wrap my arms around them. A sob escapes me. "I'm glad you're here." I point to Peter. "He's come to help. Peter will drive us to the apartment and come back to find István." I turn to search Peter's face. That's what he said he could do. "Right?"

"Yes. I will." He walks forward and gently helps Erzsébet to her feet. He rubs József's back. "Hello, little man."

I reach for the small suitcase on the floor. "Is this everything?"

She nods, and we leave the house. Although she turns the key in the lock, it won't stop anyone from taking the furnishings. We can only hope not every neighbor has lost their sense of morality.

Outside, I see poignant reminders of my brother everywhere. The barn we played in. The rope swing in the hickory tree. Now that I think about it, he was my first male friend—sharing my secrets of raiding the cookie jar, breaking Bepa's pitchfork while digging for imagined treasures, and balancing on logs in the pond. Sometimes annoying me, sometimes soothing my tears.

Little did we know István would be burying a neighbor's treasure as an adult to keep it safe. Zoltan and his family most likely were taken away too. I send a prayer skyward that they return to dig it up one day.

When we're seated in the car, Peter starts it up.

I reach into the backseat and squeeze Erzsébet's hand. "We'll find him."

She nods, her chin quivering. "It all happened so fast. They wouldn't listen to him and how he is Catholic and had already spent two years fighting against the Russians."

I struggle to hold back my own tears. I need my brother, even though we aren't children any longer. We are the ones who remember family feuds and secrets, family grief and jokes. The stories live on because we keep them alive in the retelling.

If he's gone, our memories from now on could be told from only one perspective. Mine.

And what a sad day when memories told by one are no longer shared by two.

−9−

BUDAPEST, HUNGARY

April 26, 1944

"He plans to trade us for *trucks*?" I ask Peter. "A request for money or jewels would make us feel more valuable, don't you think?"

For ten days we've been meeting to share information. He updates me on the search for István, which so far has led nowhere. I fill him in on what I hear at the Girls' Homes and the underground or through my father's contacts. Public buildings and parks are off-limits to us, so we meet in Jewish cemeteries. Today we've chosen the Kerepesi Cemetery near my apartment in District VIII. We're inside the Schmidl Mausoleum, a beautiful crypt lavishly decorated inside and out with blue tiles configured into colorful mosaics.

We hope its occupants don't mind.

"Eichmann met with Joel Brand," Peter says. He's dressed as a Hungarian military officer again. "Brand is Hungarian, a Jew, and a member of the Relief and Rescue Committee like Kasztner. The deal is that Eichmann will allow the emigration of a million Jews in exchange for ten thousand trucks as long as they're equipped to handle the wintry conditions on the Eastern Front."

"That's better." The inside of the tomb is restful with tranquil blue hues to soften everything. I'm relaxed for the first time since leaving home. "I'm worth a hundred trucks."

He chuckles. "And more. The list included two hundred tons of tea, eight hundred tons of coffee, and two million cases of soap."

"And just where will a million of us go?" Although I'm making light of this information, this could be good news. There aren't a million Jews in Hungary. If we can get out alive and avoid the gas chambers, why argue where we temporarily end up?

"Spain." Peter touches the intricate design on the wall near his line of sight. "Eichmann calls himself the transportation expert and believes he can make this deal."

"Do you think it'll happen?" I can't imagine leaving without knowing about my brother. And if Gellert is still hospitalized, I wouldn't leave, but getting the rest of the family to safety would be a relief. The noose—what we are calling the new Anti-Jewish rules—is tightening. We're forbidden to engage in any work related to the theatre, cinema, or press. All shops belonging to Jews are shut down, but owners are required to continue to pay their Christian workers' salaries. If a Christian owes a Jew a debt, he is no longer required to repay it. They've even confiscated our bicycles and typewriters.

"I doubt they'll make this deal. The Germans really need the trains and requested trucks to fight a war they're losing, so why would the Allies make it easier for them to fight on? And unless they plan to walk everyone to Spain, my sources say it won't happen, and it's a false and desperate bargain on Eichmann's part."

"Maybe not a million then, but getting thousands out is better than none." I picture what little I know of Spain. Bullfights, olives, and a civil war not that long ago. "Spain is neutral, right? Safe from the war?"

"Not completely neutral. More like weighing their options, jumping from ship to ship when the tide changes. Franco sent forty-five thousand men in his Blue Division to fight at Stalingrad. Now the United States has threatened to stop oil shipments to Spain if they don't quit supplying tungsten to Germany."

"If we could get to Spain, and I know that's a problem, maybe the ships bringing oil could carry us to the United States on the return trip."

He stands silent, studying me. Then speaks with that edge back in his voice. "Countries aren't willing to open their doors to thousands of Jews. Including the United States."

"Is that just a rumor? The United States is a huge country, with seemingly so much room for everyone." All the American westerns show so much open space.

He paces inside the small area, his face cast in shadow then light as he passes the tiny windows. Finally, he stops and turns to me.

"Five years ago, just before Hitler invaded Poland, my mother, little brother, and I bought Cuban visas, two hundred Austrian Schillings apiece to emigrate to Cuba. My father was to follow. We boarded the *MS St. Louis* with over nine hundred other passengers, all relieved to be leaving the Nazis behind."

Here is the story he stopped short of telling me weeks ago. "You don't have to retell this if you don't want to."

He shrugs. "This emigration idea. The bigger picture isn't as rosy as it seems."

"I take it you didn't make it to Cuba."

"No, we did. Steamed across the Atlantic from Hamburg in two weeks' time. I was sixteen and my brother was fourteen. That ship offered one luxury after another. Great food, games"—he raises one eyebrow—"and pretty girls." He draws in a long breath. "But, Cuba decided not to honor our landing documents, and after a week floating offshore, we sailed to Florida."

"Ah. I remember you said you gazed onto the shores."

"The United States turned us away. The idea of more Jewish immigrants wasn't popular. Then Canada followed right after, lamenting that if they accepted one ship, they'd be flooded with hundreds more. Twenty-four days after we left Europe, we sailed back under a Coast Guard escort so we couldn't jump ship and remain behind."

"Those countries couldn't take nine hundred people?" I ask. "Especially those fleeing for their lives?" Where could we go if we're offered a way out of Hungary? If this mindset still holds true, there's no safe or accepting place.

"I tell you, overnight, our celebration sure turned to despair." He slowly shakes his head. "We were dropped off in Antwerp, then auctioned off at five hundred dollars a head to any country that would have us."

"That's a lot of money. Who paid that?" Five hundred dollars almost purchases a new car, and not many people are that wealthy.

"The Jewish Joint Distribution Committee. France bought us, and the three of us lived in a crowded camp in a safe unoccupied zone. Until…" He rubs his right fist in the palm of his other hand. "Until we got separated when the French police rounded up all non-French Jews. The French Minister of State decided we'd been there long enough and should all be *repatriated* to our home countries."

"Do you know where your mother and brother are?"

"I can tell you this"—his jaw muscles flex—"they're not in Austria."

"I'm so sorry." I want to hug him, but it feels too forward. And I want to know more. How did he make it to Hungary? When did he join the Resistance? "Now you're helping others search for their loved ones."

"Revenge is all I have." He takes me by the arm and leads me to the metal door with its intricate scrolling. "I'm heading to another labor camp in thirty minutes. As always, if I have good news, I'll deliver him in person to your apartment. Otherwise, let's meet at the Griesz family tomb tomorrow."

"Same time?"

"Same time." As he leaves the crypt, he straightens his jacket, and assumes the assured stride of a military man.

Peter is confident he'll find István. Several times a day, my family and I pray he's right. But after hearing his personal story, what family does *he* have left when the war is over?

I'm heading to the Holy Spirit Church south of the cemetery, closer to the Danube. It's the main headquarters for the Sisters of the Social Service and where Sister Sára lives. We call it the Mother House. Sister called the Jewish volunteers together, those of us masquerading as Catholic girls. Because her rescue efforts have increased, I've not seen her since that day Eichmann visited the convent, and I still haven't learned Jakub and Zofia's story. The children watch me warily at the home and keep a safe distance from me. I understand. Somehow, I've scared them.

Avoiding the People's Park, I head underground and use the miles of limestone passageways under the city to navigate. Since Jews aren't allowed in the park, maybe the name should be changed to *Half the People's Park*. These tunnels are from old quarries. Arched, extra wide and high in places, large enough here and there to drive trucks through. The beer and wine manufacturing businesses use the dark cool spaces to store their goods. Different shaped doors appear at random spacing along the walls, lit by oil lamps or electricity. The doors lead to businesses or apartments above on the streets. The air is dusty in some areas and dank and stuffy in others. I startle several times at a sudden scraping or a splash in standing water, but it appears I'm alone.

When my father consulted with the transportation department, my brother and I played hide-and-seek down here. On rainy days, Father checked the drainage efficiency from the streets as we chased each other around, our vision murky in the differing shades of darkness.

I climb the stairs into an alleyway and walk quickly to the church. The light scent of smoke and incense greet me.

Sister Sára is kneeling in the nave, her head bent in prayer, the rosary beads moving through her fingers.

I've just passed the sanctuary when she calls my name. I turn back to greet her. Her smile is compassionate, her face holding the same countenance no matter the situation. Could I ever have the faith she embodies? To be at peace in the middle of the war? To be unafraid as danger lurks everywhere, especially for someone breaking the law?

"Marika." She takes my hand, hers cool and dry in my damp palms. "I've wanted to talk to you alone."

This must be about Jakub and Zofia. I need to know how to help the children and not say the wrong thing. "The children from Poland. You know their story."

Her forehead lifts slightly under her coif. She appears confused for a moment. "Oh, yes. I know you are concerned for them. But I need to talk to you about a family in your apartment building."

I'm the confused one now. I think of all the tenants and can't imagine whom she might know. "Who are you worried about?"

"The Dely family. I believe they own the bicycle shop on the first floor."

"Yes. They do. But it's mainly a father and son. Belko and Benedek. Frau Dely is rarely there. Has something happened to them?"

"My dear. I'm here because I'm worried about *you*." She brushes a lock of hair off my forehead. "Have you heard of the Arrow Cross party?"

"Sure. They're a small group…very right-wing, aren't they?" Father talked about them putting anti-Semitic posters up even before Hitler declared war. They wear their green shirts and ties and hold small rallies where they chant hate and impart fear.

"A monk, supposedly defrocked, has arrived in Budapest and has joined the Arrow Cross. Friar Kun. He is said to be very charismatic and determined to either convert Jews to Catholicism or turn them over to the Germans. And the group has grown, perhaps to as many as sixty-five thousand."

"Really? That many?" I chew on a fingernail then catch myself. "And while that is concerning, how does this tie into the family in our apartment?"

"The Dely family has joined the Arrow Cross movement. We've learned the mother is highly involved in the women's side of the group."

"I didn't know women were drawn to malicious factions like that." Raakel said she thought Piroska was dressed in men's trousers. Maybe that's part of the uniform for the hate group. And just where is Piroska Dely when she's not home? There must be a headquarters for the Arrow Cross or housing where members live.

"Evil worms its way into a beating heart, whether man or woman. She sent Friar Kun to the Girls' Home today, looking for you. Benedek tells him you are open to converting." Her tone is quieter now. "Have you had this conversation with him?"

"When he walked me home a few weeks ago. He said he was at a meeting, not for work. He brought up the conversion subject, and I thought he was joking. Even offered to marry me." Now there's a repugnant thought. "I made some noncommittal remark something like I'd keep it in mind. He knew I wasn't serious."

"That's the danger. He apparently feels rebuffed and wants to make you believe you have no choice in the matter."

"Ridiculous. He can't make me do anything." The gall of that sneaky simpleton.

"Friar Kun can. From Benedek, Kun now knows you're Jewish, working under the false premise of being a Catholic nurse." Her gaze is less intense. "This friar carries a gun, visible on the outside of his frock. He seems quite intimidating. We need to have you stay away for your safety, Marika."

Sadness sweeps through me. I love my time in the Girls' Homes and working with the children and refugees. Tears blur my vision. In the past week I've spent an hour a day typing up Aryan papers, but my first love is working with the children. Maybe Ariel, if I can meet her, will set me up with the homes the Resistance is running.

"My dear, we're so sorry."

"Could I help in another way even if I can't go there?" Her safe houses and Girls' Homes number in the dozens now. "Maybe a smaller house?" This is so unexpected. I need to have a purpose, and right now I'm like a dry leaf about to be swept away in a cold wind.

"You're a great blessing to us. But for now, you need to be less visible. You're being watched." We link arms and she leads me out of the sanctuary and to the room where we're to meet. "We believe the war is nearly over. Other countries know about the German death camps now, and God willing, will surely double their efforts to stop them. The Russians and Allies are squeezing in from the east and west. Stay home. Take care of your family."

These are the death camps Peter told me about. The gas, the burning of bodies. I'm glad to know the horrible facts are out in the world now. But my mind remains stubborn. Using the underground passages, maybe I can sneak back to check on some of my favorite patients. "I'll miss you all and the wonderful work you're doing. Before I go, will you tell me about Jakub and Zofia? I did or said something wrong last time to really upset Zofia, and I don't want to make that mistake again if I have the chance to work with other children."

She stops and leads me to the corridor wall. Her upbeat countenance is gone. I've never seen her so serious.

"Those poor dears. There are only a handful of Jewish survivors from their town of Jedwabne."

"Jakub was clearly burned. Was the town bombed?"

"This happened before the bombings, early in the war. A few German soldiers arrived and asked the town leaders to round up the Jews to prepare them for resettlement." Her face blanches. "Hatred was ripe in that town. Neighbors turned on neighbors and murdered the Jews instead of corralling them as asked. Zofia's family was herded into a large barn with a hundred or more citizens. It was locked and set on fire. Her father and another man found loose boards and broke out and managed to escape while the townspeople shot at the fleeing men, women, and children."

"Oh, my goodness!" I shake my head, remembering how I placed the small barn over the horse and Zofia yanking it off and throwing it. "I reminded Zofia of that day with the toy farm."

"You couldn't have known. No one could foresee that kind of wickedness. Their mother, baby brother, and another sister died in that fire." She shakes her head. "Zofia may never trust another person again. Her favorite schoolteacher and the teacher's husband forced Zofia's family from their home by pitchfork and prodded them toward the barn."

"Her teacher? How horrible." What makes a person turn on the innocent in a few short moments? I release a long breath. "That kind of evil. Sister, I lose faith when I hear what has happened to so many. Where is the justice for the persecuted? The divine intervention?"

"In Romans we learn, 'Beloved, never avenge yourselves, but leave it to the wrath of God, for it is written, Vengeance is mine, I will repay, says the Lord.'" She pulls me into a long embrace. "Go home, my child," she whispers in my ear. "And go with God. Have faith that you have no reason to convert. Your heart follows His teachings."

If she only knew the ill will I wished on the immoral townspeople of Jedwabne. I understand Peter's chosen path of revenge against the Germans, transporting thousands to their deaths, most likely his family included. And anyone who says it's *inconvenient* to help a person in trouble. My heart is beating streamers of vengeance through me right now, but I'll hold my tongue.

"Do you think converting will keep my family safe?" Although István switched religions when he had the chance, it hasn't saved him from whatever hell he's experiencing right now.

"Not from what I hear. Whether you follow Christ or not, the Germans are only concerned about deleting original bloodlines."

-10-

BUDAPEST, HUNGARY

May 17, 1944

Dusk comes sooner than expected tonight, the last of the sun's rays tucked behind thick grey clouds. The light rain outside our apartment has stopped, and the scent of wet stone and brick wafts through the open windows on a warm breeze. We've finished our supper of pickled cabbage, sour-cherry soup, and creamed spinach. Raakel dropped off a funnel cake earlier, and Mother served it topped with a drizzle of lemon juice and the last of our sugar.

Raakel begged off coming in, saying she needed to run more errands for her mother, but agreed to come back later for a game of dominoes.

I wonder if she still has a crush on that waiter. If he's walked her home again, I haven't noticed. My life is nothing but pent-up frustration, so I could use juicy details of a blooming romance to lift my spirits.

Tonight, as the light drains away, there's barely enough even for shadows to appear. The buildings across the street take on the appearance of an old photograph, every curtain or flower planter turning a dismal shade of sepia. There will be no stars or moon with the foreboding layer of clouds looming above. They may as well have been suspended there by the Germans with the newest round of rumors. In agreement with our parliament, the Germans want a sprawling area designated around the Dohány Synagogue turned into a ghetto for us. Prime Minister Sztójay on BBC radio announced that all Jews in Budapest, about a quarter-million, would be moved to that specific area for our safety.

How stupid do they think we are? We're completely safe in our homes.

With our banishment from theatres, eateries, and public areas, including using transportation, they rarely see us. Must we be reduced to the size of dust before they're happy?

That news does nothing to ease our fears. No longer can the Germans pretend the ghettos are a protection for the Jews. The death camps are no longer a secret, as the report from the Auschwitz escapees circulates through the underground and to each Jewish organization. Ghettos on the outskirts of our country's towns are overcrowded corrals where dirty and starving families wait for a final train ride.

And we have to chuckle at a threat from Britain that came an hour after the Prime Minister's speech about moving us. On the same airways, a spokesperson for the Royal Air Force announced it would now alter their bombing policy in Budapest. Since they've learned where the Jews are to be safely housed, they will focus on attacking other neighborhoods.

I sent a silent thank you to the RAF for their threat. The government quickly backed off on their ghettoization idea. Now we wait to hear their next confinement scheme.

I met with Peter this morning as planned. He delivered Swiss protective passes at the countryside ghettos and brought back forty lucky people—men, women, and children—in three trucks. He's heading out to Kistarcsa, another transit camp fifteen kilometers northwest of Budapest to rescue dozens more. I asked why he doesn't take a thousand Schutzpasses, and he said they have to be careful. Only eighteen hundred protective passes were agreed upon. His group and others are forging the original documents as quickly as they can and cautiously giving them out in small portions so as not to raise eyebrows.

"The International Red Cross is looking for volunteers," he said before we parted. "They need nurses at all their designated safe houses. Your family could benefit by hiding there if they need protection."

I told him I'd think about it. We don't want to leave our apartment, but I do need to do something to help. Nursing is what I know best.

Turning from the darkened streets, I retreat to the front room where Erzsébet and József play on the rug near the small fire Father built in the fireplace. The room isn't chilly, and he didn't need to light the logs this evening, but Mother asked for one.

Raakel comes back, hugs my parents, and tickles József before we set up the dominoes on the small game table.

"I have to know about your boyfriend," I say, leaning across the table.

Her wide smile tells me all I need to hear. She's enamored for sure.

"He's so interesting." She lays out a tile. "He came here as a waiter because Paris is in turmoil."

I make my play on the table. "How did he get here?"

"He says he has a car stored in a garage on Buda Hill. A distant relative is there." She raises her eyebrows. "He seems to come from money from what I've seen. He pays for our meals at the finest places."

A flicker of jealousy moves through me, but I shoo it away. "You deserve to be treated like a queen."

Her face crumbles. "I'm sorry. How insensitive of me." She quickly lowers her head and makes her next play.

"Please, as if any of this craziness is your doing." I reach across and lift her chin. "I want you to live your life, and one day again, Gellert and I will join in."

My mother speaks up. "You know we must approve of this young man, Raakel." Her tone is upbeat as always when she has her children and *second daughter* around her. János said the same to me when I first started dating Gellert.

"I think you'll approve." Raakel seems to put her guilt aside. "He's mannered, funny, and interested in learning about our culture."

"He's French, right?" I add a domino that makes Raakel draw several from the bone pile before she can continue.

"He's Austrian but raised in France." Raakel smiles. "I told him about Papa Endre and how he sold puppets to famous theatres in Paris."

"I miss traveling there," my mother says with a wistful expression. "Has he seen any of the shows at Arc-en-Ciel? Maybe one of Endre's puppets was performing."

"It didn't sound like it."

"How's Gellert?" Raakel asks.

"I think he'll be discharged soon." I draw tiles and make a play. "The doctors are amazed he's turned around so quickly."

"What do you think happened to him?" Raakel stalls with her hand in midair. "With that head wound, Marika. Clearly he was attacked."

"I haven't asked, but the head wound…it's possible he was bashed with something hard." I shrug. "I'm waiting for him to tell me what happened. And I guess I'm afraid to send him spiraling back into his nightmares if I press him. I just want him home."

"Well, I can't wait to see him again." Raakel tucks her blonde curls behind one ear. "I'll make a special cake when he comes home."

"You're so sweet," I say. "That sounds wonderful."

We finish our game, and she leaves, but not before there are hugs all around.

"She's such a dear," Mother says as she pulls István's bar mitzvah prayer shawl around her. "Come sit with me by this fire, Marika."

I take the matching chair next to her facing the hearth. "She's the best."

"The fire always makes me feel hopeful," she says, staring into the flames.

I understand what she's saying. Although destructive, we can control flames—one small success in a world that now controls us.

A glass box, holding pressed flowers from the estate, sits on the sofa table. Erzsébet packed that, a dozen family photos, and Bepa's accordion. We all appreciate she thought to save these few things in her haste to pack and hide. Who knows what will be left or undamaged when they return home?

"Mika," József says from the floor in front of me. He's always smiling, and I'm thankful he's too young to know what's happening outside the apartment. Several nights I've taken him from Erzsébet and had him sleep curled next to me on the couch. Her weeping is understandable, but his little voice pleading, "No cry, Mama," breaks my heart.

He's pushing a toy car around and making a droning noise. Erzsébet stares at nothing but keeps a hand on his back.

"We can't lose hope," I say. "We will have István back."

"He was barely home five months." Her face is drawn, her eyes defeated. "I hate waiting and worrying all over again."

I remember the torment during the time I waited to hear about Gellert. "I know what you're feeling. So hollow inside, the jitters bang from one side of you to the other. At moments, you're dizzy and can't focus, and other times you see every dust mote running away in a sunbeam."

"That's about it. And our farm—the new lambs, the calves, the horses. I have to stop thinking about how they've been slaughtered."

My horse, King. His wild-eyed look toward me as he was led away. I swallow a sob. "I hope other neighbors come forward—the decent ones—to help run the place. We'd do as much if the circumstances were switched." Deep inside, I know the animals have all been taken as food for the starving army.

Father is tapping away in his workspace. He's almost finished the puppet for the baby. It appears to be his best one yet, and any theatre would be proud to own it. He'll never sell it though. I look forward to the day when we can live our lives again. We'll go to the theatre, walk right past the bright marquee with the name of the show without being told to leave. Maybe see one of Father's puppets on stage. Gellert and I often attended two shows a month, many times with my parents. I miss it all. Gellert pocketing our tickets from the coat check counter. The rows of plush seats, and the muted conversation as the actors prepared behind the heavy burgundy curtain.

The Austro-Hungarian Emperor Franz Joseph approved and partially paid for the construction of our opera house on the condition it was no bigger than the one in Vienna. Smaller it may have been, but it's far more opulent. The emperor's reported reaction on seeing it at the grand opening in 1884 was to mutter, "These Hungarians!"

"I'm going to see how József's puppet is coming along." I stand and cross the room.

I drop my hand onto Mother's shoulder for a moment. She's been knitting scarves, hats, and mittens. Although she says she's merely using up extra wool, I know she's preparing for a long winter ahead, should the war not be over.

"I like those colors," I say. "That lilac shade is one of your favorites, isn't it?"

She pauses her needles and smiles up at me. "It is."

My heart nearly breaks at the pain on her face she struggles to control by always appearing upbeat. We say we're holding good thoughts in our heads, praying for a positive outcome, but can we really fight the terrible images that arise. Hopeful thoughts battle those of dread every hour.

"Don't give that one away, Mother. You should keep it."

"We'll see who might need it come winter." She drops her gaze. The knitting needles click against each other in a well-practiced rhythm, a sound that reminds me of winter evenings, the family huddled around the fire listening to the radio.

I head to the workroom, breathing in the scent of wood chips, paint, and glue.

My father is humped over a table, and a light above shines down on his work. His glasses balance on the bridge of his nose, and he holds a tiny shaping tool in his hand.

"How is your creation coming along?" I wrap my arms around him from the side and rest my chin on his shoulder, studying the pieces in front of him. "Performing heart surgery?" I always tease he could operate on a flea with the miniscule ends of the instruments he uses.

He chuckles and continues shaping the wooden lips. His highly mechanized puppets are capable of delicate and complex movements, particularly the eyes and mouth. He also must finesse the hands and make every part in natural proportions. Hanging around the room are some of his best—the puppets he's won awards for or made for István and me. Mine is a half grotesque, folkloric woman dressed in a richly decorated costume. Father gave her a stern expression, so I've named her *Szigorú Anya*, Stern Mother. She holds a rolling pin like a bat in one hand and a washrag in the other. A theatre in Vienna offered him twenty thousand schillings for it in 1937, a fortune. One day it will hang on the wall in my home.

István's puppet is outfitted as an 1800s Hapsburg soldier, with pale blue pants, a white uniform shirt, and collar and cuffs in orange. Its hat that resembles a black puff pastry held in place with a chinstrap. He holds a bayonet rifle in one hand and a military pack in the other. It hangs in the estate house next to the stone fireplace, high enough for the baby not to touch.

This new one will hang on the other side after some good men rise to put an end to this war.

"Everyone okay in the other room?" Father asks, shifting his weight on the chair to get a better view of the marionette. "I guess Raakel left?"

"She did. And Mother's on her fifteenth scarf, and the baby and Erzsébet are playing."

"Good, good."

My father is his most relaxed in his workroom. His father denounced his interest in art and puppet making as a childish pursuit. Father's argument that the Greeks and Romans invented the fine art of puppetry and Catholic churches used it to teach morality was lost on his father.

"I'm working on a new riddle, Marika."

"I can hardly wait to fail again," I say and chuckle. "I've solved so few over the years."

He sets his tool on the table, leans back, and looks at me, his blue eyes piercing. "You're smart, my *Schatzi*."

His *little treasure*. He hasn't called me that since I was in braids.

"This might be the most important riddle I ever tell," he says. He's serious, which is so unlike him. He's usually self-satisfied when he has a good brainteaser for us.

"An important one." I repeat his pronouncement. "Is it for a special occasion or will we hear it soon?"

"I'll wait until the time feels right," he says and turns back to his work.

"You're a man of many talents, Father." I lean down and kiss his cheek. "I can't wait to hear what you've devised."

Again, he shows no excitement for his new word puzzle. Worry has drained him, has drained us all.

I'm in the hallway headed for the kitchen when I hear him tapping again. But that can't be right. The sound is in front of me, not behind. The door!

I hurry back to the workroom and whisper, "Father. Someone is at the door."

He springs from the table and is at my side as we reach the living room. Mother has her hand to her mouth, and Erzsébet has scooped up József, wrapping him in a protective stance.

Have the Germans come for our apartment to house more bombed-out families? Have they learned I've met with members of the Resistance? I remember Sister Sára's warning about the Dely family and Benedek and his mother belonging to the fascist Arrow Cross Party. I've been careful, but maybe they are sneakier.

The tapping is more insistent. Father motions for us to huddle in the corner away from the view from the entrance. He adjusts his shoulders higher and turns the doorknob. For an instant, his face is frozen in shock, and I believe our worst fears have come true. The enemy is on our doorstep.

He reaches across the threshold and pulls a disheveled man into a hug. "Little Bear," he says, his voice cracking.

"István!" Mother cries as Father's pet name for my brother sinks in. "Thank you, God!" she says, reaching her hands heavenward before hurrying to him.

A rush of jubilation whooshes through me. The Germans have not stripped this branch from our family tree. My brother, my childhood friend, is back. Through my tears, I watch him fall into his wife's arms and kiss baby József repeatedly on the head as the baby giggles. I'm shaking inside, weeks of fear rattling its way out of me.

Father motions to someone else. Peter steps through the door and looks around until our eyes meet. "Marika. I might need your help soon."

"Sure, whatever you need." I nod my head. "We're just so grateful you found my brother."

He nods. "I'll be back in the morning and will explain more then."

As István pulls Peter into a hug to thank him, my determination to become more deeply involved in the Resistance grows.

It appears to be the only way to help people and in turn save families.

-11-

BUDAPEST, HUNGARY

May 18, 1944

Early the next morning, Peter arrives dressed as a doctor. His group must have a warehouse of uniforms and costumes for every necessity. The name tag on his white lab coat reads *Doctor Nagy*.

"Good morning, *doctor*." I smile. "I'm always wondering what new performance you will be dressed for."

"I'm a man of many disguises," he says, then hands me a bag of clothes. "And you will be yourself today."

I open the bag and pull out a bundle of white. It's a nurse's uniform complete with headscarf. "Wonderful. I'll get dressed."

Moments later, I leave my bedroom holding up an extra white coat. "There were two."

"You should wear both," Peter says, accepting the empty bag. "You'll see why."

"I'll follow your lead." Then I tap the name tag on my chest. Maria Nilsson. "I see we're with the International Red Cross?"

"We are." A yellow star is on the front of both our coats. "And we're protected Jews, working under Swiss diplomatic papers headed for Dániel Bíró Hospital." He smiles. "We'll get to meet each other's sweethearts."

"Finally," I say. "I've wanted to see what woman can put up with you, and I'd like you to meet the man I've talked so much about."

He laughs. "Me too."

He hands me a paper. Across the top is the word *Schutzpass*. "We need to get your photo, but I think this one is close enough."

The woman in the photo has my light brown hair, although she wears it longer than my shoulder length. Her eyes are blue while mine are grey. "I'll just squint if we're questioned."

"Good plan," he says and points to my uniform. "Lift the yellow star."

Under the cloth symbol is a small white cross. "Ah, and we're Christian converts." This is a new rule that the small insignia can be sewn under the star.

"We're a bit of everything today. All situations covered."

"We're leaving, István," I call before opening the apartment door.

"Keep her safe." His remarks are directed at Peter as he pokes his head around the corner of my bedroom, where he and his family now sleep. He will continue to hide in the house should anyone report he's no longer in a work camp.

"You know I will," Peter says and directs me to the door.

Father is off to a secret meeting with other Jewish businessmen. They're trying to learn what the Jewish Council is doing to prevent a mass deportation. Only days ago, Regent Horthy refused Hitler's personal request that Jews from the countryside, over four hundred thousand, be sent to Poland and Germany. Everyone who has relatives in the countryside is panicked like we were before István returned. We've learned the Germans are rarely involved in clearing Jews from the villages and steering them into ghettos outside the towns.

It's the local gendarmes who drive the villagers from their homes and allow looting of their properties. Eichmann is said to have only forty-eight SS officers available to him. Other Germans who arrived in March were here initially for a grand show of force but were soon sent back to the fight. Father and his colleagues are demanding that the Jewish Council intervene to stop the police from acting like Nazis. Like in Jedwabne, Poland—Zofia and Jakub's hometown—neighbors turned in neighbors, all eager actors in this horrible play.

Mother and Erzsébet are out for a walk with the baby, taking in their allowance of fresh air and sunshine before that too may be forbidden. Each day, they deliver a few canned goods to women whose husbands haven't returned from the Labor Divisions.

As Peter and I exit the building, I spot Raakel in their apartment window. A young man stands behind her.

I wave, and she raises her hand in return, flashing a bright smile.

She's brought her boyfriend home! This must be serious. I'd love to stay and meet him, to tell her I'm on my way to see Gellert, but there's no time.

We hurry through the streets and hop the main tram that takes us across the river. No one pays us any attention as we sit in the back. We are exempt Jews because of our Red Cross status, otherwise we'd be walking. We leave the tram at the base of the steep incline and take the cogwheel railway up Castle Hill.

We begin the fifteen-minute walk to the hospital once we reach the top.

"Eichmann's at the Majestic Hotel, right?" I ask. The impressive building sits off to our left.

"That's his headquarters, but he's taken over a spacious villa atop Rose Hill. He seized it from a Jewish businessman. Aschner, I think." He nods in that direction. "Have you heard of him?"

"I haven't"—I shrug—"but it's a big city."

"Your father seems to know everyone and has many connections, so I thought maybe?"

"He does or did, mainly when he was head of the engineering department and dealt with transportation issues. But many of those businessmen are no longer working or are missing."

"I may have him mixed up with someone else." Suddenly, he grabs my arm and steers me off the street into a narrow alley between two shops. "Don't look back."

We move deeper into the passageway and stop when we reach a shadowy area. Several sets of footsteps pass the entrance to the alley.

"Who is it?" I whisper. The tremble in my voice is hard to control. I need to appear calm and brave, or I fear Peter may decide I'm too much of a risk to take along on these clandestine trips.

"That devil Kun." There's absolute hate in his voice.

"Sister Sára warned me about him. A Friar with a gun." We reach the street again and spot a tall man in black flowing robes and wide-brimmed black hat, walking between two German soldiers. "He has German protection?"

"He's taken over a grand mansion up here and moved his parents in." He touches my back to get us walking again. "And yes, he and the Germans have the same annihilation plan."

We arrive at the Dániel Bíró Hospital and enter the main foyer.

"I have an errand here after I meet Gellert," Peter says. He stops in the doorway. "I'll take that extra coat now."

I unbutton it and he takes it from me. We head to Gellert's room on the second floor. The air feels thicker and has a sourness you can almost taste in the hallways.

Gellert sits on the side of the bed. If you ignore the deep scar along the right side of his head, he looks as if he's here on vacation, dressed in fresh pajamas and holding a newspaper.

"Hi, love," he says. His tone is bright, the words no longer slurred.

I cross to him and kiss his cheek. "You look wonderful today, Gellert." I point to Peter. "I'd like you to meet a family friend. He helped us get István back."

Peter enters the room and extends his hand. "I'm happy to finally meet you, Gellert. Marika has talked about you so many times. It's nice to put a face with all the stories."

Gellert stands, and I'm so glad he shows no hesitancy. He's always loved meeting new people, completely at home in a crowd of strangers who wouldn't remain strangers for long. He grips Peter's hand in both of his. "It's good to meet another family friend who has been so helpful."

"Glad to do anything I can. It's what makes me happy," Peter says. "That and my own sweetheart. I'll let you two have your time together as I go find her. Hope to see you out of here soon."

"Any day now," Gellert says. "I'm ready to go home."

Peter leaves and I turn to Gellert. "We should talk to the doctor. Maybe today is the day you're given a clean bill of health."

"I'm not sure why I've been here this long." His eyes darken. "I've been ready for a while."

Has he really forgotten the delirium, the yelling and screaming, the paranoid behavior? The puzzling paralysis that kept him from walking even one step?

"When you were first admitted, you had a hard time walking, sweetheart."

"I don't remember that. Maybe I was dizzy from getting bonked in the head, but that's over now."

"Is that what happened? Were you hit in the head?" He may be ready to tell me his story.

"I don't remember." He turns and steps to the window. "I know I don't want to miss another day with you."

I walk to his side and pull him into a full-body hug, something we've not had enough of during his recovery. "Let's get you out of here. I want to spend every next minute of my life with you."

What will he do while I'm working? We'll have to hide him like we do István. There's no way Gellert can be sent out to a work crew or back into the Labor Unit.

A tapping on the doorframe directs my thoughts back to the here and now. Peter waits there with a woman about my age, wearing the extra nurse's coat.

"Gellert, this is Ariel. Ariel, Gellert and Marika."

She confidently crosses the room and shakes both of our hands.

"I'm happy to finally meet you both." Her eyes meet mine. "Seems we have many…uh…activities in common, Marika."

"I think we do," I say with a smile. "And I'd like to have many more."

"That can be arranged," she says. "Nurses. We need more."

"How about a doctor?" Gellert asks. "Can you use my services?"

He has no idea we're talking about working in the Resistance, but I'm thrilled he's interested in returning to what he loved.

"We do need you." I kiss Gellert's forehead. "I'll talk to the doctor. If not today, then tomorrow." For the first time, I'm leaving him with that glimmer in his eyes I remember so well.

"I'll wait right here." He sits back on the bed. "I look forward to the four of us dining out together soon."

I don't try to correct him. He was taken away before the restaurants banned Jews. So much has changed in the last year.

"We look forward to it," Peter says.

I chuckle and kiss him once more and then leave.

At the door, Peter raises his hands and I realize the silent question about how my visit turned out.

I point down the hallway, where he and Ariel follow me.

"He's ready to come home. This is the best I've seen him."

"That's great, Marika," Peter says. Then he turns to the girl by his side.

Her open nurse's coat reveals packages of bandages and medical supplies taped around her middle. She is so slender the extra inches won't show with the coat buttoned.

"I am thrilled to meet you, and I wasn't kidding. I want to do more to help." I scan the hallway to make sure we're alone and lower my voice. "Do you work with Peter's group?"

"She organizes practically all the underground units," Peter says. "I met her in the group that smuggled me here from France."

Ariel nudges him and raises her eyebrows. "And?"

Peter chuckles and wraps an arm around her. "And I fell in love with her on the way."

"That's better," she says, then she addresses me. "Men! Why must we always be in charge?"

I like her already and am glad they're a couple. "Because they need us to be, I guess." The hospital's cleaning solution scents work to cover the overwhelming smells of sickness, blood, and rotting flesh but fail the longer I'm here. "Let's head outside. I have questions."

We move through the corridors until we reach the hallway leading to the exit. I face Ariel. "You've worked in the Kasztner group. Peter said he's negotiating with Eichmann to trade trucks for Jews."

"I did work solely for him at first. Now I see them as adults trying to make deals with the enemy." Ariel is young, but her eyes hold an intensity born of hard times. "Our group doesn't make deals. We get things done by hiding, rescuing, or providing supplies to Jews who find themselves stuck in Hungary."

"I just learned she and another resistance worker she rooms with brought Gellert here," Peter says, beaming with pride.

"Wait. You found Gellert? Where was he?" Maybe if I know what happened to him, I can help him when he is ready to talk.

"I met him in the forest in the Carpathian Mountains. He was helping about fifteen local citizens, mostly women and children, flee west." She pushes her short dark hair off her forehead. "They were traveling at night to avoid both the Germans on one side and the Russians pushing in from the other. I'm not sure what happened after that."

"Thank you for bringing him here. Now more than ever I want to help out too. Maybe not the daring rescues so far from home, but I must do something."

Ariel takes me by the arm as we walk toward the front entrance and says, "I have many ideas."

Peter stalls behind us in the front waiting area, where he's reached for a newspaper lying on a table by a blue armchair. After a moment, he shakes his head.

"What is it?" I ask. With so many possibilities, I almost don't want to know.

"The Germans have started a new research group here."

"We've heard terrible tales of experiments in the extermination camps," Ariel says.

"That's true." Peter taps the front page. "But this is different. This assembly is gathering photos and mementos from the Jews to create a museum here. It says this is a gift to *future* Hungarians. They'll be able to study the past and follow the complete cleansing of the Jewish community that will be on display there."

"Like bugs in an exhibit," I say.

"They don't have all of us yet," Ariel scoffs with an impish smirk. Then her face darkens, and she clenches her fist.

"But clearly, they believe they will," Peter adds. "We have to double our efforts." He turns to me. "You've come at the right time. We need all the help we can get, and you might as well get busy. We have a few hundred Swiss protection letters to forge today for the men held at the Óbuda brick factory."

"I'm ready," I say. And with those words, it dawns on me. I am.

-12-
Budapest, Hungary

June 1, 1944

This morning before leaving the secret printing operations on Akácfa Street, I memorize where we will set up the coming evening. The Young Zionists have dozens of locations, but the danger is that discovery means torture or death, so they move every few days.

The willingness of our citizens to turn in offenders has grown like untreated cancer, especially since the tipster is rewarded the property of the person arrested. Many Jewish families have fought false claims against them, but not before non-Jews harvested their prized possessions while the family was held in custody. When they ask for the return of their belongings after they're cleared of charges, no one seems to know where their effects are.

I leave the building through the back entrance with Ariel. I suspected she was young when I first met her, but not a mere seventeen. Peter brags about her all the time as he should. She's small but forceful, working as a liaison for many of the underground groups, organizing food and clothing donations for those rescued from ghettos.

"Remember," I say, "day or night. Just come by." I've added our family's name at the Central Jewish Agency as willing to take in refugees from the countryside. In particular, young Jewish girls. Many are saved from deportations but unfortunately are forced to travel with the Germans to the edges of the fight to be used as prostitutes. None have returned.

This is my second week working in forgery and documentation. I asked Ariel how this all works, and she explained.

"We print certificates that pass for protective papers from either Sweden or Switzerland. The paper has an official-looking seal or stamp and exempts the holder from Jewish regulations, but especially from deportation. I have the Young Zionists comb the towns and gather names of Jews held in the ghettos at the edges of cities. The next day they return with passes bearing those names." She chuckles. "Because most of the countryside police are illiterate, they accept the stamp as official proof of the person to be released and protected."

"Clever," I say.

She added that over and over, the ghetto police still transport away tens of thousands because the Jews refuse to accept the passes.

"'We're part of this country's heritage,'" they say to us. "'We're loyal citizens, and the government will protect us. You're too young to understand. They're just moving us into safe zones.'" She shakes her head. "It's all so frustrating."

It doesn't help that the few remaining Jewish newspapers carry messages from Jewish leaders urging their constituents to obey the laws, and that the Germans have promised they won't be harmed. In the meantime, they rob the complacent of their property, as well as their political, civil, and economic rights.

The assimilated Jews' general belief is the war will pass, and they will remake their lives and recover their dignity.

I believe this willful ignorance will be the end of our race if we don't wake up.

"See you tonight," I say to Ariel, and we go our separate ways. She rooms over a tailor shop on Andrássy with two other girls, all working in the underground.

I pass a bakery, where the sound of the slide and catch of the cash register reaches me as the heavenly aromas of bread and fresh pastries follow. I run my hand along the wall. The bricks are warm from the bakery ovens on the other side, and the yeasty scent hangs thick in the air.

My stomach growls, protesting against the *No Gypsies or Jews Allowed* sign that fills the front window. Besides, with the new curfew restrictions, I have less than four hours to cross to Buda and see Gellert, shop for my family, and still be off the streets by two this afternoon.

The rules restrict us from being outside from 2 p.m. to 10 a.m. the next day, allowing non-Jewish shoppers to buy the already limited supplies of meat and vegetables before we are allowed in.

My father's riddle from last night returns to my thoughts. What has white and yellow walls? To get to the yellow wall, one has to break the white wall. With a bit of a hint, István finally guessed an egg.

The analogy in that isn't lost on me.

I watch my family's determination, along with the Sisters in the orphanages, the resistance workers. Like that egg, we're all delicate, held together by fragile walls. But after three months of hate and ever-constricting rules, we're hard-boiled and won't be broken.

I reach the hospital and am wearing the yellow star. Inside, the front staff greets me. "I've come to bring my guy home. He's been cleared for discharge. "

"We're happy for you two," a nurse with large doe eyes calls back.

I reach Gellert's room. He smiles when I enter. He's dressed in a light shirt and black dress slacks, holding something in his hand.

"I have this for you." He holds up a small package wrapped in newsprint held together with a bandage.

"Just like old times," I say, fondly recalling his creative flair in how he wraps gifts for me. I peel away the bandage and start to unravel the newspaper. It weighs almost nothing. "What do we have here?"

"I want to give you the world, but this is all I have at my disposal."

I remove the newsprint to find a folded cloth napkin. He's scrawled "I Love You" on the material with a pen. "How sweet, darling. I love you too." I fold it and put it in my pocket. "The best gift is having you well enough to leave."

We hold hands, not speaking but content in our connection, waiting for the nurse and his discharge papers. As minutes move along, I selfishly forget what's happening outside the hospital and throughout Hungary and Europe. For a thoughtless moment or two I pretend we're free. I picture choosing whom we listen to, where we work, whom or what we worship. I want this vision to be real and not erased by the facts that right outside this door our deadliest enemies live among us. Watching.

A stocky male nurse enters the room. "Gellert. I wish for you a life free of horrible images and pain." He hands him several folded papers. "And a happy reunion with this lovely lady."

"Thank you," Gellert says and wraps his arm around me. "You have no idea how much I'm looking forward to that."

I reach in my pocket and squeeze his note. We'll rebuild our lives together. I know we will. As for me, I have the easier job, remembering our cherished moments before the war. But in his case, he may need to fight every day to forget the devastating memories that came after the war started.

I pin a yellow star on his shirt as we leave the building. Gellert takes long breaths of fresh air as we reach the east side of Castle Hill and wait to descend in the tram. "Even with those smoldering buildings in the distance, the city looks wonderful."

I follow his gaze. The Danube's surface sparkles with sun-kissed waves as it reflects Parliament's majesty, and in the distance, I hear church bells. "Leave it to you to see the best this city still offers."

Once we cross over to Pest, we stop at an open market near the Dohány Street Synagogue. I trade food coupons for wilted vegetables, dried fish, canned beans, flour, and eggs.

Fiora and Gyorgy Kende walk out next to us, appearing older than they actually are by a dozen years. Fiora taught my music classes in lower school, and Gyorgy was a pharmacist. They carry one small sack with leafy greens protruding from the top.

"Marika and Gellert," Mr. Kende says. "How are you and your family?"

"We're staying strong." I want to explain all that happened to my brother, the estate, and what Gellert has been through, but it's too dangerous, even when speaking to old acquaintances. "How are you?"

"We've been forced out of our home, into an unpleasant building without fresh air," Mrs. Kende says. "But many of our faith have it far worse than us, so we thank God each night for what we have."

"We heard some hopeful news," Mr. Kende says. "Regent Horthy has halted the deportations because other countries have demanded it."

"That *is* great news. Finally, someone in the outside world is listening," I say. I can't wait to get home and tell my family. István just missed being forced on a trainload of eighteen hundred Jewish prisoners dispatched to Auschwitz when Peter found him.

"From the world's mouths to God's ears," Mrs. Kende says. She smiles. "We should get going. We don't move as fast as we used to, and there's the curfew and all."

I spot their meager groceries again. I reach into my sack and retrieve the eggs, fish, and cans of beans and hold them out. "Please take these. I'll just dash back in for more."

After a slight protest, Mr. Kende nods once and accepts the food. "May God continue to bless you and your family, Marika. Gellert, stay well and take care of this girl of yours."

"You bet I will," he says.

I touch Mrs. Kende on the arm. "Be safe."

Then I watch them disappear around a corner.

"That was so sweet, Marika. Let's head back in," Gellert says.

"I used all our food coupons on those purchases. We have canned vegetables in the cellar and dried beef in the cupboard. Plenty until we get more vouchers in a few days."

"See, this is why I love you," he says and kisses me.

I smile and retake his hand. As we near the apartment, I have him head around the block to the back entrance. "I'll walk through and unlock the gate."

I stop to knock on the Schlesingers' door. My hope is to catch Raakel before she goes to work just so she can say hi to Gellert. She came by two nights ago wanting to talk with me. My parents told her I was spending a few nights a week at the orphanage, which is what I told them when I'm making false documents through the night.

The door to the Dely apartment opens, and Benedek steps into the hallway dressed in his tugboat worker uniform.

"Where have you been?" he asks, his eyebrows bunched.

My heart pounds. He cannot see Gellert here, or he'll likely turn him in. I lift the grocery bag so it catches his attention. My words momentarily stall on my tongue. "Shopping. While I can." Why is he so surly? Has he seen me sneak out late at night, heading to the newest underground location?

"Huh," he says, doubt in his voice. "How many people do you have living with you now?" He points to the ceiling. "Was outside your door a few days back and heard more than just you and your parents."

"Erzsébet and the baby are with us. And we didn't hear you knock." How *dare* he eavesdrop outside our home. If he hears István's voice, they will arrest us. "Did you need something?" I keep my voice light but inside I'm furious.

"No. I just like to get higher up in the building once in a while. The window in the stairwell on your floor has a nice view of the gardens." His lip curls. "Privilege sure has its benefits, doesn't it?"

Gellert will be waiting outside the back gate to the gardens, and I have no way to get a message to him not to come inside.

"By privilege, do you mean owning the building?" I can't control the disgust in my question. "My father worked hard for years to save enough to buy this place."

"Your mother's money, from her parents swindling the people of the countryside with their outrageous wool prices, bought this place."

Raakel opens the door to her apartment, arching her left eyebrow as her gaze shifts between Benedek and me. "What's going on out here?"

Quickly, I turn my back to him and face Raakel. "Benedek was just leaving to go play boat captain." I know I shouldn't antagonize him, but I'm exhausted from being up all night, and his new supervisory attitude rubs me the wrong way.

"You can keep your door closed, Marika, but rumors have a way of seeping through the building." He smashes his hat on his head and storms out the front door.

"Get in here," Raakel says, pulling me into their front office. János isn't at his desk, but I hear him talking to Ilona from deeper in the house. "You need to avoid that creep, Marika."

"I know. But he said he was listening outside our door, and I don't like that." I feel guilty that we haven't been able to tell her or her parents that István is back, but we can't take the chance that information slips out.

"How is Gellert?" She points to a hard-back chair, and I take it as she sits in another.

"Better." Now, I'm not sure why I don't say he's here with me. As Benedek warned, the walls may have ears, and his father could be listening for all I know. I reach into my pocket again and bring out the cloth napkin with Gellert's message. "He gave me this wrapped as a makeshift present."

Raakel unfolds it and smiles. "He's still the man you love." She squeezes my arm and hands it back. "You watch. Soon enough, we'll be double dating."

I change the subject. "How is Sándor? From what I saw when you waved the other day, he's kind of tall and handsome."

"He is." Her smile droops for a moment, then returns. "He's hard to read, a bit guarded at times, but lovely in so many ways. He's heard so much about you and your family, and says he wants to meet you all one day."

They cannot come to our apartment as long as we're hiding my brother and Gellert. "The next time he's here, ring us and we'll come meet him."

"I will." She stands. "Be right back." She returns with a loaf of bread partially wrapped in baking paper, the crust glistening and crunchy-looking. "I was able to grab two at work."

"By grab, you mean hide?" I shake my head. "Please don't get in trouble by taking food you shouldn't. Only leftovers."

"I'm careful. And I know you can't get baked goods."

"We're fine." I give her a wraparound hug. "You're too good to us."

"We really hate what's going on." She rubs her hands along her forearms as if suddenly chilled.

We both turn as János enters the room and clears his throat. "Hello, Marika."

"Hello, Mr. Schlesinger." I stand and shake his hand. "How are you today?"

"Is your father upstairs?" He runs his finger under his shirt collar, not meeting my gaze.

And he didn't answer my question. "I imagine he is since it's almost curfew time. I've not yet been home today." I move to the door. "If you like, I can share a message when I get upstairs."

"I hate to do this, Marika, but I'm being pressured. I need him to bring the telephone and radio down."

I sag. This is a low blow. How can we stay informed about the war? And what if we need a doctor or have an emergency?

As if reading my mind, János says, "You're welcome to discreetly use our telephone."

"Thank you. I'll send Father down." I hug Raakel again and leave.

I wait for them to close their door, and I scurry through the back door and across the garden to Gellert. "Hurry inside and upstairs." I close the gate behind him. "It seems everyone is home and in a talkative mood right now."

All the way up the stairs I replay János's words. I'm angry at losing our phone and beloved radio, but it's the use of the word "discreetly." *Discreetly use our telephone.*

It's apparent that it's now dangerous for anyone who associates with us.

And just like that, our lives are more complicated. If someone needs to talk to us, they'll have to climb the stairs instead of calling. It's time to speak with Father and Mother about what the resistance groups can do to help us. The most pressing problem is how to keep my brother and Gellert safe. The Győr police know who they rounded up in their area, and they must know by now István escaped deportation using false papers Peter presented at the ghetto. And that Eichmann hates to have even one name come off his extermination list.

It's only a matter of time before someone comes looking for him.

And with Benedek's threat about rumors in the building, that time may have just gotten shorter.

Inside the apartment, my parents wrap themselves around Gellert. He's been a son to them these last three years.

"Welcome home," my father says, smiling widely. The sight of their reunion thrills me. "We couldn't come see you, but Marika kept us informed on your progress."

"That's no problem," Gellert says. "I'm here now."

My mother swipes away tears. "Yes, finally we're all together again."

~13~

BUDAPEST, HUNGARY

June 16, 1944

Peter wears a dark brown leather cap pulled down over his eyes, the Arrow Cross uniform with its green shirt and dark pants, and the cross insignia and stripes on the sleeve. I must admit I'm loving this stylish figure-hugging dress, the likes of which I haven't been able to afford to buy for a while. Not crazy about the pale shade of green, though, and it's a tad shorter than I'm accustomed to wearing.

"I hate wearing this outfit," Peter says, "but it's our best chance to avoid being stopped."

We both carry Aryan identification papers—Joel and Clara, last name Conrad, brother and sister. We're on our way to Győr to see if the estate is empty and if my family can somehow secretly return. The neighbors would recognize us, of course, but we hope to be accepted if we show our intent to convert to Christianity. We also want to bring back heirlooms Erzsébet had no time to pack.

Would we even be safe if we moved out to Győr or is that too unprotected, too close to Yugoslavia and Austria? The neighbors certainly proved they're unwilling to help us. The dilemma is we have no idea what awaits us in Budapest with the new decrees.

Rabbi Sofer met with Father yesterday after the authorities tacked the announcement to our building and nineteen thousand others. It proclaims we need to vacate our apartment and move into a shared flat in a building designated as a Yellow-Star House. We have five days to complete the order, four days now, or we will be arrested. János promises to protect our belongings we can't possibly take, but Father thinks it's best we try to leave the city altogether. If we can't go to the country estate, we'll be forced to move into the area northwest of us, District VII.

The order forcing us to move into a designated Yellow-Star house is an obvious attempt to create a ghetto around the Dohány Synagogue. The apartments are smaller and in less desirable buildings than where many Jews now live. Because Jews aren't permitted to own anything, my father's argument that he owned our building and we should be allowed to stay fell on deaf ears.

Gellert says he'll come with us if we move to the estate. Or to the shared flat. Father paces the floor at night. None of us sleep well, often meeting each other in the kitchen, dimly lit by the streetlights. We don't talk much, and when we do, it's in whispers. A shared look says more than any words we might form in our sleep-deprived minds. We're scared, but we have each other and that's what matters.

"Good," I say, watching the rain begin again. "This should keep the neighbors inside while we check the house."

"I'm going to park in the bigger barn, just in case," Peter says. "We need to be in and out as fast as we can."

"I know right where everything is kept so it shouldn't take long."

We slowly turn into the drive and my heart sinks. Rain hangs about the place, like stripy grey ghosts. Behind its murky veil, the house looks forlorn, the yard and flower beds overgrown, uncared for. I'm not sure what I expected with István and Erzsébet away these past two months. I guess I hoped as if by some miracle the house and property would remain neat and orderly.

"It looks like no one's moved in," Peter says. "That's a good sign."

No more than a dozen steps out of the barn I notice a horrible sight on the house's roofline and stifle a scream.

"The stork nest," I say, swallowing a sob.

"Those dirty bastards," Peter says.

Their nest is broken in half, which would have taken some effort, and Rezi and Jeno's deflated bodies hang over the sides, apparently dead for many days. Then I spot three shattered eggs on the ground.

Rage burns through me. I want to kill for the first time in my life. Why slaughter these innocent birds? It wasn't for food. I'm ready to march to the neighboring houses and demand answers until I find who did this.

I turn to Peter. "I really want to hurt someone."

"I know the feeling." He shakes his head. "Been there myself many times. But that kind of retaliation? It'll corrode a person from the inside out, so be careful. It's why I joined the underground. It was that or murder as many as I could until I was stopped."

I nod. He's right. The secret war we fight under the Germans' noses helps more than killing a few.

We head to the front door, and although the rain has lightened, the heavy clouds above remind me of its ability to suddenly return full force.

The awful smell that greets us right inside the door lets us know people have defecated inside. We step over areas soiled with human waste and reach the kitchen. The icebox stands empty, and the cupboards gape open. There's nothing left in them. My grandmother's flower-patterned china passed down from her mother is gone. The walls are blackened with smoke where a fire was built at the base.

"Looks like they tried to burn it down but changed their minds," Peter says.

The mattress in the first-floor bedroom has been slashed down the middle and bleeds white feathers onto the floor.

"Why not just destroy these things?" I ask.

"I'm sure it's the *dirty* Jew theory. Everything we touch must be destroyed."

"Hatred makes people stupid." I can't spend time looking at more damage. I need to find the family heirlooms we want to save. "Let's get what we came for."

Peter follows me into the parlor with its massive fireplace. "Oh dear," I say. István's puppet that hung beside the mantel is gone. "Evidently the value of the puppet Father carved helped someone overcome the fact that it was made by *Jewish* hands."

"I'm sorry." He shifts his weight slowly from foot to foot, waiting for my cue as to what to search for next.

In the bedside table's drawer, I find our *Tanakh*, the family Bible, undamaged. "Thank goodness." I bring it to my chest like it's a newborn baby. "This goes back four generations." I pick up the Shofar, a discolored ram's horn, and tuck it under my arm. "And this does too."

We head upstairs, sidestepping broken glass from our once beautiful wall sconces. The handmade wallpaper Mema bought from Italy is slashed and ripped into long strips. I push down anger and try to envision our family repairing everything, restoring the house to its preinvasion glory.

In the master bedroom, I cross to the closet where István's suits and Erzsébet's pretty dresses are strewn on the floor. They've been stepped on with muddy boots. I push the soiled clothes aside, and in the back corner, I kneel. The dark brown hinge perfectly matches the color of the flooring, making the small secret compartment hard to spot. I pull up on the barely protruding brown ribbon, and a section of flooring opens.

"That's clever," Peter says. "Who built that?"

"My grandfather." I reach inside, almost expecting an empty space, but my hand touches a wooden box. I bring it out and open it. "It's all here." Inside are my great-grandmother's ruby earrings and a dainty necklace, and several small pins with emeralds and sapphire stones. My grandfather's gold watch. A diamond hatpin.

The roar of a vehicle freezes us in place. Our eyes lock. He quickly walks to the window overlooking the front drive and hurries back. "Where do they keep the first aid supplies?"

"What?" I'm confused. "Is someone outside hurt?"

"I need them now." His eyes are intense. "Keep the jewels but put the box back and close the opening in the floor."

I quickly do as he says. How will we get these out of here if he's so worried about who has arrived?

"The bathroom. There's a first aid kit. Or at least there was."

A man calls from below in Hungarian. "Who's here?"

We silently move along the hallway until we reach the bathroom. I pull out gauze and wrappings from deep inside the sink cabinet and set them on the sink as Peter surveys the room.

"Sit down," he whispers, pointing to the edge of the clawfoot bathtub. "Hold your arm out."

"Okay." I have no idea what he's planning but I'm nervous it may not get us safely out of here.

He turns my arm wrist up and sets the jewelry, one piece at a time from my wrist to my elbow and wraps the gauze around and around until it's all sealed inside the thick padding. He then winds the medical tape around the bandages, overdoing it so it's extra thick.

"Who's up there?" The man is closer, perhaps in the hallway near the foot of the stairs. "Come down *now*."

My heart's pounding. I lean closer and ask, "Who did you see?"

"A local policeman," he whispers near my ear. "Will he recognize you?"

"I doubt it. I've never been in contact with the police here."

He grabs a towel and punches the corner of the mirror, loosening a piece. Before I can say anything, he untucks his shirt and cuts a thin line below his rib cage, bringing blood instantly to the surface.

"Peter!" I say, sounding like a hissing snake. I give him a wide-eyed look as if to emphasize my next words. "What are you doing?"

He drags the underside of my bandage along his wound, and soon it's covered with his blood. "Making you authentic."

He calls over his shoulder, "We're up here," and tucks his dark green shirt back in and pulls me along the hallway to the top of the staircase, and releases my hand.

A man with a squarish head and bulbous nose comes into view. "Who are you?"

Peter descends the stairs and I follow, carrying the Jewish Bible and horn in my *uninjured* arm.

"My sister and I came on behalf of the new Jewish Museum in Budapest." Peter's tone is light. "Seems we aren't the first people through here. We're collecting Jewish artifacts, so after the race is wiped out, there will be some items in the museum."

I stand by Peter at the bottom of the steps, trying to suppress a loud swallow that may give away our lies. "We found this," I finally say, holding up the Tanakh.

"What'd you do to your arm?" he asks, moving closer.

I drop my arm to my side. It may look professionally bandaged on the top, but the thickness and lumps on the underside aren't typical.

"Last night. A terrible cut from a broken window in another building," Peter says, shaking his head. "Fifteen stitches."

The policeman studies us. "Seems like a long way to come out here in search of Jewish junk."

"Budapest has been picked over"—Peter shrugs—"and it's nice to go through these big estates and see the wealth up close."

The man relaxes his scowl. "I know what you mean. I stop by to use the place as a toilet every chance I get."

My fist clenches. Peter must sense my outrage because he steps in front of me to hide my reaction.

"Then we will leave you to it." Peter forces a laugh.

"Thanks for joining the Arrow Cross Party," the man calls to our backs. "We need all the help we can get ridding the country of the depraved."

This time I feel Peter stiffen. We exit the house and head to the car.

I force my gaze to the ground, so I don't have to see poor Jeno and Rezi again. For twelve years they came here to the safety of the farm to raise their young. They trusted their nesting grounds. How could they know evil and danger now rule the pastures?

We are well on our way back to the city before either Peter or I speak.

"If you stop the car, I can check out your wound," I say as I reach to unwrap the top layer of the bandage. "These wraps will work great to stop the bleeding."

"No, I'm fine. Keep them on until I get you home." He steers around a stalled truck with three horses standing in the back. "And I think we learned your family won't be safe in Győr."

"I was just thinking that. We'd be beaten, killed, and plowed under." I shake my head. "Now we have four days to vacate our apartment and move into the Yellow-Star building."

"We can find safe houses for all of you. Your parents would stay together, as would your brother and his family, but in separate locations. You could move into the Glass House, or we'd find another place for you and Gellert."

"Gellert is much better but has had some nightmares. He will be best living with very few people at this point. It's frightening when he slips into one of the nightmares."

Last night, it wasn't even a nightmare, but just after dinner his mind seemed to travel to a different place only he can see.

"Put a message in a bottle!" Gellert's shout startles us.
"What's wrong, dear?" I try to make eye contact but his gaze
is vague, elsewhere.
"Like you used to do with your brother. Tell them we're trapped
here."
"We're fine. You're fine." I rub his arms. "You're home."

As children, István and I wrote messages in bottles when we stayed at the estate in Győr and dropped them in the Danube, hoping for replies from people in Budapest or countries farther south.

He's shouting. "Wolves on one side, bears on the other! Get out
now before they get here."
He paces for ten minutes, ranting, and then sinks onto a chair
and finally returns to a calmer state.

He couldn't explain what set him off.

"That's no problem. We'll find a private flat." Peter looks my way. "You must be very excited he's finally home."

I quickly nod, afraid I've been less than enthusiastic. "Oh, I am. But sometimes I don't know what to do. I can patch cuts, tell you what sickness someone has, but a semi-shattered mind…I'm not sure I know how to cure that."

With a warm smile he says, "You are all he needs."

Thirty minutes later we cross the Elisabeth Bridge and wind through the streets until we park near the apartment building's front gate.

"I'll walk you up," Peter says. "I want to tell your parents that it's too dangerous to leave the city and give them some options."

Benedek appears in the doorway of the bicycle shop as we enter the building. He scowls when he sees Peter in the Arrow Cross uniform but quickly recovers, throws his right hand in the air, and yells, "Awaken, Hungarian!"

Peter returns the salute and fascist slogan.

Benedek notices my arm. "You're injured."

"I was carrying a milk bottle and fell, cutting it."

Suddenly, Piroska Dely steps from the apartment. She's dressed in the women's Arrow Cross uniform, with a black skirt and dark green shirt. She's as tall as her son, but her expression is three shades more hateful.

She addresses Peter. "Why have you not arrested her for being out after curfew?"

"As you well know, she's moving from this apartment and needs to be here packing and clearing out and not sitting in a jail cell. I think you will agree."

"I do." She smiles. "The sooner the better." Then she steps to the front door but turns before leaving. "We're ready for the air to smell a bit fresher in here." She arches an eyebrow. "The word *cleansing* has never felt so appropriate as it does these days."

"I'll see you at the meeting, Mum," Benedek says.

"Yes. Bring that young man with you." She points to Peter.

"I'm escorting some Jews out of the courthouse prison," Peter says, "and will have to pass."

"Line them up back to back, son," she says. "We've learned you save a bullet that way."

This woman is so full of hate. How did she come to think this way?

"I won't forget that advice." Peter's jaw twitches, and I recognize the signs of anger boiling inside him.

She leaves, and Benedek returns to his apartment.

Peter hurries up the stairs with me before anyone else decides to question us. He mutters, "That's the caliber of people in Arrow Cross. Recruiting from pools of the unemployed, the uneducated, and the chronic haters. But I have to say, that woman is one of the worst I've met."

"She's awful."

"Unfortunately, they're recruiting more every day."

He stops on the landing in our hallway. "I'm glad you're leaving here… even if it's only temporary."

I open the door to the apartment, anticipating my family's joy that I found the Bible and jewelry. Instead, Mother and Erzsébet are huddled at the table, eyes red-rimmed and puffy. Baby József is asleep on the couch, his tiny arms wrapped around a stuffed bear. Gellert paces off to the side, his face masked with hot rage.

I rush to them. "Whatever has happened?"

"Your father and István have been taken with all the other men in the neighborhood," Erzsébet says. "About an hour ago."

"I was in the basement getting food jars," Gellert said. "It happened so fast."

"Who came for them?" Peter asks.

"The local police," Mother says. "I recognized Mr. Storz, whose wife used to be in my riding club." She notices my arm and covers her mouth, stifling a scream. "Marika! You're hurt?"

I sink into the chair next to Mother, setting the Bible on the table. "I'm not injured." I unwind the bandages and slowly the jewelry pieces and watch drop free. "Peter did some fast thinking when a policeman showed up at the house."

"But that's real blood," Mother says.

"It's Peter's." I turn to him. "I have limited medical supplies here but can at least stop the bleeding."

"I have to leave. Your nosy neighbor is surely watching to see how long I stay."

"Where will you go to get help?" I ask.

"There's a doctor in an apartment near here." He pauses and then asks, "Did the police say where the men are being taken?"

"No," Erzsébet says. "Just that it was again time to help win the war."

"I'll try to find out where they are being held," Peter assures us.

When we're alone, I open the Bible to the Torah portion. We join hands and Gellert leads the prayer for Father and my brother's safe return. I add a small thank you at the end that Gellert wasn't here. I know this is selfish, but I don't care. I fear what the police may have done to him if he refused to go with them. One of his rants is about needing a gun. Would he have charged the men to try to take their weapons?

I'm thankful we didn't have to find out.

-14-

BUDAPEST, HUNGARY

June 24, 1944

As the sun's first light reaches the city, I sit at the kitchen table, watching the smoke floating in the streets turn into light peach ghosts. Bombs hit the city throughout the night, and sirens wailed as we huddled inside the cellar. The Dely family was nowhere to be seen. Benedek and his father, Belko, must be staying with Piroska at her other house. Wherever that is. Or they're at one of the new Arrow Cross headquarters that's sprouted up in each district in the city.

I rub my eyes. They're scratchy from too little sleep and of course the smoke. In the past, I've always enjoyed the morning hum of the city coming to life. Dog walkers giving quiet instructions to unruly pets, the rumble of the tram, and birds cooing in the eaves. Somehow, the sunrise always infuses common sense into a fresh new day and offers a sign from God that this day will be one of hope, a gift to enjoy.

But now, the morning often dawns without any joy.

I pray with my mother, Gellert, and sister-in-law, five maybe six times a day. Still I'm more disheartened than encouraged. Budapest was once a civilized world—cultured, a blending of all races—the business of hate left to a dispirited few. Then Hitler took power, and the Kingdom of Hungary joined the Axis powers. Now we live in a divided world where nothing counts but blind adherence to orders devised by madmen.

On the street below, a young woman rolls a pram back and forth, trying to soothe a fussy baby. The rubber wheels' soft *thump thump* reminds me of when I nannied for Mrs. Stern, wife of an obsessive author who needed absolute quiet to conjure words.

I pushed Baby Becca for hours, covering the city, stopping to talk to the puppet master at his tiny booth in the People's Park. Feeding her while I dipped my feet in the thermal waters of the Széchenyi Baths and eventually bumping my way up the cobblestone streets back to their elaborate apartment. I was thirteen that summer and fell in love with the idea of marrying a prince and having my own babies one day.

I have a prince, but the rest of my dreams are on hold.

A man's voice, amplified through a bullhorn, cuts the peace. "This is your final warning!"

Local police fill the street like malicious black ants spreading out to supervise the expulsion from our homes.

The Jewish relocation to Yellow-Star houses was supposed to be completed by 8 a.m. three days ago, but we didn't budge from our home. And according to whispers in the back alleys, a vast majority of the Jewish population remained in their apartments, hoping the wait and see policy would work out, and the city council would overturn the selfish decree. But wait and see brings the frightening promise of arrest if we don't move today.

In the last eight days, we've had no word from Father or István. Once again, we've experienced the most painful of goodbyes—those left unsaid and never explained.

Peter heard they may be in the group of men sent as slave labor to the Bor Copper mine, five hundred kilometers to the south. We try to meet near the Glass House each day for updates. Now that Benedek was introduced to Peter as an Arrow Cross Party member, Peter is afraid to come to the apartment again. At Mother's pleas that I not go to the orphanages—which is what she still believes—I've stopped sneaking out at night to make forged documents. I miss the camaraderie and knowing I'm doing something helpful, but I can't add any more worries onto Mother's or Erzsébet's plates.

Gellert stays inside as much as possible now that we know all Jewish men are targets. He still hasn't talked about those weeks he snuck through the countryside to return home, or how he was injured. I can be patient. We're glad to have at least one man in the house should anyone try to break in. He's back to his inspiring self, helping where he can, comforting us many times a day with soothing words, his bedside manner on full display.

There is rumor of a train headed to Switzerland if a person has enough money to buy a seat aboard. Rudolph Kasztner is trying to negotiate a deal with Eichmann, who has fallen in love with our wines and is said to be drunk more often than not. The imminent German defeat must be wearing on him, and I wish him a long bumpy road of regret.

If the deal goes through, the train leaves within a week. Mother talked about all of us going if we can get Father and my brother back. Switzerland is neutral, safe. Of course, I've not shared my thought that I wouldn't leave Gellert, as he's made it clear he won't leave. I've told him about what I've done in the Resistance, and he wants to be involved. However, we both agree my family should go.

But how do we trust Germans and trains? Every sad tale we've heard involved stuffing people into them, heading to a place of no return.

"You have four hours to move your possessions to your assigned house," the policeman on the street bellows.

I snap back to reality.

Mother enters the kitchen and wraps me in an embrace. "Good morning, my darling." She steps back and tips her head toward the window. "Here we are. The day we prayed would never come."

The proclamation, even in its inevitability, always felt ill-defined and chaotic. "I know. It's unreal."

"Ferenc will be here soon," my mother says. "We need to eat before he arrives." She moves to the refrigerator and pulls out pickled eggs, sour cabbage, and rice stuffed peppers.

Ferenc came by last night to offer his help. Last week when he heard all Jewish men were rounded up and taken away, he immediately sent a note saying if we needed anything, just ask. He discovered Gellert is home, but of course, won't say anything.

As city transportation supervisor, he promised a truck this morning and several men to help load our belongings. He's including a uniform for Gellert so he can appear to be one of Ferenc's employees.

Erzsébet feeds József while we pick at the food. The little boy is the bright light in our days, always happy, blissfully ignorant to what's happening to the adults. He asks, "Papa go?" several times a day, and we assure him his daddy will return soon.

We're assigned a shared apartment, with one private room to ourselves. We've discussed what we can take, and what we must leave. János assured us he will watch for Father and István and redirect them to our new flat. He also suggested we lock our valuable china and other heirlooms we don't need right now in Father's workroom, and he'll see to it they're protected.

Within an hour, Ferenc, two of his employees, and Gellert have a truck bed packed with one mattress, a couch, a wardrobe, select articles of clothing, photographs, the phonograph, Bible, Shofar horn, dried and canned foods, and basic kitchenware. Mother sewed the jewelry into the hem of her winter coat, which she carries over her arm as we leave the apartment.

I walk through once more, the moment the mantel clock chimes eleven. Each peal reminds me my time in our wonderful apartment is almost over. In Father's workroom, I study the marionettes. Their lifelike eyes seem to beg me to take them along. My heart stutters at the thought Father may never come back. His essence is in these puppets. Without further hesitation, I decide I need to take one in case the room is looted. My Stern Mother puppet with her rolling pin or Baby József's? And there hangs my father's first puppet—Moshe. Even though it's old, wooden, and worn, it still means a great deal to Father.

Policemen blow their whistles from the street, and the shouting intensifies.

I grab the puppet intended for József and hurry from the room, locking it behind me.

At the foyer, I draw in a quick breath as I bump into Benedek and his mother again.

"You had your chance, Marika," Benedek says, his gaze shiftier than usual. What does he have to be nervous about?

"Actually, you've been doomed from birth." Frau Dely's beefy hands are clasped in front of her, a woman someone may describe as having generous features. She resembles a spinster librarian, except for her eyes. They are full of disgust, although she *is* wearing a smile. An acidic smile.

"You'll be more comfortable living among your own kind, closer to the synagogue."

It's on the tip of my tongue that I now see where Benedek inherited his utterly fantastic social skills, but I smile and raise my chin. "Have a...nice day."

I desperately want to say a quick goodbye to the Schlesingers, but with the Delys watching and under the new city rules, I can't risk putting them in harm's way for letting a Jew in their apartment. As the building supervisor, János has spare keys to our apartment. I'm glad we already discussed the locked room with him.

Before I'm out of earshot, I turn and say, "Don't forget, justice is a sneaky thing."

I don't hear their answer because just a few steps outside I'm greeted by the chaos in the streets. People carry bags and suitcases, pieces of furniture, and personal possessions by carriage, handcarts, and wheelbarrows. And those poor souls who found no better way struggle under the weight of their bundled lives on their backs.

I'm sure the police chose this day because it breaks the sanctity of the Sabbath. Thousands of women, children, and a few elderly men are in the streets trying to move their precious belongings. Wagon and truck drivers have doubled or tripled their prices to take advantage of the dire circumstances the Jews face. Whatever can't be moved in the next four hours will remain behind.

Ferenc drives Mother in the truck, and the three men ride on top of the load in the back. Erzsébet pushes József in a buggy as we walk the nine blocks to our assigned apartment on Akácfa Street. We know nothing about it except we're sharing the two-bedroom flat with another family.

We arrive, but Ferenc's truck is nowhere to be seen. With so many people plugging up the streets, he may not get here before curfew.

I study our new *home*. The front gate is rusted, but the painted six-inch Star of David on the front door is fresh. It stands out like a yellow beacon against the ordinary four-story brick building.

A barrel-chested man with sloping shoulders and thick fingers tacks a piece of paper to the left side of the doorframe.

"I believe this is where we are to report," I say and hand him the slip of paper with our names and this address.

He glances at our names and then runs his stubby index finger down a list on the paper he's just nailed to the door.

"Yup. Got three of you and a babe in 2C, front bedroom." He gazes behind us. "Where's the third?"

"Coming by truck with our furniture"—I point back along the route we walked—"anytime now." Our moving time is nearly expired, so I don't need him causing a stir.

"Make it quick when they get here." He points to the upper floors. "I've got four apartments of non-Jews in this building who refuse to move, and they're already complaining about the place being chosen as a Yellow-Star house. They've petitioned City Hall, but I doubt a thing will change. You need to be in your rooms and to stay put during the mandatory hours."

"Thank you," I say. His snappy words prove that as the janitor of this building, he isn't thrilled to have us thrust upon him and his responsibilities and duties. This guy is no rule breaker. If I'm to bring Gellert here, or if Father and István show up, we'll have to be extra careful. "And what is your name, sir?"

"Tamás Gábor. Wife's name is Judit."

"We appreciate your insight into the other residents' feelings," I say. "We aren't happy with this move either." Ferenc's truck slowly pulls along the front. "Here they are," I add, waving my hand at them.

"I'll be up to explain the rules once you're in." He drops onto a weathered bench, a dour sentry, and lights a cigarette.

As we enter Flat 2C, we find a central room with a kitchen and another area with a washtub and clothes wringer. Our room is to the left and overlooks the street. The other room is to the right and must view the courtyard in back. Ferenc and the men make quick work of hauling up our few belongings and placing them in the room. Gellert changes out of the uniform and hands it back.

"Stay in touch," Ferenc says. "I need to know you're safe. And Endre. I want to know if…um…when he comes home."

We thank him, and he and the men leave.

"Well, we're in good company, even if we're in a less than nice place," Mother says. I see a new determination in her. She'll try to make sure this place feels like home.

Surely we won't be here long. Now that the word is out concerning the Germans' true purpose, Regent Horthy is under extreme pressure to stop the deportations to the death camps. World leaders have spoken, including Pope Pious XII, President Roosevelt, and King Gustav V of Sweden. Roosevelt even threatened a ramped-up bombing retaliation on Budapest.

The air in the room smells moldy, and the buildup of dust suggests the room has sat empty for a while. I wonder where the previous renters have gone. I prop open a window with a ruler, obviously left on the sill for just that purpose.

"You're going to need a bath," Erzsébet scolds József who's crawling around on the floor, pulling items from the lower shelf of a wire stand.

Under a few items left behind, he pulls out a cloth doll. "Baby," he says, sitting back on his pants pockets, holding up the toy for us to see.

The doll is creepy, staring with her dead button eyes and red stitching that barely attaches her head to the body as if ripped off and hastily sewn back on.

I reach into a bag and replace the doll with his favorite stuffed bear. Then I lay the doll facedown on a high shelf. "I see why they left that," I say with a light laugh.

Erzsébet nods and shivers. "I wonder if we're allowed to box up their belongings?"

"That's a good plan," Mother says and starts gathering their candles, doilies, and old books.

What must Mother feel? Raised on the estate with its thirteen-room main house, and then she and Father comfortably made their home in our five-room apartment. I never heard her complain once about lack of space. But who imagines their lives will shrink to living in one room in a shared flat? Her face gives away nothing as she hums a song and gathers the belongings of a family who, in all likelihood, will never return.

Will that be our fate as well? János promised to protect our rooms, but a gun pointed toward a person or a threat to the family erases good deeds, no matter how big the desire to do good.

I shake away the image of the Schlesingers in danger and start unpacking. Within thirty minutes, we've hung our clothes in the wardrobe and found places for our kitchen supplies, canned goods, and personal items.

Someone taps softly on the door.

We all look at each other for a few heartbeats before Gellert crawls under the bed. Then Mother opens the door. "Hello. You must be the other occupants," she says.

We step into the kitchen area to introduce ourselves to the Szabó family. We're sharing the space with three women and a ten-year-old boy named Bandin. His mother, Imre, a striking woman, has a heart-shaped face and long dark lashes and is probably near Mother's age of forty-two. The others are her mother and aunt, Eden and Eunice, twins dressed in matching navy blue day dresses with their grey hair styled in perfect buns.

"We are surely in the end times with all that's happening," Imre says.

Within minutes we learn Imre was a glove maker and her mother a women's tailor. They are Christians, Jehovah's Witnesses hated by the Germans for their unwillingness to give the Nazi salute, or join party organizations, or let their children join the Hitler Youth. They're apolitical and refuse to participate in elections or honor any government in power.

Kálmán, Imre's husband and Bandin's father, was a poultry merchant arrested a year ago when he refused to join the Army's Labor Force. They've not seen him since.

"We pray for him daily," Eden says.

"As do we for my husband and son," Mother adds.

A sharp rap on the hallway door startles us. No one moves until a man says from the other side, "It's Tamás Gábor, the building janitor."

Bandin lets him in, and we all step back forming a half-circle.

"I'm glad you've met." He clears his throat. "You are a lucky few, you know. The building next door has eleven Jews per room." He shrugs. "But who knows. The city may require more in here soon."

Is he being compensated per person? It sure sounds like it. I don't say the words, but I want to challenge him.

Gábor continues. "I need to go over the new rules with you." He pulls a sheet of paper from his pocket and unfolds it. "Everyone is forbidden to be outside their living quarters, except for medical attention or shopping. You have three hours between two and five p.m."

"Not the ten to two?" Imre asks.

"It's so you are outside when most housewives have returned home for the day. My wife and I will be at the gate between these hours to make sure you follow the schedule." He reads from the paper again. "Jews may not accept visitors to their homes or hold conversations through their windows that open onto the streets. We have a bomb shelter, but you'll only be allowed in last. If it's full, you may wait in the hallway on that level.

"Finally, you aren't allowed in the Christian apartments even if you are invited in. They had the opportunity to leave but decided not to. They've been warned not to help you in any way." He looks at each of us. "Are there any questions?"

"Will the men in our families who are returning home be allowed to stay here?" I ask. Maybe we can say Gellert is back from his time in the Labor Force.

His forehead creases. "Who would that be?"

"Our husbands," my mother says, pointing to Imre, Erzsébet, and herself.

"And my fiancé," I add. "He's already served his time."

The janitor sucks on his eyetooth before speaking. "Let me share a saying my father used all the time. 'A fool in the morning is a fool in the afternoon.' Remember that in case you think you should hide someone here who is required to help with the war effort."

When he's gone, we each return to our separate rooms. Our mood has changed, even Mother's. We can't go out twenty-one hours a day. Can't allow anyone in. How will we get a message to Father and István that it's not safe to come here when we don't know where they are?

We need to get out of here. These buildings are *not* our new homes. They're nothing more than jail cells with the keeper at the gate more than willing to make sure the inmates comply.

-15-

BUDAPEST, HUNGARY

June 26 and 27, 1944

The Szabó family turns out to be good company, and we've had no choice but to introduce them to Gellert. This apartment is too small, and we share the kitchen and bathroom.

"We're not ones to help the Germans or their collaborators in any way," Imre said.

We settle in and divide our roles. Cook, shopper, cleaner, dishwasher, and responsible person of the day. We usually leave that last job to Bandin, who is happy to spy out the windows on the lookout for happenings we should know about. Yesterday, the police went door to door asking that we hand them any books we own written by Jewish authors. We left our books behind but watched in horror as the confiscated books burned in piles along the sidewalk.

The Jehovah's Witnesses have no specified Sabbath but instead pray every day as we do. The only difference is they believe we're in the end times and pray for Judgment Day to come sooner than later, while I pray the Germans' time ends and their judgment day as war criminals is swift.

In the few hours I was outside today, I sensed more hostility. With a complete lack of reasoning, the most outlandish and stupid statements are made and broadcast to those who still own radios, all to strengthen the hatred toward us. Unfortunately, it proves again and again that no propaganda is ever too unreasonable not to appeal to the lowest instincts of the population.

As I passed a shop with newspapers on display, I saw one such headline that accused British and American pilots of dropping dolls and toys filled with explosives to murder our children. What rubbish!

The storekeeper shooed me away when he saw my yellow star. "No gloating. Move along."

Gellert and I discussed his possible move to a safe house where he can help the other doctors. Maybe we could both work side by side in some capacity. The nuns asked the government for Jewish doctors and nurses for their charity homes since they are no longer allowed to work in other facilities. Budapest is short on Christian medical workers because they are treating the wounded military men in the big hospital they appropriated. We're needed everywhere but aren't allowed to do what we're trained for.

We're waiting to hear from Peter's organization.

Tonight, it's the Szabó family's turn to clean up after our shared meal of vegetable stew and dark bread. We wish them pleasant dreams and say goodnight and return to our room.

Erzsébet rocks József as she sits on the edge of the bed she shares with Mother and the baby. I sleep on the couch and Gellert takes the floor.

She hums the tune to a popular folk song.

"One of my favorites," Mother says. "I sang it to the children when they were little."

I smile. "And you sang it when we were not so little, if I remember right."

Mother chuckles. "That's true, I guess."

"The sun has set in quiet, the city is sleeping," Erzsébet sings.

"Sleep well my son," my mother joins in. *"Above you a beautiful angel is watching. A hundred fairies by your side."*

"You close your eyes in peace," the three of us softly sing now. *"This is how your day whispers to a close. While you are dreaming in the land of the fairies, we will watch over you."*

Erzsébet chokes on those words and wipes away a tear that slides down her cheek.

Gellert rubs my back and smiles. "My mother sang this too."

Mother and I finish with the final verses. *"Love us as we love you. Good night, my little child."*

With the baby asleep, Mother, Erzsébet, Gellert, and I share in long hugs, standing in our one-room cell, quietly assuring each other that if we stay strong, things will take a turn for the better. As long as we have food, shelter, and hope, we'll be all right.

The next day, Mother and I leave the apartment right at 2 p.m., wearing our yellow stars. The janitor glances at his watch before opening the front gate as if freeing us a minute early would matter to anyone. Judit, his wife, has softer edges than her husband but stands next to him grim-faced while she writes our names in a ledger.

They take their new positions as our keepers a smidge too seriously.

Mother is heading to the pharmacy that continues to sell to Jews. The baby has a cough and fussed most of the night. As for me, I'm off to talk to Sister Sára about volunteer jobs for Gellert and me.

The sunlight gleams against the office windows, but the sidewalk is damp from an earlier storm forcing me into a pattern of leaping over pools of water. Instead of heading straight to Kerepesi Street and the Worker Girls' Home, which is almost directly to the right, I want to walk by our apartment. I probably shouldn't, but I'm curious to see if in three days, anyone has moved in.

I hope not. I try to imagine taking over another family's house, using their belongings, staring at their paintings, knowing that family is deemed unworthy of living in their own home.

Could I post a sign on the apartment door saying this is a tuberculosis ward to scare away possible tenants? I dismiss the idea because it would mean more trouble for János. The Dely family knows the truth. They've probably already invited their distant relatives or friends to move in.

I see no activity through the fourth-floor windows, but that means nothing. They could be in the living room or out enjoying the courtyard and gardens.

Then a deep ache of loss moves through me. It comes out of nowhere to remind me of what we had.

I shouldn't have come here.

Two blocks later, I turn as I hear footsteps quickly approaching me from behind. A beggar in a worn coat and torn trousers, with a hat pulled low over his face, rushes toward me. My throat goes dry. I have no time to think about who he is or his intention. I take off running, searching the shops for a place to bolt into. Will someone have mercy on me if I enter a store where Jews aren't allowed? His footsteps sound closer but I don't dare look back. I gulp air, fear depriving me of a way to get enough in to my lungs.

"Marika!" the beggar says. "Wait!"

As I wonder how he knows my name, my mind registers the voice. István!

He reaches my side and pulls me into a narrow side street where vendors park their empty wooden carts.

"Thank God!" Tears fill my eyes. "You're here."

He's breathing hard with one hand on his thigh, the other on my arm to steady himself. "Meet me in the tunnels," he says, barely able to form the words. "Near the wine casks."

He lifts his face and I gasp. He's been beaten. His eye is swollen shut and upper lip is cut. Bruises discolor his cheeks and chin.

He bolts away, but my tears flow unchecked at the thought that Father isn't with him.

I pull myself together and stare at a lovely blue piece of sky that has no business being there. Instead, boiling grey clouds should reign, chewing their way across the heavens, blotting out the sun.

I head eastward through the People's Park, and descend age-old stairs into the huge system of cellars carved into the limestone rock. The wine casks he's talking about are stored near the breweries of Kőbánya in District X. These dark rooms have whitewashed damp walls with twisty channels and passageways.

István and I don't know all the one hundred and eighty kilometers of tunnels running under Budapest, but we've explored more than our fair share. Local wineries used the caves for a short period of time. But then the

Dreher Brewery bought the abandoned cellars and uses the enormous, cool tunnels to make their beer. The giant wine barrels remain along the passageway and are probably still used for games of *bújócskázunk* by children who know the caves and want a heart-pounding game of hide-and-seek. The barrels are big enough for a grown man to fit in, so there's ample room for two scrappy children to find refuge.

My shoes are quickly soaked, the rains from this morning move through the tunnels, in places a few inches deep.

After a turn to the left, I realize I've gone the wrong way. In the distance I hear motors and the pounding of hammers on metal. Who could be working down here? These passages are storage rooms and a breeding space for rats, not workspaces.

I retrace my steps and take the tunnel to the right, and soon I'm heading where I was supposed to go. A few minutes later, I spot István in the dim light, kneeling in front of a large wine cask on its side.

"István," I whisper. "What's happened to you?"

His face is full of fear as he points to the open-ended cask. "Not to me, but what happened to *us*."

I reach his side and stifle a scream. Father is tucked in the barrel, unconscious. His face is toward us, and it's bloodied and swollen. He's nearly unrecognizable. I drop to my knees and check his neck for a pulse. It's there but weak and thready.

"Who did this?"

"Secret police in the basement at Sixty Andrássy Street." He folds his arms tightly around his midsection. "He was tortured for information."

"What information could you and Father have that they needed to do this?" I gently touch Father's face. He moans, and his pain echoes through me.

"They want to know about the Resistance."

My thoughts jump to Peter and how he worked to free István so he could come home. "Did they connect you to Peter?"

"He was never mentioned, and as far as I know, neither Father nor I named him." He shakes his head. "We denied knowing anything."

A horrible thought crosses my mind. "Maybe it was me," I whisper. "I could have been followed from one of the secret printing locations."

"Wait. You've been working with the Zionists?"

"Yes, at night making forged papers. I started by bringing refugees into the orphanages."

"They didn't mention you, Marika. But they acted like Father knows something."

"Maybe about his meetings with Ferenc and the rumors in the city."

"This was different. They asked if we owned guns. How did I get papers to get out of the ghetto at Győr? They know my Aryan papers were falsified. Who did that for me? Who do we take orders from?"

I frown. "This is our police who did this to you? Not the Germans?"

"Yes. They're killing dozens each day. They pile the bodies by the door with a death notice that says, 'Death due to measures taken by the authorities.'"

"How did you escape?" Father moves his arm to cover his head but still doesn't wake up. I need to get him and István to a hospital. They can't stay in this cold, damp air without falling ill.

"They moved a dozen of us to another building, not far away"—his face lights up for the first time—"and I recognized it. I delivered coal there during high school and knew the cellars ran for blocks under those buildings. When the police went back for more men, five of us escaped that way. They had a noose hanging in there. I'm sure we were to be next. Poor Father was on his feet for a while, and we made it here before he collapsed."

"You have to get out of here, but I'm not sure where to take you." I grab his hand. "We're in one room in an apartment on Akácfa Street, but the janitor is not friendly. He keeps a strict guard at the front gate and enforces curfew like his life depends on it. We're still hiding Gellert."

"You're all fine?" His expression softens. "How's my little man?"

"He's obliviously happy but asks for you all the time."

That brings a bit of a smile to his injured mouth.

"Can we go to the estate?"

"It's a wreck and the local police check it each day." He doesn't need to hear about the storks or our stolen belongings right now. I remember the train Peter mentioned. The one Kasztner made a deal for. "But perhaps we all can leave the city. A man on the Relief and Rescue Committee is negotiating a deal with Eichmann. Peter mentioned it to me a few days ago. A train going to Switzerland, and I don't think it's left yet."

His busted lips part but he hesitates. He stares at me with his one good eye, as if processing what I've just said. "How can we get seats on it?"

"I'll find out from Peter. There's a cost per head, but we have the jewels and money Father kept." If anyone finds out János helped Father shelter our money, he'll be the one arrested and tortured.

New energy moves through me. We can all leave together. "You need to come to our apartment." A plan comes to mind.

"You just said the janitor is unwilling to help us." He coughs, and it sounds wet.

"Wait for an air-raid siren. We've stopped trying to go down to the shelter because there's never room for us. When the others go into the cellar, come then." I repeat our address. "I'll be at the gate. From the first sirens to the all clear is usually thirty minutes but often more. Can you get Father that far?"

He takes a moment to think then says, "The brewery has a hand-pull wagon. I'll take that to get as close as I can to Akácfa Street. Then I'll wait for the sirens." He leans forward and embraces me. "You're definitely the smart one in the family."

I lean into him, cherishing the fact he's alive. "Or the one most likely to break a few rules."

"Get going," he says. "If for some reason this doesn't work out like we hope, tell everyone we love them."

My throat nearly closes at the thought. He gives me one last desperate look and waves me away before kneeling in front of Father. I hear him praying as I turn and run back the way I came.

I won't have much time to find Peter. And I need medicine from the Red Cross storehouses.

I have never wanted the Allies to dispatch more bombers overhead until now. They usually strike at night, which means, we all may be together again within six or seven hours.

We thought we were safe. István and Father's torture brings the truth home. The war may be nibbling at our lives, eating away at our freedoms, taking our possessions, but now it's found us. If we don't leave this city, it surely will devour us all.

$-16-$

Budapest, Hungary

June 27 and 28, 1944

Afternoon and evening schlep on forever as we wait for bombs to fall and our men to return. Anticipation and worry cripple the idea of completing anything useful. I never realized how many moments are in a minute, each like a miracle balanced on a ledge of possible sorrow. Back and forth. Teeter-totter.

Before returning to the apartment today, I talked to Ariel when I couldn't find Peter. She informed me the *Blood for Goods* train leaves in three days.

Once home, when I told Mother and Erzsébet about the plan to get Father and István home and then on the train, we cried happy tears. Mother unpicked the hem of her coat. We gathered and put that jewelry and the pieces I collected from the estate into a small purse.

When the bombing begins around 9 p.m., we grab each other and smile at the ironically pleasant rumble of residents' footsteps pounding down the stairs to hide in the cellar. "Be careful," Gellert says as I leave.

"I will, sweetheart."

I sneak out to the gate as sirens continue to wail, only to find the metal door locked. I panic at first until I realize no one should be in the Gábor apartment as long as the warning continues. Slowly I turn the knob on their front door and open it into a cluttered living room. Artwork leans against walls, stacked four deep, and ornate gramophones, radios, and vases cover every table. Apparently, they've helped themselves to other families' possessions.

Between the rise and fall of the siren's blare, I listen for any sound from within their apartment. I'm alone. If discovered here, I'll be arrested.

Quickly crossing to the front window facing the street, I push it open. Once I crawl outside, I drop behind a row of bushes and scan the streets. No one is out.

The siren continues. I'm so grateful for more time.

Then I see them!

Father has his arm around István's shoulder as they turn the corner, a house away. I run to them, no longer fearful anyone is watching.

"You made it." Tears stream down my face, and I support my father from the other side. "This way, through the lower window."

With my brother inside and me outside, we help Father through the opening. Stumbling across the apartment, we soon climb one flight of stairs to our door. I go in first to make sure the Szabó family isn't in the shared kitchen. They have also stopped going to the bomb shelter. The room is empty, so I wave the men inside and hold the door open to our room.

A chorus of hushed, "I love you" and "Praise God," along with tight embraces, goes on for minutes behind our closed door. We have to shush József as he yells "Papa" over and over. When was the last time we were this happy? The fear of losing each other makes the moment extra precious, a gift above all others.

I pull out my medical bag and apply ointments and bandage the men. A cold compress should help István's swollen eye. Father has a deep cut on his arm, but there's no way to stitch it up. "Knife," he says when I ask what happened. I wrap it as tight as I dare and give them two tablets of Kalmopyrin, all I have left from the Red Cross hospital nearby. The pain reliever should help through the night.

But my day isn't over. We've talked, and I need to run one more errand as the bombing continues. I slip out the window again, but this time I close it nearly all the way, leaving just enough room for my fingers to get under when I return. If the Gábors return to their rooms before I sneak back through, they most likely won't notice the barely open window.

It's dusk, that lonely time of the evening when brooding and melancholy fill the space between day and night. I send a prayer skyward for my safety as the pale stars slide into their places.

I scurry along the buildings' walls, returning to our old apartment, and slip a note into the Schlesingers' mailbox. I ask them to unlock the back gate in the courtyard tomorrow during our free hours. I don't tell them why, but we need to collect the money Father hid when János cashed that check for him. We have no idea what the cost per person will be for the train. I already told Mother I'll be on one of the next trains with Gellert, but the five of them need to take this opportunity. She's adamant I go with them. I won't argue anymore. For now.

The all-clear siren sounds, but I'm still five blocks from our one-room flat. Non-Jews are pouring out of the city shelters to return home. I need to get off the streets.

I turn around and head to the large convent next to City Park. If I must scale one of the high brick walls to get inside, I will. I warned my family that if I don't return tonight, I'll be safe in one of the many houses the underground runs. The convent will be safe.

I'm in luck when I reach the front of the structure. The nuns are still ushering children up from the cellar, using the outside stairs, and into the building. One nun spots me and lets me inside the locked gate.

It's Sister Aleksandra, the Polish nun who helped me talk to Zofia and Jakub. "It's so good to see you," she says. "The children wondered why you'd stopped coming."

"Sister Sára asked me to stay away for my safety. My neighbor told Father Kun I was working here and that I'm not a convert."

"That nasty man"—she shakes her head—"needs to stop pretending he's a Christian. He's trailing in the Devil's footsteps if you ask me."

"How are Jakub and Zofia?" I help her guide the last of the children up the wide stairs into the convent. "Are they still here?"

She smiles. "They are. They'll be happy to see you."

The pleasant scent of laundry soap, soup, and baking bread fills the hallways. I've missed this mix. "I've wanted to visit. I'll let them know that."

Other nuns greet me, and I realize I've missed being here. I help put the toddlers in their cribs before I go in search of the older children's rooms. Jakub spots me first as I enter their dormitory, rushes to me, and throws his arms around my legs. I swear he's grown taller in the last month. Then I steer him to Zofia, who sits on the edge of their bed, watching me.

"Hello, Zofia." I stroke her arm, and she doesn't pull away. She's made progress in trusting an adult. "It's so good to see you."

I point to the spot next to her and mime I'd like to sit there.

She nods, and I pull Jakub onto my lap as I plop beside her. He's almost too big to be held this way, but I love the warmth of his body clamped around mine.

"I had to stay away," I say, "but I thought about you both all the time."

Zofia watches my face. I don't know how much she understands German, so I try in my limited Polish. "I missed you."

Sister Aleksandra laughs from the doorway. "You just said, 'I washed you.'"

I chuckle. "Oh, dear. Please tell them I wanted to come but couldn't."

Even Zofia smiles when my words are translated.

"And that I'll come back more often," I add. Now that I'm not under Benedek and his mother's watchful eye, maybe both Gellert and I can work here.

"Have you moved into a Yellow-Star home?" the Sister asks.

"Yes, a shared flat." I almost slip and add the good news that my father and brother are back. "The other occupants are very nice."

"If you feel like you could take in a few children, we need homes for hundreds of them. We're overcrowded here. At least in the Yellow-Star houses, you're there nearly all day and night, so the children will never be alone."

I turn over the idea. Could I convince the janitor to accept that Gellert lives there too? He's not fit to serve in the labor force. With only us there, we could take in a few children. It would be good practice for when we have our own children one day.

"That might work, but I must make arrangements with the couple in charge of our house. They haven't been very accommodating."

"I won't say anything, but I do know two children who'd like that."

I wrap an arm around Zofia, and she leans into me. "May I stay in here with them tonight?"

"I don't see how you can leave." She smiles as she turns to go. "I'll welcome your help in the morning."

I pantomime I can sleep on the floor next to their bed, but Zofia scoots to the far side of the mattress and motions for me to take the center. Jakub curls up on my other side. This is not where I pictured I'd spend the night, but I did pray for a safe journey to our old building and back.

We're taught every single prayer is effective and answered, though not necessarily with the exact answer the petitioner requests.

Tonight, this solution works for me.

I can't leave the convent until 2 p.m., so I help with the children all morning. Sister Aleksandra is right—the rooms meant to house two hundred and fifty hold close to a hundred more now. Most of the children are orphans, missing parents who were deported or died in the bombings.

The children need so much more than a few minutes of our time as they dress, eat, or play. They come from trauma and are unable to use toys in appropriate ways. Instead, they build checkers into fortresses, hide dolls or have them threaten each other with violence, and happily-ever-after stories are too far-fetched to believe.

Sister Sára won't be here today but another lead nun, Sister Ruth, with crystal blue eyes and jutting cheekbones, listens to my request to volunteer here with Gellert.

"If not here," she says, "then the new office for the Hungarian Red Cross is looking for unpaid Jewish staff. They're acquiring sixty houses or flats in different parts of the city for the office requirements and establishing places to house juveniles and children."

"How can we come and go from there?" I ask. "We're so limited with the curfew."

"You'd be protected under the banner of the International Red Cross. Friedrich Born is a Swiss delegate in Budapest who has seen enough. He's made a deal with our government to provide Jews in Budapest with certificates showing that they're in possession of immigration papers issued by Latin American countries."

Maybe this is another option for my family. "We can emigrate to South America with these papers?"

"Well, no." She shakes her head. "It's the game we all have learned to play. The papers are for protection purposes only. Born has placed all Jewish hospitals, shelters, and community kitchens under his protection, so as a Red Cross volunteer, you'd be allowed to work in any of those."

This sounds like the best news. My family will be safe in Switzerland, and I'll be working for the Swiss Red Cross.

I arrive home that day as the Gábors are at the gate to begin their patrol, observing who goes in or comes out of the building. Have they nothing better to do? I'd suggest decluttering their apartment of everyone else's belongings, but that would give away that I'd been inside.

"Where were you?" Judit asks, her face taut with disapproval.

"When I was out yesterday, I felt ill and checked into the hospital." I raise my palms skyward. "Praise God it was nothing more than spoiled food."

She mumbles some nonsense about rules as she steps aside. I climb the stairs to the apartment. Father is awake but foggy. He slowly turns his head, studying the room, probably taking in what we've been reduced to. István holds his toddler son, who giggles as he makes faces at him. I tell them where I was and what I learned about the Red Cross houses and hospitals. I explain I'm staying in Budapest with Gellert and hopefully we'll work in one of these protected programs, then we will catch the next train or meet them just as soon as we're free to travel.

They all protest at once, but I assure them this is what I want to do.

"Will there even be more trains?" Mother asks. "It's a big gamble taking this one. Do we trust them?"

I've lost sleep over the same idea. The Germans play so many games to keep the deportations going.

"I think we have to trust this plan," István says. "Kasztner has helped with the relief and rescue program since before the Germans arrived."

My mother bites her lower lip. "But my heart aches, Marika, thinking you'll be left here as the situation worsens."

"I'll be here with her," Gellert says. "She's my life, you know that."

Mother smiles. "I do know that."

"Everyone says Eichmann and a man named Becher are eager to get all the money they can from us," I say. "As long as we can pay, we can leave."

Father has been extra quiet. I take him aside and ask what's worrying him.

"I've known of a few groups who have made plans to leave. Some have made it while others haven't."

"Where were they headed?"

"Across Romania to a ship. But one ship was already sunk by a torpedo and hundreds perished." He scrubs his hand across his face. "I've thought of us all leaving, of getting us out, but now I'm not so sure."

"Mother and István and his family. They need to be safe. And you know Mother won't go without you."

"I know." He forces a smile. "I'm worried about you. What kind of father leaves his daughter behind?"

"A father who raised her to be tough and not give up, that's who." I hug him. "I will see you soon."

We have so much to accomplish in the next few hours. Because Erzsébet can be on the streets without a problem, she'll go to the apartment and get the money. We've warned her this is dangerous and she's to act like she's shopping until she reaches the back gate to the courtyard. If it looks dangerous, she needs to come right back and forget the errand. Father tells her that if no one is around, she'll find the money taped to the inside of the large wardrobe behind a false wall he built inside the cabinet.

"Wrap the money in wax paper and put it in a sack covered with rotten food from our icebox." He hands her a key to his workroom. "And…please get my old puppet before you lock it back up."

I knew that marionette meant everything to him. It was the start of his side career, and I feel guilty for not choosing the right one to bring here.

I'm off to the Relief and Rescue building not too far away. Ariel said a committee decides who will be allowed on the train once the paperwork is filled out. My family can complete that today. I'll find out more details about what to bring and when to pay.

Part of me is relieved they can get out, but I also worry this is another German dirty trick, and they'll be taken to an extermination camp. Can a man making deals with Eichmann be trusted to know who he's dealing with?

Mother is taking the baby as she shops for dried meats and cheeses for the trip, and bread and powdered milk if she can find any. The three men are to remain hidden inside the room, and under Gellert's orders, Father and István must try to rest.

Because we nearly lost them, I make sure to give my brother and father extra-long hugs before leaving.

We three women exit the building together, each carrying our fears along with positive thoughts about what we're accomplishing to keep our family alive.

I wait in a long line outside the Swiss Consulate building. Clearly, hundreds of people are trying to leave Budapest.

Swiss policemen guard the doors under the country's flag. Twenty minutes later, I'm inside. In groups of ten, we're led to an office that smells of crisp paper, pencil shavings, and stale smoke. Rough leatherbound law books line one shelf, and the long mahogany table where we're seated is polished enough that I note my nervous reflection on its surface.

I'm seated across from a pleasant-looking man. The nameplate in front of him reads, Ottó Komoly. He brushes eraser bits off the table and leans forward.

"Are you here to gain passage on the train leaving for Switzerland?"

"Yes, not for me but for five members of my family."

"If they are chosen, they will each need to pay seventeen thousand pengö in cash, jewels, gold, or stocks." He counts out five forms from a stack beside him. "Do they have that amount?"

I believe Father has 43,000 pengö, and with the jewels and gold watch, we should have more than enough. "We have a two-year-old in the group. Will it be the same charge?"

"Unfortunately, yes. The Germans are strict on the amount they need to collect to safely move seventeen hundred passengers."

"We have the money." I lean closer. "And there is no way they won't arrive, is there?"

"Young lady, I have my reputation and the others on this committee at stake. We take this exchange very seriously." He points to the men to the right and left. "We have a chance to save as many as we can with this deal. I feel personally responsible for how many Jewish people have been transported away already. My committee brought tens of thousands here from other countries because we believed Hungary would remain safe. Hungary was an unwilling Axis power, forced to fight the Russians alongside the Germans." He shrugs. "The Germans seemed to have no interest in the Jews here, but sadly it is no longer true."

Peter said he came here from France through Kasztner and the Zionists. He trusted Hungary would work out too.

"That's good to hear." I reach for the papers. "What does my family need to do next?"

"If accepted, arrive at the Keleti Railway Station by seven in the morning on the thirtieth. Each passenger is allowed to bring two changes of clothing, six sets of underwear, and food for ten days."

The railway station is only a few blocks from our original apartment, near the cemetery. "How's my family to know they're accepted?"

"Lists will be posted at the train station tomorrow afternoon, during the hours you're allowed on the streets." He exhales heavily then gives me a certain look. "I wish your family luck in leaving. But I must ask, why are you staying?"

"My fiancé was badly injured and is unable to travel just yet. We'll get on the next train. Until then, we can work with the Red Cross." I say this with a confidence I'm only starting to accept. If my family is safe, why should I leave? There's so much to be done here with the orphans and displaced people. If given another chance to leave the country, Gellert and I may find we don't want to leave. We must do our part. I'm tired of hiding and being told what to do and when I can do it. What food I'm allowed to buy. Where I'm able to buy it.

"You need to know there may not be other exchanges." His face is grim. He slides two additional forms across the table. "Just in case you change your mind."

"Let two others take these seats." I push the papers back. "Thank you."

Outside, the line has grown longer and snakes down the block. I scan the faces to see if I recognize a neighbor or friend. My gaze stalls on a middle-aged woman who quickly turns away and disappears.

May a thousand ravens descend on my head if I'm wrong, but I'm almost positive that was Piroska Dely. What would she be doing here? Seems she'd be glad to see every last Jew shipped out of Budapest.

Then a ridiculous idea pops in my head that makes no sense no matter how I look at it. Is she here because she's tracking my family's movements?

-17-
BUDAPEST, HUNGARY

June 30, 1944

The morning arrives as a natural force, bold, needing no invitation, dropping an eerie glow onto the tops of every building.

Gellert says a tearful goodbye to everyone while we're still inside the apartment because he can't be seen on the street. He promises my family he'll do everything he can to protect me.

Tamás begrudgingly opens the gate for us after reviewing the papers, allowing the five members of my family safe passage to the train depot.

Erzsébet retrieved the money from the apartment and, as she was leaving, bumped into Raakel and Sándor. She admits she may have looked nervous as she quickly bid them hello but was sure Raakel and her suitor saw nothing suspicious in her presence there. She told them she came to collect more food, which addressed the bag she carried.

"That was so frightening, yet exhilarating all at the same time," she said, her face flushed.

I know what she means. A thrill comes with danger as long as the situation doesn't feel deadly.

It was easy enough to fake happiness while my family packed an hour ago. But now as I hug each of them goodbye, the tears I dammed up since finding their names on the list yesterday flow freely.

"I'll see you again," I say and pray this isn't a setup. "And soon, I hope."

"Godspeed to you and Gellert," Erzsébet says. "We will be impatient waiting for you."

My father pulls me in close. "I would stay, but I need your mother to leave, and like you said, she won't go without me."

"I know." I'm careful as I hold him. His cut is healing quickly, but he has bruises everywhere from the beatings. "Take care of everyone. I love you all so much."

"You're braver than you know, Marika." He pushes back and looks into my eyes. "Remember the teachings of Hillel. 'At a time when there are no men, you be a man.' Or in this case, a strong, capable woman."

I smile. "I will."

His expression tenses so I know he's serious. "Please get the Red Cross papers today. I need to know you're both going to be fine."

"I promise," I say.

We've been told the train is thirty-five cattle cars long, and each family will remain together. Some people are already accusing Kasztner of favoritism, given who's been allowed aboard. There are over three hundred from Kasztner's home city of Cluj, including his friends and family members. I'm relieved to hear this. If he has included his own family, that convinces me the convoy is safe.

My mother wraps her arms around me. "I know you're strong and brave, but remember it's better to avoid a problem than to look for one to solve."

Her words mean so much. She's describing herself, and I'm honored she feels this way about me.

"I love you, Mother. Take care of everyone. One day we'll retell stories from these crazy times, and it won't feel so awful."

My brother is next. "If working for the Red Cross doesn't keep you safe, promise you'll leave."

"I will." I plant a kiss on his cheek. "Keep baby József from growing too fast. I still want a little boy to play with when we meet again."

"That's enough time." Tamás Gábor growls out the words. "Was just supposed to let you out, not throw a family party."

István's hands close into fists.

I wrap mine around one of his and whisper, "I'm sure they must eat nails for breakfast." Louder, I say, "Go now. I'll see you soon, right after the Russians arrive."

István smiles and plays along, hoping to put fear in the Nazi rule follower. "Ah, yes. Within a few weeks."

And then my family walks off.

Seconds before they disappear around the corner, Mother stalls and turns to look back.

I paste on a grin and place both hands over my heart. She does the same, and then she's gone.

Back inside, our single room still holds this morning's echo when the seven of us filled the space. The room is too spacious now, needing their voices, whether in conversation, song, or prayer.

Remembering my family will be easy but missing them already hurts.

Gellert holds me as I cry, and suddenly worry invades my mind. What if this is a setup and they are on their way to their deaths?

"Let's get something to eat," Gellert says. "You're getting too thin."

The Szabó family is eating in the kitchen area when we enter.

"Good morning, Marika," Imre says. "Bandin tells us your family left not long ago."

I drop into one of the chairs as Eden pushes a plate in front of Gellert and me with a slice of dark bread. On the table is a canning jar of Mother's apricot jam we brought from our storage.

"Yes. They've been awarded passage on a train leaving for Switzerland." Guilt flits around in my chest as I think how this must sound to a family trapped here without money to pay for seats. "My father and brother came back two nights ago. They'd been beaten for information they didn't have."

"Where did you receive news about this train?" Imre points to the jam. "By the way, your mother makes the best preserves."

"She does. And we have another dozen jars, so please eat as much as you'd like." I put my hands on my lap to hide my case of nerves. "I have a friend who works for the Swiss Embassy, and he told me." Peter technically does work *with* the Swiss, since the Swiss have combined efforts with the Zionist Youth. "We learned of it just days ago…then it all happened very fast."

Why didn't we share this information with the Szabós? Were we wrong not to let them decide if they could buy tickets?

Imre leans toward me. "We will pray for your family. We trust no government, even those with good intentions."

Her words relieve some of my reservations about keeping the train a secret.

"The two of you will be living here now?" Eunice asks.

"I'm not sure. We may be able to work for the International Red Cross. Also, I may take in some orphan children." I shake my head. "There are thousands now who need a home. I'm heading out today to gather more information."

"We could take in children too, if that helps," Imre says.

What an admirable offer. "Thank you. I'll let the orphanages know." I turn to Bandin. "You could have other children to play with."

"I hope so," he says. "We could take turns standing watch, and maybe one of them has a chessboard."

"You play chess?" I envision Father's chess set stored in the cabinet at our apartment.

"I do. I mean I did." He drops his head.

"We gave it to a neighbor who helped us move here," Imre says and points to the bread again. "Please. That's for you."

The bread goes down hard. My throat is tight with emotion. First, because this family has so little, and second, the jam reminds me I may not see my mother for quite a long time.

I finish and touch Bandin on the shoulder. "I'm going to try to get a chess set for you, as long as you promise to play your first match with me."

His mood brightens. "You'll have to play all the matches with me. Only my father knew how to play."

"That's a deal," I say as we return to our room.

Can I get Raakel to pick up Father's set? The main office for the International Red Cross is on Mérleg Street, one street over from the Gresham Restaurant where her boyfriend Sándor works. Perhaps he would deliver a note to her.

Hours later, I leave the main office of the International Red Cross with safe-conduct papers for Gellert and me. We'll work in Department A, the children's section. They assigned us work at the orphanage on Munkácsy Mihály Street, near City Woodland Park and the convent where I first met Peter and that monster Eichmann. I mentioned to the Red Cross worker that I wanted to take in two children. He thanked me and suggested we stay in the assigned Yellow-Star apartment for now. They will send a mattress and extra bedding with volunteers to carry it over. Jakub and Gellert will have one and Zofia and I the other.

Maybe as Red Cross workers, the authorities will allow us to take the children to the nearby park. Gellert and I spent many Sundays there, welcoming the scents of greenery and flowers. We'd bring a book, and with our backs against the uneven surface of a tree, take turns reading it aloud, listening to the splash of water from nearby fountains. We'd laugh and cheer on the children as they'd run with a flapping kite, begging for an uplifting wind.

I want that back.

Next, I stand on the street across from the Gresham Hotel, hoping to spy Sándor. He's not allowed to talk to me, I know. So when a cook exits the backdoor and lights up a cigarette, I hurry across the street.

"Excuse me, sir"—I hold the folded paper out to him—"this is for Sándor Saamik, if you would be so kind."

He accepts it without issue, even as his gaze drops to the yellow star on my blouse. "Sure. You got a name?"

"Just a friend of his girlfriend."

He nods, extinguishes the end of his cigarette between his thumb and forefinger, drops it in his shirt pocket, and goes back inside.

The note asks Raakel for the chess set if she feels it's safe to bring it to the front steps of the Red Cross building on Mérleg Street. I also thank her for the help with the back gate two days ago.

I return to our assigned Yellow-Star flat.

"How did it go?" Gellert asks. He's at the tiny table organizing his small kit of medical supplies. Dressed in a shirt he must have pressed himself, he looks professional and ready to take on the world.

I relay all that I learned with the assurance we will be working together.

"That's worry I see on your face," he says and stops what he's doing. "Is there more terrible news from the outside?"

He hates being stuck in the apartment, but now with our protection papers, we will both be free to leave. "My family. I sure hope they didn't make a mistake taking the train."

He pulls me into an embrace. "Your father is a wise man. He wouldn't have done this if it didn't feel right to him." He sweeps hair off my face. "He and I had some good talks these last weeks while you women ran errands. He's a planner and is always thinking ahead."

"You're right." I smile, thinking of my father. "And I never got a chance to tell you what he said to me outside before they left."

"Was it a new riddle?"

"Surprisingly no. But he made me laugh. He said something like, 'At a time when there are no men, you be a man. Or in this case, a strong capable woman.'"

Gellert drops his head and studies his hands. "I'm sorry."

"Whatever for?" I thought he'd get a kick out of my father's words. Gellert has always said he admires my independence.

"I'm so ruined. You may one day realize you don't want me around."

"What in the world are you saying?" I swat at him. "You are so strong, so kindhearted. You've survived your family's sudden deaths. You have an amazing way with patients. And I love you no matter what has happened."

"You may not if you knew the truth." He sits at the table and stares out the window, suddenly lost in a memory.

Is he about to have another episode? He's been so calm this past week. I sit across from him. "I *want* to know what happened. Why don't you let it out? I'm here to listen. Maybe it will ease your pain."

"I most certainly was not a man when I needed to be. I was a coward… and people died."

I keep my gaze on his eyes, never flinching. I want him to tell me everything so he can heal.

"When I escaped the Labor Force with three other men, we were in the Ukraine, in Galicia. We'd sleep in barns or attics during the day and travel at night. We'd been helping groups as we met them in the forest by offering what little medical aid we could or by finding food. This one evening, we were hiding in the upstairs of a farmhouse while on the main floor were five women, all related. Three widowed. Two were about your age, never married."

"Go on," I say, keeping my tone soft.

"Russians came through the village. They were looking for anyone who fought for the Germans and had been through there months before, pushing toward the fight in Stalingrad. I was the only man in the house at the time. The other two were in the woods hunting."

His lip quivers. His hands shake.

I reach across the table and take them in mine and squeeze them. "You've done nothing wrong."

He shakes his head. "The soldiers broke into the house and confronted one of the widows at the door." He swallows. "Every Ukrainian woman was pregnant but not by their husbands. Their men had been in the German Labor Force for over a year. The Russians knew it. One soldier pointed to her swollen belly and asked, 'German or Russian?'"

It sinks in how they'd become pregnant. "Those poor women, having to admit they'd been raped by the Germans." Sadness boils in me.

"They assumed, as I did, that the Russians were upset by what happened to them as the Germans retreated." His face crumples. "I was at the top of the stairs when the first soldier stabbed the woman in the belly. The other soldiers found the four women huddled in the kitchen and butchered them. My two pals came running when they heard the screams, and they were shot." He looks at me with the saddest eyes I've ever seen. "I lay on that floor and did *nothing* to help. I don't know what happened, but my legs were suddenly paralyzed."

And he remained "paralyzed" long after. Was this his mind's way of justifying his inability to act? For letting the women die instead of helping?

I quickly round the table and take him into my arms, and he breaks down, sobbing.

"Gellert"—my voice cracks—"that's truly horrible what you witnessed. But you are not a bad person. You would've been killed."

"A far more noble act," he says. "I can never be a doctor."

"This war isn't about bullets and fixing wounds." I cup his face in my hands. "It's about demoralization and disorder and extreme brutality. And complete indifference on the part of whoever has the upper hand at the time. No one wins when that's the battle."

"I'm going back to the countryside, Marika. There are so many women left out there." He sits up straight, and with care, pushes my hands away from his face. "I didn't want to tell you what happened, but now you know why I have to do this. I will never be able to put it behind me if I don't."

He has impossible expectations for himself. But I'm not surprised this is his solution. He's kind to a fault, and watching those executions damaged him to the core of his being. They would anyone.

"As of an hour ago, we have protective passes through the International Red Cross. We are to work in an orphanage together…and live here for the time being."

"I can't do that right now." He stands and pulls me to my feet. "I must make up for this failure."

"I understand. I do. I know your heart and it's not whole right now." What can I say to convince him? "Why not work with the women brought in from the countryside instead of getting seriously injured again in the war zone?"

He's silent for a moment. "I won't be injured again."

"And how do you know that?" I touch the scar on the side of his head.

"Because I did this to myself."

~18~
BUDAPEST, HUNGARY

July 8, 1944

Calm settles into the lives of us Jews remaining in Hungary. Regent Horthy ordered a halt to all further deportations, citing the world is watching and is displeased. Eichmann snuck in one last trainload yesterday, deporting people from Kispest and Újpest, both about twelve kilometers outside the city. Eleven hundred souls added to his tally of 437,000 in only seven weeks, on one hundred and forty-seven trains. Eichmann celebrated in his confiscated house on Buda Hill with wine and women. He had succeeded in sweeping Jews out of a country faster than any other leader.

Where did I hear these facts? From Tamás Gábor who reminds us of our *specialness*, that we are protected in Budapest and safe because janitors like him and his wife are organized and care about rules.

I picture my parents and István, Erzsébet, and the baby, traveling on the train. The itinerary laid out the diversions along the way, avoiding the military trains with the right of way. What should have taken two to three days before the war will now take twelve days. They planned enough food and changes of clothes, but I'm sure they'll be glad when they arrive in Switzerland in two to three more days. They promised to write as soon as they do so I know they're safe.

The flat is so empty with them gone. I'm so empty. I hadn't realized how much our personalities create an agreeable harmony when we're together. Alone, I talked to myself and frankly grew tired of my solo voice. But it didn't last long.

Zofia and Jakub moved in two days after my family left, filling the room with a new quality, one of careful bonding, of a deepening trust.

As for Gellert and me, we've seen each other twice in nine days. He joined the Red Cross transportation department. It's for rescue missions outside the city. They follow safe leads—provided by the Zionists Youth groups hiding in the forests and countryside—regarding children left in homes after the parents are taken or killed. He's also managed to save many pregnant women and bring food from farmers who now have fewer customers. I can't help but notice he has a new spark in his eyes. At first, I wasn't sure if this was good for him, but he said his nightmares have abated and he's more outwardly focused. Less guilt-ridden.

When he returns from a rescue mission, he stays at the flat. Zofia and Jakub were wary of Gellert at first, but it didn't take long for him to charm them with his playful nature and small gifts he brought. The children spent three years hiding with their father before he drowned, but now show signs they're eager for a father figure. Gellert gladly fills those shoes.

I ask him how many more rescues he needs to complete before he decides to stay with us for good, and he merely shrugs. "There're too many out there to stop. I'm not ready yet."

Whatever it takes for him to heal. It must be on his time, not mine, although I worry about him and miss him when he's gone. He finally confessed to me that once he left the farmhouse with those butchered women behind, he threw himself headfirst off a cliff and suffered the head injury. Will he try to take his life again if he witnesses another terrible incident?

After, when he wasn't in a fog of pain, he woke up dismayed to find himself in a hospital and still alive.

"Wash your hands and faces, children," I say to Zofia and Jakub. They spend the day with me at the orphanage on Munkácsy Mihály Street. "We need to leave soon."

My protected status gets us in and out of the flat with only minor complaints from the janitor. "The Hungarian government may approve of all these free passes, but I think something fishy is going on."

He's right, of course. The seventeen thousand original documents are duplicated repeatedly, with new names added each time. May the fishiness continue.

I lock our room and meet Bandin in the kitchen. He's enjoyed having two more playmates.

"A chess match later when you get home, Miss Tausig?" he asks.

I've reminded the child to call me Marika, so it doesn't sound as if he's asking for my mother, but the boy has manners. Or he knows he'll get a thumping if one of the aunts hears him. Those two sisters are quiet until something happens that they disagree with. Then I'm reminded of chickens pecking at problems, as Mema used to say.

Raakel dropped off Father's chess set at the Red Cross headquarters as I requested. I heard I missed seeing her by a few minutes, but I'm sure she was careful not to break the rules—no contact between Christians and Jews. Yet I need to find a way to thank her.

One positive note. Our new mayor, Ákos Farkas, offers extended hours on the streets to any Jew who converted to Christianity before 1941. This pertains to only ten percent of Jews in the city but appears to be a stab at a concession for the harsh rules imposed so quickly. It's also a way to appease leaders of Christian churches who've seen their members assigned Yellow-Star houses and denied all the freedoms non-Jews enjoy.

It's a surprising move since Farkas agreed with the Jewish *resettlements* imposed by Eichmann for the last two months. Maybe his conscience gave him a good talking-to. Most likely, he's planting a few helpful seeds in the barren landscape left to us Jews in case the Germans lose, and he's held responsible for the fate of so many citizens.

Not *if*, I remind myself, but *when* the Germans lose.

Information about Allied victories snakes its way to us through the underground. The big news was the landing on northern France in June, where 400,000 German soldiers died, and another 300,000 were captured and sent to POW camps in the United States. The Allies fooled the German generals with a massive deception operation. They intended to make them think the main invasion target was in a place called Pas-de-Calais. There, the Brits and Americans built fake equipment, touted a phantom army commanded by General George Patton, and announced it all in fraudulent radio transmissions meant to be overheard by the Germans. It worked.

And as Gellert experienced, the Russians are reclaiming the East, although now more than ever, I'm not looking forward to the barbarians' arrival. We'll have to decide what to do as they get closer.

With a bag slung over my shoulders and a child on either side, I hold their hands as we leave the neighborhood. Today, the heat reigns. The hot cobblestone has us walking along somewhat faster, and the sun is intense in the cornflower-blue sky. I miss the summer rhythms of the neighborhoods. A time when music, art, and dance filled courtyards and parks. When a baby's birth or a new promotion was reason for celebration.

"We're having chicken for dinner," I say.

Money from other countries donated to the International Red Cross supplies enough food to the seventeen orphanages, although meat is often unavailable. Some farmers have defied the Germans and secretly kept their flocks and grains hidden from confiscation. The transportation volunteers, like Gellert, stop at the farms when a signal is raised. For one grower, his wife hangs the laundry upside down. Another parks his tractor next to the house instead of by the barn.

The children squeeze my hands, and I know it's because they're excited about having chicken. Their eyes gleam. Their lips pinch a smile to keep it from showing. How sad they know better than to look as if they're happy while out in the open. If you ask those in charge, Jews should have no reason to smile.

"I swing hundred times this day," Jakub says. "And chicken. Good day."

He's talking about the new tire swings added to the large trees behind the orphanage. And he's picked up English fast, the language I decided the children should learn. My hope is this will secure a permanent home for them in England or an English-speaking country.

"Yes, a good day." And it does appear as if we're relatively safe now. At least no longer in grave danger of deportation. With Swiss diplomats under Carl Lutz already handing out protective passes, a new rescuer has arrived. Raoul Wallenberg, a Swedish diplomat, with Swedish funds and the backing of the War Refugee Board established by President Roosevelt. He intends to open hospitals, nurseries, soup kitchens and designate more than thirty *safe* houses.

The Swiss headquarters is officially situated in the Glass House, where I met Peter the day I asked him for help reaching my family's estate. The Germans agree it's off-limits to attack due to its neutrality.

The walk to the orphanage takes only fifteen minutes. We have two blocks left when ahead I see four Arrow Cross women crossing the intersection, each prodding along a Jewish woman. The women are crying, their hair is in disarray, and their clothes are rumpled. Piroska Dely is there, so consumed by her importance she doesn't see me, but I hold the children back until the aggressors turn down an alley and are out of sight.

What could these Jewish women have done and where are they taking them? They have their yellow stars on their shirts and dresses, and this time period is when we're allowed out.

This is different though. The disheveled women have been detained somewhere.

"Are we okay?" Zofia asks.

I smile at her. "We are. I thought I saw someone I knew." I squeeze her hand.

I walk faster, unnerved that Piroska and her gang are out on the street someplace. The children keep up with me, and we arrive dewy with sweat. "Have fun," I say as I send the children off to the play area.

Today, I'll be in the large kitchen. With over three hundred children currently housed here, one of our biggest concerns is procuring and preparing enough food for the coming winter. We've been warned that as the weather changes, and if the war still rages, our numbers may double. Extra beds and bedding fill the sizable parlor, the thin mattresses stacked on their sides. I'm reminded of oversize playing cards whenever I pass the doorway. The orphanage receives two hundred pengő per child, but the money doesn't always arrive as it should. So we prepare for the worst and hope for the best.

Forty women and two men work here. The women offer their cooking, cleaning, and laundry help in exchange for protection for themselves and their children. Keeping clean diapers on the dozens of babies is a full-time job in itself. Men work as carpenters, haul away garbage, and keep the sewer lines flowing.

"Where do you need me today?" I ask Luca, a robust woman who ran a private school before losing everything and joining the Red Cross.

"We received twenty-seven kilograms of plums. You can make brick jam if you'd like."

"Gladly." The next hours fly by as I grind the fruit to make a mash. I spread it out on parchment paper to firm it up as it dries. Once that's done, I cut rectangles and stack them to make a brick-shaped block I wrap in paper to store in the cool cellar.

My hands are stained purple and my fingers ache, but I smile as I scan the forty-three bricks the orphanage will enjoy at a later date.

Next, I check on my two charges. Zofia waves from a table where she's drawing with another girl, and Jakub is playing with a group of boys, building a tall structure with wooden blocks. My prayer for them every day is they don't let these war years ruin the rest of their childhood and adult lives. The children have heard these same guiding words from the nuns and women in charge. "The Germans have taken so much. You must not let them take any more joy from your life."

We return to the apartment before dark, the children now tired and dirty. They get a bath after dinner. I tucked away extra food at work and offer it to the Szabós for their nightly meal. From what I can tell, they don't have much money to spend, and trips to the store are rare.

Once the children are clean and tucked in their beds, I wash my hair and change clothes. If Gellert returns, it's usually around this time. He doesn't need a fiancée smelling like cooking smoke, with her hair hanging in strings from standing over steaming pots for hours.

A memory bubbles to the surface. The two of us in the university library, staring at each other more than studying, his finger playing with a loose strand of my hair. We had a favorite study room with bay windows, where we'd watch the steady flow of students passing by, warmed by the sun shining in.

"It smells like burnt chocolate," he'd say, discussing the scent floating from an old medical book. For me, it called to mind the scent of old coffee or dried wood.

Our romance grew the more we spent time in the reference section or perusing the special collections, discussing the research and how it would help our medical careers.

There's a soft knock at the door to our room. Excitement races through me. I'm no longer tired knowing Gellert is here.

But it's Peter. He's disheveled. His eyelids droop. I spot drying blood on the front of his shirt. "Marika. I need your help."

The Szabós close their door, and I realize he's come through their side of the flat to get in here.

"Did you climb the back wall?" I say as I pull him inside.

"I did." He raises his hands. "Your janitor might as well be the Gestapo, threatening me that he had a gun."

"He's bluffing." I direct Peter to a chair at the table because he's unsteady. "I've never seen him with a gun, and I think he would have waved it around for show by now."

The children are awake, staring wide-eyed at a man they've never seen before. "It's okay," I say to them. "He's a good friend of mine."

I reach for his shirt to check where he's been wounded. I have more supplies now, taken from the Red Cross storehouses.

"Where are you injured?"

"Not me. It's Ariel. I found her hiding in a bombed-out building." His eyes are strained, almost bulging. "She's been shot and is asking for you."

"Oh, no." We'll have to sneak out the back window into the courtyard. The children will be safe with the Szabó family.

I bend down and talk to Zofia and Jakub. "Bandin is going to come stay with you while I go help a friend who's hurt."

"Will you ever come back?" Jakub says, his voice breaking.

"Of course I will…" I kiss them both on the head. "As soon as I can."

I grab a bag of medical supplies after asking Imre for Bandin's help. Peter and I cross through their living area and climb out the window and down the rusted main water pipe that supplies the upper floors.

Since the SS expropriated the Jewish hospital and ordered the patients removed, Ariel is at the Jewish school on 44 Wesselényi Street. The hospital personnel managed to smuggle out portable medical equipment and transferred operating rooms to the school. The Resistance provides the makeshift hospital with medical supplies and medicine obtained through contributions from Jewish doctors not allowed to practice.

We keep to the alleys on our way to the school.

Inside, patients lie on wooden tables in the hallway or in classrooms on mattresses on the floor. Moaning and cries come from the rooms we hurry past.

Ariel is ghost white and covered with a bloody sheet. I pull back the cover and flinch. Her right arm is barely attached at the elbow, and another bullet has ripped through her abdomen, leaving a gaping wound. Someone tied a rope above her elbow to stop that bleeding, but the amount she's losing through her midsection will soon prove fatal.

"Is there a surgeon here?" I study the room, searching for surgical tools. Anything to help close the wound.

"You and your father," Ariel mumbles. "Smart. Brave."

"You don't have to talk." I move in closer and brush stray hair off her face. "I'm going to get you into surgery. Stay strong."

Peter's face is flushed, his lips set in a hard line. He's terrified, as I would be, that the love of his life may die.

I glance his way. "Please find someone to help."

He hurries away, his boots slapping the linoleum floor.

"No time," she says and coughs up blood. "Gellert. He's ruining plans."

Gellert's missions are with the Red Cross. How does she know what he's doing? She must be out of her mind with tremendous pain. This is delirium talking.

"What plans do you mean?"

"Your father's plan"—she chokes and swallows blood—"helping the transportation department. Gellert…"

Peter returns and shakes his head.

Ariel's breath hitches. I stroke her hair as she struggles, her eyes locked on mine. "It's okay," I say.

Peter is across from me, his face a mask of pain. "I'm sorry," he whispers. "I should have gone with you."

She turns to him. "Don't. Quit." She barely chokes out the words between gasps.

"I won't," he says. "I love you."

Her breath catches, and her chest rises for the last time. Her face is still, but a tiny smile remains.

"She heard you, Peter." I close her eyes. "She knows she was loved."

My vision blurs. This beautiful, brave seventeen-year-old. The main liaison between the underground groups. Never tired, never unsure about what she was doing. I wipe tears from my cheeks and turn to Peter. His face is white, and tears stream down his face. "I'm sorry there was nothing I could do."

Peter clenches his jaw, making tendons in his neck stand out. "I knew it was too late. She asked for you, and I wanted to do that for her."

He leans close to her, tears dripping from his cheeks. "You'll always be with me, carried next to my heart." Then he turns his back to me, gathering himself, his shoulders still shaking.

I place a hand on his back, his sobs rattling me. He eventually turns, and I take him in my arms. "I am so sorry, Peter. I can't even imagine how horrible this feels."

"I can't believe it." He draws in a shuddering breath. "She was so alive, too alive to ever die."

We remain silent for a few moments before breaking apart.

"I am here for you." I shake my head. "Gellert and I are here for you."

"Thank you." His voice is choked with emotion. "She was amazing."

"I agree." I try to control the tremor in my legs. I want to be strong for him. He's lost so many in his life it seems there are no words to possibly comfort him. "She felt the same way about you and loved you dearly."

He nods and controls the tremble in his chin.

"This is horrible. Do you know what happened?"

"She was heading to a warehouse in District Six." He swallows and swipes away tears. "I'm sorry."

"I'm sorry I asked." What was I thinking? I am so insensitive. "You don't have to talk about it."

"I know you have lots of questions. I would too." He shakes his head. "We heard the local police were about to raid the warehouse. We store the plans there for several of the resistance groups, and she was warning the workers." His breath stutters as he inhales, then exhales. "She was going to move the files to a safe house."

"She was always so daring."

"I wanted to go with her, but she insisted she'd just run there and back."

"Do you know who shot her?"

"The boy who came to get me said the whole thing was a setup to flush out resistance leaders. The police were waiting." He's quiet for a moment. "Two others were killed too."

"This is so unfair." I take his hand. "What are you going to do now?"

"I'll stay until I make plans for her burial. She has no family, but the Resistance will pay for a coffin and plot."

"I'll stay too." My tears are back, and I let them flow. "I want to be here for you both."

۟○۞

It's early morning when I say my final goodbye to Ariel. I let her know she's the bravest person I know, and I'm blessed to have been her friend. I wait outside the room for Peter to emerge. When he does, his eyes are swollen, but he offers a weak smile. "She's with her family again."

"I'll bet she's reorganizing Heaven right now." I smile. "She was an expert at that."

"She sure was."

There's nothing more to say as we make our way through the hallway to the hospital entrance. Every room is in chaos, with workers yelling orders or working to save patients. The bombings last night must have hit some Yellow-Star Houses.

"They need more help here," I say.

"We need more help everywhere." Before stepping outside, he adds, his tone full of emotion, "And I need to talk to you. Ariel was right. Gellert puts you in danger too."

I recall her warning about Gellert. "We can talk about this later if you want although I am confused by what she said." I shrug. "Something about Gellert is ruining my father's plans?"

He draws in a long breath, already showing strength that must come from deep within. "Your father built a good network in the underground, using his contacts in the transportation department. He managed to get hundreds of children out of the country…some to Romania, some to Palestine."

"My father?" I remember Peter saying in an earlier conversation my father seemed to know everyone and had many connections. And Father said he knew of groups that were doing this. All along it was him?

"He's helped the Zionists for months with who to bribe, who to avoid," Peter says.

"He told me once that he thought to get us all out, but it had become too dangerous along that route."

"Yes. One of the ships was torpedoed and sank."

"You knew this about him? I'm confused why you didn't share this with me."

"Your father asked that I not tell you or your mother about his involvement."

"When he and István were captured and beaten…the police must've heard what he was doing." I can't believe my puppet-making father is involved in the Resistance. Pride swells in me.

"Does he know what I did with the underground?"

"If he suspected it, he never asked me. And you should be warned, the Dely family tipped off the police about your father. Said they overheard your father and his chess partner talking about the last group they safely moved."

"Ferenc. He's my father's best friend. Is he in danger?"

"No. The police have nothing, just rumors." He touches my arm. "But Ariel was right. Gellert is running some rescues on his own, using those same secret passages."

"The tunnels." I've told him about these and even showed him through some of them.

"And our safe houses, which won't be so safe if he leads the wrong group to us."

"He's desperate to save more people."

"I'm sure, but he's going to get himself killed, and possibly many others in the Resistance."

"I'll talk to him…the next time he returns. I have Swiss protection papers. So does Gellert. Maybe those will keep us safe." And I'm even more relieved my family left when they could. Especially since I've learned this about my father.

"Here's what I've learned. Protection papers are good as long as all the players agree that's what they are. But it can change in the blink of an eye, like my family's emigration documents to Cuba. In the end, we held nothing more than worthless, tear-stained paper."

He has a point. Eichmann is frustrated with the lack of deportations. His next move may be to overrule these outside embassies working so desperately to save us.

Then all of us will be looking for a way out.

-19-

BUDAPEST, HUNGARY

July 18, 1944

"I promise," Gellert says, holding his hands up to ward off my list of concerns. "I'll only make the rescue trips with the Red Cross."

He arrived at the flat as the sun was setting, disheveled and reeking of petrol and motor oil. I surprised him with my anger over his secret forays and how he's putting everyone in danger. Told him Ariel is dead, shot because someone found out she was working with the underground.

He tries rationalizing all he's done to help others. "Just yesterday, I used contacts from the underground to drive a mother and her daughter to a safe house outside the city. From there, they'll continue hopping from place to place until they reach Bulgaria."

"Bulgaria?" I sense the frown forming on my face. I've heard of a lot of destinations, but not that one. "Why there?"

"They thwarted Hitler early on by proclaiming that no Jews would leave the country. Period. The Orthodox Christians have blocked railroads even under the threat of death, claiming the Jews and Christians have been old friends for five centuries."

"Hungarians could take a lesson from them."

"It's too late to stop the hate here." He reaches for me, and I step into his embrace. "I have to keep doing this."

"I can't argue with your intentions"—I push him back to arm's length—"but *phew*, right now you need a bath, sweetie."

"Sorry." He laughs and steps back a few paces. "Five trips in ten days."

"Again, what you're doing is noble and feeds that need we all have to help, but Peter says these unsanctioned trips may compromise everyone if you aren't careful."

"Peter doesn't know everything." He shrugs. "And I *am* careful."

Gellert isn't like this. He rarely has an unkind word for anyone, and he admires Peter. I'm sure this remark comes from a place of exhaustion. Where else would we get information if not for Peter's contacts?

"He's been involved with the Zionists and the resistance groups for months now," I say. "And he's proven to be trustworthy. He promised to find István, and he did."

"I'm sorry. He's a good guy. I'll do as you ask." He grabs some donated clothes from a drawer. "Maybe you can come along with me on the next rescue, then we can see each other more."

It's impossible to stay angry with him. "I'd like that but not overnight. Just a day trip because of the children."

"Of course. Where are they? It's so quiet without them."

"Bandin is teaching them chess." I smile. Gellert readily accepts this is how it will be until the end of the war. The orphans will remain with us until they find new homes. "That boy is a dear with them."

"They do seem to get on well." He starts to unbutton his shirt. Paper crinkles in his pocket. Then he pulls out a folded leaflet. "Wait. Have you seen these? After the Americans bombed the oil refineries and storage tanks, they flew over the city and dropped them."

I read the paper. It threatens punishment for those responsible for the deportation of Hungarian Jews to the gas chambers at Auschwitz. "The U.S. government wants Hitler and his SS to know it's watching." I flash a broad smile. "This is good news for us."

"I think so. Let me clean up. Then I want to do nothing but hold you close and remember all the fun we've had."

"Can't think of a better plan."

Sometimes we all need an echo to hear ourselves. Gellert had been off on his own, not sharing his plans with anyone. I know he still fights growing guilt and mounting hate for what he's experienced. He thrashes at night, and I often take Jakub into bed with Zofia and me to let the boy sleep.

In the early days at the hospital, when Gellert was in and out of consciousness, he'd wail and moan in pain for no apparent reason. I always asked what hurt, and he never answered until one day he did.

"Living," he said.

And for thousands, that is the sad reality. When fear creeps into my thoughts, I chant a slogan Father started saying after the Germans arrived. "Sit tight, do what we know is right, hold out to the end."

I can hardly wait to talk to my father again. I have so many questions about his involvement with the underground. How he and Ferenc made their plans. I should've known the man who shared a daily riddle was a riddle himself.

The opportunity for Gellert and me to share a rescue mission comes the next day. We take the children to the orphanage, grab the tram, cross the river, and continue up Gellért Hill. The Swedish Embassy, with Raoul Wallenberg as its head, sits at the top, flying the country's symbolic blue and yellow flag.

A long line of shabbily dressed people, many hysterical and in tears wearing the yellow Star of David, stretches all the way down the steep hill.

"Why are they all here?" I ask.

"They're trying to obtain Swedish passports to stop them from being deported."

"But the trains have stopped," I say. "Horthy ordered it."

"Eichmann listens to no one. He's furious, we hear. Today, we're going to the Kistarcsa transit camp. But I must warn you. The conditions are horrible there. Disease is rampant, there's little food, and rumors are that the guards are getting tired and planning a camp cleansing."

"I'm not afraid," I say. "I'll do whatever it takes to help."

We show our Red Cross papers, and a Swedish guard guides us inside the embassy. He signals to someone across the high-ceilinged room. A tall man with wavy dark hair hurries to us, stops, and sets a briefcase at his feet. He has big brown eyes and offers a quick smile, then sticks out his hand to shake Gellert's.

"I'm Raoul Wallenberg."

"Gellert Varga and my fiancée Marika Tausig. It's nice to meet you."

"We've heard so many great stories about you," I add.

"Not me. Everyone like yourselves who step up to help. You're part of the recovery mission to Kistarcsa today?"

"We are," Gellert says, full of confidence.

A swell of pride lifts my spirit. My guy, a doctor someday.

"My assistant will show you to the garage." Wallenberg bends down, clicks open the briefcase, and pulls out a stack of papers. "We have three cars going, and a truck pulling a wagon with food and medical supplies." He hands the papers to me. "These are all I have right now. Bring back the children."

My throat tightens. The importance of what we're about to do sends a shudder up my back.

"We will."

Not much later, Gellert is at the wheel of a Skoda. We're following an embassy car with flapping flags and two other cars. The truck and wagon are behind us.

"Wallenberg comes from one of the wealthiest families in all of Sweden," Gellert says. "He left a pampered life to come here."

I touch his cheek. "Thank you for your kind heart. This is truly what we need to be doing together."

"It feels good, doesn't it?" He's watching the road but cuts his eyes my way. The sparkle there is evident.

"It does."

Kistarcsa transit camp sits nineteen kilometers to the northeast. The front vehicle driver hands something to the guard at the gate, and we're waved through. The stink of death, sickness, and raw sewage fills the air. The interior is laid out along several streets with three-story white-or ochre-colored long buildings.

Men wearing yellow stars on their tattered coats surround the wagon of food and form a human chain, passing the food to a nearby building with a tall chimney.

"We can take twenty-six children back," Wallenberg's assistant says after we step out of the vehicles. "Age fourteen and under."

"What do we say to the mothers?" I scan the teeming crowd of women and children, clutching each other, exhaustion etched on their faces.

"Tell them we'll take them to one of the Red Cross houses where they'll be fed and kept safe." His emotions remain flat. He's done this before. "We will be back with more protective passes as soon as we can."

"Will we?" Gellert asks.

"We might get another hundred out of here. The problem is that the Hungarian police running the place expect us to have fifteen hundred *total* passes. Of course, we've made thousands and thousands from those. So we can't use them all at one camp."

"How can we get more people out without the passes?" I ask. "There must be close to two thousand behind this barbed wire right now."

"Many times we do whatever we must do. Bribery, favors, sometimes just cigarettes. Whatever was illegal is now considered legal in the face of this inhumane treatment." He points to what appears to be the main building set away from the others. "The Germans never come here. The camp commandant, Istvan Vasdenyei, has cooperated with our Jewish organizations for the most part."

"And yet so many were deported from here," Gellert says.

"And right up until four days ago," the man says, "Eichmann tried to ship fifteen hundred away...these people you see. The leaders of the Jewish Council in Budapest alerted Horthy. The Regent intervened, and the train-load was turned back."

"But it might happen again," I say.

"We hope not. But get going and hand these out." He divides the papers among seven of us, and we split up.

I approach a woman with a green embroidered scarf worn as a shawl over her light green dress. Her once expensive shoes are covered in mud. Next to her is a boy, possibly ten, holding a tin soldier.

"I'm with the Red Cross. We're here to offer your son a safe home in Budapest."

"We hear these promises. Will I see him again?" she asks. Her chin trembles.

"The deportation trains have stopped now. We hope to come back with more protective passes for you."

She pauses then kneels and looks her son in the eyes. "Neci. You be a brave boy and go with this lady."

"But Mama," he whines. "I promised Papa I'd take care of you."

"You have. You are. And you'll go ahead and pick out a nice bed for us, and we'll have good food again."

"Yes, we have plenty of food for everyone." Then I ask for her name and hometown and write it on a card with his information.

She hugs him and stands, fighting the tears. "I'll see you soon, son."

I take his hand and give it a slight squeeze as I lead him to the cars. "Tell me about your soldier."

"It's Papa's toy. From when he was a boy like me. He got taken away to fight."

"It's a fine toy, Neci. A reminder of how strong you and your papa are." I seat him in the back of the Skoda next to a girl Gellert must have chosen. "We'll be right back."

When our car has four boys and two girls packed into it, we're ready to go. The other cars are filled with more children and babies. The drive back to Budapest takes longer, the drivers taking the roads slower, as if the precious cargo we carry can break. We stop at a Swedish safe house in Pest near the Danube and walk the children inside to introduce them to the adults in charge. As the children are led down the main hallway, Neci looks back, holds the toy soldier up high, and smiles. He then overly performs as he marches away, swinging stiffened arms back and forth, straight-legged, following the rest of the children.

"That little guy stole my heart," I say to Gellert. "But I wish we could have brought them all here."

He and I walk along the street, heading to the orphanage to collect our two charges. We nod to folks wearing yellow stars, hurrying from place to place during their few hours of free time. We no longer are required to wear ours as long as we work for Wallenberg, and guilt eats at me for the privilege.

"I'm so glad we got to do this together," Gellert says, taking my arm and linking it around his. "You can see why I was trying to do rescues on my own. There are just so many people."

"There are." I picture the hopeless faces of those we had to leave behind. "And there's hope now. Deportations have halted. The Swiss have their Carl Lutz, who's doing the same as Wallenberg, buying houses, setting up soup kitchens."

"It's getting better. Although the Germans keep trying. One of the other drivers told me the German embassy is offering to send three hundred orphaned Jewish children to Stockholm. Families there will take them in. The trade, however, is very lopsided. The Hungarian government would need to release three hundred thousand Jews for forced labor in Germany."

Aghast, I say, "That's every one of us left in Budapest."

"Quite naturally, every rescue organization is refusing to accept."

I'm surprised to find Peter waiting for us outside the orphanage. He must have important news, or he wouldn't be here.

"Peter. What is it?"

"I heard you two were on the Kistarcsa mission today." He turns to Gellert and smiles. "My good man. Wallenberg spoke rather highly of you after you left."

"That's nice to hear." Gellert smiles. "Just trying to keep up with you. Were you on a Red Cross run as well?'

"Wallenberg asked me to go with him to his first meeting with Eichmann at the Hotel Majestic. Dressed as a Hungarian soldier, of course."

"Did he remember you?" I ask. I've never told Gellert about the incident outside the convent when Peter saved me. Gellert was still in the hospital during that time. There was no reason to worry him about my brush with Eichmann.

"He asked how my fiancée was." He cuts his eyes from Gellert back to me. "He's still as cunning as ever and not to be trusted."

"Why do you say that?" Gellert asks. "What's it like meeting with him?"

"He sits behind his large walnut desk, his back to the windows, and keeps his right hand near a revolver on the desk. We all know his penchant for young girls and prostitutes, but framed photographs of a dull-haired woman with two children are on his desk. The disregarded family back home, I suppose."

"What was the meeting about?" My curiosity is piqued.

"He demanded that Wallenberg come to this meeting. And Eichmann is furious. His hands flew back and forth, swiping away the thick smoke from his cigarettes, and his eyes were menacing. The man talks as if he's a chattering machine gun, accusing Wallenberg of forging the protective passes and insisting all Jews are enemies of the Reich." He shakes his head. "And his parting words were, 'You and the whole lot trying to save them will pay for this damn mess you're making here.'"

"How did Wallenberg reply?" Gellert asks.

Peter chuckles. "He said something like, 'Your ideals, and those of the rest of the world, do not match. One person can make all the difference, and I plan to be that one.' He's lucky he didn't get shot." Peter's facial expression changes, his lips now set in a grim line. "Actually, I came here to tell you some alarming news."

What's he talking about? Every minute of every day is more than upsetting. "Go ahead."

"The Kasztner Train. It was rerouted on July ninth."

Suddenly, my legs weaken. *My family.* "Where is it going now?" My words are barely above a whisper.

"Not where is it *going*. It's been stopped. At Bergen-Belsen. The sister camp to Auschwitz."

Electricity shoots straight up my spine.

My world goes black.

-20-

BUDAPEST, HUNGARY

July 30, 1944

For twelve days, Peter tries to learn more about the train stop in Bergen-Belsen. Since Kasztner's family and friends are also aboard, we tell ourselves there's no need to worry. Or they duped Kasztner along with the other passengers, who handed over a great deal of money and valuables for a chance at freedom.

My thoughts cycle through each of my loved ones there. The baby with his innocence, giggling at almost any facial expression to tease him with. Erzsébet is a loving mother, patient but fun, and a great wife. István, my childhood friend, my protector growing up. Mother. Spunky and positive, prone to making sure everyone else is happy around her at a cost to her own happiness. And Father. Creative and intellectual but calm in all things. And now, I learn he's brave, risking his life to help the underground.

Their absence leaves a hole in my day but if we were never to meet again? I'm not sure how anyone goes on with an entire family stripped away.

Worry and work keep me going, and with double shifts at the orphanage, as well as a few short rescue trips with Gellert, I've learned a day of worry is more exhausting than a week of work.

Thousands now line the streets in front of 29 Vadász Street to get a Lutz protective pass from the Glass House. The crowd often brings normal traffic to a standstill, drawing attention. Many, perhaps most, come risking their lives, staying in line even during curfew hours.

Early this morning, I meet Peter outside there, and we enter through the basement area. While he goes to the upper floors to see if there's an update on the Kasztner train, I spend thirty minutes duplicating Schutzpasses for distribution. The noise inside the expansive open space is energizing, with phones ringing and people calling out names that immediately need to be added to rescue lists. Added to that are the continuously clacking printers and the rapid *fwap fwap* of typewriter keys, as helpers complete the blank forms.

Peter returns and we exit, moving to stand in the shadow of the alley before he speaks.

"Well, some hopeful news. The passengers are safe and being held in a special area at Bergen-Belsen. They have food and a dry place to sleep."

"But why are they there?"

"It's reported Colonel Becher insisted on collecting the money and jewels before the train reached Switzerland to ensure his payment."

"They arrived in that camp nineteen days ago." My pulse quickens. "It would only take a few hours to collect the payments."

Then he gently touches my back. "No one knows why it's taking so long, but the news is they aren't in danger." He looks around the corner. We must be careful every minute. "The Rescue Committee already demanded passengers write about their circumstances, without German censorship. They've asked for thirty letters."

"I hope my family is asked." I sigh. "All this worry serves no useful purpose but to wear us down."

"As soon as any letters are answered, I'll let you know." He glances at his watch. "I have to meet Gellert soon. Be careful on the walk home."

I like that they are working more closely together now. Peter is quieter, more withdrawn since Ariel's death, and his activities in the Resistance have doubled. Like the rest of us, he covers up pain and loss by layering his days with too much work and his nights with exhaustion.

Some days, Gellert goes with me to the orphanage. Our rescue trip to Kistarcsa brought us closer together than we've been in months. But it's a mixed set of emotions that bond us. On one hand we're thrilled for the children we saved, but now we wrestle with abject sadness for the parents left behind. We learned that after a four-day struggle, Eichmann evaded

Horthy's order to halt deportations. He sent one final train to Auschwitz, full of the one thousand fifty Jews who remained at Kistarcsa.

Neci's mother's face appears in my dreams, concerned but trusting, fearful yet hopeful I was telling her the truth. Is she in a concentration camp, replaying my deceitful promise that we were coming back for her? Or is she relieved her son is safe? I hang on to the latter thought. We haven't informed the twenty-six children that their parents were taken away. There's hope Horthy will fight Eichmann's revenge deportation move, and we'll get them back.

Gellert and Peter are off to rescue Jews holed up in the basement of St. Stephen's Cathedral in the town of Fehérvár. A dozen were able to avoid being whisked away to Auschwitz, thanks to a brave priest who didn't make their presence known, even to his deacons. But now the priest is worried someone has seen them, so he made the call to the Jewish Rescue Committee.

It's Sunday. I'm not working today after my seventy-hour workweek. Back in our assigned flat, I sit at my father's desk, reviewing my plans for today. I like this desk. His drawers are full of memories. Fading photographs. Postcards from theatre friends across Europe. Forgotten letters on yellowed paper, handwritten in our childish scrawl. I had no idea he kept the notes we sent while he traveled selling his marionettes. I read through a few.

István asked for snowshoes when Father was in Austria, and I asked for French makeup when he went to Paris. Instead, he bought my brother a telescope. He gave me a sphygmomanometer, a blood pressure meter invented by Dr. Recklinghausen. The instrument is still in its original Bakelite box, but the rubber parts hardened over time. Secretly, I was disappointed when he presented it to me but later realized it may have led to my interest in nursing. Once the gift was in my hands, I took the blood pressure of anyone I could force to sit still.

Sometimes, bravery is nothing more than gritting your teeth through emotional pain by putting one foot in front of the other on a slow walk toward the next day, the next week.

That's what I tell myself many times a day.

But some good news comes our way. Christian clergymen are steadfast in fighting off Eichmann's annihilation demands. He requested the Hungarian government begin deporting one hundred thousand Budapest Jews. The papal nuncio, Monsignor Angelo Rotta, and every neutral ambassador protested to Horthy and the deportations didn't happen.

Today, we share the midday meal—bread, cheese, and dried apricots—with the Szabó family. They remain in their room most days, ready and waiting for Jehovah's return, content not to learn what the chaos around them means. But I believe they need to stay informed, so I share the news.

"The Germans are truly losing the war. The Soviets just crossed the Hungarian border, and the Red Army is said to be amassing for a final push across the Hungarian plain toward us."

"We await the Soviets' arrival and for the Germans to leave," Imre says, running her hand down her son's back.

It's nice to see their close relationship. She and Eden take in mending for others in the area, putting their tailoring skills to good use. Laughter often comes from behind their closed door, and they never seem to worry about what may happen. I've decided if a person believes this is the end of the world, somehow they must find joy in every minute. It's a lesson I should learn. But my vision extends further than this single moment. I want a long life as a daughter, wife, mother, and if lucky, a grandmother.

"And the allied bombing does seem more ominous," Imre says. "We have friends near the river who spend every night in the shelters or cellars. One friend said they watched their neighbor's house come apart like a sandcastle at the edge of an angry sea. Afterward, the odors of cooking gas, dust, burnt wood, and death filled the neighborhood."

"This is how it will end for all of us," Eden says, cutting another slice of cheese.

I wish she wouldn't speak this way in front of the children. Bandin understands her sentiments but doesn't react. The world-is-ending message runs through his veins. Thankfully, Zofia and Jakub understand so little Hungarian.

"Also, good news," I add. "We've found people who are stockpiling food, ensuring that warehouses in various localities will be kept fully supplied. And the man in charge of the Hungarian corn exportation assured us the food would remain in Budapest for the coming winter. He reports he hasn't seen a German in his office in weeks."

"Anything is possible with prayer," Eden says.

"Amen," I say, and hurry to gather the plates and utensils and set them in the sink for my turn to wash. I chafe at Eden and Imre's doomsday attitude. My positive messages are to help ward off sadness and despair. Including my own. I know they can't change their beliefs, but I refuse to change mine either. Although the world is full of suffering, it's also full of ways to overcome it.

Throughout the afternoon, I play with the children. I've taught Zofia how to knit using the basketful of good wool Mother brought from our apartment. Near the bottom of the basket, I find the lilac scarf she knitted earlier this year. If I'm allowed to send items to Switzerland, I'll make sure she receives this when my family gets settled there.

Jakub has become a champ at jacks, snatching up the spiked pieces faster than I can see them. Both try to teach me their favorite songs in Polish, and often laugh at my many mispronunciations. If this is what it takes to hear their merriment, I'll keep messing up.

We practice English each evening, browsing through picture books the last occupant left. Or play pretend, conversing in English through daily situations they may find themselves in.

Gellert returns as the birds sing valiantly against the coming night. But he's not radiating his usual upbeat spirit.

I set up the children with scissors and a roll of wallpaper I discovered at the back of a cupboard.

"Cut out one hundred hearts, please. We'll take them to the other children tomorrow." The Sisters and I brainstormed the idea to pin a heart onto every person at the orphanage, unifying us in love.

I motion Gellert to the two chairs and small table by the window. "What's wrong, darling?"

His face is taut, pale, and the darkness I glimpse in him from time to time is back. All that pain rooted in his indecision that one fateful day as he watched those women murdered.

Tears spill, but he fights the sobs. Instead, he extends his shaky hands to me and cups them around mine. He doesn't speak, and I don't make him. I expect he'll always struggle with emotional pain. After all, a scabbed-over memory does not heal in a person's mind. And it takes almost nothing to tear off the covering and experience the rawness again.

Something definitely went wrong today.

I inhale the enticing scents of meals from the Christian apartments around us. Someone is frying sausages and onions, and the lovely aroma of paprika is in the air. How I miss our Saturday meals of chicken paprika and potatoes. Or főzelék, a thick, creamy vegetable dish that was my specialty. Goulash, tejföl, or fisherman's soup. One day, we will taste those again.

Gellert whispers something.

"I'm sorry." I lean closer. "What was that?"

"They weren't at the church when we got there."

"Oh no. Had they already been taken away?"

"Someone told. The priest was dead at the altar."

I murmur a portion of the prayer for the dead. "God full of compassion. Shelter him forever."

He no longer muffles his sobs, fisting his hand over his mouth and nose as if he can hold them at bay.

I hurry to his side and pull his head into my neck, my arms wrapped around him. "You don't have to tell me."

He's broken, barely holding himself together. On days like this, I can't pretend he's the same man who went off to the Labor Force. Is his volunteering helping him in any way? How will he heal if he continues witnessing more atrocities?

"The priest was a hero for what he did." I rub his back. "Sounds as if the people he hid got away."

He breaks down again, and I quickly turn to see what effect this is having on the children. They've crawled into my bed and pulled the covers over themselves. I don't need to peek under the blanket to know they're holding each other tight.

"To the woods." His cracked voice comes from a different lifetime. "We found them, tied together and set on fire."

"Oh my gosh! That's horrific, Gellert!" Will the ghastly murdering ever stop? Where are answers to prayers at times like this? It surely seems the sun shines on the evildoers while the rain continues to fall on the righteous.

He moans.

I whisper and try to console him, but soon I've exhausted the inadequate words I've pulled from the depths of my soul. Even I don't feel comforted.

"We must stay strong, Gellert. That's how we win. We walk out of here in the end and start over."

He gathers himself but doesn't lift his head. "I won't let you down. I can do this."

"I know you can, my dear."

Darkness settles outside the window, and a half-moon battles the thin clouds above.

"Let's get some sleep."

He stretches out on his mattress, and I snuggle into his side, my head on his chest. One arm and leg thrown over him.

Exhausted from his day, he falls asleep. His heartbeat slows to a regular thumping rhythm, calming my mind.

But the horrible visions he described—they will surely ruin my ability to sleep tonight.

-21-

BUDAPEST, HUNGARY

August 19, 1944

I hurry to meet Raakel in the abandoned puppet booth at the People's Park. I startle as a squeaky bicycle comes along the path from behind me, fearing my arrest. *No Jews in the Park* is on the signage at every entrance. Then I remember I'm a member of the Red Cross, and without a yellow star sewn on my dress, no one knows my heritage.

The wind is moving through the tall trees, and they creak and clack against each other. I lightly touch the rough wooden railing of a bridge as I cross a narrow stream. The flow has nearly dried up this time of year. The grey clouds bunched at the edge of the horizon might have other plans on this sunny yet windy day but not right now.

In 1926, Henrik Kemény moved his family's traveling puppet show to this section of the city and performed here for eighteen years in a wooden booth. He's been missing for several months, with rumors he was arrested for refusing to join the Labor Force.

Unlike the traveling puppet shows that move from town to town during fair season, and are made of flimsy wood and cheerful cloth, this is a solidly constructed booth inside a wooden enclosure. The wood-paneled walls are covered by a canvas roof. The wall the puppeteer stands behind, opens near his head to reveal a small stage. The puppets perform on a miniature proscenium-arch stage at the top. The booth opens outward to a small area where two dozen people can stand or sit to watch the performance.

That's where I find Raakel.

She looks great, wearing a fashionable blouse and skirt. The cynical part of my mind says why wouldn't she look good. She's not hunted or limited in what she does each day. I brush those negative thoughts away. We are closer to her family than any other Christian family in the city. They've never labeled us as *the other*.

"It's so good to see you," we both say at the same time as we hug and then step back and laugh.

I motion that we should scoot inside the booth for privacy.

"We're like spies," she says, her face bright with excitement in the dim interior.

"Believe me, it's not that much fun when you have to do it all day."

"I'm sorry. I'm so dense," she says. "I wasn't thinking." She holds my hand. "How is your family?"

I tell her about the paid passage on the train, how it's made an unaccounted-for stop, but the news is it will continue to Switzerland. "I hope to hear from them soon."

"You must miss them terribly."

"I do. Although I'm relieved that they aren't here, I find I have so much to say to each of them during a day." I lean my head against her shoulder. "I talk to myself more than ever when no one is around."

"Do you still feel safe here?" Her brow wrinkles. "You're crammed in that awful one-room place."

"The other family is very nice. We get on quite well. Gellert and I have protective letters from the International Red Cross. We technically work for Wallenberg, the Swedish ambassador."

"Gellert is better?" She presses her palms together in front of her mouth.

"We're working through his recovery. He was running rescues for the underground, but he can't mentally deal with it. He came upon a horrifying scene in the forest outside Fehérvár, and it set him back to the nightmares and uncontrolled nervousness." I saw him balled up in the alleyway a few days ago. I went looking for him when he hadn't come back after taking out the garbage. He was muttering he was sorry, over and over. "I'm not sure I'd be any better off if I had witnessed what he has."

"Do you think he still wants to be a doctor after this is over?"

"I do. He has the knowledge and the heart to be a great doctor. He's just not trained for witnessing executions." I've never told anyone else about what happened the day with the pregnant women when he froze up, and I never will. "But we did a positive rescue. Twenty-six children brought back from the Kistarcsa camp, and we have two orphans from Poland living with us."

"Oh, how sweet. That must help with you missing baby József." She suddenly stops talking. Men's voices draw near then move away.

When it's quiet again, I ask, "How are you and Sándor doing?"

"He's avoiding me, it seems." She shrugs, but her mouth droops at the corners. "He started acting strange after we helped you when we left the back gate unlocked, and especially after I got your father's chess set out."

"Oh, dear. That's not good. We appreciate what you did to help. But I hope it doesn't come between you two."

"It's more than that. I found him walking through your apartment, and he wanted to know why it wasn't inhabited yet."

"Really?" I immediately think less of him. "Did he take anything?"

"No. Your father's workshop is still locked. But, just so you know, my father is getting pressured to fill it with any one of the bombed-out Christian families. And get this…we'd be expected to cook for them, reimbursed by the army, they say. We all know they have no money. They're surviving on the bank accounts stolen from you and other Jewish folks."

"Sounds like Sándor is distancing himself in case you get in trouble."

"What harm is there if your family wants to have an old worn-out puppet, or a chess set? If anyone asks, that's what I'll tell them."

"Please be careful." I peek out over the small stage at eye height to see if anyone is outside. "The Delys? What's going on with them?"

"Belko's making money selling bikes, confiscated from you all, to the Arrow Cross members or the Hungarian police. Remember the Dengler kid in our grade who was always getting into fights?"

"Didn't he try to burn down the school in year six because he got caught smoking?"

"That one. His younger brother, a kid of about fifteen, just joined the party. I heard Benedek glorifying their cause with him outside the building. The kid was in uniform, in that green shirt and black pants, and he even had the armband already."

"It seems as if they're just playing army. The local police appear to keep them in check." I snort. "Their lack of any kind of achievement or recognition will come to light sooner than they think."

"I think some have guns."

"It's still illegal to shoot people," I say. "Jews included if you're not a certified policeman."

"He who dares wins," Raakel says. "I hope that's not true with the Arrow Cross."

"Me too." I glance at my watch. "I need to go. Gellert and the children are already at the orphanage, but I need to get there." I smile. "It's delousing day for the new arrivals."

She laughs. "You two know how to have fun."

We hug and agree to meet here on another Sunday.

"Be careful," I say.

"And you take care," she calls back, heading along the path to the park's entrance.

I need to stop by the Yellow-Star flat to grab my medical kit. Carrying it to the park would have been too much.

The front gate is unlocked, and I step inside the front door. The janitor's apartment door is open, and men are talking. I plaster my back to the wall in the hallway to listen. We rarely hear firsthand news, and I wonder what's so important.

"We didn't find that they were hoarding anything," in a deep voice, a man says. "Where did you get the information?"

"A family who rented below them at their last apartment," Mr. Gábor says. "Said they kept cash and jewelry, enough to pay for passage out of here."

"Well, that may be, but if it's already paid, there's nothing we can do." This speaker is a man with a nasal quality to his speech. "They've brought bare necessities with them, for all we saw."

They're talking about us! I quietly dash up the stairs and push into our room. Obviously, the men have rummaged through everything because items aren't where we left them, but nothing looks to be missing. The old puppet is on the floor, no worse for the fall, and cupboards are half-open.

That's when I realize the family Bible is missing. It sat in the middle of our table where we prayed over it each day. After a quick look through the room, I enter the kitchen. It's not there. Then I find it in the bathroom, at the bottom of the bathtub. Someone put it under the spout and ran water over it. The book is ruined, the pages wavy and damp, the leather cover warped.

Heat reaches my neck. We're taught to forgive evil but not excuse it. This is the Dely family's doing. Why can't they leave us alone? They continue to pester the authorities, snitching on my family, even getting Father and István jailed and tortured.

I carry the book back to the table, leaving it open to dry in the rectangle of sun shining through the window. I won't tell Mother or Father about this when I write. The men went out of their way to ruin a treasured heirloom. Maybe one day, I'll have the ability to get it to a book repair shop. If nothing else, perhaps I can iron the pages before my family sees it again.

Is anyone ever prepared for this much hate? A few short years ago, we all lived together in the city, a bustling beehive of energy, everyone offering their special talents and flavor to the hive's productivity. We were the cultural center of Europe, a popular destination because of our famous thermal baths and our theatres, where we would gather to hear our poets and writers.

How naïve we were to think we could stay isolated from the war, from the hate. And not just we Jews. Christians have died by the thousands, bombed out of their country homes and apartments in the city. It's why the leaders haven't confined us into a ghetto area but designated the randomization of the Yellow-Star houses around the city—the fear the rest of the city would be bombed once our section was identified. So now we all suffer together, some more than others. Not really friends but more like people clinging to each other on a life raft. We must all dance to this tune until the Russians arrive.

And I keep worrying about how the Russians will treat us. Father talked about the bad blood between our countries after what we did to them in the Great War. Will they hack us to pieces like the women Gellert witnessed, or was that just a fluke?

I have to stop distressing about this. Tomorrow's troubles sap the strength I have for today.

A knock on the door startles me.

Have the men come back to search again?

I cross the room on shaky legs and open the door.

Tamás Gábor stands there. "Some men searched your apartment because they heard your family was hoarding goods."

The *nerve*. He delivers this message as if saying, "I saw an interesting bird on the roofline today."

"I see that." I don't try to hide the disgust in my words. "Guess you can't trust all the rumors you hear, can you?"

"I have to do what I'm told." He shrugs. "Many Jews are saving items that should've been turned in."

"You should do what you feel is right." I know I'm wading into dangerous waters. "You saw what my family brought here from our apartment. You monitor the gates like you're guarding the last lifeboat on a sinking ship. It would've been easy to take our side just this one time."

He stares, his mouth slightly open. Will he turn me over to the police for my chastisement and his weak-tea values?

"A letter came for you." He pulls it from behind his back.

The Jewish Rescue Committee symbol is the return address. "Thank you," I barely say as I close the door.

Finally. It's from my family!

I wish Gellert was here. He's been just as worried as I have about them. My hands shake as I use a knife to open the top of the envelope and pull out the folded sheet of paper.

I expect to see Mother's pretty handwriting, but István has penned it.

July 24, 1944

If you've learned where our train stopped, you most certainly have been worried about us. We had a few frightening moments ourselves and thought for sure we'd been duped. Rest assured. We've been fed and housed in safety, although it breaks our heart to know what the other side of camp has meant to so many unfortunates. We are informed we will be leaving here in another week and should reach Switzerland by early August.

If this schedule stayed in place, this means they've already arrived. Weeks of worry come off my shoulders. They're safe and away from all that's happening here.

Baby József asks for Mika every day.

That's odd phrasing. He's writing the letter to me so wouldn't it say he asks for *you* every day?

As soon as we are settled, we will write again with our address. The talk of the train has been all about our parents. Everyone is calling them heroes.

What could they have done that precipitated that? I'm not surprised they're looked upon with honor. I've felt the same way about them my whole life.

The two children they paid for are thriving and excited to be reunited with relatives in Stockholm since they have no one left in Hungary.

They must have cut a deal and paid a lesser fare for two orphan children to board the train. But that can't be right. They went to the train station with exactly the money they needed to board the five of them. Then I remember the man at the Rescue Committee saying no discounts for anyone. My pulse quickens, and my eyes jump to the last lines in the letter.

Mother and Father, your sacrifice that day when you gave up your seats will be retold for years. Especially by those two boys. Until we are all together again, we love you and miss you.
Stay safe and watch out for each other, like you always have.

István

I drop to the floor.

This is a terrible moment in a long line of dreadful moments. If my parents never got on the train, then where have they been for seven weeks?

-22-

BUDAPEST, HUNGARY

September 28, 1944

An odd serenity and even security prevails on this Yom Kippur morning. Gellert and I began our fast last night. The children are too young and therefore exempt. They're sitting on the floor, speaking in Polish, playing with little figures made of candle wax. I never try to stop this. Their native language will remain part of them forever.

On this holiest of days, I plan to reflect on my sins and pray throughout the daytime until sundown. Usually, we spend the time in the synagogue for the five prayer services—Maariv, Shacharit, Musaf, Minchah, and Neilah.

Gellert led Maariv in our flat last evening. Moments like that fill my heart with so much love for him. Also, he really is one of those people who can convince you he's intent on your every word. Genuinely intrigued. Maybe he won't be the man he was before this war, but what he is now is enough for me.

They suspended our evening curfew to let us attend synagogue services. Because of that freedom, we plan to go. I've always looked forward to celebrating this holiday in our beautiful temple. A time of personal soul cleansing. A reflection on my sins and transgressions of the past year. A time to ask for forgiveness.

It's also a reminder that God grants redemption.

The day would be more miraculous if only we knew where my parents were. It's been five weeks since we learned they gave up their seats on the train. Letters to the Red Cross and the Swiss Embassy bring no news. It's as if they disappeared the second they walked away from the Kasztner train.

The Red Cross is overwhelmed with pleas to investigate missing family members. I helped sort queries sent to the Swedish Red Cross. Now the letters come in by the thousands. Within the past few weeks, we registered sixty thousand missing persons' names, including my parents.

It appears that, although Hungary's last surviving Jews will be saved, I may never see my dear parents again. István is trying from his end, and his letters are increasingly terse to me when I replied we had no luck. Are we trying everything, he asks?

His point is a good one. How far could my parents have gone when on June 30 they were at the railway station in the city?

Every day, we check in with the rescue agencies, hospitals, and resistance groups for any new information.

Every day, I lose a bit more hope. Where they once centered my life, there is now a hollowness I find myself constantly trying to fill with work during the day. Yet it empties each night, again leaving a void in the coming sunrise. Are they still alive, and if so, are they safe? I fight to push away horrible images of my sweet parents tortured, sick, or starving. I pray they come walking through the door. It's all I can do.

The good news is this nightmare in Hungary is almost over. By the end of last month, Regent Horthy insisted that Eichmann and his commandos withdraw from Budapest. Eichmann, of course, was said to hope Hitler would thank him for his extermination successes. Wallenberg reported Eichmann left here with meager recognition as Hitler shifted his focus to not losing the war.

On August 24, Berlin jumped on board and suspended Eichmann's mission in Budapest. His office closed at the request of the new head of the Hungarian government, Géza Lakatos. Since then, our restrictions have eased. This reprieve happened when the German High Command— Hitler's Oberkommando der Wehrmacht—turned its attention to holding the Eastern Front rather than monitoring us, the remaining Jews. There's hope in the air, and the incessant climate of fear has abated.

We only need to wait.

And it shouldn't be long.

Also in late August, the Romanians made peace with the Soviets, thereby speeding the Red Army's advance through their country toward us. Fully realizing the Axis was doomed, Horthy resolved to do the same as Romania—establish a peace treaty—before Stalin crushes Hungary as an ally of Germany.

It was announced that all Jewish males over fourteen were to report for forced labor to defend Budapest. We worked round the clock on September 7, running to and from foreign embassies around the city to distribute protective passes. We saved thousands, but the Hungarian Army marched others off to dig ditches and set mines to the east.

From across the room, I watch Gellert thumb through the warped pages of the Torah. The meaning of our sacred holiday weighs on him. He's remained happy this last month with his work at the orphanage, shying away from all rescue missions to the countryside. But today, he's restless, pacing, muttering to himself. He hasn't said it, but I know him and that he wonders if God's will allows the forgiveness he desires for the deaths of those women. In years past, our pleas for atonement covered minor sins such as an unintended lie, or a time neglecting to extend goodwill to a neighbor or friend. The magnitude of what we ask for this year must test the power of HaShem's mercy and forgiveness.

This evening, Gellert, the children, and I go to the Dohány Synagogue for Neilah service. The sanctity of the moments inside the impressive house of prayer is without doubt what we need. The eternal light of the Ner Tamid hanging above the Ark of the Law brings peace to my soul. There *is* a bigger plan.

I glance at Gellert sitting with his arm around Jakub on the men's side of the temple. His eyes are closed in prayer. His expression is peaceful. I pray that tonight he surrenders his pain to God and finally receives healing from all the guilt he carries.

The temple is packed. Several worshippers stand in the loft and in the back, all with the apparent need to come together to declare, *Look, we made it through this terrible time.*

The bleat from the shofar signals the end of service and the fast. We've promised Jakub that, once back in our flat, he can blow the ram's horn our family has passed down for a hundred years or more. Zofia remembers her father with his shofar on holidays past, but Jakub was too little when they escaped Poland. The boy has had a grin on his face since we asked him if he would do this for us.

It's strange to be out at night, freely walking the streets. The stars are bright pinpricks in the black velvet quilt above. The banter between groups is upbeat, encouraging. We promise to see each other soon to meet in our favorite coffee house. To shop in dress shops and shoe stores closed to us for so long.

At our flat, the door to the Szabós' side is ajar. They've just cooked food in the shared kitchen, and the aroma of cabbage and potatoes claws at my empty stomach.

We'll have food on the table soon. I prepared a goulash last night, knowing it would taste delicious this evening.

I stall before entering our room. The Szabós are entertaining someone. An additional, somewhat familiar voice mixes into the chatter.

Deep within my brain, it registers. My mother!

I rush to their doorway and there she sits! She rises to her feet, and I fly into her waiting arms.

"You're alive!" Fresh tears race down my face. In this world, there must be more tears shed over answered prayers than those that remain unanswered.

"Marika." Her voice is rough then she begins coughing. It takes a moment for her to gather herself. "I hope you knew that no matter how much I said I loved you, I always loved you more."

"Me too." I hold her thin frame. She's lost so much weight. Her hair is unkempt, her fingernails broken. "This is a Yom Kippur miracle."

Gellert enters the room, and the Szabós step out to give us space.

"Leichi!" He wraps his arms around both of us. "You have no idea how much we've prayed for this moment."

Though afraid to ask the next question that must be on our minds, I can't hold it in any longer. "Father? Where is he?"

"We gave up our seats on the train…to two of the saddest boys we've ever seen."

"István wrote that you're both heroes," I say.

Mother grabs my hand. "They made it?"

Why tell her about Bergen-Belsen? "Yes. We've written back and forth several times. Of course, we've all been so worried about you."

"We were arrested on the walk back. For hoarding money. Of course, this was true; we had stored away the money and jewels, or we couldn't have paid for our passage."

"But so few people knew that." I frown. "Really…only János and his family. The Schlesingers wouldn't have told the authorities."

She wobbles on her feet.

"Leichi…"—Gellert reaches for her—"you need to sit down."

We cross the kitchen to our room, and Gellert helps her onto a chair.

Once settled and introduced to Jakub and Zofia, she continues the story.

"Your father believes it was Raakel's boyfriend. He may have seen Erzsébet when she snuck in through the back garden that day."

Is this the reason Sándor distanced himself from Raakel? After all, his odd behavior toward her suggests he turned in my parents to the police, and he would know how close we are.

"You may be right," I say. "Raakel says he's acting strange now."

"Since Endre was still injured, we were sent to a labor camp together. To the east, near Valkó. I was on laundry detail, and he cut and carried firewood from the forests. Most of the workers are digging trenches to stop the Russians."

"And where is Endre now?" Gellert asks and sits beside her. He's assessing her health without her realizing it. I've seen this look on his face hundreds of times—a vertical line appears between his eyebrows, his expression serious.

Zofia helps me set food on the table as she answers.

"I haven't seen him in two weeks. They took him and a group of men farther east."

"How did you get out?" I ask.

"Through Wallenberg's Red Cross." She coughs again and leans over to catch her breath. "I gave them my name…told them you both worked for them as a doctor and nurse. They came back today with a protective letter."

"Praise God." I turn to the children. "Go ahead and get some food on your plates. You're allowed to eat while sitting on Jakub's bed tonight."

I act like it's a treat, but it's because we have only four chairs at the table.

The food does us all good. It renews my energy, so I wash the dishes then make sure the children are bathed and in their nightclothes.

Gellert checks out Mother. "Not pneumonia" is his final assessment.

She washes in the bathroom and returns with wet hair. Face and hands scrubbed clean.

I ready a menthol compress and will insist she share the bed with Zofia and me. Once she's lying down, I sit by her side and place the warm compress on her chest.

"If I had a single flower for every time I thought of you, Mother, I'd have bouquets that would fill this room."

She smiles. "My biggest concern was how worried you'd be for us." Then she sighs. "We had no way to reach you until the Red Cross arrived."

"I'm furious you were arrested. And I thought for sure the Dely family had a hand in your disappearance."

"We need to warn Ilona and János." She rubs the back of my hand in tiny circles with her thumb. It's soothing but lets me know she is troubled. "They could be in danger for helping us that day."

"Unfortunately, I've asked for other help from them since you left." I swallow hard. "I even used Sándor to take a note to Raakel."

She rocks her head from side to side on the pillow then speaks. "Have you talked to Raakel?"

"About ten days ago, before Rosh Hashanah."

"Oh dear." Pain fills her eyes.

"What is it?"

"As I was leaving the camp, I saw that boy, Sándor. He was with Benedek and those Arrow Cross ruffians. They were unloading men from a truck, men who could barely walk for the injuries they had."

I need to warn the Schlesingers. Sándor is more than a neighborhood spy. It appears he has embraced the ideals of the radical right. Would the police still allow me on the street tonight since they extended the curfew? Where are the American bombers when I need them?

"Not tonight." Gellert's tone is quiet but stern. It's as if he read my mind.

"Tomorrow then. On the way to work." We signed up to work in the cold-storage section of the main warehouse for a day.

I rub my mother's arm.

"The children can stay here with you if you're up to it."

"I can't think of a better way to spend my first day back." Her gaze loses focus for a moment. She blinks and stares at me. It's as if a memory surfaced. "Your father. He wrote a message for you. He said you'd know what to do with it if we're ever in danger." She points to her shoes. "Check in the right one."

I recover a rolled-up piece of paper wedged in the toe area. It's damp and crumpled, of course, so I take extreme care to undo it. At the sight of my father's neat handwriting, I choke up. Why did he send me a written message when he could easily give that information to Mother?

It's a riddle. That day in his workroom, he said he had an important one planned. I read it a second time.

Because I'm no longer colorful or passionate, no one wants to hold me up. But inside, my heart of gold is the key to life.

I return my gaze to her. "Did he give you the answer or even a clue?"

"He was so afraid I would be tortured. It was a constant threat, and many women were taken away and never brought back."

I don't like what this suggests. He doesn't believe he'll return home. And somehow, the answer to this riddle will save us.

Like so many of his riddles, I have no idea what this one means.

But I'd better figure it out soon.

~23~

BUDAPEST, HUNGARY

October 15, 1944

It's a magnificent fall day, full of bliss, yet I always find autumn brings a measure of melancholy. This is when the sun takes a step back, and the leaves start their spectacular change to royal colors before they take a final flight from the trees.

As if overnight, the trees on Margaret Island in the middle of the Danube show off their heads of copper and red. It's Sunday. We have taken the children out for a walk since we're living in relative safety now thanks to our status as foreign citizens of a neutral country.

Peter is working hard to locate Father, and we pray he returns soon, healthy, and able to enjoy this new feeling of freedom. Images of us saying goodbye in front of the apartment fill my dreams. I never suspected it might be the last time. Should have hugged him longer. Said how much I love him. How I admire his talents, his heart, and his ability to stay calm in the face of danger. I never shared those feelings enough with him while he was here. I regret that now.

The children accept Mother as their surrogate Mema and have taken it upon themselves to call her that. She beams each time they do. Having her home after thinking I'd lost her is a gift every day. With the five of us in one room, I worried we'd rub on each other's nerves. If you'd asked me a year ago if a family could be happy in our crowded quarters, I would have said no—a person needs space to be their best. Now I know that's not true. All we need is to be with people who care for us as much as we care for them.

Gellert's hand is warm in mine while we all leave the riverwalk and head back to the apartment. We bump shoulders every so often, a quiet connection that says I'm glad you're here.

Jakub plays a game of stomping on the crisp leaves blowing along the street. He still carries his wooden horse everywhere. He told Gellert he's afraid to leave it in the flat because we might not go back one day. The poor boy has been on the move too much in his short life.

Zofia walks beside my mother who has recovered from her illness. She's teaching Zofia how to embroider now that she's mastered knitting.

I make sure to tell my mother everything she means to me. We've laughed over her funny antics back when we tried on ridiculous hats in a store. Or her empathy when the hairstylist cut my fringe too short, and she reassured me it was the newest hairstyle.

And before bed, we've started a habit of sharing with each other our favorite part of the day or offering a kind word about someone or something we feel grateful for.

Sometimes Jakub's list goes on and on. He's learned to name almost everything around us and at times is compelled to be quite specific.

"I like the flowers in one window box, but mostly the red ones that are next to the white pointy ones."

Perhaps he'll be a painter one day.

Gellert and I openly share with the others, but we express our deepest feelings in private. Last night, we sat on the steps leading to the flat to steal some much-needed alone time.

He whispered he loved me with his messy heart and was glad I stuck around. I pointed out my flaws too. We agree we still have the best of ourselves to explore. That we're about to leave the storm behind and inhale the future together. He finished professing his love by saying I was nothing he ever expected but, at last, everything he ever wanted.

We were nearly broken, pulled apart between our enemies and those we called neighbors.

Nefarious neighbors, that is.

The Schlesingers are safe, although I warned Raakel about Sándor. Without question, many Christians have helped their Jewish friends throughout the city when asked. Many have children in mixed marriages.

There's no true dividing line in an integrated city like ours, even if the government tries to draw demarcations and demand the no-contact laws are followed.

Raakel agrees Sándor is not who she thought he was and says she hasn't seen him in weeks.

Today, for our midday meal, we decide to dine in the back garden at a long table the house janitors never use. We tested the theory we'd be allowed to eat there a few days ago and no one stopped us. This freedom is like pure oxygen to the soul.

We bought cottage cheese for the first time in a long while from the farmer who delivered to the warehouse. Another pasta purchase and Mother made a hefty bowl of Túrós Csusza that will easily feed us and the Szabó family.

We're barely into the meal when someone in a first-floor apartment turns up the volume on their radio. They must be Christians to still own the device. With the window open, we recognize Regent Horthy's voice.

"Today it is obvious to any sober-minded person that the German Reich has lost the war. Conscious of my historical responsibility, I have the obligation to avoid further unnecessary bloodshed. I informed a representative of the German Reich that we were about to conclude a military armistice with our previous enemies and to cease all hostilities against them."

Our silverware stalls in midair and we make big eyes at each other. Can it be true? The war in Hungary is over?

"I appeal to every honest Hungarian to follow me on the path beset by sacrifices that will lead to Hungary's salvation."

We laugh and hug each other, moving around the table from person to person, the special foods forgotten.

"We're saved!" Imre says, ripping the yellow star from her sweater. The aunts do the same, flinging them to the ground.

"Will Papa come home now?" Bandin asks his mother.

"We pray he does"—she runs her fingers through his hair—"and he'll be so surprised to see how you've grown."

On the streets, people blow horns, and rounds of cheers fill the air.

"Let's join them," Mother says, a gleam in her eyes. "We must not forget this moment."

We run the food upstairs and soon are on the streets with a few hundred people. The doors to the Yellow-Star houses fling open, while the yellow cloth symbols speckle the pavement. It's as if the sky tossed its abundance to the ground.

My cheeks ache from smiling so broadly. We wind through the city and move slower now that thousands have joined. Many stop at the parks that for so long they couldn't visit. Others grab towels to enjoy the thermal baths. Oh, a swim does sound invigorating. Raakel and I swam four times a week before the Germans arrived. I've missed it.

We join in singing Zemirot in Yiddish, especially those hymns we sing around the table on Shabbat and our holidays. The Polish children don't know the words, but they try anyway, laughing at their silliness. We join in spontaneous prayer circles, hugging friends we've not seen for months.

The celebration fills me with complete joy, more than any other festival I can remember.

Within an hour, we return to the flat. Jakub needs a change of clothes after playing in the fountains, and a nap. Although I barely notice it anymore, his mouth always droops lower from the burn scars when he's this tired.

We're all drained from so much excitement but also from the weightlessness of relief.

"The labor camps will release the workers," Mother says. "Endre can come home."

"We'll celebrate for sure," I say. "Maybe we can all go to Switzerland now."

"I miss them so much," Mother says. "I'll bet the baby is talking so much more now."

"I'm going wherever you're all going," Gellert says, kissing my forehead.

He leaves to check in with the Red Cross to see where we will volunteer now that the Germans are leaving. All the orphanages and hospitals will need help for weeks if not months to come.

Not long after, footsteps pound up the stairs, and the outer and inner doors open before I'm on my feet.

Gellert is out of breath, his face ashen. "They've kidnapped Horthy's son."

"Who did?" I close the door behind him. The Regent only had two sons. One died in a plane crash, so it's his namesake, Miklós Jr., who lives on Buda Hill.

"The Gestapo. He was tricked into coming out of the villa without guards. He was beaten, rolled in a rug, and driven off to the airport. Flown to Vienna."

"What are they demanding for ransom?" Mother asks.

"They forced Horthy to appoint Ferenc Szálasi as prime minister. Horthy's family was taken by car to Germany and is detained at an unknown location."

"Serves him right," Mother says. "For too long he tied his fortunes to the swastika. He allowed half a million of his citizens to be killed by Eichmann and the Hungarian accomplices."

"What happens now?" I drop into a chair, suddenly fearful. Only a few minutes ago, we were free from the yoke of Nazi terror, and the threat of death was lifted.

And really, the bad part of this news is not about Horthy. Ferenc Szálasi is head of the Arrow Cross Party. Benedek and his mother's unlawful group of soldiers is finally in control.

Gellert paces the small space in the room, his hand fingering the scar on his head. "The report stated Szálasi appointed himself Leader of the Nation. He has two goals. One is to make sure Hungary stays in the war to help Germany win." Gellert draws in a shaky breath. "The second is to finish what Eichmann started...purge the country of its remaining Jews. Szálasi added...a simple chore now that we're corralled in the capital."

As darkness falls, we're stunned to hear gunfire and screams outside. We three adults huddle on one bed with our hands covering the children's ears.

Moments ago, Bandin snuck to our front gate to see what was happening. His report is horrifying. The Arrow Cross thugs pulled a family across the street from their home and shot them in plain sight.

What was their crime? Could we be next?

We pray that by morning, common sense returns and the police rein in the roving bands.

Weeks ago, Peter shared that many intelligent men who joined the Arrow Cross in 1938, at the peak of the movement, recently left the party because of the type of people joining. This new group comprises those attracted to the possibility of getting rich off the spoils while strutting around in uniform and hoping for the chance to carry a gun.

Survival. I understand it now. We've been relatively safe until this evening.

Our days now come down to nothing less than the pressing business of staying alive.

"I'm not sure we're safe volunteering," I say to Gellert.

"We have our protective passes." Gellert grinds his thumb into the palm of his other hand. "Wallenberg and Lutz haven't changed their position about protecting as many as they can."

"I want all of us to stay in tomorrow." My mother's eyes are clouded with worry. "Until we know what's happening out there. We have plenty of food and will be safe here."

"I agree," Gellert says. "Besides, Szálasi may end up being a short-term puppet for the Germans. We do know the Russians are close."

I reflect on this. The word "puppet" makes me miss my father more than ever. Agony rushes through me every time I imagine him in pain or starving. All alone. I've never accepted that he's dead. My mind won't allow that dreadful idea any foothold. When István was engaged, he thanked my father for doing the greatest thing when we were growing up, and that was to love our mother. He created the pattern we could follow when we sought our future partners. Father didn't tell us how to live. He lived and let us watch him do it.

I need him here again.

The shelf across the room holds József's fancy puppet and old Moshe. Most would say they admire the newer puppet's intricate detail. It's worth more. To me, it's the first one Father made, the one that launched his love of marionettes, that has my heart. Even though it can't dance from strings like the newer one, I'm glad he asked Erzsébet to rescue it from our apartment.

Then I blink twice as I stare at the puppet. The riddle replays in my mind.

Because I'm no longer colorful or passionate, no one wants to hold
me up. But inside, my heart of gold is the key to life.

The old puppet is the answer! But why? He told Mother the answer to the riddle would help us in times of trouble.

What does a twenty-five-year-old string puppet have to do with keeping us safe?

-24-

Budapest, Hungary

October 18, 1944

"Our battle is no longer between bad and good but between bad and worse," Peter says. He's come to check on us just minutes after Raakel arrived.

Raakel had no idea the ordeal my mother and father had been through and that Father is still missing. My mother learns that Raakel's parents are well but afraid for us and their other Jewish friends.

And this is the first Raakel has seen Gellert in over a year since he was first taken away in the Labor Force. "He seems as good as new," she whispers to me when he's talking to Peter.

"This is for you." Raakel hands me a big basket of bread. "I know you must be terrified to go shopping."

The morning after Szálasi took control, we learned they shot over one hundred Jews that first night. The anti-Semitic population is reawakened. The fascist group fills the city streets. They wear uniforms—black trousers, dark green shirt, and black tie—with that pompous Arrow Cross symbol glistening on their shirt. They've organized parades and rallies while exploiting every chance to curse and denigrate Jews in the streets. Boys, aged sixteen, with Tommy guns round them up, kick them, and use whips to drive them to a loosely established ghetto in Pest.

"The worst part is the police don't interfere," Peter says when Gellert asks how they are getting away with murder. "The constraints of hatred are finally loosened."

Peter advised that we not take the children outside as dozens of Jewish corpses lay pooled in blood on the curbs in every district.

"Will no one stop the Arrow Cross?" Mother asks.

"Decent Hungarians are protesting what's going on," Raakel says. "My father went to City Hall to ask how this can be right when the killing is no longer a military action. They warned him to stop poking his nose in or he'll be in trouble too."

"It's insatiable greed and cold opportunism that's seized a sizable segment of the city." Peter drops a hand to Jakub's back and the boy leans into him. I'm glad to see the child warm up to another man besides Gellert. Although he and Zofia briefly met Peter, they haven't had any time around him. They will be out in the world one day and need to feel cautious but safe around new adults.

"Have you seen this?" Raakel hands Gellert the Arrow Cross weekly, *Összetartás*. I lean over his arm to read along.

"That's terrible," I say and step back, as if distancing myself from the words changes anything.

"Read it out loud," Peter says.

"It's a reprinted quote from László Endre," Gellert begins. "Another right-wing politician. 'We express our unreserved faith that Jewry is an undesirable element for the Hungarian people in every way: morally, spiritually, and physically. We seek out the solution which removes Jews from Hungarian life totally and absolutely.'"

"The audacity." Peter snorts and crosses his arms. "No wonder the roving bands feel safe killing any Jew they see."

"Will they kill us?" Zofia asks, tears welling in her eyes.

I rush to her and take her in my arms. "Goodness no. You're safe with us."

"The booms," Jakub says in his limited English. "Our house?" He points to the ceiling.

The allied bombings have picked up. Often we huddle inside our room, praying nothing hits our building. Every day we learn wayward bombs reduce buildings to rubble, even in neighborhoods away from the river, like ours.

"It's still dangerous on the streets," Peter says. "Posters are plastered everywhere, saying the government no longer recognizes any protective papers."

I scoff at the absurdity. "Wallenberg and Lutz will have a say in that. The government agreed to honor the foreign embassies' help with its citizens."

"The problem is, Szálasi must know we've duplicated the original passes thousands of times," Gellert says.

"He does." Peter folds his arms. "There's talk again of creating a ghetto, and this street with your flat will be inside the walls. They say they'll butcher anyone not moved there." When he sees the shock on our faces, he nods. "*Butcher* is the exact word the mayor used."

Raakel says she will be back with food in a few days.

"Please don't," I say. "We have plenty here, and I can't have you in trouble for helping us."

"It's too dangerous, love," Mother says. "Tell your family hello and that we pray for their safety and hope to see them soon."

I hug her goodbye and give Peter a quick hug.

"Thanks for coming," Gellert says to him as he shakes his hand. "Is there anything we can be doing to help?"

"Give it a few days. Let's see what Wallenberg and Lutz manage to stop. You probably can get back to the orphanages then."

"Does that uniform keep you safe on the streets?" Mother addresses Peter.

"As long as I don't bump into any Arrow Cross or police who know who I really am." He smiles, something he rarely does since Ariel's death. "The chaos on the streets works in my favor until someone tries to take me along for what they call target practice."

"Which is?" Gellert asks.

"Often drunken illiterate teenagers shooting at random." He eyes the children. "There's no judging where or why they will appear."

Peter and Raakel leave.

We're silent, each lost in our thoughts. I'm sure we're each trying to figure out how we stay safe with what's happening outside the flat.

I read another headline in the Arrow Cross newspaper. The local police announce they can't stop the killings but wish the Arrow Cross did them in less obvious areas, where bodies aren't piling up. It's a *discomfort* for all citizens.

Discomfort? Am I supposed to care about citizens *not* hunted by the Arrow Cross?

This is indeed a most dangerous moment in a long series of dangerous moments. I'm more worried than ever about Father's safe return.

And somehow, the old puppet should have an answer that will help us. We've all taken turns going over it after I announced I solved the riddle. Now we're not so sure.

I retrieve the wooden figure while Mother plays a guessing game with the children, trying to lighten the mood in the room. Gellert stares out the window onto the street, his hands in his pockets.

I open and close the puppet's wide mouth, but no pieces loosen. Nor is anything written inside. The attached arms and hands show nothing different from what I've seen before. A string that would attach it to paddles above is broken but has been for a long time. Let me think.

Based on Father's riddle, I know there's something *inside*. I drag my fingernail across the puppet's chest but find no openings. I do the same to its back, and there's smooth wood until I reach its left side. Ah, there's a tiny line here that matches the one on its other side. I try pushing my fingernail into the crack to pull it open, but it's too fine. Gently, I shake it next to my ear but hear nothing and don't want to pound the puppet open and ruin it.

I lay it face down on the table and push on its back. There's a slight popping noise. The back springs open on hidden miniature hinges. Not surprised my father made this secret compartment. He's such a genius with his tiny tools.

"Look here!" I say.

"What did you find?" Mother asks, then draws close to my side. "You were right. He did hide something in there."

I pull out a key—*my heart of gold is the key to life*—wrapped in a piece of paper. "There's a note." I read it aloud.

"Locker number seventeen, Józsefváros train station." It's a transit station in District VIII, not far from us. "He's left something for us."

"It's so unsafe to go out," Mother says. "And although I trust Endre has hidden something important, can we risk getting there? The train station is teeming with police looking for any Jewish man who can still work in their camps."

"I still have my Aryan papers from when Peter and I returned to the estate. If stopped, I'll show those."

"It's too dangerous," Gellert says. "What could be there that's important enough to risk going out? Medicine? Money? We can get those things."

"It has to be something more than medical supplies or money." I run my finger across his handwriting and miss him even more. "Maybe it's a plan for a secret way out of the city, like how he helped the Resistance. New passports, tickets?"

"Yes, we could use those," Mother says with a nod. "Especially if he's waiting at the other end."

I picture that moment, running into his arms. All of us surrounding him, making sure we never lose him again. If he's still alive. I wince at the thought.

"I have to try." I memorize the note and leave it on the table but put the key in my small purse. "He made careful plans to ensure we got this message. We can't ignore his effort."

"I don't want you to go alone," Gellert says. "We heard what Peter said. That Arrow Cross arm of Szálasi's is shooting people just for fun."

"We should have asked Peter when he was here," Mother says. "Maybe he or one of the underground members can go to the train station? They have their disguises."

"I know I can make it to the Glass House through the smaller tunnels and side alleys. I've done it before." I stand and walk to the cupboard where I've hidden my forged Aryan documents. "I'll find a new place for us too. We need to move into a safe house and get out of here before we're trapped inside a ghetto. A safe house would have guards at the gates instead of those meek Gábors. They haven't stopped *anyone* from coming in here. They let the men in who searched the place and ruined our Bible."

"But your father," Gellert says. "He'll come here looking for us."

I appreciate his positivity that Father is alive and will return.

"Then we leave him a message." I tear a strip of paper off the top of a sack and grab a pen. "What should we say?"

"That we love him," Mother says.

"I'll add that." I tap my pen against the paper. "How about, 'Find us through the Red Cross'?"

"That's good," Mother and Gellert say almost in unison.

I write the message, roll it up, place it inside the puppet, and close the compartment. Once again, no one will notice Moshe's secret door. It will have to remain here when we move out. "I hate leaving it, but we have no choice."

Then I return it to the shelf behind the newer, modern marionette hoping someone will find the bigger one more enticing if they come here. The only solace is there are bigger, finer Jewish homes to pillage. One room in a two-bedroom flat in a Yellow-Star apartment building will be less attractive.

After I reassure everyone that I'll be careful, I slip out of the apartment. The streets are now almost deserted when I leave the tunnels as they change from wide hallways to narrow passages. That is until I near Lutz's Glass House on 29 Vadász Street. The word spread that Swiss Deputy Consul Carl Lutz's responsibility was to prepare the list of emigrants. Glass wholesaler Artúr Weiss offered his Vadász Street property for the operation. Lutz opened the emigration office there too. Within months, the young Zionists seized the building for their official hiding place, base of illegal operations, and distribution center for forged documents.

The roads leading to it are swamped. Every Jew left in the city is terrified and desperate for a safe pass.

I squeeze my way through the crowd, citing I'm a nurse who works there. A guard points me to a conference room when I ask for Peter. I hope he's come back here after leaving our flat.

Lutz, Peter, and other top Zionists are gathered around a large radio. Anger rises in me when I hear Eichmann's voice.

"As you can see, my arm *is* long enough to reach you again. Every Jew will be deported now…not one will be spared. This time there are no trains, no lorries to transport you out of the city. We need two hundred thousand workers to defend Vienna, and it's up to you who have fought so hard to stay hidden. We know you've disguised yourselves as gentiles or foreign nationals. But I am like a bloodhound and will sniff out who is real and who is not."

Is he laughing at the end of the message? There's a fumbling noise like he's passing the microphone to another person.

Now what?

A man, without introduction, announces, "The Hungarian government immediately revokes the validity of any safe-conduct letter *of any kind* or any foreign passport a Jew of Hungarian nationality may have received from whatever source." He pauses. "To be accepted, Swiss or Swedish Embassies must officially validate each letter."

Lutz steeples his hands in front of his mouth and slowly shakes his head. When he speaks, it's in a quiet tone. "This means tens of thousands we thought we saved are now stripped of their protection."

"What do we do going forward?" his aide asks, with both hands on the table, leaning over the radio as if looming will make it change its message. "The safe houses are full unless we can buy more."

"Call Geneva and request more money," Lutz instructs the aide and turns to another man. "Call Wallenberg and see what his plans are for the Swedish letters." Then he sits up straight and snaps his fingers. "Get me fresh pens and a thousand protective passes to start. No more duplicating… my signature will be in ink on each of them for the police to see."

While helpers run around to follow his orders, Peter steps to my side.

"What has happened?" His eyes are wide.

"We discovered something right after you left. I have two favors to ask, though."

"Sure. If I can." He rubs the back of his neck. "With Eichmann back, whatever we thought was hard to do before will have us looking back and laughing when we see what's coming. If this war doesn't end in the next few weeks, we may all be torn to shreds," he says.

He's suddenly so serious.

"I pray it's over sooner than that."

"What do you need me to do?" He forces a smile.

"We want to move into a safe house and get out of the ghetto area if it comes to that, but from what I heard moments ago, they're all filled?"

"Very crowded, but I know of a few that can handle five more. I'll get you set up and let you know where." His eyes narrow. "Even there, you need to exercise extreme caution. Arrow Cross men fired into Wesselényi Forty-four, even though it has the flag out front. They killed four and wounded another two."

"That's terrible." Wesselényi 44 is the makeshift hospital where Ariel died. "Maybe find a less notable house then. We don't care where."

He nods. "You said there were two favors?"

"My father left a key to a locker at Józsefváros railway station. Said we should open it if we're ever in danger." I shrug. "What's happening now seems to be what he was worried about."

"If he predicted this, he's a seer because who could have foreseen the Arrow Cross Party taking charge." He checks his watch. "Do you have the key with you?"

"I do"—I pat my purse—"and my Aryan papers."

"Good. Give me twenty minutes. I need to change clothes."

Peter returns dressed as a handyman, wearing an Arrow Cross armband, and carrying a toolbox while we walk fifteen blocks to the east. The Keleti train station is just north of the Jewish cemetery while Józsefváros train station is south, near our abandoned apartment.

The temptation to return there is strong. I could retrieve warm clothes for the coming cold weather, grab more canned goods, and see the Schlesingers. But I could also bump into Benedek or his mother and that would be dangerous. Benedek would recognize Peter, and I should be in my assigned Yellow-Star flat and not here.

I push the thought away.

"You ready?" Peter has warned me not to react if we find dead bodies along the way. "Remember you're Aryan. You are one of those who doesn't care what's happening to the Jews."

A train rumbles into the station, giving us some distraction while we search for the lockers. They're off to the side of the platform, but there are enough people passing by at our backs that we need to make this look official.

He speaks up when groups pass, repeating himself each time. "These old locks get rusty all the time" or "Everyone loses keys. Don't upset yourself."

"Let's see what's inside?" He pretends to hold a screwdriver to the lock but already inserted the key and turned it.

"The sooner the better." My legs quiver. What if the locker is empty? Or holds a farewell letter?

He opens it and reaches in. On the bottom sits a bag he pulls out and unzips.

"Scheisse!" Straightaway, he zips it up and stuffs it back inside the locker.

"What?" I say, looking around to see if anyone is staring our way. No one is.

He leans close to my ear. "A pistol with a box of bullets."

No Jew has owned a gun for four years, even before the Germans arrived. And my father hated guns.

"Well, that's all fixed," he says when a couple passes by. He turns the key to lock the door. "I'll walk you home."

When away from the crowd, he hands me the key.

"If they stop you with that gun on you or if found in your house, you'll all be shot."

"What should we do with it?" Am I letting my father down, who worked so hard to have me find it?

"You know where it is if you ever really need it."

"It's better left there then. I could never shoot anyone." A shiver scales my back.

"Well, you'd be surprised what you can do when the alternative is dying."

$-25-$

BUDAPEST, HUNGARY

October 26, 1944

This morning, the rain rolls in with a confident wind and trailing cold stringers, ripping the last of the leaves from near-bare limbs.

Back at the Swedish Embassy Headquarters, they're giving me our paperwork for the move to a safe house. Designated as a Swedish Embassy annex under Wallenberg's control, it flies a Swedish flag. A plaque out front identifies it as a diplomatic facility, with hope this creates a barrier of protection from roaming mobs.

Add to that, the office enjoys connections to the police station nearby, which sends cordons of police every day. Policemen on horseback keep order, using batons. People are so desperate to be saved, they risk breaching the embassy walls.

Last night, we talked to the Szabó family about moving to a protected house. They refused, citing the Bible passage, "We must obey God as ruler rather than men." They don't trust any country's government, even those that proved their devotion to saving us.

We're moving into Pannónia Utca 8, four blocks from the Danube, a multi-floor cinderblock building. The area locals now call it the International Ghetto, although there are no walls around it. Wallenberg purchased thirty houses within this area, all protected under the Swedish flag.

I hurry home to tell my family. We will leave furniture behind since the new room comes furnished. We've invited Imre to spread out into our flat but to please not throw out anything. How odd. It's as if Moshe watched us go while sitting in its slumped position atop the shelf.

Carrying our personal items, a good share wrapped in a tablecloth, the five of us walk the fourteen blocks to Pannónia Street.

The house commander Iván Pór greets us to show our assigned room. He sports a thick mustache and even thicker spectacles, affording him a permanent surprised look.

"This place feels safer," Mother says after closing the door.

He hands us house instructions. Gellert then reads them aloud while we unpack and try to find space for our belongings.

The rules are simple. Gellert continues, "The house commander is in charge and keeps regular contact with the Humanitarian Department of the Swedish Embassy. He'll register our professions, list inhabitants without protection certificates, and take care of general janitorial responsibilities."

"Like our last janitor." Mother isn't usually the one to be sarcastic. We break into laughter.

"Yeah, just like him," I say and chuckle.

Gellert reads in silence and then says, "There's an infirmary here with a doctor and nurse." He looks at me. "Maybe we can work some of their shifts. They must be overworked."

"I'd like that." I lay out our family Bible, the words on hundreds of pages illegible due to water damage. I run my hand over the warped pages. It is ruined but still means the world to me.

The letter goes on to say the Swedish Red Cross provides two plates of warm food daily and free medical services.

This move *feels* like a good choice and our Swiss protective letters are signed by Lutz.

The children don't show any signs of fear. With all my heart, I believe as long as they are with us, they don't care where we live. But Jakub's worry that we just keep moving haunts me. What if we are on the run for years? Of course, he has his horse with him. We've tried to shelter the children from the worst stories reaching us through the Zionists. They once saw their entire town hunted and killed. They don't need a replay of what that was like.

They've already met other children in the house and play a game of hide-and-seek in the stairwells.

But horrible acts continue across the city.

The Arrow Cross seized and killed the Roman Catholic priest Ferenc Kálló, who helped Jews with life-saving documents, placing them under the direct protection of Vatican neutrality. He also set up numerous safe houses throughout Budapest. The sad irony is he didn't falsify any protective papers like we did, yet they accused him of it anyway.

No doubt his death should provoke the ire of the Pope and the million or so Catholics living in Hungary.

"Are you ready?" Gellert asks. We've decided to continue helping the Red Cross now that we have the correct papers.

We haven't worked at the Munkácsy Mihály Street orphanage for over a week but hear the number of orphans has surged to over two hundred. We won't—cannot—take Jakub or Zofia back. Not only is it dangerous on the streets, but they report an outbreak of diphtheria we hope to address.

We take to the lesser tunnels again. Currents in these tunnels, mysterious breezes, somehow find their way inside despite the fact they're mostly closed off. Today, they whirl around me and touch the back of my neck like an icy hand laid there, sending a prickle down my back.

Lajos Kraszner is headmaster of the orphanage. When we find him, he's yelling into a telephone that he needs trucks immediately. He hangs up and appears to yell at no one and everyone at the same time.

"The Arrow Cross took the children away!" He paces, punching his right fist into his left hand.

"Where to?" Gellert asks.

"They claimed they're taking them to another orphanage on Síp Street, but we just heard they took them to an abandoned house on Szív Street." Worry streams behind him like comet trails. "We believe they will kill them."

For a moment, the selfish part of me is glad Jakub and Zofia no longer live here. Then in an instant, I'm ashamed. I picture the innocent faces of children we've worked with for months. "We'll go with you."

A group of men arrive—some dressed in city police uniforms—and we rush to the building, which is back near the Yellow-Star flat we just left.

"Open the doors now, or you will be arrested!" the headmaster demands of the janitor there.

"I had nothing to do with this," he says while rushing to unlock the gate. His bristling mustache holds the crumbs from the meal he must have been enjoying. "The Arrow Cross left them here but didn't say why."

We divide the two hundred scared and crying children into groups of ten. Each of us escorts a group back to the orphanage as some ride along in the trucks. The children in my group cling to me. My arms. The fabric of my skirt bunched in their tiny hands. Or my outstretched fingers.

Gellert carries two small children, and the other eight stick by his side.

I murmur messages of love and confidence to them. "You're safe now. Those men were playing a mean joke, but we're all going to be fine now."

Once back at the orphanage, I settle the sweaty children on the floor and wipe cool cloths across their flushed faces. I ask myself the same question. "Are we really going to be fine?"

If right-wing groups are emboldened enough to attack orphanages, a place most would say is off-limits even in times of war, what won't they do?

It's almost dark when we return to our new apartment.

"I saved some dinner for you," Mother says, pulling two plates out of a cabinet.

Zofia and Jakub are asleep, worn out from a day of exploring the house and meeting new friends. We explain what happened at the orphanage while we eat.

Mother and the house manager cluck and shake their heads at the story.

After dinner, Mother, Gellert, and I circle in prayer asking God to protect the people of Budapest. We ask that He watches over my father. That the hearts of the citizens in our city soften. That compassion wins over avarice.

Long after we're asleep—the women in one bed and Jakub and Gellert on the couch—my mother's quiet sobs shake the covers. It is a rare moment when she no longer can hold on to her courage. Tears bleed from my eyes, matching her fear. I roll over and wrap my arms around her from behind, the curl of my body matching hers.

Ever so gently, she closes her hand over mine. "I love you," she says.

"Not as much as I love you."

She dries her face with the sheet. "You know, I can endure emotional pain if there is some reason for it."

"Ima, you're the toughest woman I know." I squeeze her tighter. I know she likes when I say "mother" in Hebrew. "We can't reason with injustice, hypocrisy. Truly, who could believe the rumors of genocide and that one day we'd be hunted?"

"Well, your father must have seen it could come to this." She is silent for a moment. "Do you think you should go get the gun now that we're here?"

"I remember something Father told me when I didn't make the swim team the first time, and I said I was quitting."

"You would have been about twelve. What did he say?"

"'Remember the other girl who gave up last year?' When I said I didn't, he said, 'Neither does anyone else.'"

"That sounds like him." She softly chuckles.

"We may have to change course, but we can never give up…and I don't think we need that gun."

"I won't give up. We won't. We'll take tomorrow by storm."

"Those twenty-four hours won't know what hit them," I say.

Soon she drifts off to sleep.

Gellert moans and mumbles warnings. Jakub is used to these nightmares and doesn't wake anymore. My dear Gellert's caught between wanting the war to end and dreading the Russians' arrival. Who can blame him? What he witnessed is horrifying. I've tried to reason with him that not all Russian soldiers will be that way. He also saw terrible acts done by the German and Hungarian soldiers but admitted it wasn't all of them. Groups of bad apples. Men stretched to their limit.

The Russians will search for Germans and collaborators. Benedek comes to mind. Will the Russians care about the Arrow Cross and what they're doing now? His band of marauders vowed to keep Eichmann's extermination plan on course. That supports the Germans in so many ways. If the Red Army asks me, I'll tell them just that.

Before drifting off, I go over the words István wrote in the letter we received days ago. He penned it a week earlier. The day the Germans ousted Horthy.

He writes they are doing well. The baby's getting fat. That fall is beautiful in their town near Zurich. He worries about us every day but can offer no help from Switzerland, advising we must use Lutz's channels. What István doesn't know is the channels for emigration are all dried up now.

And he wants to know why we haven't located Father, chastising that Peter needs to try harder.

I'm angry with him. *He's* not hiding in a crowded house, praying vicious mobs don't force their way in and kill Erzsébet and the baby. *He* doesn't know what has happened these last few weeks. And that's just it. Does anyone outside our country know what the Szálasi government is doing? I want to write back and give him all the horrible details, although I won't. He can hear about the atrocities when we're all together again. For now, if it's possible to get a letter to him, I'll assure him we're doing everything we can. That we're safe and praying for the day we can see him and the family.

That we still have hope of finding Father.

That we still have hope. Period.

~26~

BUDAPEST, HUNGARY

November 5, 1944

We should have known better. Just when we thought that maybe we were safe, managing our lives in the crowded safe house, the news brings conflicting threats, alternating moments of worry with minutes of hope.

The worry. Eleven days ago, the Hungarian Minister of Defense agreed to Eichmann's request to deport all of us to Austria for forced labor, exactly as Eichmann threatened in his radio message after his return. The men will build a wall around Vienna, while the women will work in war production factories.

The hope. Three days ago, Szálasi had a change of heart, realizing that marching everyone for five days as the cold winds of late fall bring rain and hail reflects poorly on his party.

So, we thank heaven for another reprieve, for someone thinking sensibly. We only need to hunker down, watch our backs when we're on the streets, and wait for the Germans to flee.

Because not that much has changed in the city. The Police Chief of Budapest intervened at the last minute to save ninety elderly residents of the Old Peoples' Home on the corner of Városmajor and Alma Streets from being murdered by the Arrow Cross.

Szálasi may have stopped the forced march to Austria, but he also issued an order to confiscate all Jewish property for the benefit of the state. Jews are allowed a two-week supply of food, fuel, and a few articles of personal use and a tiny amount of cash if we still have any.

The trucks moved through the neighborhoods yesterday, randomly entering Yellow-Star Houses and hauling out boxes, suitcases, and furniture.

Thanks to our Swedish protected status, in the end our safe house didn't succumb to a search.

"Do you think they went through our flat?" Mother asks. "Father's puppet with the message could be taken."

"I would hope the janitors would say it was evacuated and we took everything. I do worry about the Szabós though. They have so little."

"Father's chess set," I say. "We may not see that again." I study my fingernails. I've bitten them so short again.

"That's true," Gellert adds. "Poor Bandin. He cherished it."

We're finishing our midday meal at the main dining room table with twenty others. We have to eat in shifts because there are over ninety of us in the apartments in the house.

A commotion erupts outside. The guard shouts that no one can enter, but the front door flies open, and a dozen Arrow Cross men pour inside.

Mother gasps at the sight of their guns, and Gellert wraps a protective arm around me and shelters our children behind him.

Our worst fears are playing out in this moment. We're going to die.

"Everyone over sixteen is ordered to the Óbuda Brickyard immediately," an older man with a deeply wrinkled face says. "No exceptions!"

My thoughts swirl, and horrifying images flit through my head. What does this mean? And if they're taking us to the brick factory, where will we end up?

Our house supervisor rushes in from his office. "Stop right now! These people are under the protection of the Swedish Embassy."

The house guard stumbles in from outside, spitting blood as he says, "Call Wallenberg. Tell him what's happening."

"We've had it with that man," an older intruder says. "He and Lutz have made a mockery of the government's good faith."

"Line up now or we start shooting the children," a scrawny boy says around his nasty sneer.

I embrace and kiss the children, their mouths still sticky with jam. "You'll stay here until we get back."

Jakub begins to cry, his scarred lower face twisting his mouth wide open. Zofia is frozen in place, her eyes unfocused. She's seen a roundup before.

"This won't be forever," I say, forcing calmness in my tone, although that's not what I'm feeling. "I *will* find a way to come to you."

They search the upper floors, and soon all of us adults, including the elderly and sick, are forced outside into the pouring rain. Mother has the sense to grab her lilac scarf and two coats from the closet in the foyer.

We're pushed along at a fast pace. The Arrow Cross men amuse themselves by firing their guns in the air and laughing when we duck and flinch.

My chest is tight as fear nearly chokes my breath right out of me. We've heard the stories, the ease at which these men walk innocents to the Danube and shoot them.

Gellert's face is a mask of hate. I meet his gaze and shake my head no. Whatever he's planning will get him killed.

In the distance is a wailing of sirens. Our captors taunt us with ethnic slurs and beat some who walk too slowly. My nurse's shoes are nearly worn out from all the walking I do, but they're comfortable. Like other older women, Mother wears her open-toed pumps with a chunky heel.

"Mother. Let's exchange shoes."

"Mine are fine, love," she says. "I've spent my adult life in heels, so don't worry."

A woman behind us struggles to keep up, stumbles, and begs for help standing up. A teenager, not old enough to shave, shoots her.

We all flinch, and a small scream escapes me. Gellert grabs my hand and holds it tight. "The dirty bastards," he whispers.

The gun report echoes against the buildings' walls, mingled with sobbing and prayers. I try to silence my ragged breath for fear they will shoot anyone they view as not in control. I focus on Mother's poised figure in front of me and listen to the sound of hundreds of leather soles slapping and scraping on the cobblestones, the rhythm a distraction from my fears.

Our group combines with others until we must be a thousand strong. Or, in our case, weak. We cross the river and follow more city streets, and eventually reach the third district on Bécsi Road 136. The Óbuda Brick

Works is a massive plant, with dozens of sections for the different brick-making processes.

"Men line up over there," a guard calls out, pointing to a train. "You're slated for work east of here." The Arrow Cross men walk along the line, pulling out any man who hasn't moved and shoving them with their rifle butts.

I grab Gellert. He's rigid, his muscles locked, his teeth set hard. "This is not the end," I say through chattering teeth.

His expression softens as he pushes my wet hair off my face. "You have made my life worth living."

"Don't talk like that. We'll be together again." We're clutching each other's arms so tightly our fingers are white. "I'm not going wherever they think they're taking us. The first chance we get, Mother and I will escape."

"I will too." His voice holds doubt. "But remember, I'll carry you with me forever."

The blood is pounding through my body and echoing in my ears, and my hands are shaking so hard. I want to scream at him to stop talking like we're about to die. "We *will* be together soon...and forever."

"We will, Marika." He kisses me and keeps his face pressed to mine. I breathe him in, memorizing the feel of his cheek against mine.

A soldier yanks him out of my arms. "Move it, Jesus killer!"

He releases me and walks away to join a line forming near the train. I'm awed by his composure. He must be terrified but refuses to show it.

Then we're herded into the drying chambers, told to sit wherever we find room. The night seems endless as we wait in fear, crouched on the stone floors, trembling in wet dresses, reassuring each other we will be fine.

But we're lying to ourselves. If they valued us for some future job, we wouldn't be treated like cattle heading to slaughter, packed in unsanitary conditions with no food or water.

Hours of dread and uncertainty fray my nerves. Mother's right eye twitches, and she rubs her temples, perhaps trying to force the pain of stress out of her muscles.

Silent sobs shake me throughout the night, and I chew my nails to the quick. What has happened to Gellert? He must come back. Hasn't he suffered enough? And I worry about the children at the safe house, which proved not to be safe after all. Will they be kidnapped or harmed? I can't bear to think of them in fear or pain.

Just as the sun crawls its way above the horizon, a Hungarian soldier stands on a wooden platform to address us. "We are unable to requisition trains or trucks to transport you to your workplaces. You, who number close to ten thousand, have demonstrated great energy in overcoming our rules. Strong women! Just who we need to help fortify Vienna."

We're going to Austria? We thought Szálasi had said no to Eichmann's suggestion.

"You will walk forty kilometers a day, with the plan to reach Hegyeshalom in six to seven days. From there you will be transported to factories."

"My heart breaks," Mother says. "Look around. These women won't make it that far."

Many women wear high heels, silk stockings, and thin work clothes. Elderly ladies barely made it this far and lay curled at the feet of their daughters. Pregnant women and young girls without jackets look terrified.

"They can't be serious," I say. "They play these mind games to torture us."

The man in charge continues. "The Hungarian Royal Army will escort you. The catering and night stations will be provided by the Hungarian Royal Gendarmerie. We're moving two thousand through a day, so many of you will remain here until your group is called."

"We need to go first," I whisper. "There's no food or water here."

"You will receive bread and a bowl of hearty warm soup at meals. At night you'll be in a covered building with adequate latrines. In case of any contagious disease or possible death, the assigned public health officer in your group should be informed. Along the way, you'll be protected by the armed members of the local Arrow Cross Party."

"They've been planning this a while, if all of those arrangements are in place," Mother says. "Do they have any idea what the Arrow Cross has been doing?"

"We can only hope that these guards aren't the same ones roaming the streets."

"Your first day is the shortest, only twenty-seven kilometers to Piliscsaba." He claps his hands and chuckles. "You're off to finally serve the Reich."

I am suddenly enraged. We're worn down by the months of occupation, by everything we've lost or may soon lose. Where is Gellert? My father? Listening to the guards' carefree laughter, a murderous rage rushes through me. Our cruel treatment and possible demise are no more than a game to them.

Whistles blow. Mother and I weave through the crowd to be counted for the first wave to leave. I lean into her and say, "I don't know how or when, but we will escape."

"He said it moments ago. We're strong. We'll show them just how strong."

We walk the blocks in stiff and horrible silence. This is really happening. Our children are safe—I must believe that because it's the only good news. People come out of their doorways to stare as if we are on parade. "Christ haters!" someone yells. Rocks rain down on us.

Not far out of the city, a woman screams that her foot is broken. She's asked to step to the side, and soon after, a gunshot rings out.

"We can't show any sign of weakness," I say. Mother's feet must be hurting, but she's not limping. "We can do this."

She smiles and squeezes my arm for a brief moment.

The day is relatively calm with sunny weather. A blessing for sure. Kilometer after kilometer we walk on, becoming weary without water, food, or rest stops. We don't talk to the others beside us. We're united in survival, in conserving our energy, or at least most appear to be. Some people's spirits break within the first hours. They make a run for the fields or trees, knowing the bullets will soon strike them down. Possibly relieved when they do.

We arrive that night as the temperatures dip below freezing. We're directed to the fairground outside the village, a vast wire-enclosed field contaminated by excrement. There is no shelter, no food, and no latrine facilities whatsoever.

Mother and I use an area of the fence line for a toilet after others have chosen to do the same. Then we try to find the driest piece of land to spread my coat. We lay side by side on it and cover ourselves with hers.

"We've made it this far, Marika." The words arrive in a husky tone, dried out before they leave her lips.

"I'm proud of us, Mom." I kiss her forehead. "You can't stop a Tausig woman."

"No, you can't." She pulls me closer. "Try to get some sleep."

"You too."

The half-moon brightens the area enough that the field appears to be a cemetery full of broken grey headstones. I brush those thoughts away, and my thoughts turn to Gellert. We loved moonlit nights when romance bloomed deeper and fuller under the cool soft light. Why is that? The moon never changes its shape, but when it's full, we are energized, stronger. The moon will always be there and has been a steadfast voyeur forever. Did Shakespeare gaze at the brilliant orb before penning Romeo and Juliet? Did the Egyptians build the pyramids to try to harness its powers?

Tonight, the moon makes me feel uncertain, cratered by my limitations, as its own face is dimpled with imperfections.

I send prayers heavenward that Gellert is viewing this same night sky. That he's not trapped in a cattle car but is on a labor crew near Budapest. Eichmann ordered three thousand men to dig trenches to the east, deep enough to stop tanks. Out where Mother last saw Father.

My final prayer is a big one. Let Gellert find Father, and please lead them both home.

The next morning several dozen sick or elderly people do not rise to resume the march. The Arrow Cross guards hand out a piece of bread per person and bring buckets of water from a nearby stream. We pass a ladle around, but it does little to quench our thirst.

Today's destination is Dorog. Once again, villagers gather along the roads. Some set up chairs to watch us shuffle past. I tune out their jeers and hateful comments and watch my feet move along the road.

We walk on, hour after hour. Gunfire reminds us not to stumble or fall. Arrow Cross youth are trigger happy, excited it appears to kill us with any pretext. A woman reached out to a guard for support and was shot dead before she ever touched him.

The skies darken, and a cold wind bites at our faces and hands.

An hour later, my mother and I come upon Imre and the two aunts. Their story is the same as ours. Men stormed their side of the apartment, forced them out and left Bandin behind.

Eunice is doing poorly, and as they begin to drop behind us, we shed our coats and Mother's lilac scarf and hand them to our friends, who seem to be freezing to death.

An uproar off to the left catches the guards' attention, and many of them run in that direction.

Acting purely on instinct, I grab my mother's arm, and as the guards look the other way, we slip away from the road and into a tall cornfield. The risk we're taking might be unacceptable, but everything about life these days is unacceptable. Just when we adjust our thinking to follow new rules, the situation always worsens.

We crouch a dozen meters inside the stalks, not willing to disturb the corn and invite a hail of bullets.

Why no one else joins us is a mystery but also a stroke of luck. A large group making a run for it would have no chance of escape. Long after the column has passed, we follow the rows of corn to a line of trees, then to a wooded area.

Without a Star of David on our clothes, we could pass as two women out for a walk, except our hair is a wreck and our clothes droop from the rain.

We travel this way until dusk when we find a rundown building, perhaps a homestead, long fallen into ruin but still enclosed enough to protect us from the cold. Inside, weak light shows a stairwell covered in debris leading to the top floor. We avoid wires spilling from holes in the walls as we search the main level. The carpet is musty and spoiled in places where water has dripped through the ceiling. Soft spots on the floor give under our shoes as we cross the parlor.

We search for food but find nothing. At the well out the back door, we drink our fill of water. The broken dining table, with two legs supporting one end, creates a makeshift lean-to that affords some cover if anyone walks in the front door. We bed down under it.

"We've made it this far, Marika." Mother parrots her sentence from last night.

"I'm proud of us, Mom." I do the same.

We're hungry and tired, worried and frightened, but somehow we begin laughing.

Tomorrow may find us captives again, or dead. But for now, we're free, and it's worth celebrating.

~27~

BUDAPEST, HUNGARY

November 8, 1944

We start walking at sunrise, still wary of following the road, so we stick to the woods and meadows. Within an hour, we're crossing a farmer's field—the scent of wet earth and dead vegetation surrounding us—when a man calls out to us from his barn.

We see the farmer and freeze, not registering what he asked. We haven't come all this way to face capture again.

He walks closer, stepping through last harvest's corn stubble and repeats himself. "Do you need some food?"

His kindness is almost too much to believe. We nod and soon reach his side. He's beefy from the waist up with short legs, thick sideburns, and a beard that covers his neck.

"Thank you," Mother says, rubbing the chill from her arms. "You're more than kind."

"What's happened in this country is intolerable." He shoves one hand in his left coveralls pocket. "Wife and I help when and where we can. We won't share our names with you, but come inside."

We follow him into the barn. Instant warmth from his animals and stacks of hay soothes skin to bone. He moves two hay bales off the floor, revealing a trapdoor.

"Five steps down leads to a tunnel. Follow it to my house and tap three times. The wife will feed you."

My heart thumps faster. How do we trust that this isn't a deathtrap?

He must see our hesitation.

"If my count is right, you two make nearly one hundred and eighty we've helped so far."

Mother nods. I will have to trust her instinct.

Everything about him *seems* honest. If he planned to get rid of us, he must own a gun to protect his animals from wildlife. He could have gunned us down in the field.

"Again, thank you," I say.

"Come back out this way. I'm driving a load of melons into Újpest, but I've often driven by the Rákospalota Synagogue. Very friendly rabbi there. Welcoming, if you understand me."

That synagogue is one district away from our new safe house.

"We can't pay you, but know our gratitude will last forever," I say.

"Get some food in you, and we'll go."

We head down the wooden steps and crouch as we navigate the dirt tunnel shored up with boards. A stringer of lights runs down the center, but my heart races at the thought of a collapse.

We reach the door, and I tap three times.

Footsteps approach, and once again, I worry this is a trap.

The door opens into a hallway closet. We push through wire hangers and coats to greet a woman.

She's so much taller than her husband. Everything about her is sturdy, from her thick hair bun to her shoes, but her eyes are soft, kindhearted. Her smile is generous.

"Please sit." She points to the table. "I have only eggs, cheese, and bread."

"That sounds wonderful *and* filling," I say.

When the woman gets plates and serves the meal, Mother asks, "Do you have children?"

"Yes. One son. He's with Hungarian Intelligence."

My fork stalls over the food. Why would this couple help us when their son is on the side of the enemy?

"Why are you risking your lives to help Jews?" I ask.

"We believe war is one thing but eliminating whole groups of people is against God's teachings. We've helped gypsies, Catholic priests, Jews. And my son, he's had a change of heart. One of his jobs is to climb telephone poles and listen to Russian conversations, as well as what the Germans are saying. He now knows the horrors each army has perpetrated."

"Does he know what you do here?"

"He doesn't. Many a night he's visited while people waited in the tunnel below." She wipes her hands on her well-worn apron.

"God bless you," Mother says, her words full of emotion. I know she's thinking of István, recognizing a mother's love for a son.

The raw scrape of hunger leaves me as I eat. I didn't realize it, but I'd become light-headed, and now energy trickles back in.

"This is delicious," I say. "Probably the best food I've ever tasted."

"Hunger will do that." The woman laughs, a deep rumble. "I've earned the best cook label purely due to circumstances."

"You're being modest," Mother says. "I know what it takes to feed farmhands."

The woman smiles and then begins washing the pans. Getting rid of evidence, I suppose. She hangs them up from hooks on a rack suspended from the ceiling.

The interior of the cottage-style house comes into focus. Exposed wooden beams frame the inside walls and ceiling. A hutch with blue-patterned china sits to one side of the kitchen, and although rare, the kitchen has indoor plumbing. A framed photo of the Virgin Mary is on the wall next to a set of brass praying hands.

The meal is over too soon, and we thank her again and leave.

Ten minutes later, we're lying flat on our backs in the truck bed while the farmer and his wife load melons all around us. When finished, they've left only our faces uncovered.

The ride is bumpy at first until he reaches a wider highway. Mother and I don't speak because we would have to shout above the engine noises to hear each other. My mind plays through the instructions he gave us. He'll slowly circle round the back of the synagogue, and when he taps the roof three times, we're to hurry out and into the building.

His plan works. We see the temple towers, and he slows. Every muscle in my body is ready to spring. His taps come soon enough, and we push the melons aside and scramble over the sides of the truck bed and help each other out while it's still moving.

No more than twenty steps to the door, we race to it. It opens before we knock.

"I'm Rabbi Mor," a tall man with bushy eyebrows says. His body has worn thin and is bent. "Tell me of your journey," he adds. "I need to hear that HaShem has performed another miracle."

The inside of the synagogue is modest compared to Dohány, but then very few compare to its beauty. Right now, this building seems glorious, and this man is a savior. He leads us to the right side of the mechitzah divider and we sit in the pews. We share everything that has happened since the Arrow Cross broke into the safe house.

"And do you wish to return there?" the rabbi asks. "We are housing many here now and have room for more."

"We have children to watch over," I say. "Perhaps there is a safe time of day we can walk there."

"Nothing is safe. There is chaos in the streets. No one's in charge." He shakes his head. "We use a high-ranking police officer as an escort. He'll pretend he's arrested you but will walk you to your house."

"He can be trusted?" I ask. "We've heard of no policemen willing to help us."

"Deep down, he's sympathetic to our cause. It angers him to see any old troublemaker apply to the Arrow Cross, be awarded an armband and rifle, and take his place as a custodian of law and order."

"How soon can he do this?" I'm growing anxious and want to get back to Zofia and Jakub.

"Give him a few hours. He's often here by midday." With an open hand, he points to the temple's inner rooms. "You'll find all you need...to wash, and if you desire, a change of clothes. Please help yourselves to the donations."

We wash and change clothes, and Mother finds a flat pair of shoes. Her feet are swollen and bleeding from blisters that have formed and broken open.

We return to the pews and lean against each other, waiting for the escort. I'm surprised both of us fall asleep.

The rabbi gently shakes us awake. "Time to go."

A well-built policeman with eyes like flint, waits inside the grand wooden doors.

"I'll drive you part of the way, but people need to see me walking you at gunpoint in your neighborhood. The Arrow Cross has set up headquarters not far from your street."

That's not good news. We've already learned our Wallenberg safe house isn't so safe, but now the Arrow Cross is constantly nearby.

"We'll play the scared victims," Mother says.

For me, it won't take too much acting. If Arrow Cross members are on the street, what prevents them from shooting at us to *help* the police?

We've put our faith in strangers today. One more time is required.

Once he parks the car, we walk in front of him, and I make sure to avert my eyes as if ashamed every time we pass someone. A bicycle whirs by, and the rider curses as the tires crunch over broken glass. The streets are littered with paper wrappings, cigarette butts, and in places, broken concrete. The sanitation workers can't keep up with the debris in the main avenues, let alone on the side streets.

A cold breeze full of a stale-water scent lifts my hair as a line of perspiration trickles down my sides.

I count the steps up to the front door, waiting for everything to go wrong. But as soon as Iván Pór, the house supervisor, swings the door open, I burst into tears.

"You made it back!" He embraces us. "The children have been beside themselves. Do you need medical attention?" Words pour from him. He doesn't know what to ask or say first. "Where is your fiancé? Have more of you been released?"

I barely say the words, "We escaped," when the children come thumping down the stairs.

"Marika! Mema!" they shout before launching themselves at us.

I drop to my knees to meet their gazes.

"I told you we would come back." How close had I come to not keeping that promise? We hug more, unwilling to let go.

Zofia wipes the tears off my cheek. "It's a good day," she says in English.

I nod and smile, overwhelmed by my love for them. Now, to find Gellert and Father. Life will be complete when that happens.

I rise and turn to Mr. Pór. "Have many others returned?"

"Twelve before you and your mother. Wallenberg went to Brick Works with a hundred protective passes and saved those few."

Only twelve? Images of the dead in the field. Massacres on the roads. Imre and her twin aunts.

Guilt tries to consume me. We are so lucky to have made it back while thousands are still out there. "So many will perish if someone doesn't stop that forced march. Eight days with little to no food and water, and freezing to even below freezing temperatures? That's insane cruelty."

"Lutz and Wallenberg are irate. They're gathering supplies, more passes, and will head out as soon as they can."

At that moment, I decide to make a formal request to go with Wallenberg's convoy since he always has more vehicles at his disposal. Imre said she would take no government help, but her determination may have changed now. One of the women hopefully will have Mother's lilac scarf. In the sea of brown tweed or grey coats, the Szabós should be easy to spot. I pray that perhaps, while on this rescue mission, I can trade my nursing knowledge for their lives.

I secure a place in the rescue mission convoy that leaves November 10. My job is to treat those we save along the way. Wallenberg appears grim. Exhausted. Most likely, the man hasn't slept in days. He had to sign the papers individually he'll submit today to bring people back.

The volunteers gather at the Swedish Embassy. Peter is there, dressed in an Arrow Cross uniform. He has no news about Gellert or where the men were taken.

"Two of us came out looking for your family when we heard your house was raided. Went all the way to the front of the group. You must have already escaped."

"Thanks for looking. We slipped away. Late afternoon, the second day."

"And you want to go back out there?" His facial expression sours. "Reports are it's an awful sight."

"I need to help our neighbors. Or anyone. Just because I'm free doesn't mean I should celebrate. Those women on the trek may as well be my mother or my mema."

"I understand. I'll see you back at the Pannónia house later." His day involves following up on reports across Budapest. "We'll be bringing in more abandoned babies and children left after the roundup."

"How many people were taken away?"

"Rough guess…thirty thousand."

So, a distressing number of them will never return to their young ones. "Bring as many children as you can. Bandin is ten and is at our Yellow-Star flat. He should be with us."

"We're doing our best, Marika."

By evening, the rescue convoy is ready to go. Wallenberg leads in his black Studebaker. Behind him are three box trucks, fully loaded with medicine and food. They assigned me to a car at the rear with other doctors and nurses. Most of us are Jewish, and I recognize one nurse from my training years in the hospital. We don't try to catch up on what's happened in the last few years. No one has a good story to share.

It's a pitiful, unforgettable journey. The Studebaker's headlights pierce the darkness, and I witness soul-destroying suffering. We pass grey-faced children with bleeding feet tied with thin rags. Old men hold up their gaunt wives, but it's obvious many are near death.

The dead litter the roadsides, moved a meter or two away from where they fell.

"Why aren't we taking these children?" I ask, considering they warned us the young ones are top priority.

"Wallenberg knows the people farther on are in worse shape."

That would be my mother's and my group.

My stomach twists when we drive by the endless columns of people crying out for help. To make matters worse, the temperature drops well below freezing and flakes swirl from above.

Many, too tired to carry their belongings one more step, let them drop to the road. The possessions once deemed necessary are now trampled and scattered.

When we reach Gönyű, the fifth night for the marchers, we stop. The Arrow Cross packed hundreds onto steel barges anchored on the Danube. We enter the metal containers and try to put food in their outstretched hands, but many—much too exhausted—can't reach for it. I hear the faint drone of prayers I recognize as the Kaddish, coming from the masses, the unfortunates facing their last moments on Earth.

Outside the floating prisons, it's no better.

In the eerie stillness, random screams punctuate the frosty night air. A doctor investigates the cries. He returns ashen.

"People are jumping into the Danube, committing suicide. Some land on the drifting ice, but there's no way to reach them."

They couldn't stand the torture any longer.

We learn another group is ahead of this one, made to walk without rest. Eichmann purports it's meant for these Jews to work on building fortifications around Vienna—Stalin's next objective. But anyone aware of his goals can see this is his final push to eliminate as many Jews as he can. Being forced to cancel deportation trains infuriated him. His next best solution? Walking Jews to death.

We resume the drive westward, heading to the border. Faint pink and gold layers edge the horizon, presenting a sunrise that will bring the antithesis of renewal to so many.

These walkers are more dead than alive. They stagger forward under poking and prodding and blows from Arrow Cross rifle butts.

We stop in the road near the front of the group. Wallenberg sets up a table, opens his briefcase, and removes what he calls his black book of life. A register of protected Jews.

Anguish reddens his face as he shouts, his tone sorrowful, "I want to save you all, but they will only let me take a few and…and I must save the young ones first. Please forgive me."

As fast as humanly possible, he calls out our most common Jewish names and distributes replacement passes as young people are prodded forward by relatives who understand what is happening. The embassy told us most of these marchers never received an original Schutzpass, and names won't match all recipients.

I search the crowd for Imre, Eden, and Eunice. They should be here. Walking through the huddled masses, I see few people left with any hope. Their eyes dull, waiting for their bodies to give out. I shared their misery for over twenty-four hours and cannot fathom the utter hopelessness that must shroud them after four more days.

Men unload box trucks full of food. The lucky two to three hundred on the list for rescue climb aboard the emptied cargo compartments.

Wallenberg is calling out the last names when I spot the lilac-colored scarf around a woman's neck. I weave my way through the masses and touch her arm then turn her around.

Oh no. She's not one of the Szabó women. This woman is young and pregnant and may go into labor at any moment. She sways somewhat while trying to focus on my face. "Mama?"

Imre and her aunts most likely perished but passed the scarf along. My deepest fears for our friends may have come true. My heart cries out for forgiveness, for not trying harder to save them. Now, I'm committed to helping this woman.

"Come with me."

I lead her to Wallenberg's table. "You called out for Eliza Cohen, did you not?" I have no idea what her name is.

He hesitates for a second when he notices her delicate condition and realizes what I ask of him.

"Yes, here is her paperwork." He scribbles a name. "Thank you for finding her."

Two doctors help her climb into a truck.

Off to the side, the soldiers poke at people who have collapsed. They've arranged dead bodies into grotesque positions and take turns laughing and trying to best each other. How can they be so cruel, celebrating the painful death of another person?

Some guards avert their eyes, disgusted, yet don't dare stand up to the cruelest soldiers.

For me, there's no time for tears, but a steady hatred grows in me. Where are the biblical days when a good smite served evildoers their just desserts? I would feel *absolutely nothing*, watching the guards and Arrow Cross brutes zapped into spires of dust.

Gloom sets in as we leave thousands behind, knowing most will die. Even if some survive until they reach Hegyeshalom, they won't last a day forced into physical labor.

If I imagined the return trip to Budapest would be easier, it was more heartbreaking than on the drive out. Although we treat the injured in our cars with what medical supplies we have, I can't help but glance outside, heeding the desperate calls and pleas of our people.

We pass a group of men from the Bor Copper mines, looking nearly starved to death, and many are half-naked. They're all staggering. I search for Father's face in the group but thank God he's not there. To find him and watch him walk to his death would be too much.

We return through the villages where earlier, peasants laughed and mocked us marchers, especially the pretty Jewish women walking in heels in obvious pain.

Time and time again, Wallenberg stops. It's always the children he signals for when he does. We hop down and pull toddlers and babies from their dying mothers' scrawny arms. We must find homes or refuge for these innocents, but for now we load them inside like small sacks, leaving them screaming and crying, packed side by side on the car floor. We continue rescuing as many as possible until our convoy can hold no more.

Back at the safe house, I find Peter with fifteen children, including Bandin, who still has the chess set with him. I hate that shortly this child will know the pangs of death up close.

Peter lifts his eyebrows, a questioning expression I take to mean he's asking if we found the boy's relatives.

I shake my head, not knowing if they're dead. But what are the chances they will survive that vile ordeal?

I kneel before the boy. "Bandin. Your mother is so proud of you. And excited about the man you'll grow up to be."

"Where is she?" His voice sounds strained, and he appears younger, more vulnerable than I've ever seen him.

"She and your great-aunts are together, either in Austria or…in heaven."

Bandin's eyes fill with tears, but he doesn't break down sobbing. "I don't know how to get to Austria, so I hope it's heaven so I can see them again."

"And you will." I pull him into a hug, and he melts into me. "Remember, your mother loves you all the time, no matter where she is. She'll be there the first light of morning and blanket you all through the night."

Easy words for *me* to offer. My wonderful mother is across the room, soothing toddlers brought in from empty apartments.

If we lose the people we love in natural disasters—like Gellert's family in the earthquake—carrying on with our lives is tough enough. We accept there was no way to prevent it. What will haunt us now and into the future is when people we love are taken by immoral atrocities—a choice made, a preventable set of events—because someone kicked over hatred's first domino.

Now, the cascade of wooden pieces clicking against the next in line is proving unstoppable.

-28-

BUDAPEST, HUNGARY

November 19, 1944

I 've been unable to discover where they took Gellert after the Brick Works factory. In my imagined talks with him, I don't say, *I miss you.* I say, *You are missing from me.* I need him here to tell me everything will be okay. That the plans we made for our lives together are only delayed.

Only three other people eventually returned to the safe house after us, all younger than my mother. That leaves over one hundred from our house who thought they were protected, now either dead or in a horrible situation.

In the streets, the shootings continue. This time, Friedrich Born, the Swiss Red Cross chief, intervenes to save ninety elderly residents at the Old Peoples' Home on the corner of Városmajor and Alma Streets from being murdered by the Arrow Cross. This makes the second time in a week this has happened.

The Arrow Cross round up the youngest and the elderly, the most vulnerable, which shows their cowardice.

The gun remains in the train station locker, and I think about it every day. Would bringing it to the house help us if fifteen men came in with guns? One six-shot pistol against machine guns. Unlikely. But right now, even the safe houses are not protected if that's where the hordes decide to enter next.

The underground says Eichmann brags that the labor marches were a great success. He sent fifty thousand of us out of the city within three weeks, leaving one hundred seventy-five thousand hunkered down in Budapest. The underground also reports the Waffen-SS receiving the marchers are overwhelmed because the starved workers are too weak to lift a shovel, let alone dig a trench for ten hours.

The main highway from Budapest to the border was so cluttered with bodies that even hardened SS veterans were revolted and said this left a terrible impression on their request for workers. The Hungarian government received a few terse calls. In particular, Szálasi's office is now forbidding further deportations of this type, emphasizing *no more women and children*. He outright opposes the label "Death Marches," but it's too late. It's what the mass march to Austria is called by outside countries and inside saviors.

When Peter comes by, dressed in a Hungarian police uniform, he shares today's news.

"Get this. To show they're making an effort to keep the Jews safe, the Hungarian government is establishing what they are calling a *protected* ghetto covering twenty city blocks around the Dohány Synagogue."

"We would have been inside that perimeter if we'd stayed in the Yellow-Star flat run by the Gábors."

"Doesn't that all sound *so* nice? They want to keep us *safe*," Peter says sarcastically. "We calculated it out. This will cram about fourteen people in every room available in those buildings in that new area. They've begun building tall wooden fencing along the periphery streets."

"That area has mixed racial buildings too," I say. "Just like the Yellow-Star flat we left to come here, about half the Christian families didn't want to move."

"They've told the Christians to move out immediately or risk arrest. The government supplied them with a list of evacuated Jewish buildings they can move into."

"I wonder if anyone has taken our original apartment."

"Let me swing by there and check." He smiles. "I'll have to break out the green and black uniform in case Benedek is around."

"Please be careful. I'm sure Benedek knows you're not in his party by now." Then I get an idea. "Would you take a note to the Schlesingers?"

"Sure." His face darkens for a moment. "I forgot to tell you. I checked into that Dely woman. Piroska."

"I saw her marching some women away awhile back. She must add vinegar to her coffee to get her face properly adjusted each morning. What a bitter-looking woman."

He chuckles. "That woman's more than bitter-looking, she's bad news. She and her husband are divorced, and she lives on Dob Street with a German soldier. Witnesses say she may be the woman that led armed men into an apartment on Csengery Street the first night Szálasi took over."

"Really? What happened there?"

"It's an affluent area, as you know. It seems Piroska made a deal with the janitor that anything they stole from the tenants, he would receive a portion. She arrived wearing the Arrow Cross armband, and along with her German-soldier boyfriend, robbed the eighty-plus residents, leaving eighteen dead and seventy deported."

"What? Was she arrested?"

"No, but we're watching her. Seems this isn't her first robbery."

"I'm sure that wasn't her first murder either." She might have started her reign of terror on my family if we hadn't been forced to move out of our apartment and into the Yellow-Star flat.

"No telling what she's done, but stay away from her."

I'm not surprised by any part of that story. She and Belko were never like a real couple the few times she came to the bicycle shop. Those visits must have been to see her son.

I write a quick note to Raakel, telling her I miss her, but it's too dangerous for us to meet. "Here's my prayer that the New Year brings freedom, lunches, shopping, and love." I fold it and hand it to him. "Thank you, Peter."

"See you at number four Mérleg today?"

"I'll be there in about an hour." I tilt my head toward the living room. Bandin sits at a game table, setting up Father's chessboard. "First, a promised game of chess."

"How's he doing?"

"Like all of us, grief continues to trip us up in unexpected ways. It's unpredictable and so deceptive, isn't it?"

"After my family was rounded up, disbelief was my closest companion, until anger followed in its wake."

I quickly hug him. He's lost so much too.

"I tell myself that my family and Ariel walk with me each day. And you shouldn't think it's the end for your father and Gellert. We just don't know where they are."

"You're right. I'll stay positive. It's the only way."

When he leaves, I play several matches with Bandin. I used to let him win, but no longer. The boy has bested me more than once, even when I try my hardest.

"You're a champ at this, Bandin." Gently, I take him by the forearms. "And thank you for being a good friend to Zofia and Jakub. They really are glad you're here."

"Will I always live with you now?"

"I won't let you out of my sight."

Every day we make promises to these orphans, including Bandin, who most likely is now alone in the world since I never learned of an extended family outside of Budapest. I'm guilty of deferring future decisions about where the children will live after this war. They have so little and deserve days when they aren't in constant fear of being abandoned.

The few blocks surrounding our safe house are designated the International Ghetto, protected by both the Swiss and Swedish Embassies.

Every Jew must move into one of the two ghettos, so the stringent curfew is lifted to allow time to transfer. But after, Jews will not be allowed in the streets except between 10 a.m. and noon.

Now I have no idea how I'll keep volunteering when that happens. Mother is happy to remain at the house, especially since we have more children here now than adults, but I need to keep helping.

The spacious six-story building at 4 Mérleg Street is now a temporary asylum, especially for the masses of abandoned children whose parents were taken away by the Arrow Cross. And although we volunteers can still go out to pick them up, sometimes with police escort, a dozen or more are dropped in front of the gate every day like bags of refuse. They are dehydrated to the point of listlessness with swollen eyes, a few near death. How long had they lain in their cribs or on the floor, wailing for comfort? It all hurts to imagine.

The Red Cross also established a gathering and selecting office at 4 Perczel Mór Street. That's where we take the children to further place them among the different orphanages. I helped bring children there this past week with no end in sight.

Is it just luck that keeps me safe when I'm out on the streets? I've been with the group twice now and we've been stopped by the local police. They warn us that our protective papers may not keep us safe and once steered us around a roaming band of young thugs.

So yes, luck, but I'd like to think the hand of God steers those who serve his children.

Today, one of my trips takes me near the Mother House so I stop in. Sister Sára warmly greets me.

"How are you moving around on the streets, Marika, without fear of being grabbed by the Arrow Cross?"

I explain my theory of luck and divine intervention. "Also, I work for the Red Cross refugee department, mostly with the children, although I know the Arrow Cross isn't impressed with our safe passes." This woman who defies the Germans and their orders to shield Jews wonders how I am safe? "Like you. I can't stop helping."

"In Psalm Nine, it says, 'The Lord is a refuge for the oppressed, a stronghold in times of trouble.'" She clasps quivering hands around my right hand. "We are in those times, my child."

She's never expressed this level of fear before. "What am I to do?"

"Not everyone in the city is evil. Some don't want to be here any more than we want them here." She raises her right index finger. "I have someone to walk you home."

She disappears and then returns. I startle, seeing a young German soldier following her.

"This is Frederik. He loves Mozart, painting, and the Lord." She turns to him. "Frederik, this is Marika, a nurse who helps at the orphanages. She needs an escort."

"Hello," he says with a mellow German accent, "it will be my pleasure."

I give him the side-eye as I reach over to hug Sister Sára. "Stay safe and I'll see you at one of the orphanages."

"Each day I want you to recite this short request," she says. "God, help me rise to my feet...a fall is what I can do all by myself."

There's her upbeat disposition I've come to know. "I will."

We leave the convent. I study the soldier, trusting Sister Sára's assessment of his mindset and his character. He must be around my age, nineteen or twenty. His upper lip has blond fuzz, but his face is smooth. The boy has a polished air about him—someone suited to the arts. Perhaps even ballet as a dancer.

We walk a block before I thank him for the escort, then ask, "Do you need to pretend I'm your prisoner as we get closer to my house?"

He laughs. It's a merry sound. "We're in charge of this city, not those local boys playing army."

He must have his head in a prayer book not to see what's going on.

"I'm sorry to disagree. Have you not noticed the random shootings, numbering in the thousands?"

That puts a scowl on his baby face. His blond eyebrows try to meet in the middle of his bunched forehead.

"We're doing our best, but we have a war to fight on the plains. There are so few of us here. We've pleaded with the local police to step up and stop these killings. It's not right and not what our commanders want to leave behind as a legacy."

I scoff. The Germans believe they have any chance of redeeming themselves? I don't address his remark. This is a dangerous conversation. For both of us.

When we reach the safe house, he touches the brim of his hat. "My advice to you would be to gather food and store water. And don't leave your house until this war ends."

"When do you think that might be?"

"I pray for a Christmas miracle. I want to go to my parents, to our farm, to my studies." He flashes a smile. "For you, that will be a Hannukah miracle."

I watch him walk away. Why can't there be a thousand more like him? He can't be the only German with a conscience and desire to do the right thing.

But to stay in the house, hunkered down, for over a month? It sounds impossible.

Sister Sára didn't warn me to stay home. She gave me words to get back up. Now that I know one soldier and the policeman from the other day who will help, I will keep saving children. I must.

Inside the safe house, I help feed nineteen children and put some down for a nap.

Mother has been extra quiet, but we all rotate through waves of hope and despair like a weathervane in a shifting wind. She's holding a baby over her shoulder and patting the back of another on her lap.

"You always were a natural, Mother." I drop next to her on the sofa.

Her smile is forced. "You'll find being a mother is the easiest and hardest job you'll ever have."

I feign shock. "When were we ever hard?"

"Let's see. Anytime you two would go upstairs, it turned into tripping or pulling someone back down. You both seemed to have some unspoken rule that going up the stairs together meant you were racing."

"Okay, one thing we did." I smile at the memory.

"The time István told you we found you in the trash behind Dohány." She lifts her eyebrows. "It took weeks and a visit to the nurse who delivered you to convince you to believe us."

"That was all him!" I nudge her. "Did he even get punished for lying?"

"He got the black pepper treatment."

"Oooh. That happened to me too." I remember I lied about a candy, saying a neighbor bought it for me when I actually stole it from the market. "Sat for five minutes with black pepper on my tongue."

"Worked every time."

We're quiet for a few moments.

"I miss them terribly," Mother says. "I hate having my family divided like this, even though I know István's family is safe. And your father. We've never been apart for more than a week in our whole marriage." Tears slip from her eyes. "I'm lost without him, Marika."

My eyes burn with fresh tears. "I miss them all too." We've written letters, but now the mail isn't functioning, and we've heard nothing from Switzerland for weeks.

"Can you take this one?" Mother hands me the baby boy from her shoulder.

He can't be more than nine months old, still asleep. Poor darling was covered in a rash when he arrived, and like all the infants, had burns on his bottom and legs from staying in the same diaper for days.

I hold him under my chin and drop my nose onto his head. What is it about babies that makes us want to just breathe in their scent? I can't wait to have a brood of my own one day. Will they have my lighter features or favor Gellert with his darker coloring? I *must* keep the faith that Gellert will return.

"You looked sad earlier," I say. A beam of sunlight comes through the window, bathing my mother and the infant in soft gold tones.

She nods. "We had the radio on while making dinner."

"Oh dear. Now what?"

"The city published a new decree. Not only do all unprotected Jews need to go into the big ghetto, but they want the orphanages emptied into that awful place too."

"Peter just told me the buildings there will be overcrowded. Something like fourteen people per room. And it's such a small area they're fencing off. The mayor will need to extend it." I stick my finger in the tiny, curled hand on my chest. "Why can't they stay in this ghetto or in the orphanages? They aren't hurting anyone. Aren't costing the city money since the Red Cross or the churches support them."

"I don't know, but I can't imagine thirty thousand children added to that crowded space. Once the walls go up, no one can leave. Who will be able to take care of them when everyone there is starving, desperate for food?"

"And the sickness that's bound to spread with winter coming on." I now understand why she looked sad. "Nothing gets easier."

I repeat Sister Sára's prayer in my head.

Can we even make it through to the end? I worry that one day I may fall and forget how to get up.

~29~

Budapest, Hungary

November 28, 1944

Cold rain lashed across the empty avenues these past few days, and rarely does anyone dare leave their homes. But not me. I've volunteered the last nine days, carefully moving from rescue apartments to orphanages. Then the Jewish Council sent out a new warning today. The previous Arrow Cross goal was to drag Jews off for slave labor. Now they've resorted to a more straightforward solution, poking them in the direction of the Danube, and in a shooting orgy, mowing them all down. These daily executions have increased, and no one is stopping them. The warning? Stay inside.

The Arrow Cross is also plundering all the food the Swiss and Swedish embassies stored around the city. Most of their raids happen at night, on both warehouses and apartments.

Bombing continues over the city, with stray shells landing in residential areas and incinerating anyone who remained on the upper floors. The cellar in our house has benches, but we've brought down two mattresses to lay the children on if we end up spending the night.

Concerning all the orphans moving to the big ghetto and emptying orphanages, a man named Weyermann managed to get a six-day postponement and is now granted another six days. He hopes to keep the move from ever happening.

Five days ago, last Saturday, I was leaving the Glass House with forged papers, skirting the busy areas on my way home. The Margit Bridge was packed with automobiles, streetcars, and pedestrians—people traveling back and forth between Buda and Pest—when I heard a thunderous boom.

The bridge exploded. Three pillars on the bridge's Pest side blew apart, and the structure collapsed into the Danube. The river's chilly waters suddenly became an icy coffin for hundreds of civilians and over six hundred Hungarian soldiers. The Germans had set the explosives to use in the future in case the army needed to retreat to the Buda side of the river.

Was Peter on the bridge?

Recently, he's either been dressed as a Hungarian soldier or an Arrow Cross Party member traveling around the city, gaining information about the enemy. I'm trying not to worry, but I haven't heard from him since the bridge collapsed, and no one at the Glass House has seen him.

He's often gone for days but never this long. Between moments of too busy and much-needed rest, my anxiousness takes over. Then I remember how capable he is in every situation and push the worry away.

Some good news. The Red Cross seized a large file of Jewish names from an Arrow Cross building and stored them in Wallenberg's offices away from enemy eyes. The Arrow Cross used the lists to trick people. They'd find out where they were staying, arrive dressed as local police, and tell them a family member was headed to the hospital. Once lured into a waiting vehicle, they would disappear.

Today, I'm going to make a quick trip to a protected house on Váci Street, a hundred yards from the Danube, to bring back two girls. We have their sister staying with us. The children were separated after the mother sent them to a Christian friend's house before the Arrow Cross took her away for the Death March. The friend grew worried for her own safety and gave the children money and put them out, abandoning them to the streets. They scattered to separate public bomb shelters during a raid and lost track of each other.

Frederik is my escort again. We've worked out a messaging system when we need him. We tie a red ribbon to the gate in front of our house. The number of knots tied on the right side indicates an hour in the morning between nine and eleven when he should arrive. Knots tied on the left are afternoon times, one to five, always for the next day.

He was forced to enlist like so many these last months of the war. And he's not the youngest—some barely fifteen. His strong Calvinist family found everything about Hitler and his regime reprehensible. They protected Frederik from the fight for a year by offering his tailoring skills when troops came through their town traveling to Berlin.

You must look respectable for the high command when you arrive in Berlin, he told everyone. And it worked for a year, until March when the Germans decided to take Hungary.

He proved his tailoring skills here and has the luxury of moving about the city, delivering mended uniforms and suits, and he poses as an escort for the nuns and a few others.

It's the Germans' own fault their clothes are falling apart. Every quality tailor in the city was Jewish.

We hear shooting and then laughter when we draw near the river. Arrow Cross men stand along the banks among the piles of shoes from weeks of victims, and more men are below on the ice. They're arranging the dead bodies on the ice to form a Star of David.

Instantly dizzy, I grab a light pole to steady myself. This is the closest I've come to witnessing the shootings, although it's all the Jews can talk about. Who's next? How can this be right?

The ice is smeared red closer to the bank. Pink trails across the white ice reveal that some tried to crawl away.

The thugs on the ice have left, but they're still laughing as they climb the embankment.

Frederik pulls his pistol and fires it above their heads. "Get away from here!"

They stare him down, but the seven finally leave.

I'm relieved to see they'll listen to a German foot soldier. However, the Nazis under Eichmann are the opposite. We hear they accompany the Arrow Cross Party on raids when they're in the city, treating the trip like a chance to hone their hunting skills.

There is nothing worse than the sharp image of a horrible sight. A second ago, I sent a prayer skyward for the dead on the ice. Then I spot someone's leg move in the human-made Star of David.

"Look!" I point, directing Frederik's line of vision to the movement. "I have to go get her."

"If they come back, they'll shoot you," he warns, and turns his head side to side, taking in the people around us. Thank goodness, hardly anyone is around after hearing the gunfire. "I'll go."

Blood pounds in my ears while he slides down the embankment by holding on to bushes. Now I feel vulnerable, standing on the river's edge as if inviting someone to take a shot.

He crawls out to the scene of the fascists' grotesque arrangement and lifts a young girl off the ice, carefully carrying her back.

He slowly hauls her up the bank until I can reach her arms. I tug her the rest of the way, stumbling through the hundreds of shoes the previous victims were made to discard before dying. One of my nurse's shoes comes off in the scramble, but I have no time to search for it. This girl's skin is already bluish-white when I get her to flat ground and turn her over to assess her wound. Her eyes are open, but she's dead.

"Too late?" he asks, squatting down next to me.

Anger is like a flame blazing and consuming my self-control. I can't speak. This girl appears to be a young teen, and the bodies stiffening on the ice are most likely her family.

"I don't understand how they can shoot innocent people," I finally whisper.

"It's tragic. It comes from a stupid conviction that these gang members probably can't even articulate." He gently closes the girl's eyes. "My father taught us there is limited atonement available when men do evil."

"I'd like to believe there's zero chance of atoning for this." My bravery has come and gone in waves over the last ten minutes, but now I make a decision I'm confident with. "We can't leave her here. I'm taking her to the Dohány Synagogue where she'll receive a righteous burial."

I reach to lift her but realize I can't carry her. Frederik is a guard, not a Jew-enabler, so he can't be seen holding her up here in the open. And I can tell by his expression, he realizes this too.

"I'll get a cart," he says. "The restaurants around here should have one."

He leaves, walking fast but not so quick as to draw attention to himself.

I sit with the girl, brush her hair off her forehead. "You didn't deserve this." My throat is tight. "You should have had a first kiss, fallen in love, built a life with someone amazing."

My mind jumps to Gellert. *Where is he?* Am I doomed to go on without him?

Shots ring out in the distance. It's never-ending now, but worse at night.

My stocking foot is wet and cold, but I welcome the pain it creates. I've not suffered at all compared to this young girl.

A prickling rises across the back of my neck, and I soon conclude someone is watching me.

I stand and turn.

Piroska Dely. Dressed in an Arrow Cross uniform with a pistol on her hip.

"Leave the girl," she says. The woman, far from ever looking feminine, is more manly than ever.

"I'm taking her." Who was this woman speaking so bravely into the face of danger? I've seen glimpses of her over the last few weeks, but it's as if I don't care anymore. "At least one person deserves a proper burial."

She snorts but doesn't speak.

"How do you justify what you've been doing? Killing at random? In war, men take a life in self-defense. But not you. Or the fascist group you've joined." I may be pushing her too hard. Her face reddens, but I refuse to stop. "Don't you think you'll answer for this one day?"

"Jews are an abomination." She moves her hand, resting it on the handle of her gun. "And just who do you think will care once the war is over?"

"Men of good character. War tribunals."

"We will be lauded for what we've accomplished in Hungary." She drops her gaze to the dead girl. "Go ahead and move her. All these bodies are plugging up the river anyway. Before the river started freezing over, my son had the hardest time at work. Could hardly navigate the tugboat through all the floating *refuse* on some days."

She is repulsive.

"Speaking of men of good character, I have two stories for you. The German boy who dared to help you just now won't be back. I may have shot him on the next street over." Her smile is wide. Her eyes gleam. "Breaking the rules of war. Aiding and abetting the enemy…*tsk-tsk*."

A sour taste hits the back of my throat. Poor Frederik! Kind, with a single desire—to treat others well and return home. It takes all I can muster to reply.

"You are incapable of recognizing good character." I wait to be killed. And maybe that would be all right. Because of me, Frederik is dead.

Her eyes bore into me. "And the second story. I think you'll like it even better since I see no reason to kill you once you hear it."

My legs shake. Is it Peter? She and Benedek may know of his involvement with the underground by now. Is that why he's missing?

"What have you done?" My tone is nearly a growl.

"I just saw Benedek. He was going to investigate the noises coming from upstairs in your apartment." She smooths her black skirt. Or is she nervous and drying her palms?

Oh no. I sent Peter to the building with a message for Raakel. And I asked that he check to see if anyone lived in our apartment. Dread fills me. My vision wavers then returns to pinpoint clarity. I don't want her to speak, to say the words that will make me sink into even more guilt.

But the evil woman continues.

"Of course, an intruder would be breaking the law, and Benedek would have no choice but to kill that person."

Forgetting all sense of danger and my desire to help the dead girl, I take off running with no shots fired but only her rusty laugh at my back. Our apartment is several districts away, and I'm weak from too little sleep and less than adequate food. I pray for protection and the strength to keep going, but several times I stumble and grab onto building edges and railings to stay upright. I beg God, something we should never do, that I'm not too late. Peter can defend himself but not if he is taken by surprise.

Benedek is running from the building, going in the other direction.

I pull myself up the stairs, my lungs burning. What has Benedek done?

The door to our apartment is closed, but I burst inside and stall in my tracks.

I'm too late.

I don't have to look too far before agony rips through me.

It's Gellert! He lies on his back in the hallway, in front of Father's workroom. He's moaning as I reach his side and drop down next to him. I lift his head to my lap. "Darling," I gulp, seeing the enormous chest wound and the amount of blood soaking his shirt. "Stay with me."

He doesn't open his eyes. His lips move, but he has no voice behind whatever he's trying to say.

I try to decipher his words as his body stiffens then sags. Blood flows from his mouth, and I realize in horror his chest no longer rises. He can't be gone!

"No, no, no…" I say, weeping as I rock back and forth, gently touching his face and hair. Why did he come here and not to the safe house in the International Ghetto?

God? Where are you? Where was I? Gellert didn't deserve this. Benedek! He's wanted to kill Gellert from the very beginning. Did he lure him here somehow?

My beautiful Gellert. The war broke him, but he bounced back. He was healed, ready to heal others once the madness ended. Now he's gone. Forever.

The harsh reality hits me, and darkness overtakes my exhausted mind until I tumble into complete oblivion.

$-30-$

BUDAPEST, HUNGARY

December 10, 1944

During the day, the mere act of surviving takes so much energy that sometimes memories of those I miss are just background noise beneath the unceasing panic. Often, I imagine a reunion where I turn a corner, and Gellert is there, his upbeat personality winning over my sadness once again. In the worst of times, the sad truth is life takes on a heartbeat of its own, and the days blur into one another. I do nothing but collect days, but for what purpose?

After I left our apartment that day, I tried to find János to help me get Gellert out. Their apartment door was open, and they weren't there, but the inside looked like a scuffle had taken place. So absolutely broken by Gellert's death, my mind hardly registered that they must be in trouble. I barely made it home, almost unable to walk the distance. The dead girl's body remained where I left her, and although unavoidable, I am still guilt-ridden about it. Most likely, she ended up back in the river. At the time, I wasn't thinking straight and only knew I needed to get to the safe house, to my mother. Once home, we wept for hours.

Mother loved Gellert like a son. After his parents died, he reached out to her, and she gladly stepped in as a second mother. I haven't told the children yet. They believe he's still missing.

During a bombing raid that evening, four young men recommended by our rabbi agreed to cross town and remove him from our apartment and bury him in the Salgótarján Street Jewish Cemetery. His grave will remain unmarked for now. I couldn't go because Mother nearly lost her mind and begged me to stay inside, crying that she couldn't lose another person.

We pray over our ruined Bible, remembering Gellert's commitment to helping others, how alive he made a person feel, his love, patience. He would have made a great doctor and a fantastic husband and father.

I dream about him at night and remember our times together during the day. But losing the person who can share those memories worries me that I'll eventually lose the memories themselves.

Over the weeks, I learned where he'd been after they took him from Brick Works. Gellert and other laborers dug trenches and cleared rubble the weeks he was gone. Eichmann convinced the Szálasi government to let him send a thousand laborers to build defenses around Vienna. Because all new forced marches were forbidden, Eichmann found a free train he was in the process of loading when Wallenberg arrived. Wallenberg rescued him and eighty others from the Józsefváros railway station with protective documents. Gellert received a pass while nine hundred were deported.

Gellert may have gone to the apartment because he needed a hiding place, and it was closest to the train station. Maybe he sought the Schlesingers' help. But there is no one to ask, and it doesn't matter in the end.

And we fear the worst has happened to Raakel and her parents. The men who went back for Gellert said their apartment was still empty. But Belko Dely came out to say he was acting as the new janitor since the Schlesingers were taken away.

Taken away means imprisoned or killed.

So much loss hurts right down to my hair roots. Every fiber in my body is inflamed with agony. And I've learned grief and love are conjoined. My mother and the children are my focus, but I move through daily activities like a stranger, new to an unexplored world. The routines are familiar, yet how I perform them is foreign.

The ghetto between Wesselényi and Dob is sealed off and called the Central ghetto. Although both the Swiss and Swedish Red Cross fought the forced resettlement of all orphans there, they lost the fight, and the small innocent ones are moved into the area full of squalor and despair.

Of course, total safety in the streets was not expected. Still, I decide to volunteer in the new hospital set up inside the walled Central ghetto. Am I testing the grim reaper? Daring him to take me next? I simply know I need to keep helping everyone I can, pretending Gellert is by my side.

The Central ghetto area is in the old Jewish Quarter, encompassing the two main synagogues of the city—the Dohány Street and Orthodox Kazinczy Street synagogues. Stone walls or high fencing reinforced with wooden planks surround the designated blocks. Police guard the four gates to prevent people from sneaking food or weapons into the complex or people getting out.

Seventy thousand Jews are packed into a quarter square kilometer zone, now with sometimes twenty to thirty people in a room or dank basement. Understandably, within days, dire living conditions threaten everyone inside.

But the leaders of the Arrow Cross Party aren't happy. They want every last Jew, protected or not, inside that ghetto, and they still hunt those who've chosen to hide in cellars and abandoned buildings.

I walk through Klauzál Square, dressed in a nurse uniform, passing empty suitcases strewn about. The Arrow Cross stopped everyone when the Jews were first forced to move inside the walled area. As they passed through the square, the rogues demanded all valuables they may still have.

As if this miserable year hadn't brought enough hardship our way, winter comes early and with brute force. Frozen bodies of those who disobeyed handing over their last possessions are stacked like logs off to one side. They are bound together, forming solid inseparable blocks of ice that only a thaw will loosen.

The only positive, and it's a tiny one compared to the suffering, is that the bitter cold helps eliminate the real danger of cholera or typhoid outbreaks and reduces the urgency for quick burials.

I show my Red Cross papers to a city policeman at the gate, allowing me to work in the hospital. He opens the gate for me.

A young boy yells at me, "Trying to help the kikes? You dirty Jew-lover!"

I walk on in my dress shoes, the shiny leather now ruined. My feet hurt every day since I no longer have my nurse's shoes, but I refuse to stop walking. Of course, I have no choice—all transportation is either not working or off-limits. My protective papers are just that—protection from deportation. They no longer allow me the non-Jewish privilege of city transportation. Today I surmise my almost-Aryan features and a simple nurse uniform are why I receive these epithets from the child.

Without armed guards inside the ghetto, I hear that some SS soldiers and fascists have seized the expected Red Cross trucks on their way here. They're stealing the meager food allotment meant for prisoners, increasing the death count without firing a shot.

Our makeshift hospital is already over capacity once I arrive today. With so many patients and inadequate supplies, infection is rampant. They take the deceased outdoors and quickly perform temporary burials in bomb craters.

I brought fresh bandages from our central warehouse. On my last visit, we had to take them off dead bodies and try to sanitize them to reuse on new patients. Many had survived beatings or gunshot wounds. These are the hardest for me. If Gellert had been shot in a less vital area, he might have lived.

"This permanent stink gets to me," a woman beside me says.

Gyula is a doctor who is fastidious and never shows signs of tiring.

"We have to provide sanitary conditions but without enough water—"

"Or disinfectant," she adds.

Dirty water runs under the ice along the gutters, and the snow barely covers the garbage, dead rats, feces, and urine on every street. Orphan children roam through this filth, dirty and scared. Many people took in infants, but with massive overcrowding, older children are not welcomed since thousands of adults never found rooms to live in themselves. People lie curled in doorways or alleys. An unfortunate number are dead, simply left to be picked up later by the collection brigades and buried in massive pits in one of our parks or the garden behind the Great Synagogue.

There's no time for identification, so a short prayer ritual is offered.

On display inside this walled ghetto is all the misery, poverty, and suffering without much mercy. Everyone's worn down to the point of having so little to offer.

Disease is our biggest issue at the hospital. Currently, smallpox is besting us, chasing after patients before we can separate them from the others. Lice and dysentery are nearly unstoppable.

Surprisingly, many people pretend life hasn't changed for the worse. The sidewalks are lined with individuals trying to sell all kinds of useless merchandise, remnants from a distant yet normal life. Books, embroidered pillowcases, hats, even the rare typewriter or violin. Crowds fill the street during sunny days. Even the cold winds don't prevent citizens from leaving their packed rooms to walk along the ramshackle tables. No one has money, but perhaps acting as if this is an ordinary shopping day helps ward off the cold hard facts of their situation.

An elderly man arrives with a pushcart. His wife is slumped inside, her arms hanging off its sides like a life-size doll.

"She fell over after we woke up. Caught a bad cough first night we were stuck outside before we found a room."

"We'll take care of her," I say. The fear in his eyes tells me he's afraid to leave her. "You can wait inside for her."

"If she passes, I want to be there." His voice is reduced to a squeak as it fills with emotion.

I understand that. As futile as it was, I'm glad I held Gellert in the end. He knew I was there.

I squeeze the man's bony shoulder. "I'll do that." By the looks of his wife, I'm sure I'll be right back to get him.

I work long days and try to wall myself in from the increasingly gruesome updates, but some get through. The Arrow Cross must have decided nothing is off-limits and broke into the Sacred Heart Church. They terrorized the nuns until a Vatican diplomat, Monsignor Rotta, arrived to stop the death threat. The nuns added their own names to the fifteen thousand baptismal certificates that offer Vatican protection in hopes of staying safe.

Today, the story a doctor tells piles on another layer of pain and sets me on another step on the path to losing my mind. How can we bear so much loss?

He said Arrow Cross men broke into the orphanage where we took the twenty-six children we saved from deportation that day at the Kistarcsa camp. They killed everyone inside, roughly one hundred twenty—including the boy Neci I promised would be safe—by either shooting or bludgeoning them.

We also promised the parents we were doing the right thing by getting the children into safe houses in Budapest. They would be safe even while the adults were shipped to their deaths. May God welcome their tiny souls into his embrace.

The fight in the city is for the children as one side tries to save them, and the other wants to annihilate them all.

There are times when I understand why so many wanted to end their lives. But then I think of Mother, my brother's family I long to see again, and Zofia, Jakub, and Bandin. How could I do this to them?

Thankfully, more food makes it past the front gates while I'm here, and I volunteer to help distribute it to those too sick to leave their rooms. I enter an apartment building where the hallways are dim, but its courtyard is filled with skinny children. They all eye me with suspicion. The entire place has such a dismal atmosphere. Perspiration and other odors thicken the air. I go into apartments, every inch of which is used. It's hard to move around. Residents sit or stand everywhere and must sleep side by side on the floor.

These were educated middle-class Jews who after only three weeks of ghetto confinement are living in unbearable conditions. We always thought such living conditions existed only in the most primitive villages. Stripped of all civility, what remains for these people is the struggle for their most basic subsistence.

Mother and the children will be worried if I don't return soon. The afternoon sky is brittle blue, and the air freezes my nose. I wait at the gate to be let out as a group of soldiers ignore me, talking with great excitement.

"...ten kilometers north of the city, just this morning," a German soldier says.

General Otto Winkelmann ordered his Waffen-SS to protect the gates. He's worried about what will happen to him after the war if seventy thousand more Jews are killed by the Arrow Cross under his command. Only a few dozen men are assigned this task while others try to hold off the Russians.

"We have sixty thousand fighters out there," another guard says. "Some small Russian squad won't last long."

I move a step closer. Is this the news we've prayed for? The Russians are nearby?

"It's their full army combined with the Romanian troops that broke through to the Danube," the first guard says. "I may not stick around to welcome them here."

I clear my throat, and they startle and step aside so I can leave.

I don't walk far, trying to sort my emotions. Am I elated or scared? I decide both. Gellert witnessed the Russian soldiers' brutality firsthand. He often warned us we must leave before they get here.

There's no escape for us now that they're so close.

Suddenly, I'm hopeful. It's only after we've lost almost everything that we're free to do *anything*. Bravery roars inside me. I *will* protect Mother and Zofia from the Russians' disgusting actions if it comes to that.

I head to the Józsefváros railway station.

It's time to get the gun.

-31-

BUDAPEST HUNGARY

December 24, 1944

"I'm going out to try to find food and batteries," Mother says while we wash dishes after our meager breakfast of a thin soup and hard biscuits. We don't complain. We still have some peas and beans, and at times can top it with tomato puree. However, the children need more. And when the lights go out, which is a few times a week, we still have a box of tallow candles to provide some illumination. Our hand torches give off a less eerie light but need batteries.

Like so many, we sit in the cold and dark, wasting away, eating dried fruit and vegetables.

"There's no safe place on the streets…even getting to the shops we're allowed in." I wipe the table. "When I went by the Glass House, I learned they're also low on food and basic supplies. 'Course there are a few hundred packed in there now, sleeping in the cellar and corners."

"Any word from Peter?"

I shake my head. "Someone said he was picked up and may have been taken to work behind Russian lines." The three strong men in our lives are gone—Father, Gellert, and most likely Peter.

"I'm sorry to hear that." Mother picks up a baby from an open kitchen drawer. It's padded with a quilt and works as a cradle while we cook. "You said Eichmann left again. This has to be a good sign that the Germans know they are about done here."

"Maybe not. Eichmann made the Arrow Cross Party promise to fulfill his dream of killing us all."

Before he packed up and flew out of the city, he achieved one last "Death March." They sent twelve hundred Jews held in detention barracks near Teleki Square to Austria, with no hope of surviving the frigid weather. He told the fascist party that if they want to be effective, they need to ignore the demands of neutral diplomats and do what they want.

And they have.

The new party activists, the most uneducated and greedy, are obliged to take part in tortures and executions to test their loyalty. Then they're set free.

In his black cassock and carrying a giant crucifix and snub-nosed revolver, Father András Kun leads teen groups. By his admission, he's personally *liberated* more than five hundred Jews who refused to convert in years past. He orders his followers to line up Jews on the banks of the Danube. As they take aim, he cries out, "In the holy name of Jesus, fire!"

Lutz and Wallenberg remain in the city. Other neutral countries evacuated their ambassadors to keep them safe before the coming battle, with the people of Budapest caught in the middle.

"I know the back streets and tunnels better than you, Mother." We *are* down to a limited food selection, and I remember our canned goods in the apartment. "On the way back from the Central ghetto, I'll go by our place and grab what I can."

I want to avoid seeing Gellert's spilled blood on the floor again, so I won't go upstairs. Most of the canning is in the cellar if not eaten or taken.

"Please take the gun," she says. Worry lines have deepened around her eyes. We've all aged years in these past months.

And we had a surprise. At the bottom of the bag with the gun, Father left instructions and rail passes on how to get to Romania and seek passage on one of the rescue ships. We've talked it over and decided this was too risky now that we're watched so closely. And if Father had thought it was safe, he would have gotten us out earlier when there was still a chance. I remember when he said a rescue ship was torpedoed and sunk. That must have changed his mind about moving us in that direction.

"I have it and it's loaded." I wear the gun wrapped across my stomach, barrel down. They search my bags and coat, coming and going to the ghetto, but no one thinks to pat me down. At least not yet.

Rockets light the grey skies with streaks of fire and explosions. Shellfire is continuous now, and at night, searchlights crisscross the city. The acrid smoke seeps through the window and door cracks and burns our eyes and throats.

I leave and avoid the grotesque characters roaming the streets, plastering their posters everywhere, warning they will shoot anyone caught helping Jews. Horse carcasses lay bloated on nearly every street, killed during the bombing and frozen in place. Today, I count fifty-three dead citizens left along gutters or piled in alleyways like garbage.

The Danube embankment is still the right-wing groups' favorite kill-spot, where they slaughter hundreds a day. Then they dump the bodies in the river, and with a recent thaw of the ice blocks, their remains float away.

I entered the ghetto several times in recent weeks, encountering ever-worsening conditions. The piles of dead bodies grow higher. The barely alive women, children, and old men, too weak from hunger to move, stare straight ahead. The hollows in their cheeks expand and deepen every passing day. The Young Zionists and Red Cross are doing their best to get relief inside the walls—there are just too many people to feed.

Like myself, the hospital staff is discouraged. How long can seventy thousand people hang on until the ghetto opens and they can return home?

I finish a shift and head to our old apartment. What if I bump into Benedek? I've had to push away thoughts of killing him or wanting him to die by a Russian gun, or maybe after the war, hanged for his crimes. Because what if there is no punishment? According to anti-Jewish laws, Gellert was in the wrong, not confined to a Yellow-Star house or safe house. But I know this was Benedek's way of exacting revenge because I showed him no interest in a relationship. This was his chance to hurt me the best way he could.

Anticipation as I approach our house has a way of distorting moments, somehow inflating them. I'm moving in slow motion, or my mind is toying with me. My heart pounds so hard in my chest I fear people on the other side of town will hear it.

The gate is unlocked, and I quickly scoot inside the entryway. There are no lights on in the Schlesinger apartment. I had hoped the story that they were taken away was false, but I know deep down they've died because they helped us.

I say a silent prayer for them.

No sound comes from the other side of the hallway as well. If I never see Benedek or his mother again, it will be a blessing. It's just as easy to hate them from afar.

Once in the basement, I grab a small suitcase and load jars of pickles and beets. There's not much left. Behind the jars, Mother always kept our smoked sausage in a long wooden box. To my surprise, no one discovered it. I pack the remaining two eighteen-centimeter lengths around the jars and snap the suitcase closed.

I am so tempted to climb the stairs to our apartment but can't make my feet go in that direction. Then I hear someone coming down. I hurry out the front door and duck in an alley, waiting for my breathing to return to normal. It may have been our Christian neighbors leaving the building, but there's no way to trust anyone.

I navigate the tunnels and back streets as I return to the safe house.

Dinner is like a special occasion with meat for the first time in weeks. From what I can see, Iván, the house supervisor, seems happier than usual. Once the older children are set up with a hastily improvised checkers game made from stones, and the babies given rattles and teething toys, Iván takes Mother and me aside.

"I was taking trash out when an SS soldier stopped me," Iván says.

"Oh dear." Mother bites her bottom lip. "What did he want?"

"They're putting a machine gun on the balcony at the end of our street and several others to help protect the houses in this area."

"Seriously?" I ask. "All of a sudden they want to keep us safe?"

He laughs. "My thoughts as well. They're trying to honor the international laws."

"Sure, now that the international diplomats have left and are most likely reporting the atrocities that have transpired here," I say.

"Deathbed forgiveness," Mother says. "They're hoping for amnesty at the end of the day."

"The Germans are saying they need better laws in the city, or they won't be able to defend Budapest with all the internal Arrow Cross chaos." He picks at a stain on his dark trousers. "And the Day of Judgment might be closer than they think. I hear the Russians have managed to close a ring around Budapest. Sixty thousand German soldiers are stuck in the city proper with all of us now. The fighting won't be overhead any longer. It'll be in our streets, and possibly house to house, room to room."

Will my handgun with a few dozen bullets even matter if the Germans have machine guns ready to open fire? The Russians must have the same. "We must be prepared to take all the children to the basement and lock ourselves in if they take this house."

"I'm way ahead of you," Iván says. "I've broken open the old door down there. Behind it leads to the next house over, but we can barricade ourselves in the hallway in between."

The thought of huddling in the dark for who knows how long, trying to keep children and babies calm, worries me.

"Let's hope it doesn't come to that," I say. "We can move everyone to another safe house if we have to."

"The SS officer I talked to said he and his soldiers never thought they'd be fighting a war within a war." He raises his hands as if to say *Dummkopf.* "What did they think would happen when they let the fascists run wild for weeks?"

"The leaders created chaos and now are running through a maze, trying to stomp down the murderers they let loose," I say.

And because they never stopped the killings, Gellert is gone. My heart twitches with an aching loss so raw it makes me wonder what the point will be to go on when this is over. I shake away the feelings. How selfish. I have children to care for, and most of my family is still here. We have food and are not suffering like so many.

I wasn't prepared though. When Gellert died, I didn't just lose him all at once. I lost him in bits over time. His scent faded from his pillow, and his shaving brush dried and no longer carried his shaving crème's wet spicy scent.

I still talk to him in my head.

Death ends a life, not a relationship. He always was a good listener. I miss his responses, but I think I know what he would say after over three years together.

"You're the strongest woman I know, Marika."

And I've replayed his final words and realized he said, "Be Happy."

I'm not sure that will ever happen.

-32-

BUDAPEST, HUNGARY

January 4, 1945

The fight for the city began Christmas Eve and hasn't let up. Every evening, the sky gleams in red and purple shades over the capital. The thud of shots and clatter of machine guns mingle with the muffled rumbling of aircraft circling over Budapest.

The twenty-six of us often cower in the basement, not ready just yet to barricade ourselves behind the old wooden door. Mattresses or quilts cover every centimeter of the floor. We play word games, try to make up funny dance moves, or Mother leads the nineteen children in Hungarian folk songs. The words in unison appear to soothe the youngest of the group. Perhaps it's the comfort of unity they pick up on. Although forced at times, cheerfulness calms us even as we flinch at the echoing, ear-splitting blasts on the streets.

But we appreciate the blessing of whatever brief moments of happiness we're given. We hear news tidbits from the resistance workers as they check on all the safe houses. It is enough to doubt a God in Heaven. Yet, in our hearts, we know better.

The orphanage we worked in on Munkácsy Mihály Street was invaded by the Arrow Cross even though it was guarded by the military. They fired their guns around, killing about twelve children and some adults. They justified their actions, claiming children tried to defend themselves. The faces of the children I fed and played with there flash through my mind. Which ones are gone forever? The terror they must have experienced at the end knifes through me.

On New Year's Eve, the hooligans broke into the Glass House, anxious to finally drag out some of the two thousand Jews hiding inside with forged protection papers. They succeeded in killing Artúr Weiss, the kind owner who turned his building over to help save so many. And Ottó Komoly, the Jewish organizer of the rescue activities and the man who gave me forms for the Kasztner train. The Danube was their grave.

Peter wasn't there because no one has heard from him.

I've become numb inside after losing Gellert, Raakel and her family, and most likely Father and Peter. It's too much.

But the most shocking of all atrocities happened before the break-in at the Glass House. On December 27, rabid members of the Arrow Cross Party surrounded one of the convents Sister Sára ran and arrested the Jewish women sheltered there, along with Christian volunteers. Sister Sára arrived during the raid. She identified herself as director of the house and demanded they all leave. They arrested her immediately and took her with the other women to the banks of the Danube. They were forced to strip naked and were tied together to children rounded up from an orphanage. Only the women were shot, but as they tumbled into the black waters, they pulled the children to their deaths.

Sister Sára would have gladly martyred herself to save everyone else, but to be unable to prevent the deaths of the children and others will surely haunt her through eternity.

There is no hell hot enough for these monsters.

And we learned today, the Arrow Cross seek the houses they were told are off-limits—the protected houses in the International Ghetto. On Andrássy Street, not that far from us, they marched nearly two hundred protected Jews to the Danube.

Szálasi orders the International Ghetto closed by tomorrow, and we're all to move—twenty to thirty thousand of us—by police guard into the Central ghetto.

Bombing now comes from both sides of the river. The buildings along the waterfront are nearly all in rubble and no one dares venture out. A police guard will provide nothing in the way of protection as we are forced to move once again.

The poor souls still trapped in the Central ghetto suffer from acute starvation. Hundreds die a day. Nearly all Red Cross food transports are blocked by the Arrow Cross. They've also resorted to climbing the barrier wall and shooting inside until driven away by the SS guarding the four gates.

We're not moving to the big ghetto. I won't put mother and these children through that. We've plotted the entire day about where we can safely take the nineteen children and seven adults who survived the death march.

With most of the city's residents living in tunnels and basements, we know some upper apartments are empty. Even if we need to keep moving from one to another, we believe it's only a matter of days that we need to stay out of the occupants' way. The Germans can't hold the city much longer.

We choose streets away from the river and then identify houses the Zionists know are partially vacant where no janitor would turn us in.

Our apartment sits along this area.

Mother turns my way as I change a diaper on a skinny baby boy. "Are you thinking what I'm thinking? We can barricade the door with furniture and do our best to stay quiet. Do you think you could return there again?"

I've said goodbye to Gellert, but perhaps his spirit waits there. "I want to go back. And it's still not occupied. Also, I'm not sure the Delys are even in the building now."

"That would be helpful," she says. "We'll be five with Bandin, Zofia, and Jakub. But should we take more?"

"Without a doubt, if they don't find a place."

An hour later, it's settled. The remaining sixteen children are divided into groups of three and four and assigned to five adults in five buildings.

The Red Cross paid two local policemen to escort each group, one at a time, to our new hiding places.

We take the children aside. "We're going back to our own apartment building." It wasn't a familiar home to the children, but they're excited because we are. The constant moving and reorientation to a new situation have affected them. More headaches, skin sores from picking at nothing but still sensing an irritation there, and sleep problems.

I'm not sleeping much either. Gellert's final moments haunt my dreams. In those, he reaches for me or asks for my help, and I remain stuck in place, never able to help him as he dies.

"Pack your things." That's almost silly for me to say since we have so few belongings left. Father's chessboard is still with us, and our Bible and our clothes fit in one suitcase.

As soon as I can, I'll go to our Yellow-Star flat to retrieve the old puppet and shofar.

The two men assigned to us are young but not in their late teens like Frederik was. One day his death will come back to knock on my conscience because he'd still be alive if I hadn't asked for his help. I don't want to be, but right now, I'm only reserving love and heartache for those closest to me.

Out on the streets, I take note of the clouds adorning the sky, a bunchy blanket of white and grey. In sad contrast, the view of the ground is catastrophic. We weave around piles of stone, the dead, and sewer water. Blown-apart houses expose the inner workings of tangled pipes, drooping wires, and visible rooms with their walls peeled back, like enormous dollhouses for all to see.

"Are we going to die like them?" Bandin asks.

It's impossible to avoid the stacks of bodies, mainly carried to the parks and open squares.

"We're not," I say and pull him closer. "We're going to be safe."

The streets are eerie without the constant tram noise. They've stopped to save power.

"Wallenberg and Lutz have ordered over a hundred of us to guard the big ghetto," one young soldier says. "Are you sure you don't want to go there?"

"We're sure," I say. He's obviously never been inside to experience the slow decay of humanity.

"The actual leaders of the Arrow Cross have fled," the other soldier says. "The worst elements of that group have taken over and are listening to no one."

"I would say the worst elements have been running the show since October," Mother says.

"Regretfully, yes," the first soldier says.

We move from the safety of one building's edge to another and cross the streets behind quickly erected barricades.

We finally reach our apartment and hurry inside the unlocked gate. The familiar scent of home reaches me—for sure every home holds its cooking and laundry scents within.

"I can't believe they're gone," Mother says as we pass the Schlesingers' door.

"I know. Their kindness to us…" I start. "I feel so guilty."

"As do I." Mother shakes her head. "As do I."

We climb the stairs and enter our apartment. The five rooms seem beyond spacious, and in a flash, the children quickly take off exploring.

Like a puppet hung from irregular string lengths, my legs feel disjointed as I move inside the room. Gellert's blood stains the blue-and-gold-patterned hallway runner in front of Father's workroom. I stare at it, the last place he existed. Why are the dead more present in our lives than the living? My image of him as lifeless is too unbelievable, even in my dreams.

Mother unlocks Father's workroom, and for a brief moment, I expect to see him at his workbench, tapping on a puppet with his tiny tools. We'd say, *"So this is where you've been!"*

The air inside is stale. The workspace *feels* abandoned.

The puppet heads stare at nothing, perhaps trying to understand their demise. They will never be attached to a body, never live to dance at the whim of a theatre master.

And the same goes for half a million Hungarian Jews. The music has ended.

Over the next few days, we roll the hallway runner up and drag it out behind the apartment. Then we transfer the rest of our food from the cellar and barricade the door with the couch. We keep the lights off but light a small candle at night and sleep in the room that overlooks the garden.

Two Christian families remain on the second floor. Although they said they are afraid to offer us protection should we need it, they've also let us know they won't tell anyone we're here.

Thankfully the Dely apartment is quiet. They must have moved into any one of the confiscated houses in a nicer neighborhood. That's a relief.

The children know we never speak above a whisper, and they can't run or jump. The wonderful tradeoff is we need to be next to each other to have a conversation. We've invented a game we call Close Talk, where we must hold each other to speak. The hugs weave our souls together, and every muscle loses its tension wrapped in the warmth of a reassuring touch no matter what words we share.

There's fighting below in the streets, and Russians come through the courtyard but never climb the stairs. The gun is out and ready, but thankfully I don't need it. The rest of the time, wearing extra sweaters hides the weapon always on my body.

Drawn to my father's workroom, I pull open drawers and browse through his special sketchbook. On one page, he's scribbled some words and circled them.

I am an instrument in the hand of Elohim, who played a few songs on me.

Tears prick my eyes, and my lips tremble. If he doesn't return, it is sad how true these words will turn out to be. I miss his riddles, the pleasure he took from stumping us, his quiet presence that masked a deep thinker, a planner.

On a bookshelf, he has a photo of István and me. Our faces are chapped with cold, our smiles wide after sledding in the park with him for hours. Another is of us in our matching red boots, splashed with mud up to our thighs. Mother pretended to be angry when he brought us home that day, but when she heard the excitement in our story about sailing paper boats along the creek, she warmed mugs of milk so we could sit and tell her more.

My parents' wedding photo is there—a handsome man and a beautiful woman—their faces bright with adoration, a promising beginning to their life's journey together. I used to imagine eternity must be like a set of bound photographs, where we flip through snapshots of all we've lived through.

Now I pray that's not how it is. Never again do I want a glimpse of the horrors of this last year, and I sure don't want to carry them into eternity with me.

"Stalingrad!" a man yells from the front street. I arrive at the window the instant two Russian soldiers open fire on several German soldiers.

We hurry to my parents' bedroom, the most protected from the street, and lock the door.

Gunfire and running footsteps play out below us, even on the stairs inside our building, and doors bang open and shut.

"We're fine," I continue to reassure the children. "They don't want us."

An hour crawls by before quiet prevails.

"Let me go see," I say. I carefully peek out the kitchen window. The street is littered with German corpses, many resembling statues in outlandish positions already frozen in place.

A soft tapping on the door startles me. I creep closer and listen.

"Marika," a woman says. "It's Raakel. I need your help."

Her voice is strained and shaky. Throaty. Could she still be alive?

I push the couch to the side and pull open the door.

No one is framed there.

Off to the side, I spot a portion of someone's coat. It's dark green. The Arrow Cross!

I push the door shut but not before Benedek shoves his boot inside, stopping it from closing.

In the same falsetto voice, he says, "Fooled you."

Mother and Zofia enter the room behind me.

"Why are you here? You live somewhere else now, I hear. With your *mommy*, right?" A vein pounds in my forehead.

"I followed you. You're not in a safe house anymore, now are you?" Then he scowls. "And no, I don't live with my mother."

"What do you want?" I ask.

He peeks around me. "I see you got what was left of your boyfriend scrubbed away."

I refuse to absorb his message, to let the words register in my mind. And I won't utter what an evil lowlife he's turned out to be.

"Aren't you worried?" I ask.

"About what?"—he laughs—"Following orders?"

"Yes. Exactly that. The Russians see you as the enemy."

He points to a red ribbon on his shirt sleeve, tied above the Arrow Cross armband. "I've switched sides. Which is why I'm here."

"To protect us from the Germans?" I ask.

"No. I promised a couple of Russians outside I'd get them some women." He holds up the gun. "Three of you, especially that young one, will do."

The rumors aren't good. Gellert was right about the Soviet forces, especially those who came in after the professional soldiers. The lower ranks walk into houses without knocking, confiscate everything they see, especially watches, and take the women away, saying they will help peel potatoes. The women and young girls are brutalized for hours.

I can't let this happen to Zofia or my mother.

So I go with the lie. "We have money stashed in the cellar. That's why you found Gellert here." I lie, trying to calm my quivering insides. "We'll pay you to tell the soldiers you found no one."

He smiles with a glimmer in his eye. Greed obviously feeds his actions. "How much do you have?"

"A lot. Follow me and let's count it." I turn to face my mother and Zofia and tap my midsection where I carry the gun. Mother pales, tenses. "Be right back."

He follows me downstairs but stops when we reach the bottom floor before the next level descends to the cellar. "Hey. Have you heard about the Schlesingers?"

I swallow hard and pretend I've heard nothing. "What about them?"

He cocks his head to the side. "Sándor had them arrested for helping you." His eyes light up. He's pleased with himself.

"He was just a waiter." But I know the truth.

"SS spy, pretending he was a French waiter. The city is full of them."

"You're right. The city is full of scum." I want to confront him and tell him I know he killed Gellert, but his gun is at my back.

He's annoyed and pushes me forward. "Stop talking and get the money."

I lead him into the cellar, but must get him out of this building. "Over here," I say, crossing to the empty wooden box where we stored sausage. "No one ever sees this box back there."

He's next to me and leans across the shelf to see where I point.

"Just take the whole thing," I say and step back. The moment he has the container in his hand, I take off running up the steps. There's not much of a delay before I hear him pounding up behind me.

"Marika!" he calls. "I *will* shoot you."

And I have no doubt he will. My heartbeat hammers my insides as I race out the front door. No Russians waiting like he said as I head for the cemetery and then the tunnels.

No one stops me or seems to care that I'm running with an Arrow Cross man a half-block behind me. The cold air is hard to breathe, and the sky spits coarse snow, stinging my eyes. The cemetery is huge, but I know all the paths and those that don't come to a dead end. I exit the east end, holding the stitch in my side, a pain that's growing.

I hear him behind me, and he's not that far behind.

A few more streets and I disappear down the set of stairs, the heels of my dress shoes clacking against the steps. I hold the railing on one side not to lose my balance.

It's strangely warmer inside the tunnel as the depth protects it from the winter air above.

I have no plan. I can hide in here, but he's likely to go after my family when he doesn't find me. If I can knock him out, it would give me time to move everyone out and into another safe house. I head toward the winery area, where I know there are loose boards I can use to hit him.

I stop near the large casks and am now more worried because I can no longer hear his footsteps. Where has he gone? Has he turned back already? I panic and call his name.

He appears from a different direction. "You didn't think I'd know my way around down here?"

"There's a lot I don't know about you." I'm stalling, the damp air closing in. The boards are behind me, and the second I reach for one, he'll see what I'm planning. "You've changed in my eyes over these last few months."

He likes this, although I did not intend it as a compliment. This gives me an idea. "Perhaps, I've not appreciated you like I should have."

He probably doesn't trust my words, but I see a lift to his eyebrows. "You're *just* figuring this out?"

"I can't believe it's taken me so long." I nearly gag on my words. "Could you ever be happy with me, a Jew?"

He licks his lips. "I'd overlook that." He moves closer to me, and I take a slight step back. His eyes burn in the dim light. "I just might give you a try right now to see what I think."

"Here?" I ask. Panic fills me. I need to get out of this place. If I can get past him, I'm betting he doesn't know these tunnels as well as I do. "Come—"

He strikes, punching me on the side of my face. I land hard on my back on the concrete floor, momentarily seeing stars. He drops to his knees, straddling me.

In full panic, I try to buck him off, my cheek and jaw screaming with my every move.

His legs shift and pin mine open with a move that tells me he's done this before.

"Now, let's have some fun," he says, snarling. Then he leans over me and holds my chest with one hand while fumbling with his belt with the other.

This is not happening. Rage surges through me. He's taken so much from me already, and I won't let him have this too.

I touch my blouse and find the gun's trigger through the cotton cloth.

With a mighty push upward, I lift my hips high enough that when I pull the trigger, the bullet catches him in the abdomen.

The blast echoes against the limestone walls.

I roll him off me. Now his screams reverberate through the tunnels, and it won't be long before someone decides to track the sound.

I've committed a sin I never fathomed I'd be able to do. There's no turning back, so I point the gun at his head. "This one's for Gellert." And I shoot him again.

~33~

BUDAPEST HUNGARY

February 21, 1945

Six weeks have passed, and I never told Mother what happened in the tunnels, although I came home covered with blood, my cheek swollen, and my left eye puffed up. To get rid of Benedek's body, I rolled him into a wine cask I found on its side and hefted it upright, no easy task, and sealed it by pounding the lid in place. I'm sure Mother figured out I killed him.

By January 18, the Russians liberated the Central ghetto. Days before, Wallenberg narrowly stopped an Arrow Cross massacre there. The fascist group planned to machine-gun every last Jew until General Schmidhuber, the German commanding officer in Budapest, prevented it.

Startled and dirty figures slowly staggered past the broken-down fencing, starved and near death. At the sight of them, some Soviet soldiers, veterans of the slaughter on the Eastern Front, burst into tears and ripped the yellow stars off the Jews' coats, saying, "Now you're free."

Wallenberg was last seen in Budapest the day before the Central ghetto liberation. The Red Army arrested him when he approached the army commander, asking him for food supplies for his Swedish protected houses. No one has seen him since.

The Hungarian soldiers refused to blow up our beautiful remaining bridges, so the retreating Germans did it for them. To cross the river, the Russians use captured soldiers to build pontoon bridges. It will be years before the city rebuilds.

Were we free to start life over on that day? No. Every Jew stayed hidden in their houses and cellars, and the Arrow Cross Party's murdering rampage continued.

They massacred one hundred thirty patients and twenty-four staff members, including the head physician Andor Sulzer, in the hospital Gellert was in on Városmajor Street.

Ninety elderly residents of the Old Peoples' Home, previously saved twice by Wallenberg, were shot to death in their beds.

Entire blocks of Pest have disappeared into fields of broken bricks and rubble. The remaining buildings have hollow eye sockets where windows once held glass panes. Conditions throughout the city remain grim. The cold penetrates everywhere, electricity is out, and we scramble to find firewood to burn, often taking from our dead neighbors' houses. Food is scarce, and Mother or I go out to cut meat from the frozen horses more than once. Jakub never learns we are eating horse as we say we've traded for beef. We melt snow for water when the pipes stop flowing.

And we never venture out again until today when all of Budapest is finally liberated. Our clothes are dirty. We're malnourished and somewhat disoriented, but we survived.

All anti-Jewish laws are rescinded by the Budapest National Committee, and the Arrow Cross is warned they will be imprisoned if further killings ensue. And the news that made me the happiest? Along with the top Arrow Cross leaders, they arrested Piroska Dely.

When is killing justifiable? I've carried this question around since that day in the tunnels. Peter once said I'd be surprised what I would do if it came down to dying or pulling the trigger. The question is, was he going to kill me or rape me?

I'll argue being defiled by Benedek would have killed me inside.

And I was unprepared for my emotions after. Relief—not shame—filled me when I sealed the wine cask. Murdering Benedek was my solution when self-defense was about to fail. But deep down, I know it was revenge for all the poison bottled up in me after he killed my Gellert. In the long run, I suppose I failed. Killing him did away with a hater but did nothing to erase the hate that started neighbors turning against each other in the first place.

Many tribunals are scheduled in the city, but I'm only interested in one. Piroska's first hearing is a week later in the courthouse near the Parliament. I find a great seat in the second row for spectators, anxious to see this woman answer for her evil deeds.

"You are accused of entering a house on Csengery Street on October fifteenth, and along with other members of the Arrow Cross Party, shooting eighteen innocent people to death. You are accused of robbing wealthy families at gunpoint and of killing orphans under the protection of the embassies of Switzerland and Sweden. How do you plead?"

"I was never part of the Arrow Cross Party. The armband and pin were put on my jacket by someone else."

The tribunal judge clears his throat. "You mean to say you and your son, Benedek Dely, were not involved daily in the rounding up and shooting of hundreds of Jewish citizens?"

"My son is a tugboat driver," she says. "If he was seen by the river during the shootings, it's because that is his job."

I gasp then quickly cover my mouth.

Her head swivels my way, and we lock eyes.

"Where is your son today, Mrs. Dely? We'd like to question him too."

"I don't know," she says, not turning her gaze from me. "He never returned home."

Slowly, I smile and nod.

The astonishment on her face tells me she understands. Benedek is dead.

She's sent to jail to await her sentence.

No one sees or hears from Belko Dely again. We clear out their apartment and lock it shut even though we no longer own the building according to the government. We can remain and pay rent to the cooperative the Russians set up throughout the city, which we do.

Thirteen months later, on March 23, 1946, I stand in a back alley behind the courthouse in a gathering crowd. The newspapers ran the headline,

The Servant of the Gestapo to Receive the Noose

The article continued, claiming she wasn't a woman but a bloodthirsty beast in human skin.

Piroska is dressed in a dark grey sweater and long navy skirt, and if the situation were different, she could pass as a matron for young children. She climbs the stairs of the hangman's platform with her hands tied behind her back.

She will die like so many others—hands bound. Unlike the estimated twenty thousand whose bodies disappeared into the Danube between October and February during Szálasi's reign of terror, she deserves this.

The evil woman offers no last words as the thick hangman's rope is draped over her head and tightened at the nape of her neck.

The drop comes fast, but no satisfaction for her death comes with it. She suffered too little, and it doesn't erase the pain of all who are gone.

Father, Gellert, the Schlesingers, thousands of orphans, and hundreds of thousands more.

I turn to leave when a man calls my name. Peter? It's really him emerging from the crowd!

We stare at each other in silence before rushing forward, embracing as if this is a final goodbye instead of a welcoming hello.

And just like that, when my pain appeared to be at its worst, it dissipates, like fog off a lake when the sun rises to show off a new day.

His feet are bare, ravaged, and he's thin, in terrible shape. I've seen others return in this same poor health. They'd been held in labor camps.

"Where were you?" I ask.

"I'll tell you everything"—he takes my arm—"but just know Siberia isn't any place you'll want to visit. But right this minute, I need to know… do you know any nurses who can help me?"

"I do. She'll also be there to hold you close." I smile, wondering if he recognizes his own words. "That's all the medicine anyone needs."

Epilogue

Teaneck, New Jersey

June 1, 1962

MARIA WASSERMAN

While pinning the nurse's cap into my upswept hair, I hear the broadcaster on the radio announce a special news story out of Jerusalem.

"War criminal Adolf Eichmann, charged with crimes against humanity, and in particular the Jewish people of Hungary, has been executed."

A tremor rattles through me, and I grab the dresser to steady myself. My heart leaps into my throat. If only I could dance with ghosts. Surely the dead, if they could, would want to celebrate with me. The Architect is dead. My husband Hans—whom I still like to call Peter—left only minutes ago for his high school job as a theatre teacher but should be here to celebrate this news. We've waited seventeen years to hear it.

I rush to our new Admiral television set and nearly knock it off its stand as I hurry to find which of the three networks may be covering the story. We've followed Eichmann's trial during the last year, ever since they arrested him in Argentina and secreted him back to Israel to answer for his role in the Holocaust. Each day, hundreds of journalists from around the world packed the courtroom and hallways for the trial.

The television warms up, and a newsreel of Eichmann at his trial comes into focus. He has spent the past eight months inside an assassination-proof glass cage.

Eichmann's a slender, balding man of fifty-five. The once self-assured Nazi wears a pencil-thin mustache above a mouth set between protruding ears, a long narrow nose, and often-wrinkled forehead. Resembling an ac-countant more than a butcher, he appears feeble in contrast to the two burly, blue-clad Israeli policemen in that glass enclosure.

A *TIME* magazine article reported that when Eichmann stood during the trial, "he resembles a stork" instead of a soldier. He could never be as noble as Jeno and Rezi, the storks from our country estate. This birdlike human spent eight months in court, pleading he was no more than a small cog in a vast war machine. That he never killed anyone because he had no real authority. That he was merely a loyal servant to his fatherland. A "timetable technician" following orders to ready trains for a safe transfer of the Jewish population.

We Jews of the Kingdom of Hungary knew the truth. He was rabid for Hitler's approval. The announcer continues with a review of Eichmann's escape from Germany and his comfortable life in Argentina with his family. How the Israeli Mossad captured him. The witnesses who came forward at his trial and the sentence handed down by the panel of judges.

"We find you to be a key perpetrator in the genocide of European Jewry. You have admitted that you are guilty of arranging the trans-port of millions of Jews to their deaths. You revealed to another officer that you could go happily to your grave, knowing you did your best to rid Europe of its Jewry problem. We are all in agree-ment that your death is the appropriate punishment."

I'm weeping before I realize my tears are spilling, and I sink onto the hassock, watching the blurred black and white scenes they show from the extermination camps. Every image ghastly, even when distorted through my watery vision. Lines of unsuspecting citizens forced onto trains. Each carrying meager possessions they pray will shore them up when they *start over* in their new location. City after city, country after country. My country, Hungary, was the last swept into the all-consuming furnaces of hate.

Under Hitler, Eichmann worked hard to strip us of our immortality. For immortality is only found in family. Not only did he destroy branches and roots but entire family trees. He also took out small woods and whole forests. All gone.

My gaze travels to the display box on our wall. Behind the glass sits Moshe and my family's shofar. Below, on a table, is our warped Bible. My only cherished mementos from those days of terror. The puppet's hollowed-out figure matches the emptiness that at times courses through me. It happens less and less often as the years have ticked by, but the guilt of surviving and the grief of loss come in separate waves, set off by the simplest sights or sounds—horses in a field, footsteps thumping up a stairway, children's voices lifted in song.

"Nearly six months after his sentencing, Eichmann was hanged in Ramle Prison," the announcer continues. "His body was cremated, and his ashes are being scattered in the Mediterranean Sea, beyond Israel's territorial waters. There will be no burial site available to commemorate this man or the extreme beliefs of Nazism."

I turn the knob on the television, and the picture slowly winks off.

The children have never complained that we don't own a color television like their friends. My husband and I see no point in that extra expense when we already have a perfectly functioning appliance.

Of course, our children aren't spoiled. They've known deprivation and fear. How to stay silent while listening to a clock's maddening tick, wondering if it was the last sound they'd hear before death or other tragedy found them.

As young adults now, they're compassionate without being naïve.

I think of my father. He was an artist at heart and always said, "Like music, color is also a language." During that last year of the war, I'd seen enough images in color and remember every sad word those colors spoke. Even now, when they are shown again on newsreels in black and white, I know a color TV would be too much.

I must get to the hospital for my shift, but the memories have momentarily crippled me, and I'm unable to move. Those ten months from March 1944 to early the following year are indescribable. Those who didn't experience it cannot possibly understand. To be so powerless. To have almost no one you could trust.

When Peter and I arrived in America with the help of the Church World Service, we learned people didn't want to hear the gory details of what we and the three children had been through.

He and I married soon after he escaped a Russian gulag and returned to Budapest, and we adopted Bandin, Zofia, and Jakub. Peter gave up his resistance name and became himself again—Hans Wasserman. I became Marika Wasserman, and then Maria when we reached America.

People who questioned our choices weren't there for the worst of it, which makes it so easy for them to judge the choices we made. Our rabbi says the faultfinders wrestle through their own guilt because they were for-tunate and escaped the tragedy. While it's his calling to always find the good in others, I remain skeptical about people's intentions and choices under duress.

István, Erzsébet, and the baby stayed in Switzerland. István refused to understand or accept why we didn't do enough to find Father. "Why didn't you try harder to get out of there instead of letting the Arrow Cross hunt you all down? Maybe Mother would still be alive."

We lost her to pneumonia in the fall of 1947 while we waited and worked in a displaced persons camp in Germany. We couldn't remain in Budapest under Communist rule—another controlling force. Honestly, when Father didn't return, she withered a bit each passing month until I believe she seemed relieved to have a disease take her. I picture her reunion with Father. My imagination convinces me shooting stars marked the night skies that day.

We never learned how Father died or where he was buried but we know he's not coming back. I realized a few years ago, I am my father's daughter, a planner, always thinking a few steps ahead in case the worst happens. I wish we'd known each other was working with the Resistance. The discus-sions we could have had.

Mother's ashes sit on our mantel, so she is always with me. She's beside me when I pickle and can vegetables from our garden. She's in the flowers we grow in the beds by our front steps. Every year, I knit two dozen lilac-colored scarves and donate them to the Sisters of Social Services program here in New Jersey. I do this in remembrance of the time Mother handed her scarf to our freezing friend on the Death March. I'd like to believe I'm carrying on her acts of kindness, but I'll never measure up to her.

And my first love, Gellert. I dance with him in my mind and replay our moments together before he was emotionally broken. His grave in the cemetery where he was first buried has a headstone that reads, "A good and kind heart is the best of all qualities. Here lies such a man."

We couldn't figure out why he went back to our apartment the day he was killed. He couldn't have known that in Father's workroom we'd find two secret stashes of cash. One in our music box that refused to play when we turned it on and one inside a puppet's head with a joker's face.

I think that hiding place was more than fitting.

And our children.

Zofia is thirty now. She lives in a small apartment not far from us and teaches first grade. Recently awarded teacher of the year, she seems content to surround herself with children but steers away from forming too-close relationships with adults. As much as Hans and I would like to see her marry, she may never, and we accept that.

Bandin is twenty-eight and teaches mathematics at Northeastern University outside Boston. He put himself through college on a chess scholarship. He proudly displays Father's chess set in his office. His religious views have changed, and he calls himself a Universalist. He'll attend any church he's invited to, voicing his opinion that one religion can't be right while all the others are wrong. His parents and aunts were never found.

Then there's the youngest. Jakub. He's twenty-five and studying to be a plastic surgeon. We paid for his facial surgery with some of Father's hidden money when we arrived in New Jersey. Although he's permanently scarred, he can now close his mouth and has a near-normal smile. On the weekends, he invites emotionally damaged children to his farm to ride horses.

Hans's mother and younger brother, along with fifteen of his relatives, all died in concentration camps. He wasn't thrilled about moving to the United States after his ordeal on the *SS St. Louis*. Because it was turned back, his mother and brother died. But options for a new place to call home in war-torn Europe were limited, so he agreed to our move. His choice of a career in theatre was no surprise after he proved in Budapest he could be the master of disguises and play any part.

I've not had another best friend like Raakel. Losing her was too painful, and I don't trust that another person could fill her shoes. Acquaintances suit me fine.

And I have learned it is possible to equally love the two men in my life because I love them in different ways. Gellert was a young love, full of kindness and peace, while Hans is creativeness and strength. We fit together, and I treasure the time I had with Gellert and what I have now with Hans. We're imperfect but wonderful. We embrace our differences, remembering to cherish each other every day, but more importantly, we've learned to let go and lean on each other.

This isn't the family I imagined I'd have, but I wouldn't trade them for any other.

The memories of the war circle back, and that won't ever change. On any given day, one of us in the family may buckle under the weight of traumatic memories, but we have each other to hold us up.

And although I rarely speak of those days to anyone outside the family, I've never told Hans about Benedek and what happened that day in the tunnel. I want to privately own that moment and never share it.

Sometimes people ask what Budapest is like, and if I'm in a down mood, I'll say, "The city was lovely…once called the Queen on the Danube. One day it'll be rebuilt, but even then, I'd suggest you not drink their wine."

Back then, how could we know what was coming and what we were capable of?

I'm determined never to forget the bitter truth, even now with Eichmann dead. In the spring of 1944, we feared too little, and we hoped too much. We certainly underestimated the evil nature of the enemy. And worse than that, we overestimated the humanity, the wisdom, and the sense of justice of our neighbors.

THE END

Author Notes

When I visited Budapest in May 2019 with my niece and husband, we toured the Dohány Synagogue. There I bought a locally published book titled, *YELLOW-STAR HOUSES: People, Houses, Fates – Budapest, 1944* published by Nádor and Partner Consulting Office 2015. I couldn't help but think that all that happened to the Jews of Hungary, it all happened so late in the war. The Jews of Hungary almost made it. In only nine months they went from living under restrictive regulations to wholesale mass deportations and the murder of 565,000. One hundred forty-seven trains were sent to Auschwitz, where most deportees were murdered on arrival. Because the crematoria could not cope with the number of corpses, special pits were dug nearby to dump the excess, and they simply burned them. It has been estimated that one-third of the murdered victims at Auschwitz were Hungarian.

The Hungarian populace and gendarmes' devotion to Hitler's cause, known as the "final solution," surprised even Eichmann. After the first surge of German troops, he successfully supervised the operation with only twenty officers and a staff of one hundred, including aides, drivers, and cooks.

This was the shocking part of the story I wanted to tell. Hungarian citizens turned on their Jewish neighbors and were eager actors in the deportations. Later they turned a blind eye to the Arrow Cross killings. Or they joined in the slaughter.

What arose was collective violence against those who were labelled "not us." Neighbors pilfered the belongings of the Jews, often within hours of them being deported. Was it hatred or greed, or a bit of both?

Winston Churchill said on July 11, 1944, "There is no doubt that this is probably the greatest and most horrible crime ever committed in the whole history of the world... ."

But not every Hungarian turned on the Jews. Hundreds of Christians hid their Jewish friends at risk of death. Church leaders—but not all—spoke out against the deportations, and as I write in the book, both Carl Lutz and Raoul Wallenberg, diplomats with the backing of Switzerland and Sweden, were absolute heroes. Carl Lutz returned to Switzerland where he died in 1975, at age 79. Raoul Wallenberg was taken away by Soviet officials on January 17, 1945. The exact date and circumstances of Wallenberg's death are unknown and may never be clarified, but he's thought to have died in the infamous Lubyanka Prison in Moscow. He was 32 years old when they took him away. In October 2016, 71 years after his disappearance, Swedish officials formally declared Wallenberg legally dead. An impressive memorial dedicated to him is in Dohány Synagogue's courtyard.

Adolf Eichmann lived a good life in Argentina with his family until captured by the Mossad in 1960. While awaiting trial in Israel, he was heard to say, "To sum it all up, I must say that I regret nothing." Then, concerning the 400,000 Jews sent to Auschwitz within four months' time, "It was actually an achievement that was never matched before or since" and "My heart was light and joyful in my work, because the decisions were not mine."

For more on him you may wish to read, *Eichmann Before Jerusalem: The Unexamined Life of a Mass Murderer* by Bettina Stangneth (2015).

I had never heard of the Death Marches in Hungary, only those surrounding the bigger concentration camps as the Germans began losing the war. As written in this novel, mostly women and the elderly were sent off on foot with no food or water and in poor weather conditions to work in Austria. Thousands died. For more on what was said at Eichmann's trial about the Death Marches, here is a good link: https://www.jta.org/archive/ death-march-of-50000-hungarian-jews-described-at-eichmann-trial

Sister Sára was shot on the banks of the Danube on the date mentioned in the novel, but she was not tied to children when she fell into the river. However, the Arrow Cross killed many others in this cruel manner, and I used my literary license to show that evil act through her death.

The Arrow Cross Party was as cruel or worse than I write about. They were also nearly unstoppable once the killing fever took hold. Even the

Germans left in command of Budapest were ashamed of the rampant acts of murder and atrocity. Here is a link to a dissertation that nicely sums up what led to the growth of this fascist group and their activities. https://www.ceu.edu/sites/default/files/attachment/event/14210/szelearon.pdf

Father András Kun roamed the streets of Budapest wearing his monk's Cossack and a gun, randomly shooting the Jews who would not convert to Christianity. He was hanged on September 19, 1945.

Yes, Piroska Dely is a real person. I didn't find information about her children although the research mentions she had two, so I invented Benedek for my story's purpose. She and her husband divorced by the time the war ended and she went on trial. Nothing is ever said about him after that. They hanged her as portrayed in this book.

Below is the cover to *Invisible Perpetrators: Women in the Hungarian Arrow Cross Movement*, a book by Andrea Petö, showing Ferenc Szálasi with women of the Arrow Cross. Called the "Hungarian Hitler," he was publicly hanged in March 1946.

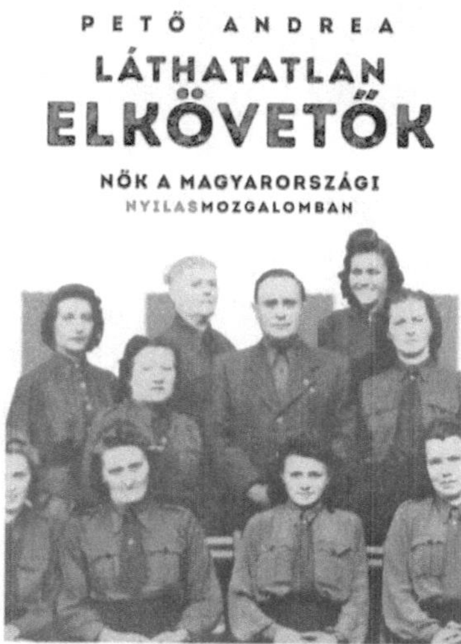

Hundreds of Arrow Cross leaders fled west as the Russians arrived and escaped accusation and trial.

The Kőbánya Caves and the huge tunnel system fascinated me. At one point in the book, Marika is in a tunnel and hears motors and someone hammering metal. A secret factory was built there to manufacture aircraft engines and assemble fuselages. The plant under the 10th District was so classified that only rumors existed about it for a long time. It was protected during the last months of the war—partly because the allied bombers didn't even know there was a military plant under the ground. Since 2017, you can tour the tunnel system.

After World War II, approximately 27,000 people were convicted for war crimes and genocide in Hungary. Its People's Courts passed 322 death sentences before March 1, 1948, but only 146 people died by execution. Regarding the number executed after final sentencing, of all the European countries, Hungary is listed midway with follow-through executions.

The Kasztner Train that transported over 1700 Jews to Switzerland, with a stop in Bergen-Belsen, made Otto Komoly and Rudolph Kasztner heroes at the time. The Arrow Cross killed Komoly just before the arrival of the Red Army. Kasztner was assassinated after the war. Here's a brief history about Kasztner and the deal he made with Eichmann. https://encyclopedia.ushmm.org/content/en/article/rudolf-rezsoe-kasztner

The Jedwabne, Poland story—where I have Zofia and Jakub surviving the town's massacre—is true. During my research what I found most frightening was in a book, *Neighbors: The Destruction of the Jewish Community in Jedwabne, Poland.* It is a detailed account of what occurred there. Neighbors turned on neighbors, schoolteachers on their pupils, the butcher on his patrons. Check it out here:

https://www.amazon.com/Neighbors-Destruction-Jewish-Community-Jedwabne-ebook/dp/B009AKK8VC/ref=sr_1_1?keywords=Neighbors+a+book+of+Jedwabne+Poland&qid=1638326690&sr=8-1

At war's end, an estimated 119,000 Jewish people were liberated in Budapest—25,000 in the small "international" ghetto, 69,000 in the big ghetto, and 25,000 hiding with false papers—and 20,000 forced laborers in the countryside. It's estimated that from an original population of 861,000 people considered Jewish inside the Kingdom of Hungary's borders between 1941 and 1944, about 255,000 survived. Those numbers amount to a 29.6 percent survival rate.

Acknowledgements

Once again, my trusted band of beta readers came through for me. Delving into a dark tale during an ongoing pandemic is not an easy task to take on. I'm indebted to Kristy Pappas, Bill and Kate Chabala, Lynda Smart-Brown, Robert Dean, Jeff Lowder, Linda Orvis, Andy Walker, Rick Christensen, and Brittani Jay for your great input.

Thank you to Z.J. Czupor and Gordy Peifer for talking to me about their Hungarian roots, and sharing some stories of their parents. Marika is Gordy's mother's name and her family's farm had storks that returned every year to nest. Fortunately, they didn't suffer the same fate as the storks in my story.

Thank you to my editors, Ann Riza and Ann Suhs for your expertise in catching the flaws, suggesting better options, and making the book much better.

My critique group cheered me on as always. Your comments are very valuable when building a new story from scratch.

Always a given, an immense thank you to Emma F. Mayo for the various creative options that ended with this beautiful cover, and for your willingness to read through the manuscript many times. You've seen what my eyes can't, and I'm blessed to have you in my life.

And to Winston, our faithful dog, who spent hours and hours with me while I brainstormed, typed, fretted, and edited. I hope I rewarded your patience enough with your favorite game of playing ball.

And to my husband, John Hardy. Your enthusiasm for what I write means the world to me. Thank you for supporting the days, weeks, and months I spend at the computer creating another story of injustice, and for always letting me bounce ideas off you so the plot doesn't get mired in unimportant details.

Author Page

Karla M. Jay lives in Salt Lake City with her husband, and one large gray dog. When she's not writing or reading, she's gardening or planning a trip, hoping to discover another story that needs to be told.

You can follow Karla M. Jay at:
Her website~ http://www.karlajay.com
Twitter~ https://twitter.com/KarlaMJay1
Facebook~ http://www.facebook.com/AuthorKarlaJay
Instagram~ https://instagram.com/karla.m.jay

Want to read more by Karla M. Jay? Click on the highlighted words in the titles below to check out *When We Were Brave* and *It Happened in Silence*, both international award winners.

When We <u>Were</u> Brave
It <u>Happened</u> in Silence